"A lyrical, gorgeous novel about fractured family, racial tensions, and the way the past flows right up through the present. Bryant's eloquent tale may be Southern at heart, but it's universal in its powerful message."

—Caroline Leavitt, *New York Times* bestselling author of *Pictures of You*

"Poignant and redemptive, *Alligator Lake* immerses us in the murky waters of a shifting Southern current, where the push and pull of racial boundaries redefine love, loyalty, and heart-wrenching pride. Lynne Bryant writes beautifully about the challenges and choices that divide a family in a predominantly segregated Mississippi town, yet delivers us the promise that hope and forgiveness can be found where we least expect them."

—Eileen Clymer Schwab, author of *Promise Bridge* and *Shadow of a Quarter Moon*

"Lynne Bryant's *Alligator Lake* is a gutsy examination of Southern race relations. Bryant is provocative and unflinching as she reveals her characters' private hopes and fears. Her abiding love for Mississippi shines through as she wrestles with its troubled history. Ultimately, *Alligator Lake* is a commentary on the redemptive power of love and friendship."

—Natalie Baszile, author of *Queen Sugar*

"Set in a picturesque Mississippi town, *Alligator Lake* is a powerful and compassionate portrait of love, secrets, prejudice, and redemption in the intertwined histories of four generations of Southern women. Bryant deftly weaves a tale steeped in the atmosphere, charm, and complex racial relationships of an evolving South. *Alligator Lake* is a compelling and memorable read."

—Lynn Sheene, author of *The Last Time I Saw Paris*

continued . . .

Written by today's freshest new talents and selected by New American Library, NAL Accent novels touch on subjects close to a woman's heart, from friendship to family to finding our place in the world. The Conversation Guides included in each book are intended to enrich the individual reading experience, as well as encourage us to explore these topics together—because books, and life, are meant for sharing.

Visit us online at www.penguin.com.

Catfish Alley

"Hailing from Mississippi, Lynne Bryant provides the ring of authenticity that only a native daughter can bring, with a fascinating tale of murder, friendship, racism, and the hope of renewal. . . . *Catfish Alley* brims with humor and pathos in equal parts, with realistic, three-dimensional characters sure to delight and intrigue from the start. Of all the novels set in the South, Lynne Bryant's debut novel deserves an honored place on any bookshelf."
—Southern Literary Review

"Outstanding . . . a poignant novel, rich with historical detail of the Old South."
—*The Historical Novels Review*

"In the tradition of *The Help*, Lynne Bryant's *Catfish Alley* tackles the racial divide of both 1930s and current-day Mississippi in a page-turning narrative that has, at its heart, the search for personal connections as the path to both survival and understanding." —Lalita Tademy, author of *Cane River*

"A tender, wise, unique story of life, love, and Southern women crafted by a skilled writer who understands the struggle to find happiness and the healing power of friendship."
—Lisa Wingate, author of *Beyond Summer* and *Larkspur Cove*

"*Catfish Alley* is a bittersweet love song to the union of women and a heartfelt meditation on the old and new wounds of a South that still must tiptoe, still doesn't always know how to move forward, but is determined to try. Lynne Bryant writes honorably and earnestly about women facing each other and themselves."
—Barbara O'Neal, author of *How to Bake a Perfect Life*

"Bryant's sprawling tale of segregation, perseverance, and interracial friendships is heartfelt."
—*Kirkus Reviews*

"Will appeal to readers who enjoyed *The Help*. The author accesses her own tumultuous Southern history to lend her enchanting tale much local color."
—*Publishers Weekly*

"Told in numerous distinct voices, Bryant's debut novel moves seamlessly through three generations, both black and white, as eventually Roxanne realizes that friendship has no color boundaries." —*Delta Magazine*

"This beautifully written and extremely poetic novel is told from multiple viewpoints. The descriptions of people and places in this novel will transport readers back to Mississippi during the 1920s. Full of tales of courage and endurance that may bring you to tears with their intensity, this is not a novel you'll soon forget." —*Romantic Times* (4½ stars)

ALSO BY LYNNE BRYANT

Catfish Alley

Alligator Lake

LYNNE BRYANT

NAL Accent
Published by New American Library,
a division of Penguin Group (USA) Inc.,
375 Hudson Street, New York, New York 10014, USA
Penguin Group (Canada), 90 Eglinton Avenue East, Suite 700, Toronto,
Ontario M4P 2Y3, Canada (a division of Pearson Penguin Canada Inc.)
Penguin Books Ltd., 80 Strand, London WC2R 0RL, England
Penguin Ireland, 25 St. Stephen's Green, Dublin 2,
Ireland (a division of Penguin Books Ltd.)
Penguin Group (Australia), 250 Camberwell Road, Camberwell,
Victoria 3124, Australia (a division of Pearson Australia Group Pty. Ltd.)
Penguin Books India Pvt. Ltd., 11 Community Centre,
Panchsheel Park, New Delhi - 110 017, India
Penguin Group (NZ), 67 Apollo Drive, Rosedale, Auckland 0632,
New Zealand (a division of Pearson New Zealand Ltd.)
Penguin Books (South Africa) (Pty.) Ltd., 24 Sturdee Avenue,
Rosebank, Johannesburg 2196, South Africa

Penguin Books Ltd., Registered Offices:
80 Strand, London WC2R 0RL, England

First published by NAL Accent, an imprint of New American Library,
a division of Penguin Group (USA) Inc.

First Printing, April 2012
1 3 5 7 9 10 8 6 4 2

LIBRARY OF CONGRESS CATALOGING-IN-PUBLICATION DATA:
Bryant, Lynne, 1959–
Alligatot lake/Lynne Bryant.
p. cm.
ISBN 978-0-451-23578-7
1. Single mothers—Fiction. 2. Racially mixed people—Fiction. 3. African Americans—Fiction. 4. Family secrets. 5. Domestic fiction. I. Title.
PS3602.R949A44 2012
813'.6—dc22 2011045423

Set in Bembo • Designed by Elke Sigal

Printed in the United States of America

PUBLISHER'S NOTE

This is a work of fiction. Names, characters, places, and incidents either are the product of the author's imagination or are used fictitiously, and any resemblance to actual persons, living or dead, business establishments, events, or locales is entirely coincidental.

The publisher does not have any control over and does not assume any responsibility for author or third-party Web sites or their content.

For Sue

Alligator Lake

Chapter 1

Avery

December 2000

Why does watching my daughter open her gifts on Christmas morning make me miss my mother? For ten years I have avoided being in the same state with her. Drifting through my mind come thoughts of my childhood Christmases, typically balmy Southern days when my brother and I couldn't wait to get outside with our new toys, which were guaranteed to keep us busy and out from underfoot for most of the morning. I wonder, as I often do on holidays, if Marion Reynolds Pritchett is capable of softening toward her grandchild in ways she never could toward me, her own daughter. Not likely, I conclude, as I watch Celi rip into the gifts Santa has left under the eight-foot-tall Douglas fir, which is sagging under the weight of every glued and glittered decoration ever created by Celi and Aunt Lizzie's grandchildren.

In the bright Colorado sunlight pouring through the windows of the still-chilly living room, Celi moves on to plunder her stocking with typical nine-year-old zeal. Aunt Lizzie and I sip coffee and watch indulgently, oohing and aahing over each discovery. Alvin leaps with feline grace, surprising for his bulk, over the growing mountains of wrapping paper and he bats the tossed-away bows across the glossy hardwood floor.

My heart aches a little, knowing that this might be one of the last years that Celi believes in Santa Claus—another milestone I have kept her grandparents from experiencing. Today must be a day for guilt. Do they feel deprived? Probably relieved, at least in my mother's case. After all, how would she explain Celi's caramel skin color to the members of her all-white Garden Club?

For good measure, and to keep up the myth, I made sure to wrap a gift for Celi from me. I've kept it hidden in the trunk of my car for three weeks. When I quietly let myself into Aunt Lizzie's grand old Victorian house on Downing Street this morning after my night shift at the hospital, Celi was still sleeping. I stuffed the large package wrapped in candy-cane-striped paper behind the tree. Since Celi has spent the weeks leading up to Christmas memorizing each gift and knows whom each one is for, in her post–Santa Claus lull she recognizes the new addition. She dives behind the tree and studies the tag.

" 'From Mom to Celi,' " she reads. "Can I open it now, Mom? Please?" she asks, giggling as she watches Alvin crouch behind the box with her name on it, waiting to attack the curly red ribbon snaking across the floor.

"Sure," I say. "But that's it until everyone else gets here."

Aunt Lizzie and I exchange glances as Celi tears back the wrapping paper and tugs at the flaps of the large box. Aunt Lizzie knows how I struggled over this gift, which for Celi represents normalcy and for me represents my attempt to overcome my constant state of maternal overprotectiveness. She reaches in, her small hands quickly pulling away the wads of newspaper that hold the gift in place. As soon as she sees what's there, her face lights up with joy and she turns to me, green eyes sparkling.

"A basketball! This is so cool, Mom!" she says as she pulls out the orange Spalding ball, the same kind Daddy gave me at her age. I still remember Mother's pursed lips and expression of disapproval for this not exactly ladylike gift. Celi almost trips over Alvin, hiding among the discarded bunches of newspaper, as she hurries over to wrap her arms around me.

"Thank you!" she says, plopping down beside me on the sofa. "Can we go to the park later and shoot baskets?"

Aunt Lizzie laughs. "There's a foot of snow on the ground, kiddo! You'll have to wait for it to melt a little bit. Besides, you've got to help me make the pies." Aunt Lizzie and Celi have been baking Aunt Lizzie's traditional Southern pecan and pumpkin pies together since Celi was old enough to stand on a stool at the kitchen counter.

Celi looks at Aunt Lizzie, shrugs her shoulders, and sighs. "Okay," she says, and immediately turns back to me. "How about tomorrow? Can we go tomorrow?"

"That sounds great," I say. Aunt Lizzie and Celi head for the kitchen to prepare for the annual Christmas feast. Aunt Lizzie's son, Felix, and daughter, Lana, and their spouses and kids will be joining us. Alvin trails behind them, hoping for a treat. I move around the living room, picking up wrapping paper and bows and stuffing them into the empty box that held Celi's basketball. I think of my conversation with Dr. Hardy. She's always so reassuring, especially when my maternal angst gets out of control.

"Sports are okay for her, Avery. As long as she doesn't get overheated," Dr. Hardy said.

"Yes, but what if she does? What if she goes into sickle-cell crisis right there on the basketball court and I'm not there?" I said, frantic with worry over something that hadn't even happened yet.

Dr. Hardy patted my arm. "You've got to let her be a kid, Avery," she said. "Keep her hydrated and let her play. She'll pace herself."

I've never known my daughter to pace herself. She approaches everything she does at breakneck speed. I've lost count of how often each day I say, "Slow down. Where's the fire?" How can those words fall out of my mouth when they remind me so much of what my mother used to say to me?

The fatigue of having been up all night starts to hit me, and I shiver with a deep chill. I reach for the thick wooly sweater Aunt Lizzie keeps draped over the back of her rocking chair and pull it on over the thin hospital scrubs I'm still wearing. The sweater smells of Aunt Lizzie's favorite Cotton Blossom lotion and makes me feel like I'm wrapped in one of her nurturing hugs. I stoop to light the gas-log fireplace and the orange flames spring to life. I collapse into my favorite corner of the welcoming sofa.

The flickering flames mesmerize me, and I tuck the shabby old homemade quilt tighter around my knees, snuggling into the warmth of Aunt Lizzie's well-worn sofa. Alvin wanders in from the kitchen and jumps up onto the sofa with a heavy thud, and I pull him in close against me. He curls his fat yellow body into my hip and his purr almost drowns out the soft drone of Celi's and Aunt Lizzie's voices drifting from the kitchen. My mental replay of last night's patients and their emergency surgeries finally starts to wind down as I drift into my much-anticipated cinnamon-and-clove-scented Christmas-morning nap.

I'm dreaming of my grandmother's holiday cinnamon rolls and hear Mother scolding me for scraping the frosting off with my fingers, when the ancient rotary-dial phone that Aunt Lizzie keeps by her chair jolts me awake with its jangly ring. I've tried for years to convince her to get a cordless, but she always says, "Now, why would I want to walk around the house and talk on the phone? One thing at a time, I always say. One thing at a time."

"I got it!" I yell toward the kitchen as I pull myself out of my warm nest, uprooting Alvin, who looks at me with disgust and jumps to the floor. I grab the phone before it can send any more shock waves of sound into my weary skull, and plop into Aunt Lizzie's rocker as I say, "Hello. Merry Christmas."

"You don't sound very merry, Sistah," Mark drawls. I'm instantly awake. My excitement at hearing my brother's voice is immediately followed by wariness. I allow only two members of my Mississippi family into my life: Mark and my grandmother Willadean. But Mark is not like Will, who faithfully writes down my crazy schedule and calls every Sunday evening that I'm off work. Usually I'm the one who calls Mark. He's either completely preoccupied with law school—following in Daddy's footsteps—or too busy partying with his friends to call me. I haven't talked to him in probably nine months.

"You woke me from a carefully planned nap," I say. "How are you? To what do I owe the honor of having my little brother call me on Christmas morning? I can't believe you're out of bed already. It must be only, what? Ten o'clock there?"

"Funny, real funny," he replies. "I'll have you know that I get up nowadays at six a.m."

"Six a.m.? There must be money involved."

"Ah, you know me too well. No, it's not that. I'm interning at Daddy's office over the break, getting ready for the real thing."

Thoughts of the skinny sixteen-year-old boy, whose life the last time I saw him, ten years ago, was already so completely different from mine, race through my mind. I picture Mark's smile, his laughing brown eyes; him as my sidekick as we grew up together in Greendale, Mississippi; the times we covered for each other with our parents so that one of us could sneak out of the house and drive around town with our friends. That was before everything changed. Questions that seem to be surfacing more frequently lately nag at the edge of my consciousness. What have I given up? Did I do the right thing in leaving and never going back?

"Look, Ave, I know it will seem out of the blue, but I've got something to ask you. But first, how the heck are you?"

I'm filled with curiosity about what Mark could possibly want. When I left home at eighteen he was already hitting all the expected benchmarks—good grades, star baseball player, plans for college at Ole Miss. I tried halfheartedly to be the proper Southern debutante and move in the exclusive social circle, as Mother expected. I had good grades. I was even somewhat athletic—a characteristic Mother could have lived without; I made a feeble attempt at basketball on our decidedly average private school team. I certainly was no beauty queen, however—tall and skinny like my grandmother, with her freckled skin and stringy hair. But, despite all of that averageness, I was playing with fire. Oh, I knew the risks when I started sneaking around with Aaron Monroe. I thought of myself in those days as such a rebel. I was smug with my own little secret.

"I'm doing okay," I answer, pulling myself into the present to focus on the conversation. Mark and I chat about the usual comfortable topics—my nursing work, Celi's school, Aunt Lizzie's latest travel adventure.

"How is Daddy?" I ask, thinking of our father's love of Christmas and wondering as I always do at this time of year what kind of grandfather he would be to Celi.

"He's good," Mark says. "Pouting a little bit, I think. He finally lost the battle of the Christmas tree. Mama got an artificial one this year."

"No kidding?" I say, sad that one of my favorite childhood traditions, of cutting a tree with my father, has ended. "Are you going over there today?"

"Yeah," he says. "It's expected. Besides, we have to do the family gift exchange."

"I gave Celi a basketball for Christmas."

"That's great. If she's got your long legs and Aaron's coordination, she could be a star." I stop myself from thinking, and from saying, that's not likely. Mark doesn't know about Celi's disease. None of them do. Since her diagnosis five years ago, I haven't been able to bring myself to tell him or Grandma Will. I haven't even considered telling Mother and Daddy yet.

Mark's casual mention of Aaron jars me. Celi's questions about her father have escalated in the past few months. The stories I've been creating to avoid talking about him are wearing thin in the face of her persistent curiosity. I decide to change the subject.

"So, what do you need to ask me?" I say.

"I want to know if you and Celi will come home for my wedding."

"Your wedding?" I must sound really dense, because he laughs.

"Yeah, where you walk down the aisle, guy wears a tuxedo, girl wears a white dress—you know the drill."

"You're such a smart-ass," I say, surprised by how much I enjoy talking to him today. It's almost as if we've picked up where we left off ten years ago—only without the anger.

"The last time I talked to you," I say, "you were never going to get married. What happened? Who is she?"

"She's a girl I dated off and on in college. We ran into each other at a party last summer, and things fell into place. Sort of unexpected, but really right." He says this tentatively, as if he's afraid I'll burst into laughter. Actually, I'm touched. He sounds like a man in love.

"I always knew that when you found the right woman, you'd fall hard," I say. "What's her name?"

"Nicki . . . Nicole . . . Nicole Collier."

I can't have heard him correctly. "That's funny," I say. "I thought you said Nicole Collier." I laugh. "That would definitely be God's idea of a joke." He doesn't respond. "You didn't say Nicole Collier, did you? Not Seth Collier's little sister?"

"Right. Why? What's the problem?" He sounds defensive. My harsh response must have hurt his feelings.

"I'm sorry, Mark. The name caught me off guard. The Collier family was the last family on earth I would have expected you to say you were marrying into. You really don't know anything about what happened, do you?"

"No, and I don't care. And I'm sure Nicki won't, either. We both agreed. We want you here for our wedding, and we want Celi here, too. It's time, Ave. It's time for you to come home."

"I don't know, Mark. It's been so long."

"Avery, I know I said some stupid things that really upset you right before you left—"

I interrupt him. Surely he doesn't believe he had anything to do with my leaving, or cutting them all out of my life. I feel a familiar twinge of guilt. "That's all past now. You were only sixteen, and I was crazy with anger then—"

"No, wait, Avery. Let me say my piece," he interrupts. "I was wrong to even mention . . . You had every right to have your baby. It's just that I . . . I hated what was happening, and I didn't want to lose you. I didn't know how to say that then. Now—maybe it's law school, maybe it's this wedding and realizing what's really important to me; I'm not sure—but I've figured out how to say what I mean, and, if you're willing, I want y'all here. We're family. Besides, somebody has to help me deal with Mama!"

I don't know whether to laugh or groan. We always were united in our mission to avoid our mother's watchful eye. Even now, the thought of being around her, under her roof again, causes a lead-like heaviness in my stomach.

And yet, I can feel that buried part of me starting to surface, the part that has always missed my family, that old longing to belong to them again. I squash it down. I have to think about what's best for Celi. "I can't have Celi experience all of that racism, Mark. I want it to be different for her. She hasn't had to deal with that here in Colorado."

"Not everybody in Mississippi is a racist, Ave. Some of us are a little more enlightened. And, as for the others, I say to hell with them."

I surprise myself by actually considering the idea. I've worked so hard to take care of myself, to be independent. "Do you really think we could come?" I ask. "I mean, I'd really like Celi to get to know Will." I think of our grandmother, Willadean Reynolds. I'm not ready for the T-bone collision with sadness I'm feeling. "Have you seen her lately?" I ask, realizing I haven't given Mark a chance to speak.

"I've seen Will a couple of times since the summer. I don't get out there much. She's still as hardheaded as ever, and she and Mama are still keeping up the cold war. Nicki loves her. Every time we go out there, they spend the whole visit talking about fishing, or Will's tomatoes. And, yes, I think your coming can work. You've got to come down here and give us a chance."

"I still can't believe you're getting married," I say as Celi comes into the living room, swallowed up in one of Aunt Lizzie's voluminous aprons, dusted with flour, and holding out a handful of pecans for me to sample.

"Who's getting married?" she asks excitedly. Lately it seems she vacillates between dressing up her dolls for their imaginary weddings and wanting me to take her to the gym or park to shoot baskets. She goes from princess to tomboy, and I can't keep up.

"Is that Celi?" Mark asks in my ear as I'm distracted by her question. "Let me talk to her," he demands.

I hand the phone to Celi. "It's your uncle Mark."

She dumps the pecans onto the table and immediately takes the receiver from my hand. "Uncle Mark, are you getting married?" she asks, her eyes bright.

Whatever Mark says, Celi's response throws my neatly ordered world into a tailspin.

She pulls the receiver away from her mouth and is almost breathless when she says, "Mom, Uncle Mark is getting married and wants me to be a flower girl! Can we go to Mississippi for his wedding? Can we, please, please, please?"

I managed to put Celi off, feeling a little bad for stifling her excitement, and she's wandered off to play a new computer game until the rest of Aunt Lizzie's family arrives. I'm still staring at the fire with the phone in my lap when Aunt Lizzie comes in from the kitchen.

"What was all the commotion?" she asks, looking at me over the top of her glasses in that way she has that says, *You'd better shoot straight with me.*

Elizabeth Hughes, Grandma Will's cousin—or Aunt Lizzie, as Celi and I call her—took me into her life here in Denver ten years ago. She has been my salvation. She never asked any questions, and when I was ready to talk, she listened without judgment. Aunt Lizzie was widowed and had two children who were already grown and gone from home with children of their own. She tucked me safely into the apartment over her garage and made sure that I had everything I needed.

Mother was appalled when Will insisted on releasing my inheritance from Grandpa Jacob before I was twenty-one. I think Mother thought that if I had to suffer more, I might change my mind, come back home, maybe even get rid of my baby. But Will was smart. She released only enough money each year to make sure that I could pay for health insurance, groceries, and Aunt Lizzie's small rent.

Aunt Lizzie became the mother I needed to get through a pregnancy at eighteen. She supported my feeble attempts at starting a new life in Denver. I cried on her shoulder when Celi had colic; slammed around her kitchen when I was completely frustrated trying to date boys my age, who had no clue about my life as a single mother; complained about how bored I was with community college classes; and generally grew up, slowly, in her welcoming presence.

It was Aunt Lizzie who finally said to me, "Avery, why don't you go to nursing school? You're smart, and you've been floundering around trying to find something that satisfies you. I think you might have a knack for it."

Turned out, she was right. I discovered that I had most of the prerequisites already done, and within six months, I started nursing classes. I graduated three years ago and went straight into pediatrics. I poured myself into that job, the kids, the parents, and, as always, into Celi. Those first few years after she was diagnosed were rough for her. I never knew when she might wake up in the middle of the night screaming in pain, her swollen joints making every movement excruciating. I never knew when a simple cold would land her in the hospital on IV antibiotics. The crises came regularly for a while, until I learned more about what triggered them and how to ask questions that would get her treatments started before her symptoms became full-blown.

Celi and I moved into our own house two years ago, and as much as I love having my own place, there are times when I don't want to be as grown up as I try to be. Somehow, Aunt Lizzie always understands that. I wonder vaguely if she would go with us to Mississippi this summer.

"Where's Celi?" she asks.

"Playing her new game," I answer. "I think she's a little upset with me."

"Why's that?"

"Mark called to invite us to his wedding. She's beside herself with wanting to go. He asked her to be a flower girl."

"Oh, my," she says in typical Aunt Lizzie fashion, no judgment, just a simple observation while she waits for me to continue.

"I don't think I'm ready to face my family. Not even for Mark."

Even though I might have let my mind play from time to time with the idea of going back, usually triggered by something that reminds me of home, I am usually bombarded with fears that outweigh the pleasant memories.

I left under a cloud of secrecy and guilt—guilt because I had caused irreparable damage to someone I loved by being foolish. How can I face Aaron's grandmother, knowing how she feels about me? Then there is my anger at my mother, which I've worked so hard to defuse. I find myself left with an indifference toward her—a cold, numb feeling as if my heart's gone to sleep. At least it keeps the pain at bay. How far did my mother go to stop Aaron and me from seeing each other? How could she have ever thought that I would give up my child because it would be difficult for *the family*? How far would she or others in her social set go to ostracize Celi? There is not a single place I can think of in my parents' world that is integrated.

And what if they all find out that Celi has sickle-cell disease? The thought of someone hurting her with an expression or a look that places her in a *less than* category makes my blood boil. Yes, I have an intense curiosity to know how my family—how I, specifically, carry the sickle-cell trait. But how will I find that out? What will I stir up in seeking the truth? What if I give them a chance and end up with another disastrous mess? Is Celi ready for a place where neither the black majority nor the white minority will welcome her?

Chapter 2

Willadean

May 2001

"I'm telling you, I'm not wearing it!" I say, pushing away the ridiculous-looking hat that Sally is holding out to me. As is our tradition on the second Sunday of the month, Sally has come by Oak Knoll to pick me up for church. "I wear a hat for fishing and for gardening, not for church," I say.

"Willie," Sally says in that tone she takes when she's exasperated with me, "how long you been going to church with me?"

"You know as well as I do that I've been going with you once a month since Henry died," I answer. She's trying to rile me up. So far, she's successful—usually is. "And you also know that in that entire fifty-nine years I have not worn a hat! We go through this every Mother's Day. When are you going to stop pestering me?" Sally sighs and picks up the bright blue flowered and feathered contraption.

"I reckon I'll just keep trying. Figure maybe someday you'll want to cover up that old wiry gray head of yours—look more like the other mothers."

"You and I both know I'd still stick out like a mule in a pen full of ponies. A hat would just make it worse. Fitting in is not why I go to church with you."

"Lord knows that's the truth," Sally mumbles, shaking her head.

I feel a little remorse then. Church with Sally is one of the highlights of my month. "Y'all look good in those hats," I say. "Like a flock of those budgies they have in the cage down at the nursing home come to roost on the church pew. And when I listen to the choir sing, it almost makes me want to shout right along with you."

"Ain't nobody telling you not to shout, Willie."

I reckon Sally never will understand that I'll always feel like an outsider at the black Baptist Church. Oh, they make me feel welcome. I've been the only white person there for all these years since I started attending at sixteen—the same year I married Jacob. As close as Sally and I are, the black folks have a common bond that I know I can't ever quite share. I decided a long time ago to make my peace with that.

Even with the air-conditioning, the women sitting around me have got the funeral home fans cranking today. This new fan, I notice, has a particularly pretty picture of Jesus and the children—all colors of little children. Reminds me of that song we used to sing: "Red and yellow, black and white, they are precious in his sight. . . ." It's hot for May, and it being Mother's Day and all, the church is packed. I'm stuffed in between Sally, who's not a small woman, and Olivia Hacock, who makes Sally look small. The feather on Olivia's hat keeps tickling my face when she leans over to shout, "Amen!" and I'm trying not to sneeze.

The preacher is waxing eloquent about the virtues of motherhood, while the congregation peppers his sermon with "Yes, Jesus!" and "Tell it!" I relax and enjoy the peace I feel in the midst of this noisy service. I gave up the white Methodist church a long time ago—too stiff and pretentious. All of my daughter's friends buzzing around after services like they give a tinker's damn about me, Marion acting all tense like she's worried I'll say something wrong. In my opinion, Marion goes mostly for the social contacts. But I reckon I shouldn't judge her too harshly. Most of the folks there are doing the same thing. And it always was important to Marion to fit in.

Nope, except for coming here with Sally, I don't have much use for church. Me and the Lord do fine spending time together in my vegetable garden.

I'm a little bit preoccupied today, trying to figure out how I'm going to tell Sally about the phone call from Avery. It's taken my granddaughter five months to make up her mind, but she has finally agreed to come for Mark's wedding. I reckon I'll tell Sally while we're fishing this evening. That decided, I can focus on Elmira Hicks. She's singing "His Eye Is on the Sparrow," and I could listen all day to that deep, rich voice of hers. I can feel her vibrato in my bony old chest, and my heart swells as she fills up the little church with the words "I sing because I'm free. . . ."

Sally and I have settled into our usual fishing spot on the east side of Alligator Lake. We piled our lawn chairs, a small cooler, and our bait boxes and poles into my old truck and drove here on the dirt back road that cuts around the lake. Even though my house overlooks the lake on the west side, we've always liked fishing on this side. The trees are thicker and the roots in the water give the fish more places to think they're hiding from us. Both of our kids insisted on us coming over for dinner today, so after we tended to the graves in the cemetery, Sally went to her grandson's, Aaron's, and I drove into town to see Marion and Holt. It was pleasant enough, but the whole time I was looking forward to being out here fishing.

Now that it's getting on toward evening, it's started to cool off a little bit, and I'm hoping the fish will be biting. We're trying out a couple of brand-new lawn chairs Holt and Marion gave me for Mother's Day. They're not broken in like the ones we've been using for twenty years, but Sally says her rear end was starting to fall between the webbing of the old ones, so I reckon it was time. These are right fancy, with a cup holder in the armrest. I've got an ice-cold Nehi grape sitting in mine, and Sally's sipping on an IBC root beer. We're munching on parched peanuts and watching our red-and-white bobbers float slowly across the green water of

Alligator Lake. There's a slight breeze and the air smells sweet from the great big honeysuckle vine that's growing in the trees near the water's edge. Heaven.

I've spent so much of my life working for one cause or another, I never thought I'd find myself so contented with idleness. But at seventy-five, I've decided to let the young folks take up the torch. And things are better now between blacks and whites, they say. Look at Sally's grandson, Aaron, going into practice with one of the oldest white doctors in town. Thinking about Aaron reminds me. . . .

"I got some good news," I say as I see that my worm has gotten nibbled off the hook without so much as a tug on the line. I pull my line in to bait it again. My big old floppy hat is pulled down, covering most of my face, so Sally sits up, turns, and leans forward so she can see me better. She raises her eyebrows and pushes those big old red sunglasses she wears up on her frizzled gray head. She's perking up like this because I'm not usually a person to have news. I don't gossip much, and I don't poke into other people's business.

"What's that?" she asks, and I stop digging around in the bait box for a worm and look up at her.

"Avery Louise is coming home for Mark's wedding," I say, and then I watch her. I can honestly say that my granddaughter is the only subject Sally Monroe and I have had harsh words over in the sixty years we've been friends. I reckon Avery was too much like me as a girl: strong willed and hardheaded. And, unfortunately, sweet on Sally's grandson, Aaron. Sally and I both saw it coming that summer they met at Oak Knoll. We already had so much history at that place—what with all that happened in the summer of 1942 with Sally's brother, Henry, and Jacob and Jerrilyn and me. It's no wonder Avery and Aaron's sparking made Sally fearful.

Sally was so angry with Avery back then, she didn't want anything to do with her. And soon as she heard there was a baby coming and Aaron wasn't going to be part of the child's life, it got worse. I tried to tell her we had to look at it through Avery's eyes, but Sally didn't want to hear it. So we stopped talking about Avery and Celi. I wonder if she's softened any over the years.

"Avery Louise?" Sally asks, acting like maybe she hasn't heard me right.

"Yes, ma'am," I say, nodding, and Sally's chair creaks as she shifts her weight in it.

"Lord have mercy," she says, staring out at the water like she's looking back in time. "It's been ten years since that child left here. I was beginning to think she was never coming back. She going to stay out at Oak Knoll with you?"

"Avery called me last night. Says she talked to her daddy about staying in town with them. Said Holt was so excited, he was beside himself. He always did have a hard time losing his baby girl that way, her being so far from home and never calling."

"Is she bringing my great-grandbaby with her?"

My bobber disappears under the water. "Hold on a minute," I say, tugging back a little on my line.

"You can't throw something like this out there and then expect me to wait while you pull in a fish!" Sally hollers. "Tell me the rest of it!"

"Hush up, Sally! You're going to scare them all off." And then I proceed to pull that catfish in. Sally can wait for a minute.

"You can catch another fish. You don't need that one," she says. "Now, answer me. Am I going to get to meet my great-grandbaby or not?"

I slide my hand down the catfish's body and pull him off the hook with a snap, then reach to pull the stringer out of the water. "You surely will. She's bringing Cecelia," I say. "Mark and Nicki want her to be a flower girl."

"Well, praise be to Jesus!" Sally says. "I got to tell Aaron." Her eyes are all lit up, and she's getting up like she's going to fold up her chair and head for the truck right now.

"Ease up there, Sally," I say, real stern. "I don't think we need to tell him yet. Don't you think Avery needs a little time to settle in before she has a line of people out the door?" I reach into my bait box and pull out another fat worm.

"That's my great-grandchild you're talking about," Sally says, and then she frowns and plops back down in her chair, and I think it's begun to set in with her how complicated this situation is.

"She's my great-grandchild, too," I say. "But Avery's got to decide how to handle it, not us old folks. Avery doesn't even know that Aaron's back in town." I finish baiting my hook and stand to swing my line out over the water.

"You mean you haven't told her?" Sally looks at me accusingly.

I sit back down to take a sip of my grape soda. "Avery told me not long after she moved out there to Colorado that she'd decided it was best for Celi and Aaron if Aaron went on with his life and they didn't have contact. So Avery didn't want to hear anything about him—not about medical school, not about him marrying Lacretia, not even about his boys. And I had no idea she would be showing up here not three months after he decides to move back. So what was I supposed to do?" I yank off my old hat and smooth back the wiry gray hairs slipping out of my braid.

"It's wrong, her not letting that child know her daddy," Sally says with a stubborn fix to her mouth.

"I know the way Avery handled things has never set well with either of us, Sally. But you got to remember how scared she was for Aaron. After all that happened, that child lost every notion she had about things between the races improving around here." As I speak, I feel the old heaviness of working so hard, so long, for changes that come so slowly.

"Still not right," Sally mutters. "Child's got family here."

Sally getting angry all over again is not going to help matters. "The facts are these," I say, knowing I sound like an old schoolmarm, but I've got to talk some sense into my friend. "Cecelia doesn't know that Aaron is her daddy. Avery has never introduced her child to any of us. And Holt and Marion—well, especially Marion—have not had to deal with Avery's situation for ten years. So it's all a tangled mess! And you and I can't straighten it."

Sally and I know when we need a little silence between us. We each look out over Alligator Lake, letting ourselves follow the gentle ripples as water striders dip up and down on the surface. I know she's as lost in her thoughts as I am in mine. What will this return home be like for my stubborn, independent-minded granddaughter? Will my own daughter, Marion, publicly accept her mixed-race granddaughter? And most of all, I wonder, how will little Celi fare in a place where racism reaches as deep and dark as the bottom of Alligator Lake?

Chapter 3

Avery

June 2001

Driving across the flat, treeless plains of Kansas gives me time to consider what I'm about to do. The past five months have had as many highs and lows as the peaks and valleys of Colorado. One minute I was elated at the possibility of reconnecting with home and family, and the next I couldn't tolerate the thought; fear set in and I would tell myself there was no way I could pull off a reconciliation. Celi's consistent pressure and Aunt Lizzie's persuasive comments gradually wore me down, and I finally agreed to go.

Since then, I've focused on what I had to do to make this trip possible. First, I had to secure a leave of absence from my job. Thankfully, this worked out well and I have enough money saved to get us through a few weeks. Next was arranging for the house and Alvin to be cared for. That turned out to be simple. Aunt Lizzie insisted on staying home and watching over them, even though I begged her to come with us.

"Avery Louise," she said, "you need to do this on your own." When I shrugged and nodded, knowing she was right, she wrapped me in one of her soft, bosomy hugs and added, "I'm a phone call away, hon. Just a phone call away."

Of course, I had to check in with Dr. Hardy to be sure Celi

could travel safely. Celi, who has been beside herself with excitement, was thrilled when Dr. Hardy said, "I think she'll be fine, with a few precautions." Naturally, Celi heard the "fine" part and I heard the "precautions" part. "The heat is the main thing you have to watch out for," she said. "She'll need to stay well hydrated."

I turned to Celi and asked, "Do you understand what Dr. Hardy is saying?"

She nodded eagerly, her springy brown curls bobbing up and down, her eyes sparkling with happiness. "I have to drink a lot and not get too hot," she replied. I thought then about the sticky, thick Mississippi heat and wondered if Grandma Will had gotten air-conditioning. My plan is to visit with Grandma Will a lot. Daddy talked me into staying with him and Mother, even though I still have huge reservations. I know that they have plenty of room. The house on Crepe Myrtle Street in Greendale, the house I grew up in, is a huge Tudor-style with five bedrooms.

When I called the number for Daddy's office last month, I was surprised by the soft Southern voice that answered.

"Merle?" I asked.

"Yes, this is Merle. May I help you?" she asked politely.

"It's Avery," I said.

"Well, great day! I can't believe it!" she said, and I felt that old familiar warmth rush over me. Merle has been Daddy's secretary since before Mark and I were born. Merle bought the favorite pink baby blanket that I carried around for years.

I wasn't ready for a long chat, so after some preliminary updating, Merle transferred me to Daddy. "Avery, is that you?" he asked, as if he couldn't believe his ears, and my heart melted. Somehow talking to Daddy always puts things right. I asked myself for the millionth time why I keep him at arm's length. Probably because he sided with Mother. "Are you all right, darlin'? You're not sick, are you? How's Cecelia?"

"No, Daddy, we're fine. I called to let you know that Mark has talked me into coming home for his wedding," I said, holding my breath, wondering what he would say.

"Whatever it takes to get you here," he said. "I would have gotten married again myself if I'd known that would bring you home!"

I laughed then, imagining Mother's response to that statement, picturing her shaping her lips in a tight line and shaking her head.

Daddy and I talked about when Celi and I would arrive and our roles as part of the wedding party, and, of course, he proceeded to insist that we stay with him and Mother.

I faltered, realizing how my stomach clenched when I thought of seeing my mother again. "Um . . . well . . . do you really think Mother will be okay with it? I know she'll be busy with the wedding and everything. I was thinking we'd stay out at Oak Knoll with Will."

"Nonsense," he said, and in his usual persuasive way, he convinced me that everything would be fine. At least I thought I was convinced. Now that I've had time to contemplate the possibility, I'm not feeling as certain. As a matter of fact, I'm pretty sure I can't do it. Call it carrying a grudge against my own mother for ruining my life, call it protecting Celi—any way you slice it, I'll phone Will the next time we stop for gas. I'm sure she'd love to have us. Her house is more than a hundred and fifty years old, and with all of those live oaks providing shade from the sun, it's bound to be comfortable enough. I've been spoiled by cool Colorado summers. But I remember as a child climbing the back steps to Will's house, coming in hot and sweaty after walking up the long slope from the lake. The screened-in back porch always offered a welcoming drop in temperature.

Mark and Nicki's June wedding date, after his Christmas Eve proposal, is apparently relatively short notice in the Greendale wedding-planning circuit. How that must completely frustrate our mother and Laura Elise Collier, Nicki's mother. Celi and I will arrive just under a month in advance of the wedding. I decided that if I was going back, then I was going to spend enough time in Mississippi to sort out some relationships and get straight some of my own family history. I'm uncertain whether my probing questions will be welcomed. After all, there's a lot at stake. Clearly, Mother hasn't distanced herself from Will for all these years without reason. Will I be unearthing secrets that are better left buried?

At eighteen, I had not yet reached an age when knowing about the past mattered to me. Who begat whom was boring to an adolescent girl focused on being Miss Change the World and secretly spending time with Aaron Monroe. But now that I have a good reason to want to understand the genetic makeup of our family, I have to figure out a way to ask questions without tipping anyone off to why I'm asking.

I'm not sure why I feel compelled to keep Celi's disease a secret. I've told myself it's because of her fierce independence and need to fit in as a regular kid. And she'll have enough going against her in my mother and father's segregated world without adding a widespread knowledge of her sickle-cell disease.

Celi has been full of questions since I told her we were taking this trip. For the whole two weeks before we left she bragged to her friends about being a flower girl. I, on the other hand, am not thrilled about being a bridesmaid.

"Why me?" I asked Mark. "Nicki doesn't even know me. She was still a freshman when I graduated from high school."

"Doesn't matter," Mark said. "You're family, and she wants you to be in the wedding." Nicki got on the phone herself then, and ultimately, how could I refuse?

Over the years, I've managed to answer vaguely, or skirt altogether, Celi's questions about my family. When she asked, "Why don't we ever visit your mom and dad?" I usually gave some excuse related to work, the long distance, or not having enough time. I've never been able to figure out how to tell my child that I'm protecting her from people whom I'm afraid might see only the color of her skin. Even now, glancing in the rearview mirror at her in the backseat, settled into a nest of pillows, books, and stuffed animals, I wonder if I'm doing the right thing. As I exit and head south through Arkansas, I recall my conversation yesterday with Aunt Lizzie.

"What are you expecting in going back there, Avery?" she asked me.

"I have no idea," I answered. "I doubt things have changed much. Mark sounds great, though. I think he'll be a good influence in Celi's life. And, of course, she'll get to meet Will." I wavered then, apprehension welling up inside me. "I expect Mother will be polite. She's always polite. But I don't plan to give her any opportunity to hurt me—or Celi."

"Is it possible to give your mother a chance to respond differently?" Aunt Lizzie asked.

I snorted with a wry laugh. "That's not likely."

Aunt Lizzie chose to ignore my sarcasm. "And what about Aaron?"

I went cold then. Cold with the perpetual guilt I feel over my foolish actions that caused Aaron so much pain; and because over the years I've forced my own heart, which once warmed at the mere thought of Aaron, into frozen submission for my own emotional survival. I've poured into Celi all of the love I once felt for him.

Aaron is the part of my own personal puzzle that I have absolutely no answer for. I didn't then, and I don't now. When Celi was diagnosed, I briefly contemplated contacting him. The doctors explained all about transmission of the disease and suggested I might want to inform him. I came close. I even dialed information, but I stopped myself—or something stopped me. Selfishly, I told myself I didn't need to complicate Celi's life with a father just then—especially one so far away. I allowed myself to get caught up in her treatments, and time slipped by. Somehow, I never got around to contacting him.

In north Mississippi, Celi and I stop for gas at a convenience store. I use my cell phone to try to call Will, but she doesn't answer. And, of course, she has no voice mail. I can hear her craggy old voice saying, "What use do I have for an answering machine? If I'm not in the house, then I don't want to talk." I debate with myself again over whether to stop in Greendale at Mother and Daddy's.

We go inside to get some snacks, and I'm paying the attendant when three little black girls gather around Celi and stare at her as if she were a goldfish in a bowl. Celi is usually impatient with ogling strangers. It's unbelievable to me, the number of people who feel perfectly comfortable asking me if my daughter is adopted. Celi and I have developed our own response to this—somewhat sarcastic, granted, but we get a wicked chuckle from the reactions. It's not that I hide the fact that Celi's father is black; it's that I resent the intrusive curiosity. At least, this is what I tell myself.

"No, I found her in the cabbage patch," I'll say, and Celi will nod innocently and smile. Usually, this is off-putting enough to forestall any more questions. Today, Celi is as fascinated with these girls as they are with her. As usual, I have to stop myself from stepping in. Celi can hold her own.

The girls range in age from three to around eight and are all dressed in brightly colored sundresses, with tight plaits all over their heads held with beads and colored bands. They look like a flock of small, exotic birds. There are very few black kids in Celi's school at home, but here the population is seventy percent African-American. I'm interested to see how she responds.

"Where's your mama?" the tallest girl asks as she reaches out to touch Celi's honey brown braid.

"That's my mom right over there," Celi replies, pulling away from the girl's curious fingers. The girls all look at me and then at one another, wide-eyed. Celi seems a little defensive, which surprises me. Her caramel skin and kinky brown hair seldom arouse curiosity in Denver, since we frequently encounter mixed-race kids.

I move over to the girls and smile at them, saying, "Hi." The girls shift their attention only briefly to me. A large black woman rounds the end of the store aisle, carrying three loaves of white bread and two boxes of Little Debbie's Oatmeal Creme Pies. She is wearing the brightest pink tank top I've ever seen. The contrast with her amazingly smooth dark skin is striking. Her hair is swept up in a swirl of parallel braids, and her fuchsia lipstick emphasizes full lips and white teeth. She smiles and nods toward me before gently slapping one of the girls on her tight braids.

"Chicena," she says in a high voice, "get over here and help me with these groceries. Y'all quit bothering that little girl. Citrine, Sonja, y'all help, too. Get away from that child." The girls obey, each taking an item. All three of them move to stand behind their mother, who turns to me.

"This your little girl?" she asks, as if she is in charge of who comes and goes in the store and I have missed the check-in procedure.

"Yes," I say, reaching down to put a protective hand on Celi's small shoulder, which she immediately shrugs off.

"She's so pretty with that light hair and skin. She must have herself a black daddy, huh?" asks the woman, echoing her daughter's directness.

Before I can say anything, Celi answers for herself. "I'm nine and a half years old, lady, and it's none of your business who my daddy is. You got any more questions?"

The woman raises her painted-on eyebrows. Her daughters put their hands over their mouths and try not to laugh as their mother orders them to put their items on the counter. I pull Celi out the door and steer her toward the car. Will such questions be a constant theme for the next few weeks? I don't think I'm ready for the South.

The wide expanse of the delta cotton fields opens up before me and I look out over the vistas of my childhood. Five years have passed since Celi's diagnosis. I've vacillated between telling myself that the origin of her disease doesn't matter and that getting her the best treatment possible should be my focus, and being completely immersed in anger and helplessness over the fact that my daughter, my beautiful little Cecelia Louise Pritchett, has a disease that, in this country, is predominantly an African-American disease.

For a brief time I blamed Aaron for Celi's condition. After all, he's black and the gene for the disease had to have come from him. But Aaron wasn't sick. He was a star high school basketball player. I knew none of his family, except for Miss Sally, the grandmother who raised Aaron and who is my own grandmother's best friend. Did members of Aaron's family have the disease? Did Aaron know about it? Then I blamed myself for getting pregnant by him. If only I'd been smarter, more cautious.

Then I learned that each parent must carry the sickle-cell trait in his or her genetic makeup for the disease to present itself. There's a one-in-four chance that a child born to two carriers will have the disease, and Celi is part of that twenty-five percent. The quandary I find myself unable to ignore is how *I* contributed the other gene carrying the sickle-cell trait. How could that have happened when my family is white?

I've speculated endlessly in the long hours while sitting in uncomfortable hospital room chairs watching Celi's fitful sleep, listening to the barely audible drone of the IV pump transfusing healthy new blood cells into her veins. Where along the way was the genetic trait for sickle cell introduced into our family? The thought of it being my mother or father seems completely implausible. Mother doesn't associate with blacks in any way except as required for the services she needs. Mother having had sex with a black man and getting pregnant with me is so unlikely it doesn't even bear thinking about. Daddy's folks were Polish immigrants, now dead, so that rules him out. Maybe Will, but how? Who?

The closer we get to the exit for Greendale, the heavier grows the bowling ball of anxiety in my stomach. With a sudden flood of relief, coupled with no small amount of guilt, I decide that Will's house is where I want to be, not Mother and Daddy's. We need to be where Celi will be at ease and embraced fully, where I can easily strike up conversations with my reticent grandmother and solve this family mystery. Feeling much more comfortable with my own decision, I happily take the Greendale exit, knowing I'll be driving through town without stopping. I punch Daddy's office number into my cell phone, hoping he'll understand, and knowing on some level that I'm adding one more brick to the wall between my mother and me.

Chapter 4

Avery

As we drive past the last few buildings in the Greendale business district and return to the country roads lined with fences, pastures, and soybean or cotton fields, I glance in the rearview mirror at Celi. She's staring out the window and seems to be lost in thought. When I found myself pregnant, I hadn't even considered the idea of having kids, but when Celi was born my heart melted into a puddle that I've never been able to mop up. Whenever she looks up at me with those big green eyes and asks one of her off-the-wall questions, I fall in love with her all over again, even though she completely exasperates me with her endless curiosity. Not surprisingly, she breaks the silence between us.

"Mom?"

"Yes, sweet pea."

"Why don't cows sit down?"

She's obviously been watching the cows grazing in the pastures that line most every road in Mississippi.

I don't know why cows don't sit down. But I always try to give her some kind of answer. "They like to do their grazing standing up, I guess. They do lie down sometimes in the shade to rest, especially when it's really hot."

"It's probably because their hips aren't made for sitting," she says with her usual analytical approach. "They're not built like dogs, you know."

I nod, matching her level of seriousness. "You know, that makes sense. I've certainly never seen a cow sitting."

We drive on for several more miles. I am lost in a memory of an afternoon when I was seventeen years old. A summer afternoon, a pasture, and a boy. I can still feel his sleek bare chest under my fingertips, the pressure of his lips on my shoulder as he kisses it, the way he wraps his arms around me as we laugh hysterically. A black Hereford comes out of nowhere. We are apparently under her favorite tree, occupying her afternoon nap spot.

"Mom?"

"Yes," I say, startled.

"I said, does Grandma Will have cows?"

"Um . . . I don't really know. I think she and Grandpa had a cow or two when I was younger, but I don't know if she could take care of a cow now. She's pretty old, you know."

"Like old enough to die?" Celi asks. She's been preoccupied with death lately, and I'm cautious about how I answer her.

"That's not easy to say. But I don't think that Grandma is in danger of dying anytime soon. She's pretty healthy for an old lady."

"If she died while we were visiting, would we have to plan her funeral?"

Why is she thinking about funerals? I'm at a loss. Images of my mother's penchant for planning the perfect event pass through my mind: the perfect luncheon, the perfect dinner party, the perfect debutante ball . . . and now that I think about it, probably the perfect funeral. From what little I know about my grandmother, I doubt she would want the classic Southern funeral, complete with carnation sprays on the casket and long lines of mourners shaking hands and discussing how long they've known her people.

"I think my mother and father would plan things, honey. Hopefully, they would do everything like Grandma Will wanted it done."

"Does Grandma want to be buried or cremated?"

I really don't want to be having this discussion with a nine-year-old. I have absolutely no idea what my grandmother has planned. I answer Celi that I really don't know, and I'm relieved when that seems to satisfy her for the moment. She goes back into another of her reveries and then dozes off. Now I'm wondering if she constantly thinks about death. Is that normal for a girl her age? Is it because of her sickle-cell disease? I know her life expectancy is likely to be shortened because of it, but I've managed to find two adult women with the disease in an online support group who are well into their fifties and living happy, productive lives. And there is ongoing research into new treatments—all of that gives me hope. I don't want my little girl thinking about death.

I take a deep breath as we top a small hill, and Alligator Lake spreads out before us, shimmering green in the late afternoon sunlight. Turtles sun themselves on cypress knees, and the trees lean in around the shoreline, creating pockets of deep shade. I roll down the window to catch the muddy scent of the water. Memories ripple across my mind like the circles a fish makes as it surfaces to eat a water strider. We are close now to the road leading to Oak Knoll. The trees become more dense as we approach the turnoff to Will's house. Everything around here looks like it did when I graduated from high school. I thought it would be different, but it all looks the same.

"Mom?" Celi calls, abruptly awake from her nap. "Are we almost there?"

"Yep. We're getting close. The turnoff to Grandma's house is just a few miles from here."

"Those trees are spooky," she says, pointing to the twisted live oaks laden with Spanish moss. "They look like they could reach down and grab me with those long fingers. Are there ghosts in Grandma's house?"

"Nope, no ghosts. Just probably a lot of dust and clutter."

"Do you think Grandma will be glad to see us?"

I have to pause to consider this. I'm sort of counting on that, actually. I know that I'm taking a chance by showing up unexpected, but I'm hoping Will is home. She has mentioned in our Sunday night talks that she seldom leaves home these days.

"Mom?" Celi asks again, and I realize that I haven't answered her.

"Yes, I think she'll be thrilled to see us. You have to remember, though, that Grandma Will is a quiet woman. She doesn't get very excited about anything, so don't expect her to be all gushy over us."

"That's okay with me. I don't like gushy."

I smile. That is so true. For all of her short life, Celi has been an independent child. As a baby, she would push to get off my lap and check out whatever was on the floor. Even now, cuddling is allowed for only a few minutes, and then she's off again, always busy, always exploring. It breaks my heart to think that sickle-cell disease will continue to change her life, that treatments and doctors might limit her natural curiosity. We've gotten her past the most dangerous years—the first five. And she's lucky. Some of the kids we see at the hospital have crises once a month. At this point, Celi's occur only a couple of times a year. But being sick, for Celi, is not just a phase; it's a life sentence.

I'm not surprised when we turn off the main road and Celi asks again where we are.

"We're still on the road to Grandma's house. We're getting closer. Help me look for a clump of mimosa trees." But she has no idea what those are; there's no such tree in Colorado. "They'll be sort of feathery looking and they'll have fuzzy pink flowers." I remember my five-year-old self having tea parties with my dolls and serving them the tiny green mimosa leaves as imaginary salad.

"There they are!" Celi says, pointing to the slick-bark trees covered in delicate pink blossoms that each look like a fireworks explosion.

"Good job, Celi," I say, turning to see the excitement on her face. "We should be close now." She leans forward to try to see beyond the canopy of trees that darkens the gravel road we're on.

"This forest looks like the one in my fairy-tale book. You know, the one with Hansel and Gretel—" Suddenly Celi stops midsentence and gasps, frozen in place, her eyes wide and staring out the front windshield.

I turn back just in time to slam on my brakes. A young white-tailed deer is standing in the middle of the road. For seconds we are locked in to her brown-eyed stare. Celi murmurs softly, "Wow," and I don't move a muscle. Then the doe blinks once and springs away into the woods, crashing quickly through the dense undergrowth.

"She was so beautiful!" Celi says. "Do you think we'll see her again?"

"I don't know, honey. If we don't see her, we'll probably see others. There are thousands of white-tail deer in these woods."

"Mom, I read in my Mississippi book that they shoot the deer here. Is that true?"

"Yes, I'm sad to say it is true. Hunting is a popular sport here."

"Are the deer mean? Do they fight back?"

"Oh, goodness no. Deer are the most gentle creatures you could imagine. They run away when they see humans. Like the one we just saw."

"I don't understand how people can kill an animal that's gentle and not hurting anybody," Celi says sadly.

"There are so many deer now that if they weren't hunted, some of them would die of starvation," I say, trying to keep my voice informative, objective. History of Hunting 101, I think. How many times did I have this discussion with my father while growing up? It's going to be a long summer of explanations. As I'm about to launch into a talk on animal population control, the house comes into view and Celi is distracted. I breathe a sigh of relief.

Almost completely hidden behind a curtain of Spanish moss that hangs from the six live oaks that surround it, Oak Knoll sits peeking through at us like a wary old white-haired woman checking on the activities of her neighbors. Memories of times spent in this house and on its sweeping grounds come flooding back, and I remember now that at Celi's age I always felt as if the house were watching us approach. I offer up a small prayer that

Will is home today, maybe working in her vegetable garden or dozing on the porch.

The house looks a little shabbier than I remember, probably because Will is not concerned with upkeep. Mother always complained about Will's complete disregard for appearances. I can still hear Mother's shrill, complaining voice: "That woman doesn't have one iota of concern for what people think. It's simply appalling. She lives out there in one of the oldest homes in this area, yet she might as well be living in a single-wide in a trailer park."

Oak Knoll is certainly no house trailer. Situated on a low rise overlooking Alligator Lake, the house was built by my grandfather's ancestor in the popular Greek Revival style of nineteenth-century plantation homes. The eight-sided cupola rises two stories above double front doors flanked by floor-to-ceiling windows, all of which circulate air to cool the house on even the hottest summer days. The wide front porch is completely screened so that in the shade of the oaks it's difficult to see through. Is Will watching us from there? Flowers grow everywhere. I recognize roses and daylilies, but there are many more I can't name.

As we pull into the circular drive, I watch for any sign of life from the doorway. I'm suddenly nervous, uncertain of how to approach my own grandmother. She will remember me as an angst-filled, angry adolescent. Have I changed? I park the car, get out, and walk around to meet Celi as she climbs out of her seat. I brush stray cookie crumbs from her sundress and arrange her books on the car seat, delaying our entrance.

Celi reaches for my hand and grips it tightly. I bolster my own courage, knowing that she's counting on me. It's all going to be fine, I tell myself. This visit will be great for Celi, and it will give me a chance to get a few much-needed answers. And I can put off facing Mother for a little while longer.

As Celi and I are about to climb the steps to the front door, Will comes around the side of the house. Loping close at her heels is, unbelievably, my grandfather's black-and-tan coon dog, Rufus. I do a mental calculation and place him at around fourteen years old. Will and Rufus are both focused on the still quivering string of fish in her hand. In her other hand she clutches a long bamboo fishing pole with the line wrapped neatly around it, and a small tackle box hangs from her little finger. She's wearing a wide-brimmed straw hat and a loose flowered cotton dress with big patch pockets, one of which I can see is holding her bait box. I got my height from her, and she is not stooped at all. Her thin white legs, crisscrossed with thick blue veins, extend from her tall white crew socks and shockingly pink Converse tennis shoes. I hear Celi's appreciative giggle as Will approaches.

I worry that we'll startle her, since she seems so focused on whatever it is she's looking for, so I call out to her. "Hello, Will."

An expression of confusion crosses her features, and then a big smile splits her deeply lined face as she stops to stare at us. I can barely see her eyes under the floppy hat. She leans her fishing pole against the side of the house and drops the fish into a bucket she suddenly spots near an outdoor spigot. Still clutching her tackle box, she approaches us with long strides. "Avery Louise? What a nice surprise! Child, you've hardly changed a whit!"

Those words are balm to my ears, and I relax for a moment, thinking that maybe I've done the right thing in coming here. Will pulls me into her warm embrace as Rufus sniffs around my knees. She smells of sun-warmed cotton, slightly of fish, and of worms dug fresh from the ground. Smells I'd forgotten, along with the places of my childhood. Sadness and relief flood through me, and I hug her tighter. She pats me gently, not bothering with words, not asking questions. After a few seconds, she asks, "Who is this smart-looking little youngster you have here with you?"

I pull away and admonish myself for forgetting Celi, standing patiently watching. I pull her small body forward and stand behind her, holding her shoulders. "Grandma Will, this is my daughter, Cecelia Louise Pritchett." Celi thrusts her small hand out toward Will.

"I'm very pleased to meet you, Grandma Will."

Will chuckles and bends to set her tackle box down, motioning Celi toward her. "You are a fine young lady. How about a hug for your ancient great-grandmother?"

Celi moves tentatively forward and smiles sweetly as Will hugs her. She reaches out to scruff Rufus's inquisitive head as he tries to push his nose between them. I'm amused by my daughter's silence. She seems so demure and timid right now—not at all like herself. But I was premature to admire her diffidence.

"Why were you carrying those fish on a string? Won't they die if they're not in the water?" Celi has pushed back from Will's embrace and is looking up at her.

"Do you like to eat fried fish?" Will asks, picking up her tackle box and heading toward the bucket she left near the house.

Celi follows her, leaving me watching them together, marveling at how quickly my daughter moves from an introduction to asking questions and how my grandmother has already taken her in, as if she's been answering her questions for years. I'll be interested to see how long she has the patience for Celi's relentless curiosity. I listen to their conversation as I retrieve the suitcases from the car.

"I don't know if I like fried fish," Celi says. "I've only ever had fish sticks. Do they taste like fish sticks?"

"Oh, much better than fish sticks. I caught these fish in Alligator Lake, so they're fresh."

"How did you catch them? And is Alligator Lake near here?"

"Well now, you see that pole right there . . ." Their voices fade as Celi picks up the pole as instructed by Will and follows her around the side of the house. Rufus trails along behind them, nuzzling Celi's hand for more pats. They seem to have forgotten me, so I troop after them, lugging the suitcases. As I round the corner, I'm stopped dead in my tracks. I knew I shouldn't have come here without warning. Ahead of me, Will and Celi have paused in the cool-dirt shade of one of the rambling old trees. Their backs are to me and they're talking to someone. I see Celi reach out as if to shake hands and as I move closer I can see around them. Sitting in a dilapidated wooden lawn chair, smiling widely and shaking hands with my daughter, is Sally Monroe, Aaron's grandmother and Celi's other great-grandmother.

Chapter 5

Willadean

I can tell right away when I look up and see Avery standing there with a suitcase dropped in the grass on either side of her, her mouth a little bit open like she's about to say something but doesn't know quite what, that Sally Monroe was the last person she was expecting to see when she decided to show up here today. I'm mighty glad to see Avery, although I'm not sure why she's out here instead of in town with her mama and daddy. At least that was the plan last I heard. And I know Sally wants to just eat up this beautiful little great-granddaughter of ours. I'm praying she doesn't say anything foolish. Avery comes rushing over, probably because she's thinking the same thing I am.

"Cecelia, this is my good friend Miss Sally Monroe," I say. "Sally, this here is Miss Cecelia Louise Pritchett, Avery's daughter." I deliberately avoid saying "my great-granddaughter" so Sally won't feel left out and in hopes that she'll take the hint. Cecelia reaches out to shake her hand; she's such a polite little thing, small for her age. She didn't get Avery or Aaron's height, but she's skinny like Avery always was.

"Pleased to meet you," she says. "You can call me Celi. Everybody does." She watches us with those doe-like, long-lashed eyes—Avery's eyes—like she's trying to take us in. Rufus sits on his haunches beside her, letting her rub his head. That old dog has taken to her already. That's a good sign.

"Hey, Miss Sally," says Avery, looking nervous. "How are you doing?"

"I'm doing just fine," says Sally. "This is a mighty pretty little girl you got here," she says, and I see her wink at Avery. I could kiss that old woman for trying to put Avery at ease. During that last couple of years Avery was here, Sally started getting cold with Avery once she and I figured out Avery and Aaron were meeting each other down at Alligator Lake. Said she didn't want to encourage her. I reckon Sally saw trouble coming. She always could spot it quicker than I could. Seems like it was always me dragging us into trouble. She's put up with a lot from me.

I know it's killing Sally right now not to acknowledge this child as part of her family, but it looks like she's going to do as I asked and let Avery figure when to tell Celi—if she does. We chat about this and that—their trip, how things look the same, what Celi thinks of the heat—and then Sally takes her leave. We wave good-bye as she rattles off in her old Ford, and I turn to Avery and say, "I don't have much cooked, since I wasn't expecting y'all until tomorrow, but I've got a package of chicken in the refrigerator I was planning to fry and a few leftover purple-hull peas. What say we slice up some tomatoes from my garden and make ourselves a little supper? And you can tell me why you missed your stop in Greendale." Avery nods, looking a little sheepish, as we head for the house.

Avery doesn't seem to want to talk about why she didn't stay in town, at least not in front of Celi. So I go on and act like nothing is wrong. Those rolling suitcases of theirs clickety-clack across the kitchen floor as they follow me through to the back hall. "I think it'd be best if y'all stay here," I say, opening the door to the old sunporch. It smells a little musty, and I reach to turn on the ceiling fan, hoping it doesn't spread too much dust. The white beaded-board walls still look fresh. I need to sweep these old pine floors.

"Wow!" says Celi. She's dropped her suitcase and headed over to the tall crank-out casement windows to look out over the back lawn toward the lake. Avery is beaming. You can see her love for that child written all over her face.

"Will, you can't give us your room," Avery says. "We can sleep in one of the upstairs rooms."

"Oh, it's fine, honey," I say. "I don't sleep in here anymore. After your granddaddy died, I stayed in this room for a few years, but it got to feeling too big, so I decided to take the smaller one up by the parlor." I smile, glad to be sharing this room with them. "This one will always be my favorite."

"I've never seen a bedroom like this," says Celi. "It looks like a porch. And the lake is so beautiful."

"Your great-grandpa and I shared many a night here over our forty-two years together," I say. "This room still makes me miss him the most." I wish that Celi could have known him. I sigh to myself as I push back the white cotton curtains, thinking they could use a good wash and hanging out on the clothesline.

"This was my favorite room, too, Celi," says Avery. "When I was a little girl, younger even than you are now, Grandpa Jacob would let me crawl up in that big four-poster bed with him in the mornings when I stayed over. Grandma Will would bring him coffee and me hot chocolate, and we'd look at the lake."

"Yes, Jacob loved his coffee in here on those weekend mornings." I walk over to the little daybed at the end of the long room. "Celi," I say, "my in-laws, the Reynoldses, had this room built as a sunporch at the same time they added the kitchen back in the twenties. The breeze off the lake through those windows is especially nice in the spring and fall. You can sleep in this little daybed. This is where your uncle Mark and your mama slept when they visited us." I sit down on the edge of the bed, remembering those rare Sunday mornings when Jacob convinced me to stay in bed long enough to watch the sun come up over Alligator Lake.

"Just a few more minutes, Willadean," he'd say.

"But I need to get the coffee on. Your mama will be hollering for a cup."

"Oh, let her holler." And he'd pull me close under his arm, with my head against his chest, and we'd lie there, waiting for that first ray to bore through the trees across the lake. When it rose high enough, that sun shone straight into our eyes and lit up the white walls of that room with a glow like a beacon focused right on us. It really was a miracle, just like he said. As I sit here remembering those mornings, I wonder why I didn't do that more often, and as I look out over the back lawn, I wonder if Avery and Celi will appreciate that sunrise.

Celi is asking me a question. "What was that you said?" I ask.

"Is that the lake where you fish?" she asks.

"It sure is," I answer. "That's Alligator Lake. This week I'll take you and your mama out fishing if you'd like. We had already planned to have a big catfish fry out here tomorrow night. The whole family will be coming." I look over at Avery and, as I expected, she doesn't look near as excited as her daughter.

"Really?" Celi asks, her face lighting up. "What's a catfish fry?"

Avery sits down beside me on the daybed and says, "It's a party. Grandma Will will fry up the fish she's caught, and there'll be hush puppies and coleslaw and sweet tea. . . ."

Celi interrupts, "What's a hush puppy? That sounds weird."

"Nothing but cornmeal and buttermilk and a little onion fried up," I say. "You mean to tell me you've never had a hush puppy?"

"No," she says, shaking her head and looking serious. "But it sounds gross."

Avery laughs. "Believe me, Celi, hush puppies are the best—you're going to love them. Now, let's get ourselves unpacked, and we'll go out and play with Rufus."

Back in the kitchen, I pull the package of chicken and the leftover peas out of the refrigerator. I put the peas in a pan to warm. I look out the window for Avery and Celi as I wash the chicken. They're playing fetch with Rufus. That old dog is as happy as a pig in a wallow to have somebody to toss a stick for him. He moves about as fast as I do these days, but at least Avery and Celi can throw for him. I can't get my arm to move that fast anymore. Just as I'm putting the chicken on to fry, Celi bursts through the back door.

"Hey, Grandma Will," she says, her little face flushed with sweat. "That smells good. What are you cooking?"

"These are purple-hull peas in this pot," I say, pointing to the pan on the stove.

She peers into the pot. "They're not purple."

"No, the hull around them is what's purple. I'll have to show you my garden tomorrow. You can see them growing—maybe help me pick a mess."

"How do you pick a mess?" she asks, her face all screwed up.

The look of disgust on that child's face is keeping me from laughing out loud. She's so serious. Bless her heart, she's got to learn a whole new language, and I'm going to have to figure out how to answer a lot of questions. "A mess is what we say for a picking of peas that's less than a bushel and not quite a peck, just enough for a meal. You know what a bushel and a peck are?" I ask.

She wrinkles up her little nose and acts as if she's thinking about it real hard. "Nope," she says.

"No, ma'am," Avery says, coming in the door right then and heading over to the refrigerator, where she knows I still keep the jug of cold water. Puzzled, Celi looks up at her mama.

"Down here in Mississippi, Celi, you say 'yes, ma'am' and 'no, ma'am' to your elders. Isn't that right, Will?"

"I reckon. Although children aren't taught that like they used to be."

"Why?" asks Celi.

"It's a sign of respect," her mama says. "A way of being polite."

"Oh," she ponders. "You mean like saying 'please' and 'thank you.'"

"Yes, like that," Avery says as she plops down in a kitchen chair and scoops Celi up in her lap. "I think we wore out old Rufus, Will. He's gone out there under that big old live oak down by your garden. Looks like he's collapsed."

I peer out the window. I can see his favorite spot from here. "Yes, he's got a nice spot dug out under that tree. Keeps his belly cool. When it gets hot like this, that's the first place you'll find him."

"I like Rufus," Celi announces. "What kind of dog is he?"

"He's a hunting dog, sugar, a black-and-tan hound. Belonged to my late husband, your great-grandpa."

"When did Grandpa die?" she asks.

"He died about thirteen years ago. He got Rufus a few months before he died. I told him then he was too old to be getting another coon dog. But I think getting a puppy meant hope for him. He'd never been without a hunting dog. So I didn't argue. But Grandpa got sick shortly after Rufus joined us. So Rufus and I spent many a long night sitting up with him."

Little Celi gets off her mama's lap and walks over to me. She wraps her little arms around my hips. "I'm sorry, Grandma Will. That sounds really sad."

I'm not quite sure what to do. I'm not used to affection, especially from little children. But she's such a sweet, serious, strange little thing; I find my old heart warming to her. I reach down and give her head a pat. The feel of her springy hair under my fingers reminds me of Sally's and Henry's hair. "Yes, I reckon it was. Now, how about you help me set the table for supper?"

"Yes, ma'am," she says, looking to her mama for approval. Avery smiles wide.

"There you go," says Avery.

"You'd better watch out," I say. "You might be making a little Southerner out of her."

"Humph." Avery snorts. "Not likely."

"Will, that was absolutely fabulous!" Avery says, groaning a little as she leans back in the glider. We're sitting out on the back porch having a cool glass of sweet tea and watching the colors in the lake change as the sun sets. The crickets are singing to us and it's finally cooling off. Celi is wandering around the backyard looking for lightning bugs. Rufus is trailing behind her. She doesn't believe me that there are bugs whose rear ends light up at dusk. That child has to see everything for herself. She's quite a challenge for an old lady.

"So what happened to you staying in Greendale with your

mama and daddy?" I ask, knowing that both of us are wondering who'll bring up her mother first.

Avery sighs and pauses a few seconds. "The closer I got, the harder time I was having with the thought of seeing Mother," she says. She pulls one leg up to her chest and wraps her arms around it, propping her chin on her knee. She doesn't know it, but her mama used to do that same thing—before Marion got so hell-bent on being ladylike, that is. Avery smiles as she watches Celi flop down on the ground in a heap. Rufus stretches out beside her with his head on his paws.

"I guess I'm afraid," she says.

"Afraid of what?"

"I don't know, really. Maybe of how Mother will react to Celi, of me getting too defensive or protective. . . ." She trails off and looks down, studying her toes. I wait for her to say more when she's ready.

Avery looks at Celi, who is faithfully studying the sky for the first flicker of light. "I don't have anything to say to Mother. You know she and I never got along—even before I was pregnant. When I left here, I swore I'd never come back. I've only talked to her maybe once a year since then. And if Daddy is the one who answers the phone, she usually relays messages through him. We exchange cards at holidays. That's about it. I have no idea what she tells her friends about me. I can guarantee she doesn't talk about Celi."

"Your mama has some definite ideas about what makes for a good reputation. That's always been really important to her," I say. "I reckon I didn't help her much with that when she was growing up."

"Why does it matter so much?" Avery asks, setting her foot down and leaning forward. She's restless, this girl who's turned into a young woman since she left here.

I think of all the years Marion has distanced herself from me in her mission to make herself one of Greendale's elite. I've never understood why fitting in with that group is so important to her, but I stopped fighting it long ago. It makes me sad to think that

Marion would lose her daughter and grandchild over something as fleeting as what people think. Should I interfere? I'm pondering how to respond to Avery when she says, "Will?" She turns her back to the arm of the glider so that she can look at me, pulling herself into a cross-legged position. "I don't know much about my family . . . not about you and your history, or Mother's and why y'all have always seemed sort of . . ."

"Crossways with each other?" I ask.

"Yes, exactly," she says. "Take you being friends with Miss Sally, for instance, and you being so comfortable around blacks. How did that happen? How can you be so open and Mother be so closed?"

"Whew! That's a lot of questions at one time, child." It's one thing for Avery to understand her family origins, but quite another for her to go digging into memories that I've put to rest. I'm not ready to pull out everything that happened all those years ago when my impetuousness changed our lives. Nor do I think she's ready to hear it.

"I know. You're right," she says. "But we've got lots of time . . . and if you're willing, I really want to know."

"I don't have anything but time these days," I say.

"Seems like growing up, I didn't know anybody who had black friends—none of the kids I knew, and especially no one from your generation, or Mother's, for that matter."

"Oh, Sally and I go way back," I say. "I was not a high-society girl, you see. I wasn't born on the other side of the tracks, but right close to them."

"What do you mean?" Avery asks. She truly doesn't know anything about my childhood.

"Back in those days, the black folks lived at one end of Washington Avenue, and the white folks lived at the other. The railroad tracks were the dividing line. Daddy and I lived back off the road right near the tracks, barely on the white side."

"What about your mother?"

"I wasn't but a year old when the great 1927 flood came through here. Daddy said that he and Mama were trying to get out of the house and make it to higher ground when the Mississippi River levee broke. He was holding me, and a big rush of water came through and Mama slipped. Daddy couldn't save her and hold on to me both. I don't remember much about my grandmother, but I do remember her saying, 'Your daddy's got a broke heart, honey.' I stayed with her in Water Valley while Daddy went to pharmacy school at the University of Mississippi. After he finished school, he moved us back here to Greendale. Let's see, I reckon I would've been around five years old by then.

"Daddy bought a storefront on Main Street and opened up Franklin Drugs. I grew up running wild, playing with white and colored children alike. Daddy was always busy with his medicines and all. I reckon some of the ladies in town must have told me he needed to get me tamed down a bit. I remember one day, in particular. . . ."

Chapter 6

Willadean

Summer 1941

I was sitting out back of the drugstore watching Leroy stir up a new batch of tonic. It was as hot as blazes, so he set up the washtub on two sawhorses in the shade of the wide-spreading oak. That live oak was my favorite because it had a limb that dipped almost to the ground, with a curve just right for a seat. Leroy had been working for Daddy mixing up the tonic for as long as I could remember. I always had Leroy to count on, and by then he'd gotten so old, about all he could do was mix the tonic. Daddy had told me that morning at the breakfast table that he planned to hire a new boy to run deliveries and help stock the store. Me and Leroy hadn't met him yet, but I was having a hard time seeing how anybody could take Leroy's place. I liked talking to Leroy because he didn't treat me like a little girl. That day, he was telling me about an alligator gar that got caught out of the lake the day before.

"That thing was the ugliest fish I ever did see, Miss Willie," he said. "Big old long snout like a gator, long fat body like a fish. And teeth? Lordy, those teeth could snap a man's arm in two like kindling." Leroy shook his sweaty head and pulled out his red bandana handkerchief to wipe his brow.

I stopped making circles in the dirt with my bare toes and looked up at Leroy's shiny black face.

"How'd they catch him?" I asked.

"Said they had to use a piano string, that thing was so big. And when they got him in the boat, they used a shotgun to kill him. Look like he was going to turn that boat over with all his flailing around," Leroy said. He pointed at the base of the sawhorse sitting about four feet from my tree limb. "That gator gar was as long as from here to there. I ain't never seen a fish that big. And he not even Big Ugly, the biggest one of all."

"Who was it caught him?" I asked, knowing there'd been a stiff competition in Greendale for years for who was going to catch Big Ugly. I'd heard the old white men who sat on the bench outside the drugstore say Big Ugly was a ten-foot-long, two-hundred-pound alligator gar that lived in the murky east side of Alligator Lake.

"Dr. Collier, he's taking the credit," Leroy continued. "But I heard tell he didn't do the catching. His colored man, Jarvis Lee—he be the one what caught the fish." Leroy pulled the wooden paddle toward him, creating a liquid furrow in the murky brown tonic mixture. The heat made the bitter scent of the vitamins he added roll toward my nose, and I felt my stomach turn. I didn't know how folks could drink that stuff. But Daddy was famous around the county for making it. Folks came from all over to buy his special Franklin Tonic and Home Remedy. I always heard people say, "It'll cure what ails you." Even the church ladies bought it. They said it helped their constitutions.

My mouth was so dry I could hardly work up any spit, and I wondered if Daddy had put more root beer in the cooler last night before he closed up the store. If I was quiet I could sneak in and grab one for me and Leroy. The breeze picked up a little bit then, and Leroy reached behind him to pull a Mason jar full of clear liquid from a wooden crate. He unscrewed the lid and poured the contents into the washtub. He'd add about five more jars full before he was done. It was supposed to be a preservative, but me and Leroy knew it was the secret ingredient that made

Daddy's tonic so popular. Especially, Leroy said, since folks couldn't buy liquor in our county. The tiny bit of wind carried the fumes from the homemade alcohol and I decided it was time for that root beer.

I thought about Dr. Collier taking credit for catching that fish. Me and Leroy, we didn't like Dr. Collier much. Leroy said he wouldn't treat the colored. Daddy, on the other hand, sold medicine to anybody who needed it—colored or white. Leroy always helped wait on the colored folks when they came through the alley to the back of the store. Maybe the new boy would do that now. I knew Leroy wasn't going anywhere. He lived in a room above the store, but Daddy kept saying how Leroy was getting old and his rheumatism had him so stove up he could scarcely move some mornings. I couldn't bear the thought of not having Leroy around. He was my best friend.

I opened the back door and stepped into the room where Daddy kept supplies. The shelves were lined with glass bottles, and I remembered that I needed to bring some of those out to Leroy, along with a funnel. But first things first. I tiptoed past the area where Daddy compounded medicine and peeked around the corner to see if he was busy. His head was bent over a mortar and pestle, the radio was playing Jimmy Dorsey, and he was humming, not paying me any attention.

I opened the side door that led to the soda fountain and peeked in to see who was working. When I saw who it was, I shrugged. Daddy had hired two soda jerks—one I liked. The one I couldn't stand was working, Beauregard Waverly, the smarmiest boy I'd ever met. He always made crude comments about what I wore. Just because I didn't like frilly dresses and bows in my hair, he seemed to think that gave him an excuse to harass me. The week before, he'd cornered me in the supply room and unsnapped the fastener from the bib of my overalls and said, "Let's see what you got under those overalls, Willadean." He leered at me and came so close I could smell his Beech-Nut chewing gum. "Let's make sure you're a girl." I slapped his hand away and pushed past him. He lost his balance and fell against the shelf. Boxes of straws and paper napkins went flying. Daddy heard the commotion and poked his head out from his compounding room.

"Everything okay?" he asked. Beau glared at me, daring me with his eyes to say something to Daddy. I didn't. Beau might be a creep, but I could handle myself. Besides, things would get worse if I tattled on him to my daddy.

"Everything's fine," I said. "I knocked some stuff off the shelf."

"Watch out for the merchandise," Daddy said, distracted.

Ever since that little incident, I'd been trying to avoid Beau, and as I saw his bony back turned toward me, I almost reconsidered that root beer. But it was hot outside, and I had promised Leroy something cold. And then I got lucky. The bell over the front door jingled as Adda Jenkins came prissing in. Only God knew why, but she had a crush on Beau Waverly—probably because his daddy had money and she thought she could marry into it and maybe get out of the Bottoms.

Around Greendale, white folks like the Waverlys and the Colliers lived on the north end of Washington Avenue in their fancy houses with maids and butlers and yard men—all colored. On the south end of Washington, the colored with money lived. They had nice houses, too. Not quite so fancy, but they were neat and tidy and they kept their yards swept clean. The poor white folks like Adda Jenkins lived in what people called the Bottoms, named for its low-lying area, which was too wet to grow cotton. The houses out there were mostly shacks for what the church ladies called poor white trash.

Adda was only about five feet tall, so she had to hitch up her dress and stretch to anchor her fat bottom on the green-vinyl-covered stool in front of the soda fountain counter.

"Afternoon, Beau," she said, batting her eyes at him and placing her handbag on the counter so she could pull off those ridiculous white gloves she was wearing. She crossed her arms on the counter, which she could barely reach, and plopped her large breasts on her arms. Adda and I were both fifteen, but as different as night and day. She had those big breasts that boys mooned over and she sneaked her mama's lipstick. Me, I couldn't have cared less that I was skinny and flat chested. Daddy said I was beautiful like my mama, but I didn't believe him.

Beau went all goofy, trying not to stare at Adda's breasts and falling all over himself to offer her a treat. "What'll you have, Adda? We got chocolate malts on special today."

Since he was distracted, I took the opportunity to slip behind the counter and open the ice case. I was reaching in for two root beers when Adda said, "Hey there, Willadean. Whatcha doing?"

Damn! I turned, holding the two icy root beers down by my side, and tried to smile politely at her. Beau scowled at me. He didn't want me interrupting his trying to sweet-talk Adda. "I'm just getting a couple of root beers. It's mighty hot out there today and I'm powerful thirsty," I said, sidling toward the door. Adda was temporarily distracted by Beau holding out a spoon with a small amount of chocolate ice cream on it for her to taste. She took the spoon daintily and closed her cherry red mouth around it.

"Mmm . . . yummy. I'll have a chocolate malt. And put some of those sprinkles on it, please," she said. He grabbed a soda glass and scooped chocolate ice cream into it like his life—or at least his next kiss—depended on it, and I tried to make my exit without being rude.

"I'll see you, Adda," I said, giving a little wave.

"Wait, Willadean," she said. "Are you going to the Methodist church hall social tonight? There's going to be swing dancing, you know."

"*I* am. Soon as I get off work," Beau said eagerly. Adda ignored him and continued to look at me. Swing dancing was the last thing I had any interest in doing. Me and Leroy had already planned to go fishing on Alligator Lake.

"Um . . . I don't think I'm going to be able to go, Adda," I said. "I've got a lot of . . . um . . . studying to do." I cursed myself for that feeble excuse. I couldn't seem to think quick enough to come up with anything else.

"You silly goose," she said, with that annoying nasally giggle of hers. "It's summer. Besides, don't you think it's time you put on a pretty dress and did something with us girls?"

Beau snorted at this and I glared at him, wishing I could conk him on the head with his ice-cream scoop. Adda was still talking.

"My mama says that she would be perfectly willing to sew you a dress for free. Not that your daddy couldn't buy you a dress, but you should know. . . ." She leaned forward like she and I shared some girl secret. "Mrs. Collier and Mrs. Cole, who are two of Mama's best customers, think that you need to be more ladylike."

Beau nodded with a leer on his face. "I could've told you that, Willadean. I've even heard my own mama say you run around like a banshee."

A red heat started to creep up my neck. It always happened when I was mad or embarrassed, and right then I was both. How dared they? What business of theirs was it what I did? I was so angry I knew better than to try to say anything. Leroy always said, "If you so mad you want to hit something, then just make yourself go the other direction." But before I could leave, Adda got in one more dig.

"It's not right hanging around the colored all the time like you do, Willie," she said, like she was some sage adviser helping a poor miserable ignoramus. "Maybe if you spent more time with white people, you'd get more comfortable with—you know—being a lady."

I couldn't stand it anymore, and I was about to give both of them a piece of my mind, and maybe more than that to Beau, when Daddy stuck his head out from the pharmacy window. I suddenly had a sinking feeling that he might have overheard the entire conversation. I was so humiliated, I could hardly breathe.

"Willie, is that you in there?" he asked.

"Yes, sir," I responded, grateful for the distraction.

"I think Leroy needs you to bring him some bottles and the funnel," Daddy called.

"Yes, sir, right away," I said, and fled before Adda or Beau could say anything else and before they could see the hot tears of anger that were stinging my eyes. I flung myself out the back door, still clutching the sweating root beers, and as the screen door slammed behind me, I ran headlong into a tall colored boy standing with his right hand poised in a fist as he was fixing to knock on the door.

My story is interrupted when Celi hollers, "I saw one, Grandma Will! I saw one!" She takes off across the yard, chasing lightning bugs with a glass jar held open in one hand and the lid in the other, and Avery and I both turn to watch her running like a gangly colt, all legs. Avery stands up to follow Celi, turns back to look at me, and says, "Just one question. Who was at the door of the drugstore?"

"That was Henry Johnson, Sally's brother," I say.

"There's so much more I want to know," she says, backing toward the yard. "But right now, if you'll excuse me," she says, holding up a finger, "I've got some lightning bugs to catch!"

After Avery helps Celi fill her jar, she uses my pecan pick to poke some holes in the lid and shuttles a complaining Celi off to get a bath and prepare for bed. This is definitely a different Avery from the girl who left here, but I'm not so sure if *here* is any different. I guess we'll start finding out tomorrow night. My house will be full of family again—Marion and Holt, Mark and his fiancée, Nicki, and Avery and Celi. It's been a lot of years since we've all been together in this old house.

Chapter 7

Marion

"Not coming? What . . . Why . . . What happened?" I can't believe my ears. I thought that maybe she was running late. I've been waiting all afternoon—she always was late everywhere she went—but not coming? I feel hurled from the roller coaster of emotions I've been riding the past two weeks. It's like I've landed on my back and I can't breathe.

Holt tiptoes around me in that way he does when he doesn't want to deal with my reaction. "She called the office this afternoon," he says. "I'm sorry, honey. Avery's decided to stay out at Willadean's."

"But I had their rooms all ready," I say. I should have known better than to get my hopes up. She's still blaming me for what happened to Aaron Monroe. She still thinks I won't acknowledge Cecelia. "I even bought those new pink sheets for Cecelia . . . and Avery's favorite tamales from Jack's. . . ."

"I know, I know," Holt says, pulling me into his arms and tucking my head under his chin. I allow myself to stand there for a moment, breathing in the scent of his cologne and the starch from his shirt. "I'm disappointed, too. Maybe we can talk her into coming into town when we go out to Willadean's for the fish fry."

I push back from his embrace and reach for a paper towel from the holder on the kitchen counter. I blot my mascara before it has a chance to run and try to get control of myself. But it's pointless trying. I can't stop the tears; the letdown is too strong. I was so ready to face her, to meet her daughter, and Holt knows that. He knows how hard I worked to prepare for their visit, to open my heart to Avery. Now she's slammed the door in my face once again.

"I'm not going," I say. How can he expect me to grovel at her feet when she treats me this way? Like lightning flashes, I feel the electricity of my old anger prickling my skin.

"Now, Marion," he says. Before he can patronize me any further, I hold up my hand.

"Just stop right there, Holt," I demand. "What do you expect from me? Avery leaves here, practically in the dead of the night, to move halfway across the country. We speak maybe once a year for the past ten years, and when we do neither one of us knows what to say to the other. And now, when I think she's finally coming home, finally going to give me a chance, she snubs me for Willadean." I jerk open the cabinet and pull out a highball glass. "I'm making a drink. Do you want one?"

"Sure," he says. "I'll help you." He reaches for a lemon from the bowl on the counter and pulls a knife from the holder. I know he's giving up on what were going to be his arguments—that Avery got cold feet, that she didn't know how to approach me, that she's worried about how I'll respond to her daughter. Haven't I had all of those same conversations over and over with myself? It's been five months since we found out about Mark's engagement, and I've spent every waking moment and a lot of sleepless nights worrying over this visit. As I pull ice from the freezer I think about the night he and Nicki told us.

It was two days after Christmas, and Mark and Nicki mysteriously decided to have us all meet at Sid's, Mark's favorite Italian restaurant, for dinner. We were seated at a large table in the back. Mark was at the end with Nicki to his left seated beside her mother, Laura Elise. Holt and I were to his right and Mason was at the end opposite Mark. We had just finished ordering drinks when Mark spoke over our chatter.

"Everyone, could I have your attention, please," he said. Laura

Elise and I looked at each other. We both suspected what was coming. I looked over at Nicki and she was beaming at Mark. So young, so in love. I envied her. "I want you all to know that I have asked Nicki to marry me, and to my amazement, she has agreed," Mark announced, with a silly grin on his face. Everyone buzzed then, all talking at once.

"Oh, I was hoping that's what you'd say!" trilled Laura Elise.

"Good job, son!" said Holt, reaching over to clap Mark on the back.

"Welcome to the family, Mark!" said Mason, who actually got up out of his chair and strode to the end of the table to shake Mark's hand. My son in Mason's family . . . How much stranger could my life become? The irony almost made me laugh. This served me right for making a best friend of the woman who stole the man I loved. And now I had to play the mother of the groom—show up, shut up, and wear beige. All these thoughts raced through my mind in a split second. I knew I had to say something.

"Oh, Nicki," I said, hoping my expression was holding up better than my heart. I reached across the table, feeling Holt's eyes—everyone's eyes—on me. I squeezed her hand. "This is wonderful news!" Mason's daughter, my daughter-in-law. I willed the thoughts to stop. . . . She should have been my daughter . . . our daughter. The old buried hurt must not surface, not then, when I was supposed to be so happy.

Laura Elise sparkled with excitement as she wrapped her arm around her daughter's shoulders and squeezed her. "This will be so much fun, planning a wedding. Have y'all set a date yet?"

Nicki and Mark looked at each other, and he nodded.

"We've decided on June thirtieth," she said hesitantly.

"So soon!" responded Laura Elise. "Why, Nicki, that's hardly time to get an invitation list together." Laura Elise turned to me. "Don't you agree, Marion? That's not enough time. . . . There's the dress, the flowers, the church, the parties. . . ." Laura Elise was working herself into a panic, but Nicki, the levelheaded one in their family, intervened.

"It will be fine, Mother," she said calmly. "Mark and I don't want anything huge and blown out of proportion. We want to keep it relatively small—family and close friends. June works best for us." The way she looked at her mother when she said these last words essentially communicated, *Don't argue with me.*

"Oh," said Laura Elise, looking crestfallen. Round one—Nicki. I had to admire her spunk. She reminded me of Avery. Since I couldn't have my own daughter in my life, maybe I would enjoy having a daughter-in-law. Her next words, however, erased that thought from my mind. I wasn't sure why she was looking directly at me. I couldn't read her expression. When I glanced over at Mark, he was watching me, too. What was going on?

"We've invited Avery and Cecelia to the wedding," Nicki said. "I've asked her to be a bridesmaid and we want her little girl to be our flower girl."

My mouth went completely dry. I looked at Holt. For one very brief instant his eyes pleaded. I reached for my water glass and hoped no one else saw my hand trembling. *Say something, Holt, please!*

"That's great, kids," he said. "It will be so good to have everyone together again. Isn't that right, Marion?" Holt reached over and engulfed my hand in his broad, strong grip. He gave my hand an almost imperceptible squeeze. I felt everyone waiting to hear what I would say. They were blaming me for Avery's staying away. I knew they were. Except Laura Elise and Mason—they both understood; they knew how impossible it would have been here for Avery.

I swallowed hard and found my voice. "Yes, that's great," I said, as I searched for something else to say. "Did Avery agree to be in the wedding?" I asked. *Oh my God! What will I do? Please say she didn't. Say she refused. How will I do this? I can't bear the gossip again, the whispering behind hands. . . .*

"She's thinking about it," Mark said. "I called her on Christmas Day to give her the news and to ask. She's not sure, but I'm hoping I can talk her into it."

"Yes, of course," I stammered. Thank God the drinks arrived then and Mason called for a toast.

As I went through the motions of a joyous toast to my son's engagement, I wondered what Laura Elise and Mason thought of having a black child in their daughter's wedding. My granddaughter . . . a black child . . . I was simply not prepared.

Am I any more prepared now, nearly six months later? I thought I was. I've decided that I will try to make this reunion successful, although I'm unsure how. I finish making the gin and tonics and Holt puts a lemon wedge in each one. I point to the plate of cashews I had already prepared, and he picks it up and brings it with him. We remain silent as we take our drinks into the early evening light of the glassed-in sunroom overlooking the garden. I had even looked forward to showing Avery's daughter my roses, thinking that maybe we could talk about flowers. Will Cecelia be interested in flowers? Avery never was.

We're settled into our chairs before Holt tries again. "What about Mark and Nicki? Don't you think they'll be disappointed if you don't come to the fish fry?" I don't answer. I can't. If I speak right now, I'm likely to explode, and this is not Holt's fault. Railing on him to vent all my pent-up frustration would only cause a rift between us again. The last time we fought over this was ten years ago when he agreed to allow Avery to go to Colorado.

"She needs this, Marion," he said then. "She needs to get away from Greendale. Too much has happened here. Too many tongues are wagging. Avery needs a fresh start."

"What if she doesn't come back? Doesn't she know that keeping this child will only cause her pain?" I shouted at him. "Why must she always fight so hard against everything we stand for?" I shook with rage, knowing everything I had planned for her from the first day I held her in my arms was destroyed. "She could still have had a good life here, if only she'd try harder to fit in." I didn't dare speak what I was hoping with all my heart that Avery would do—have an abortion. What I said instead was, "Why must she always be so different?"

What he said then cut so close to my fragile heart that it stopped me. It completely took the wind out of me. He rose from his chair and looked down at me with pain in his eyes. "Being different is your issue, Marion, not Avery's. Always has been. You're the one who can't accept her as she is. Nor can that group of women, including Laura Elise Collier, that you call your friends. Maybe if you had let Avery be herself, none of this would have happened."

It took a very long time for Holt and me to get past that night. He had never talked to me like that before, and hasn't since. We managed to go on with our lives after Avery left—him continuing to develop his law practice, me pouring myself into community projects, and both of us devoted to Mark. With Avery's deliberate distance from us, particularly from me, it became easier to leave her out of our everyday existence.

Now, the sudden prospect of her return home, her daughter in tow, to be in Mark's wedding, has me in a complete dither. Worst of all, it's bringing up my own past. As I near sixty, I find myself recalling my life like an old movie with scenes I'd forgotten. I feel stuck in the middle between my mother, whom I've never understood and never will, and my daughter, who doesn't understand me. We seem to be re-creating the same mother-daughter dynamic for completely different reasons.

As the cocktail begins to take effect on my raw nerves, I fall into what Willadean would call woolgathering. That damnable idea of *differentness* . . . my struggle with it is so old. From the time I was a young girl, I knew my mother was different. I've developed a keen eye for the facial expressions of women. I can read a Southern woman's disdain through the sheer curtain of courtesy that she draws around her words. It was Daddy who took me to church most of the time when I was little. That's when I first began to notice that the ladies would ask after Mama.

May 1949

"Good morning, Jacob. Good morning, Marion," the lady said, reaching down with her white-gloved hand to pat my head. "How is Willadean doing?"

"She's doing fine," Daddy answered, not offering any explanation. "I'm sure she'll be here next Sunday."

"You be sure and tell her we asked about her, you hear?" she said.

Daddy nodded and the lady moved off into her Sunday morning after-church huddle with the other women. I noticed that every now and then they glanced our way. I began to wonder if there was something about Daddy and me that interested them. By this time, Daddy was usually shuffling me off to the car. After church, he never seemed to want to talk much with other grownups. But that Sunday a man caught Daddy in the churchyard and they got into a long conversation, so I decided to wander around behind the church, where the kids played while their parents visited.

I stopped to stand near a group of giggling girls who were watching the boys throw a ball. They looked about my age. I was always shy, and so I was surprised and pleased when the girls walked over to me and said hello. I had just turned six that November. I had yet to start school because of when my birthday fell, so these girls were still strangers to me.

A girl with long, curly blond hair reached over and took my hand. "Hi," she said. "My name is Laura Elise Reed. What's yours?"

"I'm Marion Marie Reynolds," I replied. One of the other girls, who was wearing the most beautiful blue satin dress that I'd ever seen, whispered to the girl named Laura Elise. I was still so thrilled that the girls were talking to me that I didn't notice the change in Laura Elise's expression.

"Marion," she said politely, "is it true that your mother goes to church with niggers?"

I was so taken aback that I found myself unable to speak. I knew that Mama went to church one Sunday a month with her good friend Mrs. Sally Monroe. Mama and Miss Sally, as we called her, were together a lot. They worked in the garden together and fished together, and Miss Sally often brought us her special black-bottom pies and peach cobblers. I didn't think anything of Mama going to church with Miss Sally. Of course, I knew that colored people didn't come to our church, but that was different. This was the first time I had an inkling that Mama going to Miss Sally's church might seem strange.

One of the other girls spoke up—I later learned that her name was Mabel Allen. "That's right," she said. "My mama saw your mama going into the nigger church over on the other end of Washington Avenue."

I stayed stock-still, not knowing how to respond, but certain that my mother had committed an egregious breach in social etiquette and that it was going to cost me the friendship of these girls. Just then, thankfully, Daddy came around the corner of the church to tell me it was time to go. As we walked away I remained silent, giving only a small wave and feeling desperately that something was wrong. A moment before we got out of earshot, I distinctly heard one of the girls whisper, "Nigger lovers," to another.

Chapter 8

Avery

I wake from a refreshing, dreamless sleep to the soft drone of the ceiling fan, the smell of coffee brewing, and the old familiar crazy mixed-up song of a mockingbird choosing his melody for the hour. A gentle breeze from the lake moves the cotton curtains and the sun is just reaching the bottom of the windows in its slow ascent. My first thoughts are memories of happy times in this house with Will and Grandpa Jacob; of the carefree little girl who played in the lake and chased lightning bugs, as Celi did last night. What I'm noticing most this morning is the difference in the air. The deep shade of the live oaks around the front of the house, along with the twelve-foot ceilings, keep the house cool, so Will has never installed the air-conditioning that most Southerners depend on, which requires a completely closed-up house. With all the casement windows cranked open, the room is suffused with the balmy morning air dense with moisture—so unlike the crispness of a dry Colorado summer morning.

I look over at Celi sleeping peacefully in her daybed. She's clutching Frog, a threadbare pale green stuffed frog left over from her babyhood that she's never given up. Frog's long, spindly leg is draped across her arm. She sleeps flat on her back, her angelic face serene, her hair splayed across the pillow in tightly curled ringlets, her sweet lips parted slightly as she draws deep, even breaths.

Watching her sleep never fails to fill me with a pang for the innocence of childhood, followed closely today by my ever-present maternal angst. I think about seeing my family this evening and wonder how that experience will affect Celi. She's the mystery child—the part of my life that is least understood by my family. They've never known me as a mother; for them I'm probably fixed at eighteen. I've never asked any of them, including Will, who in Greendale knows that I was pregnant when I left town. Does it matter now? I'd like to say that it doesn't, but what if I run into people from high school? What will I say? *Hi, remember me? I'm Avery Pritchett. Yes, the one who ran away to Colorado the summer after my debutante ball. Yes, the one who tried to sneak a black boy into the all-white dance—yep, that was me.*

I slip out of bed in a T-shirt and pull on the ratty old pajama pants I tossed over the footboard last night. Tiptoeing so I won't wake Celi, I ease our door open and cross the wide hallway to the bathroom. When I make my way to the kitchen, Will has her back turned to me. I stand in the doorway watching her long fingers, covered in flour, rolling biscuit dough into a thick circle with an ancient whiskey bottle. Her braid is twisted into a neat bun, and she's wearing a blue flowered bib apron with rickrack across the bottom. Beneath her apron she's dressed in faded blue jeans and a thin plaid cotton shirt with the sleeves rolled up. Her familiar pink converse tennis shoes peak from beneath her jeans. She's humming to herself, a song I think I recognize . . . something about a sparrow.

"Good morning," I say softly so I won't startle her. "I see you still haven't gotten a rolling pin."

She turns and warms my morning with a big smile. "Good morning, sweet girl," she says, and looks down at the flour-covered whiskey bottle. "You remember my friend Leroy I told you about last night?"

I nod and answer, "Yes, ma'am," as I head for the coffeepot. Will still uses the same electric percolator she was using last time I was here. I reach into the cabinet and search for a mug that's not chipped or cracked. Finally finding one that says *See Rock City* in faded red letters, I pour coffee from the tarnished stainless-steel pot into my cup.

"Leroy taught me to roll out biscuits with this old bottle. Never have needed a fancy rolling pin," she says, returning to her work. She uses a juice glass turned upside down to deftly cut biscuits out of the floured dough and places the thick white discs on a blackened cookie sheet. "I hope y'all like grits and tomato gravy. I thought I'd make us a big breakfast today. We've got lots to do before company comes this afternoon."

"Sounds wonderful," I say, my mouth watering at the prospect of Will's biscuits and gravy. I stir sugar into my coffee from the bowl on the kitchen table. "What all do we need to get done?" I ask.

Will opens the oven and slides the biscuits in, then stirs the grits in a saucepan on top of the stove. "Well, let's see. I want to mix up a batch of ice cream and get it to chilling in the fridge. Mark and Nicki gave me a newfangled electric ice-cream freezer for Christmas. I thought we'd try it out this evening. Holt said he'd bring me some of those Chilton County peaches to go in the ice cream. And we need to go over to Sally's and pull some sweet corn. Her neighbor plants a field of it behind her house every year. He lets her pull as much as she wants. It's the best sweet corn you've ever eaten. You know your brother, Mark, can eat his weight in sweet corn."

"I remember that," I say, laughing at the memory of Mark mowing across ear after ear of buttered corn on the cob. "Mark says you and Nicki get along well," I say casually, hoping she'll pick up the cue without a lot of prompting. I really want to know what she thinks of Nicki. I'm still having a hard time imagining anyone related to Seth Collier being married to my brother.

Will sets the butter dish and a jar of what looks like strawberry preserves on the table. "Nicki is a nice girl," she says. "She likes to fish, you know." She walks to the refrigerator, opens it, and pulls out a package. "Y'all like bacon?"

"Thanks, but I don't eat pork, so Celi and I have gotten used to eating turkey bacon," I say.

"Turkey bacon?" she asks, looking incredulous. "Turkeys don't have bacon. How can that be?"

I explain turkey bacon to my confused grandmother before I slip in, "So, you like Nicki? I mean . . . do you think she'll be good for Mark? You know . . . being a Collier and all."

Will turns to face me with her back to the sink and I notice that the morning sun coming through the window behind her halos her head in light. The windowsill is lined with African violets in colors ranging from frothy pink to rich royal purple. As a kid I wondered if violets would taste good; their purple color always reminded me of grape Popsicles.

Will crosses her arms and pulls her mouth down into a thoughtful expression. "I've known a lot of Colliers in my time, starting with Dr. George Collier when I was a girl, and I didn't think much of him. His son Ralph Collier was a lawyer and your grandpa didn't care much for his business dealings, not to mention his views on civil rights. . . ." Will seems hesitant to speak of the Colliers; it's as if she's hiding something. Her voice is flat and cold. Is it simply because Mason and Laura Elise are such snobs, or is it something deeper? I wonder what happened to cause Will to speak so bitterly of Mason's grandfather. Everywhere I turn there seems to be another link in the web of connectedness they've all spun. Where do I fit?

I find myself temporarily distracted. I've never heard my grandmother talk about civil rights, and for some reason the slight edge to her voice seems at odds with her usual quiet, calm demeanor. I make a note on my already long list of questions to ask her about what she meant.

". . . and then there's Mason and Laura Elise. I've personally never had any dealings with them. They're part of your mama's set—all doctors, or lawyers like your Daddy, or wealthy businessmen, and their wives. I never did see how your mama could be such good friends with Laura Elise after what happened with her and Mason."

"What do you mean?" I ask.

Will suddenly looks uncomfortable and turns to open the

cabinet. The plates rattle as she stacks three and carries them to the table. "I reckon that's not my story to tell. I shouldn't have mentioned it," she says, effectively closing the subject. "Anyway, I've never known much about Laura Elise and Mason's kids. Their boy, Seth, I've never even met. But I have to say, of all of them, Nicki seems to be a down-to-earth girl. Looks to me like she loves that brother of yours to distraction. And I'd have a hard time not warming up to a girl who wants to talk about tomatoes."

I'm intensely curious about my mother's relationship with Mason Collier, but I decide not to push it any more right now. I consider telling Will about my high school experience with Seth Collier, but I choose not to let her in on my reservations yet. Celi appears in the kitchen doorway, dragging Frog by his leg and rubbing sleep from her eyes. Her hair, which just brushes her bony shoulders, stands out wildly around her face, and she is already wearing a bright smile.

"Look who's up," says Will as she opens the oven to pull out the golden brown biscuits.

"Morning," Celi says to both of us, watching Will intently. "What are those?"

"Biscuits."

Celi points to the other two pans on the stove. "And those?"

"Tomato gravy and grits," Will answers. "You hungry?"

"Yes, ma'am," Celi answers with enthusiasm, and I'm a little shocked to watch how my city-raised Colorado daughter tucks in to Southern buttermilk biscuits with tomato gravy and a huge serving of grits drowned in melted butter, neither of which she's ever seen or tasted before. I can only hope the rest of her Southern experience is as good.

When we have finished our breakfast and cleaned the dishes, Will suggests, "Why don't you take Celi down to the dock and introduce her to Alligator Lake while I'm mixing up the ice cream?"

"Can I swim, Mom?" she asks. "Are there alligators in the lake?" Before I can reply, Will answers, laughing.

"No, sugar, not anymore. There used to be, though, when I

was a girl. That dock over the lake was your mama's favorite place when she came out here to visit me in the summers."

Celi and I pack a couple of apples and some water. I have to insist on the water; she's already become enamored of sweet tea, which has way too much sugar and caffeine for her, especially with sickle cell. We dress in our swimsuits and flip-flops, grab some sunscreen, and head to the shed out back, where I'm pleased to find one of my and Mark's old inner tubes, covered with cobwebs, but not too much the worse for wear. I dust it off with an old rag, and Celi and I scurry down the long, sloping back lawn to the shore of Alligator Lake, laughing as we roll the black tube between us.

The sound of the water lapping against the dock, the clean morning scent of the water, and the way the sun creates ripples of light across the lake overwhelm me with memories of summer days I shared with Aaron. I can feel again that craving for something I couldn't understand. Aaron seemed to embody both my fears and my hopes—all in a boy like none I'd ever met before. I remember his flashing smile, his seriousness, the way his eyes lit up when he shared his dreams. Celi and I station ourselves on the end of the dock and swing our legs over the side, letting our toes drag through the cool water, and I hold the memory of being seventeen selfishly close. . . .

August 1990

That summer I found myself spending even more time at Oak Knoll. The previous year, when Daddy bought me my first car, I had discovered that the delicious freedom to leave Greendale and drive out in the country was more seductive to me than the shopping malls, movie theaters, and country club swimming pools where the other girls hung out. Will said she enjoyed having me around, and she didn't require me to talk. Mother was always trying to get me to chat about drapery colors or help her prune her endless roses. Will's house was old and comfortable, and she didn't worry about a small spill or my feet tracking in dirt. As long as I helped her with chores if she needed me, she didn't care how long I read or dozed in the sun.

It was so peaceful on Alligator Lake, away from the noise of town, away from Mother trying to get me to attend one of her teas or lunch at the country club. I brought my book, a small cooler with Dr Peppers and Little Debbie's—breakfast of champions, I thought sarcastically—and my Walkman to the end of the dock Grandpa had built out over Alligator Lake. Will could call to me from the back porch if she needed me. I unfolded the webbed chaise lounge chair, stretched out, and spent hours reading and sunbathing.

That day was different. When I arrived at Oak Knoll and pulled my Datsun into the circular drive, I noticed a tall muscular black boy climbing a ladder to the eaves at the front of the house. He pulled a putty knife from the back pocket of his faded jeans and started scraping the chipped paint, sending it like a snow shower into his hair and onto the flower beds below.

He stopped scraping and looked down at me as I approached the front porch steps, lugging my little cooler and an armful of library books. His smile was a white flash in his dark, sweaty face, and his eyes were warm.

"Hey," he said shyly.

"Hey," I replied, feeling self-conscious of my greasy hair jerked into a ponytail and the grungy T-shirt and cutoffs I'd thrown on over my bikini. "I see Will finally decided to get the house painted."

"Yep," he said. "Looks like it's going to be a big job."

"You painting it all by yourself?" I asked, wondering if there were going to be workmen around all summer, which would interfere with my plans.

"Just me. Miss Willadean hired me for the whole job. Probably take me a while, but I'm saving for college, so I need the money."

I was keenly aware of how his muscles rippled under the sleeves of his torn white T-shirt and how handsome he was, with his strong jaw and deep brown eyes. And his voice; I loved the timbre of his voice. I remember thinking that I'd like to have him read aloud to me.

"What year are you in school?" I asked. I was vaguely aware that I'd never had a conversation with a black boy before. I didn't know any black kids since Greendale Prep was private, and we didn't have any blacks in our neighborhood since we lived in Oak River, the wealthier part of town. I heard there was once a black doctor who looked into buying a house near us, but somehow it mysteriously got taken off the market before he could make an offer.

"Senior this coming year, Greendale High," the boy answered, turning to lean against the ladder, his long leg stretched out in front of him. "You?"

"Greendale Prep," I answered. "Senior next year, too."

He nodded knowingly. "Yeah, thought so." I was a bit offended by what seemed to be his assumption that I was one of *those* white girls. I was different. I was thinking that I didn't want him categorizing me. I probably sounded annoyed when I answered his next question.

"How do you know Miss Willadean?" he asked.

"She's my grandmother. I'm Avery," I said, remembering my manners. Before he could tell me his name, Miss Sally walked around the house, trailed by Will. They were both holding fishing poles and appeared to be headed for Will's truck.

"Aaron, you'd better stop jawing and get to working," Sally admonished. "You got to finish this job before school starts back, you know."

Aaron looked sheepish. "Yes, ma'am, Mama Sal, I'm working." So this was Miss Sally's grandson. He flashed me another of his disarming grins before turning back to scraping. I couldn't help but smile back, feeling a strange sensation of butterflies in my stomach.

"Good morning, Avery," Will said. "You're early today. You want to go fishing with us?"

I may not have been a girly girl, but fishing from the bank on the swampy east side of Alligator Lake where Miss Sally and Will liked to go was not my idea of a good time. The last time I had agreed to go with them, I'd come back with thirty-two mosquito bites. I'd counted them.

"No, thanks. Y'all go ahead. I'm going out to the dock and hang out. Anything you need me to do?"

"There's some butter beans on the back porch in a bushel hamper you can start in on shelling if you're a mind to," Will said. "And stay out of this young man's way, now."

"That's right," echoed Sally. "I can't have a grandson of mine not doing his work proper."

"Yes, ma'am," I replied, and looked back up at Aaron, who laughed and scraped furiously as he yelled over his shoulder.

"Don't you worry about me, Mama Sal. I'll get the job done."

I found myself rereading the same lines over and over that morning; I kept getting distracted wondering what Aaron was doing. Finally I finished the chapter, packed up my stuff, and left the dock to go back to the house and start shelling those butter beans. Will and Miss Sally always returned in time for Sally's favorite afternoon soap opera, so I wanted to get busy. When I peeked out the front window and saw Aaron taking a break under a tree, I hurried to grab the last Dr Pepper from my cooler and join him.

"Would you like a drink?" I offered tentatively.

He took it gratefully. "Thanks. Dr Pepper's my favorite," he said. I grinned, pushing a stray hair behind my ear, feeling awkward.

"Mine, too," I said, and I searched for something more to say to him. It was Aaron who started the conversation, who made me feel as if he was interested in what I had to say.

"You know what you want to major in yet?" he asked.

I was surprised by his question, pleasantly surprised. "Um . . . I'm not sure. I was thinking maybe physical therapy. How about you?"

"Premed," he answered. I was impressed with his certainty. We talked about school and grades and about our favorite subjects.

Aaron noticed the earphones from my Walkman, which were still dangling around my neck.

"What kind of music you like?" he asked. I reached into the pocket of my cutoffs, pulled out the cassette I'd been listening to, and handed it to him. The shock on his face when he saw that the artist was Aretha Franklin made me grin. "Whoa," he said. "I was expecting Bryan Adams or Michael Bolton."

"Will listens to her all the time, and I sort of got hooked," I said, taking back the cassette and feeling an electric sensation when his fingers brushed mine. We talked more about music, learning that we both liked older blues and jazz more than the pop stuff. He made me laugh, telling me about sneaking into the Desiree Club to hear B. B. King.

"I've always wondered what that place is like," I said, then instantly worried he might take that wrong, since it was located on Fourth Street in the black part of town and supposedly a dangerous place for white people to go. When he casually said maybe we could go someday, I nodded, not wanting to be rude, knowing the outrage my mother would rain down on me if she knew I was even talking to a black boy, much less considering going someplace with him.

Aaron was telling me about his mom dying when he was born, and how Miss Sally had raised him, when we both heard Will's truck turn into the drive. Aaron scurried back up the ladder, calling out, "Maybe we can talk again next week?"

"Sure, that'd be great," I said, as I hurried to the porch to pretend I'd been shelling butter beans.

Much later, I wondered: If I hadn't run into Aaron that day, would I have gone my whole life without ever really knowing a black person other than Miss Sally? What I didn't expect was that I would have so much in common with Aaron. I had dated a few boys from Greendale Prep, and most of them had bored me to tears. All they talked about was football, hunting, and Daddy's big plans for them. Aaron was the first boy I met who carried on conversations about what was going on in the world outside of Mississippi and what it would be like to live somewhere else.

At first I was uncomfortable about him being black. It seemed weird that I would be drawn to him. But the more time we spent talking and getting to know each other, the more natural it seemed. He was so smart and funny. It was the laughing that made me love him. Aaron's part-time night job at Pasquale's Pizza had him making deliveries all over Greendale. The way he could imitate everybody in town, from the white Baptist minister to the ancient spinster librarian, was amazing. I kept asking him if he had thought about acting. He smiled and said that would be a dream come true, but he'd promised his grandmother that he'd be a doctor.

As I help Celi lower herself into the open center of the inner tube, and smile when she gasps as the cold lake water soaks her bottom, I wonder about Aaron. Did he finish medical school? If he stayed on track, he should be done by now. I'm pretty sure he was planning on Tulane. He probably set up a practice in New Orleans. I'm sure he would never come back to Greendale. Not after what happened our senior year.

Celi and I finish our swim and return to the house to change for the afternoon. We all load into Will's truck to go over to Sally's house to pull the corn for supper. Rufus jumps into the truck bed and Will drives the gravel back road to Miss Sally's. Her cottage is scarcely a mile from Oak Knoll. As we rattle along on the deeply rutted road, Celi says, "This is like the roads where we go camping, isn't it, Mom?" I agree, thinking how far away the Colorado mountains seem right now. I wonder how much Celi will begin to miss home.

Sally's blue clapboard house appears through the trees, its white shutters glowing in the late morning sun. The house sits close to the road and the front yard is filled with flowers of every color. The aching familiarity of Sally's house washes over me.

"Mom, look at all the flowers," Celi gasps. "Miss Sally's got more than Grandma Will." Celi doesn't hear Will snort in response to her comment. I have to laugh. Sally and Will have always been rivals—over fish, flowers, tomatoes. Flowers line the short walkway and drift like swirling dancers around both sides of the petite house. The front porch holds two rocking chairs and two straight-back wooden chairs. As we tumble out of the truck, Sally appears on the front porch to greet us. She wears a blue bandana over her hair today and a faded cotton dress.

"Good morning!" she calls. As we all greet one another, Sally focuses on Celi. "I hear you're going to learn about pulling corn today," she says, and I'm surprised when Celi walks straight over to her and gives her an enthusiastic hug.

"Yes, ma'am," she says, allowing Sally to hold her small hand.

"How you doing this morning, young lady?" Sally asks. "You like Mississippi?"

"I do," answers Celi. "I've never pulled corn before."

Sally points to a basket beside the porch steps. "Y'all can use that basket for the corn you pull. I had me some for supper last night, and it's sweet and juicy. That juice will dribble down your arm if you're not careful," she says, smiling at Celi.

"Are you coming with us?" Celi asks.

"No, my arthritis is acting up today, but I'll be here waiting for you when you get done," Sally answers. "I'll fix us a glass of tea, and I got some of my peanut butter cookies made."

"Sally makes the best peanut butter cookies you ever tasted," Will tells Celi. "You're in for a treat."

We troop through Sally's grassy backyard and make the obligatory stop to admire her fat, ripening tomatoes. I'm beset with memories of the last time Aaron and I were here. I want to share those sweet moments with Celi, to tell her about the summer days and nights when I recognized how special her father was. But I've effectively cut us both off from these memories. I've made her father a nonentity in my fierce pursuit of being independent of everyone, of trying to be both parents for her. As we file past Sally's dilapidated barn, the scent of freshly turned earth wafts toward us and the memory comes unbidden, of the first reckless night we sneaked out together.

Aaron and I had talked whenever we could during the summer he was painting Will's house. Then school started and we lost touch, both becoming immersed in our senior years. But the next spring when I ran into Aaron once again at Will's—he was tilling her garden for her—we reconnected instantly. That spring we were bolder.

March 1991

"Be quiet. Your grandmother will hear us," I whispered, hushing Aaron's low laugh and reaching to pinch his arm.

"Ouch!" he whispered back and grinned, his white teeth glowing in the moonlight. "Come on," he said, and reached for my hand. We scampered across the yard like puppies released from a pen.

We reached the barn, Aaron stopped to grab a shovel, and we circled around to the black darkness in back. "Over here," he said, and I followed him to the spot where he pointed. He turned over a shovelful of the rich, dark dirt and I held my flashlight over the spot. The night crawlers heaved themselves in slippery ropes over and under each other, and I squinched up my nose at the sight. But Aaron reached down, his dark fingers almost matching the earth, and pulled out a handful of worms.

"Hold that box open," he ordered, and I obeyed, taking the lid off the cardboard carton and holding it out, far away from me. He dumped the handful of worms, along with a small amount of the dirt, into the box.

"Is that all?" I asked, hoping no more worms would have to give their lives tonight.

"Yeah, that ought to be enough," he said. He wiped his hand on the back of his jeans and propped the shovel against the barn wall. "I've already got the fishing rods and tackle box in the boat. Let's go."

We trudged through the deep grass until we reached the barbed-wire fence that surrounded Sally's pasture. Aaron stepped on the bottom wire and pulled up the next one for me, so I could slip through. This was a move I'd made since I was a little girl, but this time I was conscious of Aaron's arm and the warmth of his skin as it brushed my back through my thin shirt.

As soon as I was through the fence, I turned and held the fence the same way for him. He slid through smoothly and easily, his movements, as always, fluid and effortless. In my eighteen-year-old mind, I was on a grand adventure. Fishing at night with a forbidden boy. What would my mother say if she knew what I was doing?

We circled the lake, avoiding the road, and reached the small rowboat Aaron had tied up on the far side, hidden under the willow with its weeping branches that tickled the water. Where the boat was hidden felt like a secluded room—darker because the moonlight couldn't make its way under the curtain of leaves. It was like going into our own hidden sanctuary. I yanked off my flip-flops, stuffed them into the back pocket of my shorts, and stepped gingerly into the murky water.

Aaron was already in, having not worn any shoes. He pulled the boat close to the roots of the tree where I waited, feeling the squishy mud between my toes and hoping the movement I saw in the water was only tadpoles and not a water moccasin. Just as I was about to step into the precariously shifting boat, Aaron wedged it between two cypress roots and lifted me in one smooth movement into his arms. I gasped at the unfamiliar feeling of allowing myself to be that vulnerable. When I looked into Aaron's eyes, I saw a mixture of fear and desire. It confused and frustrated me. I didn't want him to be afraid. Being afraid spoiled the adventure. It reminded me that we had reason for fear, and I didn't want to feel it that night.

So I decided that I would cure Aaron's fear once and for all by doing something we'd never done. I leaned forward in his arms and pressed my lips against his. I had kissed boys before, making out in the backseats of cars after football games, but I'd never kissed a black boy. I'd never been this close to a black boy. I was close enough to feel the powerful muscles in his arms against my back, close enough to see how each tiny hair on his head curled and twisted individually and made up a million little curls all woven tightly together.

His lips were full and soft, and I could feel the scratch of the black stubble above his upper lip. He didn't respond to my kiss, but I felt his arms shift slightly and I worried for a second that he was going to drop me into the water. In response to his weakening arms, I tightened my grip and pressed against his chest, keeping my lips against his, willing him to kiss me back. After what felt like forever, but was only seconds, his lips moved slightly and I felt them pull toward mine, returning my kiss. It was brief but so exciting, and he pulled away suddenly, as if he was stopping himself. He almost tossed me into the boat.

We laughed nervously at our awkwardness as we both finally got into the boat. We pushed aside the fishing poles and Aaron rowed us smoothly out to the middle of the lake. It was quiet out on the lake. All I could hear was the lap of water against the boat and the tree frogs and crickets surrounding us. The moon rose high and shone down, reflecting off the water in white pools. A fish jumped up and Aaron said, "Yeah, you'd better watch out, Mr. Crappie, I'm coming for you."

I laughed at his voice and expression. He baited my hook for me and cast the line out into the water. I allowed him to do it, even though Will had shown me how to carefully thread a worm onto a hook. He handed me the rod and our hands touched, making me shiver slightly even though I was sweating in the unseasonably warm air. I slid off the seat into the cool wet bottom of the boat, feeling the water seeping through the back of my shorts. I leaned against the seat and held my rod loosely, slowly turning the reel, and leaning my head back to look at the stars.

Feeling Aaron watching me, I opened my eyes to return his stare. The energy between us was so intense I was finding it hard to breathe. I had never felt such desire before and it was scaring me. Suddenly, Aaron was distracted by a strong pull on his line. I sat up and watched as he deftly reeled in a fish, using the net to scoop it up. The fish flopped blindly around in the bottom of the boat and I felt sad, as I always did, as it took its last breaths.

"Mama Sal can fry him up for supper tomorrow," he said gleefully, and I noticed he seemed to have forgotten all about me.

Men. One stupid fish and they forget the girl sitting across from them in a boat under the romantic moonlight, waiting for another kiss.

Soon Aaron caught two more fish and the few moments we had kissed were forgotten in the hullabaloo of getting the fish into the boat and then onto the stringer. I was a bit disgusted by Aaron's bloodlust, but mostly I was disappointed because I was hoping for a little more romance and a lot less fishing. But Aaron seemed to view fishing as serious business. So I didn't argue. I was happy simply being with him in a place and time where we didn't have to worry about being seen or heard.

We decided to take a dip in the lake. Our laughter rippled out across the surface and for a few minutes we were carefree, just two kids going for a night swim in the cool black water of Alligator Lake, defying the possibilities of snakebites, alligator attacks, and sinkholes. We splashed and flirted, wrestling with each other in the water. Eventually, we climbed back into the boat, and Aaron rowed back to shore. We stretched out on a blanket on the grassy bank, feeling the sweat mixed with lake water drying on our skin as we lay there exhausted from lack of sleep and the excitement of being together.

We must have talked for hours that night. Aaron finally finished telling me about his mother, Cleome, who had died giving birth to him. He knew she had some kind of illness, but he wasn't sure what it was. He'd never known his father, who left before he was even born. He swore that if he had children he would not become the stereotypical black man who deserts his family. We talked of our dreams, and I spoke about getting away from Greendale, how I hated the debutante scene. He talked about finishing medical school and coming back to Greendale to practice.

I turned to him then, flinging my arm across his bare chest. "Don't you want to run away, Aaron? Don't you want to leave Mississippi?" He kissed me then, this time without fear, and when we turned and lay on our backs staring up at the stars over Alligator Lake, I thought nothing could ever change what we shared.

· · ·

In the cornfield behind Sally's home, as I trudge between the swaying rows of corn, memories of Aaron accompany my every step. His strong brown hand used to reach up, squeeze each ear of corn to check for readiness, and pull the silky-topped green cylinder from the stalk. His melodic voice and warm laughter filled the air around me.

Will takes Celi under her wing, showing her how to part the silks and carefully pull back the husks to check for ripeness. Celi squeals when she sees her first earworm buried in the top of the ear, gnawing on the tender yellow kernels.

"Grandma Will, it's got a gross ugly green worm on it!" she says, dropping the ear into the dirt at her feet.

"That's all right, sugar," Will says, walking over to her. "Most of them do."

"But how can we eat them if they've got worms in them?"

"We'll get rid of the worm and cut that part off after we shuck it. It'll be just fine," Will says, reaching down for the ear. She picks out the writhing worm and drops it on the ground, crushing it under her foot while Celi watches in disgust. Will hands the ear back to Celi. "Now, go put this in the basket," she instructs. Celi doesn't look too sure, but she dutifully carries the corn, held at arm's length, to the basket.

After we've filled the basket with corn, I carry it to the bed of the pickup while Will and Celi plop down in chairs on Sally's porch for the promised iced tea and cookies. I watch Celi carefully, trying to surreptitiously make sure she's not getting overtired. She hates it if I say anything. Plus Will and Sally have no reason to understand why I'd be worried about an energetic nine-year-old getting tired. I feel myself becoming a little tense, hoping Sally doesn't invite us inside. In the short time Aaron and I were seeing each other, I didn't go into Sally's house. Although I'm pretty sure that both Sally and Will suspected what we were doing, we thought we were keeping our secret. What if there's a picture of him and Celi asks who he is? Would she suspect? I chastise myself for not anticipating this situation, for not planning how to handle it.

I turn to them more abruptly than I intended. "I guess we'd better go," I say too quickly. "Sounds like we've got a lot to do before this afternoon's get-together."

Back at Oak Knoll, we finish shucking the corn and stash it in the refrigerator for later, when we'll boil it to eat with the fried catfish. I convince Celi to rest for a while; she agrees as long as she can bring Rufus with her. When I peek into our room after I shower and dress, he's lying beside her on the daybed and she's reading to him from *Hank the Cowdog.* Will watches her afternoon soap opera, then goes off to her room for a nap. I find myself on the back porch, sitting in the glider watching the shadows on the lake change as the clouds drift and change patterns overhead.

In less than half an hour my mother will arrive.

Chapter 9

Marion

I trudge slowly up the stairs to my bedroom. I am filled with anger and resentment. I am fleeing to my room because it is my only sanctuary from the constant stream of my mother's embarrassing guests. This time it is another black sharecropper she is teaching to read. I open my bedroom door and notice a lumpy, misshapen form in my bed. Fear grips me as I take a step forward into the room. That's when I apprehend that the shape before me is a human body. I stop and start to turn and run back downstairs when the body sits straight up. His black face is swollen and purple with ugly bruises. He opens his blood-covered mouth to speak to me, and his eyeball falls from its socket, leaving a gaping black hole.

I startle awake, and I'm immediately aware that I'm drenched in sweat. My silk summer pajamas are stuck to me like a second skin. I haven't had an episode like this since I was going through menopause. My heart is racing, and it takes me several seconds to comprehend that I've been dreaming. I'm not in my upstairs girlhood bedroom at Oak Knoll as I first thought; I'm in my own home, in my and Holt's bedroom, snuggled into the cool softness of Egyptian cotton sheets in the elegant antique mahogany sleigh bed that Holt gave me for a wedding present. The rising sun is brightening the sky and I can see light through the narrow vertical lines formed where the heavy linen drapes almost meet. I turn my head to see Holt's wavy black hair and his strong, broad, comforting back. His soft snores and the quiet hum of the central air-conditioning are all I hear now, not the sound of my own scream ringing in my ears.

The images of the dream float through my mind and I shudder as I sit up on the side of bed and slide my feet into my slippers. The sound of my own sleeping scream must have awakened me, because I can still feel the ache in my throat. I glance at the clock and notice it's after six. In my haze I wonder why Holt's not up and getting ready for work, and then I remember it's Sunday.

I reach for my robe and slip down the back staircase to the kitchen, trying to shake the nightmare from my mind. Why are all of these old ghosts haunting me again? As I glance out the kitchen window, I notice Mose enter through the back gate and walk toward the potting shed. He moves achingly slowly these days, but he keeps insisting he's still fit to work.

"It's just a little rheumatism, Miz Pritchett," he tells me. He's scheduled to clean and restart the fountain today. Mose has been working for Holt and me since we bought this house when we married in 1965. Mose helped me plant my first roses.

Mose Bradley is the first of many black men and women Wil-ladean taught to read. I was eleven years old when Mama set herself on a mission to educate Washington County's poor black sharecroppers. She left me at home to fend for myself and drove to classes at Sunflower Junior College to learn about teaching reading. She was so frustrated with the reading primers—the same ones I had used in first grade.

"What black man wants to read a bunch of hogwash about Dick and Jane?" she'd say, stomping around the house like she always did when she was frustrated. "I can't use that silly stuff to teach a grown colored man to read!" So she used the *Old Farmer's Almanac* instead. Mose must be in his seventies now, but in 1955 he was still a young man. Young and angry, and one of the reasons I still have these nightmares.

. . .

September 1955

I ran breathlessly in the front door. Laura Elise Reed and her mama had just dropped me off in front of the house. Mrs. Reed said she couldn't come inside because she didn't want to disturb Mama and she needed to get home to check on Mr. Reed. I ignored the fact that it was only one o'clock in the afternoon, and I knew from Laura Elise that her daddy didn't get home until after dark most days. Mrs. Reed had always been nice to me, even though it was obvious that she avoided my mother.

I was allowed to spend the last week of the summer with Laura Elise while she visited her aunt Dora Jane in Memphis. Mrs. Reed drove us there in her beautiful green-and-cream-colored Chevrolet Bel Air with its green leather upholstery. It was so luxurious. Aunt Dora Jane lived in a grand house on Cooper Street. Her house was not as large as ours, but it was much more elegant. She had a butler, a cook, and a maid. Every morning breakfast was served on fine china on the terrace. That week I fell in love with roses. Laura Elise's aunt had the most beautiful rose garden my twelve-year-old eyes had ever seen. Every color and variety adorned ornate iron trellises, scrambled along iron fences with sharp-pointed finials, and filled every corner of her Memphis yard, both front and back. I vowed then and there that I would have a beautiful rose garden like that someday.

Mrs. Reed took Laura Elise and me shopping at a beautiful department store called Goldsmith's. Daddy had given me two whole dollars to spend and I bought the prettiest pair of white gloves with a dainty pearl button at the wrist. We had lunch in the elegant tearoom of the Peabody Hotel. I felt like such a lady. We got to see Mr. Edward Pembroke bring the ducks into the fountain. We watched those adorable ducks waddle in on the carpet. I couldn't wait to show Mama my new gloves and tell her all about how exciting Memphis had been.

Only now, as I stepped through the front door, clutching my overnight bag, my childish excitement turned to fear. I could hear voices coming from the kitchen—Mama's and Daddy's voices—

and right at that moment Mama let out a wail of sorrow so awful I thought for sure someone in the family was dead. Then I thought that maybe she and Daddy were having a big fight. I had never heard them fight, so the prospect was even more frightening. I tiptoed through the door that led into the back hallway to listen. I heard another voice, a colored man's voice. After listening at the door for a few minutes, I determined that they weren't fighting. Daddy and Mama were listening to the colored man tell about something horrible that had happened. What I heard Mama say made me get a sick feeling in my stomach.

"Jacob, that boy was only fourteen years old!" Mama cried, and I could hear her pacing up and down the kitchen floor. "Fourteen and his only crime was to say something silly to a white woman. I'm not convinced he even did that. Do you know what they did to that boy?"

"No, Willa, I'm sorry to say I don't," Daddy replied in his quiet voice. At times like these Mama was loud enough for both of them. Daddy usually got quieter.

"Mose," she said, "tell Mr. Reynolds what those men did."

"They pistol-whipped him with a Colt .45, Mr. Jacob," said the colored man softly. I knew Mose. He was a young sharecropper who worked for Mr. Reed. Mama was teaching him to read. "They gouged his eye plumb out of the socket. Then before it was over with, they shot him in the head. To get rid of his body they tied a cotton-gin fan around his neck with barbed wire and threw him in the Tallahatchie River."

"Oh, my God," I heard Daddy say, his voice cracking in sorrow. "This is bad. Real bad."

"I just can't stand it anymore, Jacob," Mama said. "First they kill that preacher in Belzoni who was trying to get coloreds registered to vote. Then that man in Brookhaven who was trying to organize voters—the sheriff was in the car with the man who shot him! And now this. If you won't do something, Jacob, then I've got to," she cried.

"Now, hold on, Willa," Daddy said. "These boys are dangerous, and they won't stop at anything to keep the colored in their place. You don't need to go getting mixed up in it."

"That's right, Mrs. Reynolds," said Mose. "Them white men mad as hell."

"Willa, you're already doing your teaching. That'll make as much difference to these folks as anything else you could do," Daddy said. I heard the chair scrape then, and Mama sat down hard. I heard her hands slap the table.

"It's not enough, Jacob. It's just not enough." She sounded dejected then.

"If you won't think of yourself, then think of Marion," Daddy said. "You know how sensitive she is."

Sensitive? Is that what I was? All the sparkle of Memphis hissed away like air out of a balloon, and I turned and walked quietly back to the stairs, the beautiful world of roses and fancy department stores and precious waddling ducks on red carpet replaced by the reality of my world at Oak Knoll. Other families, like the Reeds, kept the bright, shiny modern world close. They had a television. Laura Elise and I had watched Lee Meriwether crowned Miss America right there in her living room last September. But my mother wouldn't let that world into our house. Instead I was surrounded with the dark, ugly plight of colored people that my mother refused to ignore. And now I had to think about a boy, not much older than me, with his head bashed in and his eye gouged out, washing up on the banks of the Tallahatchie River.

Holt finally convinced me to go to the fish fry at Willadean's this evening. I'm sitting on my terrace taking a few minutes to collect my thoughts before it's time to leave. The late afternoon light fills my garden, and some of my favorite roses, the early June bloomers, are glowing. Mose got the fountain cleaned today, and the trickling water sparkles as it trips from one level to the next. The sound follows the rhythm of my thoughts as they leap from my mother to Avery to her daughter, Cecelia. When I learned a few short weeks ago that they'd be coming, I was thrown into a tailspin. And to hear the news at the same time as Laura Elise gave me no opportunity to consider my reaction. It was all so public.

So much has changed since I was a girl, yet I'm aware of how little it has affected me directly, until now. Laura Elise can continue to stay in her all-white world, but my daughter is forcing me out of mine. So, what now? I am not my mother. I can't imagine going to the extent that she does to mix my life with blacks. I have no desire to. The blacks have their own garden club, their own social venues, their own churches. They like that separateness as much as we do. I don't consider myself racist, but I am certainly not the civil rights champion that Willadean is. I've spent a lot of energy distancing myself from her extremist actions. And when I found out about Avery's crazy scheme for her debutante ball, I acted so as to save her from pain.

But the fact of the matter remains, I have a black granddaughter and she will not be hidden away in Colorado any longer. She has arrived and met her great-grandmother, and today she will meet me. I wonder vaguely how Cecelia will compare us. I have to face that, too. No more hiding behind the excuse that Avery doesn't want to visit. She's here—well, not here at my house, which is another matter entirely, but here in Mississippi. The other ladies don't know about Cecelia. Laura Elise is the only one I've trusted with her existence. Well, I really didn't trust her with it. Doctors talk to each other, and I knew that Mason and Dr. Boggess talked when Dr. Boggess confirmed Avery's pregnancy. After it was decided that Avery would leave for Colorado, Laura Elise and I never talked about it.

Now Laura Elise is acting like I've been diagnosed with a terminal disease. "How can I help?" or "What will you do?" or "What is your plan now?" she asks. She's starting to irritate me. Haven't I always been able to make things work for myself? Haven't I always overcome obstacles to get what I needed?

It doesn't take a genius to surmise that I will not be able to hide this child. Now I feel awful for even considering it. This is my granddaughter, but she's not real to me. I didn't have the experience that Laura Elise had with her sons Seth and Robbie and their children, of watching the pregnancies, buying baby clothes and nursery items, then holding the babies in her arms, watching them grow up. Cecelia's coming into my life as a prepackaged nine-year-old.

Holt tries to make conversation on the drive out to Oak Knoll, but I'm not in the mood to talk. He, of course, is elated that I changed my mind and agreed to go. He even suggested I call Avery and talk to her, but I couldn't bring myself to do that. We'll have to see what happens when we get there.

I look down at the box in my lap and adjust the pink bow. Avery probably would have called it gaudy, and it was the biggest, pinkest bow in the selection. I've been deprived of nine years of gift giving, and I want to see Cecelia open it. Holt and I always send gift cards at Christmas and birthdays. Since we know almost nothing about their lives, I always feel it's for the best. But I had this gift waiting for Cecelia in the room I fixed up for their visit, so when they didn't show up, I decided to bring it with me. Why should the child wait when it's her mother who won't darken my door? Besides, it will give us something to focus on if I can't think of anything to say. It's a silly gift, but aren't little girls allowed to be silly? A childhood should have room for playfulness. A little girl should have time to let her imagination fly, to dream of being a princess, to dream of her Prince Charming. At least that's what I wanted at nine.

Mother never understood that about me. Everything was always so serious. Always a purpose to everything she did. The closest Willadean Reynolds came to play was fishing with Sally Monroe. I think that's the only time I ever heard her laugh. I tried to get Avery to take an interest in pretty clothes and home décor and fine china or even rose gardening, but without success. I've determined I will try with Cecelia for that little-girl experience. I'm worried about her being black. But I've had nine years to contemplate her mixed race and I'm at that point in my life when either I must accept my granddaughter or I will lose them both.

I want to experience my grandchild before I become one of those doddering old fools who can't do anything but sit in her chair and sleep. Of course, if I'm anything like my mother, that's not likely. She can run circles around me with her activities. But then, I'm as different from my mother as Avery is from me. What will Cecelia be like? I don't know anything about her father,

Aaron Monroe. I assumed that young man would never return to Greendale after what happened. So when Laura Elise showed up at my house last Friday to tell me about the announcement in the paper, I was shocked.

"Marion, have you seen this morning's paper?" Laura Elise asked, without so much as a hello. Leona was cleaning that day and had let her in. Laura Elise came rushing out onto the terrace and called to me from the edge. She had that excitement she gets in her voice when something particularly disastrous has happened. I really wasn't in the mood for a disaster.

"No, not yet," I answered from the garden, annoyed at Laura Elise for interrupting my quiet time with the roses. Their scent gives me a pleasure I don't find in anything else. "I wanted to finish trimming before it gets too hot." I walked back through the still dewy grass, sat down in one of the terrace chairs, and set my hat and gardening gloves on the table. I studied the David Austin Ferdinand Pichard and wondered about moving it to complement the pale pink of the New Dawn, but I do love it close to the terrace with its wonderful fragrance.

"Well, go and get your newspaper, right now," she said. "I'll wait." Laura Elise arranged herself on a chaise lounge near the fountain and propped her feet up as if she was planning to stay for a while.

I shook my head as I checked my shoes for dirt. I decided that I'd rather not mess up Leona's clean floors, so I opened the French door a crack and called, "Leona, could you please bring me the newspaper? I don't want to track up your floors."

"Yes'm," she said, dropping her mop and walking into the dining room, where Holt had left the paper after breakfast. She handed me the paper, and I brought it back outside, pulling a chair toward the chaise where Laura Elise was reclining.

"I'm so exhausted with all of these wedding plans," she said, as if she had been doing hard labor. "Yesterday, I drove all the way to Memphis just to look at a particular white peony." She opened her eyes to find me waiting with the paper in my hand. "Oh, yes."

She sighed, as if she'd forgotten why she came here. "The business section, page three, the lower right-hand corner," she said with a precision that surprised me. To my knowledge, Laura Elise doesn't read the paper very often.

"Mason was reading the paper at the breakfast table, and I happened to be going through on my way to a tennis lesson, and he pointed it out to me. We both thought you might find it interesting." She chuckled, which caused me to pause and look at her. Her expression was both smug and curious. I'd seen that look on her face when she was telling of someone's impending divorce or torrid affair.

I located the article and swallowed hard, knowing Laura Elise was watching every move.

DELTA DEMOCRAT TIMES

June 1, 2001

Native Greendalian and Tulane Graduate Joins Boggess Family Practice

Dr. Harold Boggess, of Boggess Family Practice, Greendale's oldest medical clinic, proudly announces the addition of a new physician to the practice. Dr. Aaron Monroe, a recent graduate of Tulane Medical School, will join the Greendale Family Practice offices this week. Dr. Monroe is a native of Greendale and may be remembered by many as a star athlete of the Greendale High School basketball team and the valedictorian of the Greendale High class of 1991. Dr. Monroe has returned to Greendale with his wife, Lacretia, and their two sons, five-year-old Brandon and one-year-old Louis. When interviewed, Dr. Monroe stated, "I'm enjoying being back home and reconnecting with my extended family." Dr. Monroe is the grandson of longtime Greendale resident Mrs. Sally Monroe, and the son of the late Cleome Monroe.

I was able to maintain a calm composure that day. I simply placed the newspaper on the table and observed, much to Laura Elise's disappointment, "Isn't that interesting?" I refused to discuss it any further with her, making an excuse that I had to get back to my roses, and I haven't brought it up since. But now, as Holt turns the car into the deeply shaded driveway to Oak Knoll, I become conscious that all of the shadows that have kept Avery's life from public view are about to be chased away. Avery and Cecelia are here. Aaron Monroe is back in town along with his family. All of us are about to face one another, one way or another.

Chapter 10

Avery

Celi and I watch the driveway for the family's approach from our vantage point on the front porch. All the preparations for supper are done and Will shooed us out of the kitchen so she could work her crossword puzzle in peace. Celi is so excited to meet my family that she can't sit still. She keeps getting up from her chair to peer through the screen door into the late afternoon shade of the trees lining the drive. I've bolstered my courage as best I can, stayed as busy as possible all day, and now, with a cup of coffee in hand, I'm pretending to read a newspaper from last week that I found on Will's kitchen table. I'm turning to the business section when Celi spots a car approaching.

"They're here, they're here!" she shouts, squirming with anticipation. I set the paper and my cup on the table beside my chair and watch the navy Lincoln Navigator pull into the driveway and park under the trees. With the tinted windows and the glare of the sinking sun, I can't see at first if it's Daddy and Mother or Mark and Nicki. With Mark's love of sports cars, I'm assuming Mother and Daddy. I'm proven right when the driver's side door opens and Daddy unfolds his tall frame. He waves as he steps around to open the passenger door for Mother. I open the screen door and Celi and I walk partway down the steps. I find myself hesitating. My father looks older. The wrinkles on his forehead have deepened, and his thick black hair is peppered with gray. He still seems fairly fit and walks with that same confident stride. After Mother's door is open, he opens the back car door and pulls out a basket of peaches.

I'm so torn right now, I feel as if I'm going to explode. The little girl inside me wants to run to my daddy and throw my arms around his neck. I want to feel the safety I always felt in his presence, like I did all those years ago. I want to ask him what I should do, how to handle all of my questions. I'm paralyzed because the realization hits me like a freight train: This feeling of having reached safe harbor, this rush of relief that floods through me at the sight of Daddy, is something I've denied Celi. How can I rush into his arms, allow him to take care of me, when I haven't given my own daughter that opportunity?

Mother gets out, straightens her perfectly pressed linen jacket, and smoothes her capri-length slacks. I'm surprised to see her reach back into the car for a large package brightly wrapped in pink paper with a huge pink bow. A gift for Celi? I feel a twinge of guilt, wondering if she had the gift waiting for Celi's arrival in Greendale.

Rufus lopes around the side of the house. Going first to Daddy, he nuzzles his knees, wagging his tail happily. Daddy sets the peach basket down and squats to rub Rufus behind his ears, while Mother makes sure to steer clear of Rufus's busy rear end. That small gesture of Daddy's so endears him to me that I can't wait on the steps any longer.

"Come on, Celi," I say, reaching down to grasp her hand. "Let's go meet your grandparents." We descend the porch steps. Mother looks toward us and smiles, holding the gift precariously in one hand while she digs around in her purse with the other. Is she uncomfortable? She pulls out glasses and perches them on her nose, peering through them as if to study us better. As Celi and I approach, Daddy rises, dusts off his jeans, and walks toward me with his arms open wide.

"There's my baby girl, finally home after all these years," he says, and I notice as he takes me into his warm, Old Spice–scented bear hug that there are tears in his eyes. Again, I feel the old tug of wanting to melt into his embrace, let him smooth over all of my worries, let the power of his openly displayed affection make up for Mother's chilly stillness. I push back from his arms, still holding Celi's hand, and gently pull her toward him. Mother comes to stand beside Daddy.

"Marion, would you look here," he says, looking down at Celi. Mother nods and looks expectantly from Celi to me. Her lips are fixed in a thin straight line.

"Daddy, Mother," I say, willing my voice not to tremble with the surge of emotion I'm feeling, "this is Cecelia Louise Pritchett, but we've always called her Celi for short." Celi stands very still, and it's obvious to me that she feels my mother's scrutiny. She's not acting nearly as excited now as she was earlier. I remember Aunt Lizzie's words: "Can you give your mother a chance to respond differently?" *Okay, Mother, here's your chance.*

Mother stiffly holds out a hand toward Celi and says in her most polite tone, "Hello there, Cecelia. It's so nice to finally meet you." Daddy watches as Celi carefully shakes her grandmother's hand, and then, as if he can't stand it anymore, he kneels in front of her. The tears are sneaking down his cheeks now. Since when did he get so emotional? This is strange.

"How about a hug for your grandpa?" he asks, opening his arms toward Celi. She moves shyly toward him and he gently embraces her. Mother watches them briefly, then looks back up at me. In the split second that our gazes meet, I see my mother through different eyes. Eyes that now understand the struggle of raising a daughter, of watching her grow and change in ways that often mystify. What was that like for my mother with me? I think briefly of trying to explain why I chose to stay out here with Will but think better of it. I'm not ready for such honesty, and I don't think Mother is either.

I stoop to hug her, and I remember how I had already towered over her for several years at age eighteen. I remember the scent of her Chanel perfume, the smoothness of her dark brown hair against my cheek. It's shorter now, chin length and tucked neatly behind her ears. Her skin has a few more wrinkles but still possesses the same softness and olive-toned glow.

"Hey, Mother," I say, my voice cracking as I release her, remembering that I promised to start off on the best foot possible. "It's so good to see you. You look beautiful." I clasp her small hands in my larger ones and force myself to smile even though my lips are trembling with emotion.

"It's good to see you, too, Avery," she says, squeezing my hands and looking unflinchingly into my eyes. She seems so sincere right now, but I feel the slight tremble in her hands. "It's been too long. I've missed you." Three simple words—"I've missed you"—are enough to begin to thaw my heart, enough to make me want to believe that we can be a family again.

Before we have a chance to say more, Mark's vintage red MGB comes roaring up the driveway and we all turn to greet him and Nicki. They jump out of the car and rush to greet us. Mark looks the same, a younger version of Daddy, lean and muscular with a ball cap covering his wavy black hair. I'm happy to see that Mark and Nicki are dressed as casually as Celi and I. Mark's wearing baggy cargo shorts and a Panama City T-shirt that I would swear I recognize from high school, and Nicki's in a simple sundress with her long blond hair in a loose braid.

"It's about time you came home," Mark says, pulling me into a hug, while Nicki goes first to Celi.

"There's my little flower girl," she says. "Aren't you beautiful?" Celi blushes with pleasure. "Are you excited about the wedding?"

"Oh, yes," says Celi. "What does my dress look like?" Nicki launches into a description, and I notice that Mother is quietly watching Celi. What is she thinking? I'm certain she's studying Celi's wiry plaited hair and brown skin, her petite slender body, and the ordinary T-shirt, shorts, and flip-flops she's wearing.

"Avery, this is my fiancée, Nicki," Mark says, as he interrupts the dress description and, grinning proudly, pulls the petite Nicki into the circle of his arm. Nicki reaches to hug me warmly.

"Avery, you look the same as I remember you in high school," she says.

"Thanks, I think," I say, laughing. I thought maybe my looks had improved at least a little bit, but then, Nicki doesn't know all of my old high school baggage. I watch her warily for signs of Collier snobbery and am pleased not to see any.

"So, how was the trip, darling?" asks Daddy, moving from side to side as a happy Rufus winds among the group of legs.

"Yeah, that's quite a drive from Colorado, isn't it?" Mark asks.

"Long," I answer. "Very long."

"And boring," Celi chimes in. "I saw lots and lots of tumbleweeds and corn." Everyone laughs, even Mother.

Will, who has come out to the top step, breaks into our chatter in her usual fashion, giving orders. "Well, now that everybody's said hello, how about y'all come on in the house. It's hot out here." We all troop obediently up the front steps. Daddy holds the door for us and then follows us through the back hall and into the kitchen.

"Willadean," says Nicki, setting down a bag and pulling out a container, "I made the coleslaw like you told me, but I couldn't remember how you said to do the dressing. Could you help me?"

"Sure, hon," Will says, and brings Nicki to the refrigerator where she starts to instruct her about what to pull out. Over her shoulder, Will says, "You boys can get the outside stove lit so we can cook the fish and hush puppies out there."

Daddy and Mark nod, and Daddy pulls open a kitchen drawer and rummages through it for the lighter. Mark turns to Celi, who is standing near me, watching everyone with curiosity. "Hey, peanut," he says, already picking a familiar endearment from our childhoods for Celi. "How about you come outside with Grandpa and me to light the stove? Maybe you and I can throw a stick for Rufus."

"Okay." Celi nods, flushed with excitement.

Mother and I stand in the midst of the busy family. I'm trying to decide what to do with myself, and Mother looks uncomfortable.

Daddy locates the lighter. "Got it," he says, and he reaches out to Mother, gives her a squeeze and a kiss on top of the head. "Off we go. We'll leave you ladies to the cooking and gossiping," he says, laughing and getting a smile from Mother like he always could.

"Daddy," Mark says as they start out the kitchen door, "I've been meaning to ask you about this pro bono case you've got me working on. . . ." Celi and Rufus follow them. As I watch them all leave, I feel a tiny bit of jealousy at Celi's ease in joining the men at their task. That was me once, and now I feel compelled to remain in the kitchen with the women—a role that still doesn't quite fit.

"Will, can I help with something?" I ask.

Will hands me two knives. "You and your mama can peel those peaches for the ice cream." She turns to Mother. "Marion, there's some aprons in that drawer by the sink. You don't want to mess up your clothes." I grab a bowl and flop down in a kitchen chair, not worried about my T-shirt and shorts and glad to have an assignment, while Mother searches through a drawer for an apron. After examining several with holes, stains, and various faults, she finds one she's satisfied with—in a style that slips on over her shoulders and covers her silk blouse and linen capris.

I smile as she sits down, picks up her knife and a peach from the basket, and says, "I know what to get your grandmother for Christmas this year—new aprons. Those are atrocious." Some things never change. The sweet smell of fresh peaches fills the kitchen as Mother and I peel the slippery fruit. I stop to eat one of the peaches, biting into it and feeling the chewy skin between my teeth and the soft, sweet fruit underneath. The peach is so juicy that I have to reach for a paper towel to wipe my chin. Mother watches and smiles. "I see you're still a messy eater."

"I guess so," I answer, feeling a little of that old awkwardness of being the gangly, all-hands-and-feet girl. But Mother's tone is not as critical as it seemed in those days, and I can tell her next words are deliberate. I'm a little surprised at her directness.

"I want to hear about your work and about how you like living in Colorado," she says.

"Yes, me, too," Nicki says from the counter where she is stirring the coleslaw dressing. "I think it's so cool that you're a nurse."

I tell them about the work I've done, ending with my most recent stint as a pediatric surgical nurse, and I describe Colorado and what Celi and I love about it. They are fascinated to hear about the snow and how I learned to ski.

"How about a glass of tea, y'all?" asks Nicki. Everyone accepts the offer. Nicki pulls ice from the freezer and pours tea into tall glasses, plunking a lemon wedge into each. She passes the tea around and then comes over to sit at the table with Mother and me while Will prepares the hush puppy batter. The pungent aroma of the onions Will is chopping joins the peaches and I'm reminded of peach chutney and Indian food.

"Have y'all ever eaten peach chutney?" I ask, trying to continue the casual conversation. When they answer that they haven't, I describe the Indian food I've eaten in Denver.

"I never had anything like that, either, until I moved away," I say.

"I guess Colorado's really different from Mississippi, huh?" Nicki asks.

"Oh, yes," I say. "Different weather, different landscape, different people."

"I bet that's true," Nicki says wryly, and I wonder what she means. I glance up at Mother, and she raises her eyebrows slowly with this comment but doesn't respond.

I'm having a hard time associating Nicki with the rest of the Collier family. For one thing, she seems so authentic, so different from the Collier brothers. Robbie, two years older than me and an obnoxious football jock, moved away to somewhere . . . Atlanta, I think; and Seth, who was my official escort for our debutante ball, proved to be an even bigger jerk than his older brother. When I was a senior in high school, Nicki was a plump freshman, all bouncy energy and smiles—a girl I instantly classified as the cheerleader type with a head full of blond curls and air. But I'm quickly finding out today that I misjudged her. She's warm, friendly, and down-to-earth—still beautiful, of course, with her mother's blond hair and blue eyes, but dressed simply and genuinely interested in each of us. She's such a contrast to her mother,

Laura Elise, whom I consider to be one of the biggest snobs in Washington County.

"Avery, Celi is beautiful," Nicki says. "I can't wait to see her in the dress I've picked out for her for the wedding."

"Oh, she'll love that," I say, trying to believe this casual conversation is really happening, me sitting at my grandmother's kitchen table with the women, discussing a dress that my daughter will be wearing for a wedding.

"So she likes pretty dresses?" Mother asks, not looking up from the peach she is peeling. Is this a trick question? If I answer yes, should I mention that she loves basketball, too, or will that make Mother uncomfortable?

"She does," I answer. "Will," I say, trying to change the subject, "the peaches are all peeled. Do you want them cut a certain way?"

Will sets Nicki and me to dicing the peaches, and Mother gets up and goes to the sink to wash her hands. As she looks out the window, she says, "I'm not sure Celi should be around that old propane burner. It gets awfully hot."

"Oh, she'll be fine," Will answers automatically. "Holt will keep an eye on her."

"I'm not so sure about that. Those boys get to talking about work, they're not going to be watching a little girl."

"She's probably playing with Rufus and not even near that burner," Will says. "You worry too much, Marion. Let the child play." I can feel the old tension between them. Nicki and I look at each other across the table and I roll my eyes at Nicki's quizzical expression. I can't escape now that I'm one of the mothers.

"I'll check on her," I say. I get up and grab a towel to wipe my hands, and I'm headed toward the back door when Celi comes bursting in. Part of her hair has come loose from its neat plaits and forms a curly halo around her flushed face, which is smeared with dirt. More dirt is streaked down the front of her T-shirt, shorts, and legs.

"Uncle Mark says to tell you that the fryer is ready for the fish," she calls. Before she can run back out, I stop her.

"Celi, you're covered in mud. What have you been doing?" I ask. I can't help but glance at my mother. Is that disapproval on her face? I can't read her.

Celi looks down at her clothes and then back at me. Her wide smile shows her lack of concern for neatness. "Me and Grandpa and Uncle Mark went down to the edge of the lake, and I was throwing a stick for Rufus. He likes to fetch it out of the water. You should see him," she answers. Without missing a beat, she looks at my mother and asks, "Grandma, want to come see Rufus fetch the stick out of the lake?"

Memories of Mother's warnings about the lake surface in my mind. *"Don't go down there by yourself! Watch out for snakes. You get out of the water if it clouds up. There might be lightning."* It was always as if the lake was the enemy, and I never understood why. It was Will who took Mark and me to the lake to swim or float when we were young. Mother never wanted to come; she always had some excuse.

"Um . . . how about I watch you from the picnic table while we're getting it set," Mother says, smiling at Celi.

"Okay." Celi grins. "Are you coming now?"

"Well . . . yes," Mother says.

"Go ahead, Mother," I say. "Nicki and I will bring the catfish and the other stuff out."

Mother joins Daddy outside at the picnic table and they wave and laugh as Celi and Mark throw the stick out into the lake for an eager Rufus, who shakes each time he retrieves the stick, showering Celi with lake water. No wonder she's so muddy. Nicki and I make trips back and forth from the kitchen, hauling out the catfish, hush puppy batter, and coleslaw, and setting a large pot of water on the grate to boil for the corn. Then we bring plates, condiments, and flatware, while Will starts placing the catfish dredged in her special cornmeal preparation into a black iron skillet on the burner.

Mark and Celi trudge back up from the shore of the lake, laughing at an exhausted Rufus. The dog collapses under the picnic table for a nap and to watch for stray crumbs.

"Mark, you and Celi come help me figure out this new ice-cream freezer," Nicki calls. The three of them head for the kitchen in search of ice and rock salt. Will and Daddy stand by the stove chatting about an elderly black man whom she's sending to see Daddy, as Will drops hush puppies into the hot oil of the deep fryer.

"You know they're not treating him right, Holt," she says angrily. "He's worked for that company for forty years, and now they want to say he's not doing his job. It's wrong."

"I'll look into it, Willadean," Daddy promises. Listening to them reminds me of all the times I've heard this same conversation. Will always had a person—usually black—who needed assistance; Daddy was always willing to do what he could. Daddy's law practice is lucrative and well established. He counts among his clients some of the richest and most powerful businessmen in Greendale. Yet power like that never seemed to taint him. He always made time for Will's "personal projects," as Mother referred to them. And it sounds like he still does.

Mother and I set the table. I'm feeling the awkwardness of the silence between us. Mother breaks the tension. "I have a gift for Celi," she says.

"Yes, I saw that huge box," I reply, smiling. "I thought it might be for her."

"I had it waiting in the room I fixed for her at our house. It was her welcome gift," she says, studying a fork and then placing it beside the plate.

So she is going to bring it up after all. I feel my guilt hovering over me like a black cloud as I search for an explanation. "I was . . . I didn't . . ." I'm completely frustrated now, unable to find words to express my fears to my mother.

She reaches for a package of paper napkins and tears it open. As she pulls out each napkin, folds it neatly in half, and places it under each fork, she waits for my response. When it's obvious that I can't find words, she stops and watches me fiddling with the ketchup bottle until I look up at her. "Avery Louise," she says calmly. "You and I can be enemies or allies. I would prefer that we be allies. A lot happened before you left here ten years ago, and I'm sure that you and I will need to talk about it all eventually." She has a fierceness about her, a determination that's different from what I remember.

"Yes, ma'am," I say, uncertain of how to respond. I desperately want to avoid a confrontation with my mother about the past. Will and Daddy's conversation fades. I'm only vaguely aware of Mark and Nicki's friendly bickering from the porch as they attempt to start the ice-cream maker. Celi's tinkling laughter carries down to me like a lifeline, reminding me why I'm here, why I must face my family. Mother's brown eyes are illuminated by the citronella torches that surround the table.

Mother stops fussing with the napkins and takes a deep breath. "I want . . . I hope . . . you'll allow me to be part of yours and Celi's lives." She breaks eye contact then, as if it took all she had to get those words out. She busies herself with the place settings, fussing over the flatware. I am at a loss for words. This direct, no-nonsense approach was the last thing I expected from my mother. She must take my surprise as hesitation because she doesn't give me a chance to answer before she turns to Daddy and Will and asks, "Is it ready? Should I call everyone?"

All through a dinner marked by Celi's first delighted experience of catfish and hush puppies, and by our collective groans of satisfaction as we push back from the table after the last hush puppy is consumed, I puzzle over Mother's intensity, over the determination in her eyes. Now it almost doesn't seem real as we adjourn, laughing, to the screened porch after Celi gets her first mosquito bite and tries to avoid scratching the large red welt forming on her leg.

"Let me go find you some calamine lotion, honey," says Will, and she heads off to search for the itch remedy that I remember from my childhood.

"Avery, do you remember the time you and I decided to go night fishing down at the dock?" Mark asks.

I laugh. "I don't remember any fish, but I remember the mosquitoes that night." Mother shakes her head and Daddy sits back, listening contentedly as Mark and I regale Nicki with our story of sneaking out to the dock at night to fish in Alligator Lake and how Mark got bitten by bloodthirsty mosquitoes.

"That poor child's little legs were so covered with bites, you couldn't see even a space between them," Mother says. "He scratched them until they bled."

Will returns and sits beside Celi on the love seat to gently smooth the pink calamine lotion on the itchy bite and then wave her hand over it to dry the medicine.

"Better?" she asks.

Celi nods and I resist the urge to pull out disinfectant and antibiotic cream, realizing that would be overkill and would make my family wonder if I've lost my mind. They have no idea how prone Celi is to infection, or that I'm kicking myself for not remembering to bring bug repellant. Celi lounges back on the cushions, allowing Will to pamper her; both of them are acting out of character.

"That ice cream ought to be about ready by now," Will says, and Celi pops up, her mosquito bite forgotten, which makes everyone laugh. "We'll see how that newfangled electric ice-cream freezer worked," Will continues.

We line up with our bowls at the kitchen sink and Daddy volunteers to dip out big spoonfuls of the cold, creamy confection dotted with fresh peaches, which we take back to the porch to eat. I've missed the food of home, but more than that, I've missed being with my family, eating together, telling stories, laughing. I notice that Celi's eyelids are heavy, and she's fighting to stay awake, not wanting to miss a second of this evening.

"I think it's about time for someone to get to bed," I say, rising to take my bowl to the kitchen.

"No, Mom. Not yet," she complains. "It's too early."

"Oh, Avery," Mother says suddenly, "I almost forgot." And she disappears into the front hall, returning seconds later with the pink package. "Celi," she says, "this is a little 'Welcome to Mississippi' gift from your grandpa and me."

"Wow!" Celi exclaims as she tears into the beautifully

wrapped package and pulls from it a pale pink satin dress with a narrow bodice covered in an open-weave lace and a full just-below-the-knee skirt, trimmed with the same lace. The short puffed sleeves are pink satin with lace cuffs, and the bodice closes all the way up the back with tiny pearl buttons, completed by a wide sash at the waist. Celi stands and holds the dress against her small body, preening like a peacock. "I've never seen such a beautiful dress," she exclaims, and before Mother can fully prepare herself, Celi rushes over, still clutching the fluffy dress, and almost bowls her over with a hug. "Thank you," she says, and moves on to Daddy for the same treatment.

Mark must see my expression, because he dissolves into laughter. "What?" I ask, realizing I've been caught.

"Your face," he says, turning to Nicki. "This is exactly the kind of situation that brought Mother and Avery to blows when Avery was Celi's age. She hated fancy dresses."

"Oh, what do you know, Mark?" I say, irritably. "You were too busy playing ball."

"I know," he says, laughing. "I heard the fights."

"Really?" Celi asks, looking at Mother. "My mom didn't like pretty dresses?" I can't believe how incredulous she is.

"No, honey, she didn't," Mother replies, looking at me and smiling. "Your mother and I had very different ideas about how little girls should dress."

"Can I try it on, Mom, please?" Celi begs.

"But you're grubby and coated with calamine lotion," I reply. "How about after your bath—it's time for you to get to bed, you know."

Everyone tells Celi good night and I shuttle her off to the bathtub still complaining about having to leave the party. When I return to the kitchen, everyone is preparing to leave. Mark and Nicki are the first to go.

"Listen, Sis," Mark says, "Nicki and I want to take you out to Desiree's on Wednesday night. They've got boiled crawfish and great jazz. Maybe Celi could stay with Will."

"Or she can stay with us," Mother interjects.

Before I can recover from my shock at this offer, Nicki jumps in. "And we're having lunch with my mother on Friday. Right, Marion?"

"Yes, at the Randolph."

"And you and Celi will need to go by the Southern Belle and get your dresses fitted," Nicki continues.

By the time I've hugged and kissed everyone good night, my head is spinning with invitations, plans, command performances, and obligations. I sit at the kitchen table after everyone has left, enjoying the quiet and thinking over the evening. What did Mother mean when she said we should be allies? Allies against what? Or whom?

Will wanders into the kitchen wearing an ancient pale blue dotted Swiss housecoat and black slide-on house shoes. Her braid is unpinned and trails down her back.

"Headed to bed?" I ask.

"No, not yet. I don't sleep well if I go to bed too early," she replies. "Thought I might make a cup of tea. You?"

"Not yet for me, either," I say. "I was thinking back through the evening."

"And?" she asks, uncapping the teakettle and holding it under the tap to fill it.

"You know, I think it went pretty well," I say. "Better than I expected—especially with Mother. No major conflict. Seems as if she's watching, biding her time."

"Maybe Marion's trying to figure out how to start off on a new foot with you," Will says.

"Hmm," I say. "Maybe. I don't know about that. I guess I'll have to see what happens." I wish I felt as casual as I'm trying to make myself sound. "You know, Will, it's amazing the memories I have of this place. I thought I'd left Alligator Lake and Oak Knoll and Greendale far behind me. But I guess I haven't. I can't imagine how it must be for you when you've spent most of your life here."

I decide to take advantage of this opportunity in the quiet of the night and the lull after everyone's gone, not to mention the fact that Will and I are both wide-awake and I really don't want to think about my mother any more right now. "Last night you were telling me about Henry Johnson when Celi spotted the lightning bugs. We never got back to the story."

Will nods. "That's right. Let's see—where was I? Oh yes, the summer I met Henry and Sally . . ."

Chapter 11

Willadean

Summer 1941

The colored boy backed up as I came barreling through the door. He reached up and yanked his cap off his head when I stopped and said, "Hey."

Leroy called from over by the washtub. "Miss Willie, that there is Henry Johnson. He come to see your daddy about a job." The young man named Henry nodded politely. I noticed his clothes were old and faded and his pants were too short, but they were clean, and his boots had been wiped off.

"Yes, ma'am," he said. "Mr. Leroy done talked to your daddy about me. He's expecting me."

I was suspicious of this Henry Johnson, even if he was polite and nice-looking. He might be taking Leroy's job, and that made me mad. I walked past him and handed Leroy the root beer. I felt bad then because Henry looked so hot and thirsty.

"I'll go get Daddy," I said, turning around. I held the root beer toward him. "You want a root beer?" He licked his lips like he was so parched he could practically taste it, but he shook his head.

"No, thank you, ma'am," he said. "I'm fine."

"Suit yourself." I shrugged and took a long swig before I set the bottle down beside my tree seat and slammed through the back door, hollering, "Daddy! Somebody named Henry Johnson is here to see you. Says Leroy told you about him." I reached for a box of tonic bottles on the shelf near the door and set the tin funnel on top. Daddy came from his compounding room, held the door open for me, and followed me out back.

Leroy and I set about getting the bottles ready, but what we were really doing was eavesdropping on Daddy's conversation. Daddy peered at Henry over the top of his thick black-rimmed glasses. "J. W. Franklin," Daddy said, extending his hand. Henry looked like he didn't know what to do with it. I didn't know any other white men around here that shook hands with the colored like my daddy did. But he always said you could tell a lot about a man from his handshake. Henry shook his hand. From where I stood it looked like Henry had a firm grip. Daddy would like that.

"Henry," Daddy said, "how old are you?" Daddy was a tall man and I noticed that he was looking Henry right in the eye.

"I'm seventeen, sir," Henry answered, fiddling with his cap but pulling himself up straight and squaring his broad shoulders.

Daddy pulled his pipe out of his shirt pocket, stuck it in his mouth, and crossed his arms—his thinking pose. "Who are your people?" he asked.

"My mama, sir, she's Clarice Johnson. She cooks for the Reynoldses out at Oak Knoll. My daddy, he was Clyde Johnson. He died near about five years ago. He was a cropper for Mr. Olan Reynolds."

"I remember Clyde," Daddy said. "He was a good man. Killed in a tractor accident, wasn't he?"

"Yes, sir, he was," Henry said, looking down. Leroy and I looked at each other and Leroy shook his head as he stirred the tonic, mouthing the words, "Bad, real bad."

"You read, Henry?" Daddy asked. My daddy was a big believer in reading. He said a man, white or colored, had to learn to read to get along in this world. I reckon he extended that to girls, too—at least he never said any different. I was always going to our little library to check out books for me and Daddy. That's how it came about that I taught Leroy to read. There were a lot of folks in Greendale who didn't think the colored ought to read—said it would give them ideas about taking over the government and such. But Daddy said that was horseshit.

"Yes, sir, my mama, she made sure me and my sister, Sally, learned to read when we was little," Henry answered, and I could hear the pride in his voice. "And I went to school up until the year my daddy died."

"Can you drive a truck?" Daddy asked.

"I can drive a tractor. That's what I was doing for Mr. Reynolds since I was big enough to reach the shift, only he don't have much work for me no more, him being sick and all. I figure if I can drive a tractor, I can drive a truck, sir."

Daddy looked at Henry then for several seconds. Daddy does that when he's making an important decision. Henry stood quietly and waited. I admired that. A lot of boys his age would be talking to fill up the space. I reckon Daddy had enough information, because he hired Henry on the spot.

"You'll be stocking the shelves in the back," Daddy said, "mopping up and cleaning the store at night after we close, and making deliveries when I need you to, so you'll have to learn to drive my truck."

Henry's wide white smile flashed and I thought how handsome he was when he smiled. "Yes, sir," he said. I looked at Leroy, who was watching Henry and smiling, too, so I decided if this was okay with Leroy, Henry taking over his job and all, then I reckoned it was okay with me. At least it wasn't going to be Dr. Collier's son, Ralph, whom Miss Inez tried to get Daddy to hire. He was about as big a jerk as Beau Waverly. I had overheard Daddy tell Leroy, "I don't care how much his daddy, the good Dr. Collier, wants him to learn honest work. I don't like his attitude and I'm not hiring him."

"Pays a dollar a week, every Friday," Daddy said to Henry.

Henry's eyes lit up. That was probably more money than he'd ever seen. "Yes, sir! Thank you, sir," he said.

"All right, then," Daddy said, and he turned and looked at me and Leroy. I busied myself with the box of tonic bottles, and Leroy studied his stirring. "Henry, you already know Leroy. He'll show you around, explain what to do. This is my daughter, Willadean." I nodded. "I reckon she'll be clerking in the store here soon, but she can answer questions if you have any." I almost dropped the bottle I was holding into the washtub of tonic. Clerking? I looked at Leroy and he shrugged his shoulders like he had no idea what Daddy was talking about. Daddy was already turning to go back into the store. "You can start tomorrow," he said to Henry as he looked back over his shoulder. I marched in the door right behind him.

"Daddy, what's this about . . ." I started.

He held up his hand and said, "Come on in here, and we'll talk about it."

That's when I found out that according to Miss Inez, the old-maid clerk who had been working for us since Daddy opened the store, certain ladies in the community—namely, Mrs. Collier and Mrs. Waverly—were concerned for my personal dignity. They had made sure that Daddy heard, through Inez—whom I never liked; her breath smelled of onions and Lady Pinkham's tonic, and all she did was gossip all day with every female customer who came into the store. They thought it was time that I started associating more with white girls and dressing appropriately for a young lady approaching marriageable age.

"Inez thinks, and I agree with her," Daddy said, working with his mortar and pestle and not looking at me, "that it's time you started dressing in something besides those overalls and learning a ladylike job in the store."

"But, Daddy," I whined, "I don't want to work at the counter. And Miss Inez hates me!"

"She doesn't hate you, Willadean. She's trying to make sure that you . . . well, that you learn how to act. You spend too much time with Leroy, and now that I've hired Henry, he can take over what you've been doing."

"But, Daddy . . ."

He stopped me again. "Now, Willadean, I've made up my mind. I don't want to hear any more arguing."

I stormed out and spent the rest of the day complaining to Leroy as we bottled and labeled the tonic.

There was no changing Daddy's mind after that, even though I tried. Three days a week, I was stuck behind the counter, wearing a dress, fending off Beau Waverly's hands and rude comments and learning the boring jobs of waiting on customers, organizing the shelves, and helping Daddy fill prescriptions.

Henry started that very next day. I liked him from the start. When I was able to escape Miss Inez and the counter, I would sit with Henry and Leroy and listen to them tell stories while they worked. Not long after Henry started he was mopping the floor one evening, and I hung around after Miss Inez left. Daddy had gone to make a delivery and I knew he wouldn't be home until late.

"Henry, what's your favorite book?" I asked.

"Mr. Hemingway's *A Farewell to Arms*," he said instantly. We started to talk about our favorite books when there was a knock on the back door.

"I'll see who it is," I said, wondering who could be coming to the back door this time of night. When I asked who it was, a small voice said, "Sally." I figured any voice that small couldn't be anybody too threatening, so I opened the door.

"Hi," she said. She looked to be about my age, but shorter and rounder, and her eyes were bright and smart and looked just like Henry's. "I'm Henry's sister," she said as he walked up behind me.

"We walk home together in the evenings after we get off work," he said. "Sally's working over at the King's Daughters Hospital in the laundry. She waits for me to finish up here. I hope that's okay."

"Sure," I said. "Come on in. Would you like a cold drink? Daddy lets Henry and me have a root beer at the end of the day. I'm sure he wouldn't mind you having one, too."

Sally's face shone with a wide smile as she followed me to the soda fountain and carefully placed the ragged carpetbag she carried on the counter. "Yes, ma'am, that sounds good."

"No need to 'yes, ma'am' me," I said, reaching into the cooler. I popped the top off and handed her the cold drink.

"Thank you," she said, taking a generous swig. "That's good."

We both watched Henry, who had gone back to his mopping, and I searched for something to say. "Henry and I were talking about books. Do you like to read?"

Henry laughed as he moved around us to mop behind the counter. "What you think is in that big old carpetbag she carts around? She's worse than me. Can't go to work without a book to read on her supper break."

"It's true," she said, her black eyes sparkling. "Miss Beatrice lets Mama borrow books for me from their library, as long as I take real good care of them."

I was fascinated by a family that had their own library, and that solved the puzzle for me of where Henry and Sally got their books, since colored people couldn't use the town's public library. "What kind of books?"

"All kinds," Sally said, her initial bashfulness disappearing. "Mr. Reynolds has a lot of war history books that are kind of boring, but my favorites are the mystery stories by Miss Agatha Christie. Those belong to Miss Beatrice."

Henry snorted. "Yeah, since she discovered those, I don't get to read near as much. She goes through them like they were the funny papers. Sometimes she'll stay up all night finishing one."

"Can I see?" I asked.

Sally opened the bag and pulled out a parcel wrapped in a white dish towel. She unwrapped it carefully, revealing a book with a blue-and-orange cover. The title read *The Mystery of the Blue Train* and I was instantly enthralled. I had never read a mystery story before. Soon Sally and I were immersed in a conversation about Agatha Christie's stories, and before we knew it, Henry had finished all of his work and was nudging Sally toward the door.

"So that's when you and Sally met?" Avery asks.

"That's right," I say. "I knew the minute I met Sally that we'd be friends. She had laughing black eyes and a hardheadedness to match my own. And she liked books—she and Henry both did.

We'd read the same ones and talk about them. I would go to the library and check the books out, since there was no library for black folks, and then I'd share them with Henry and Sally. Before the summer was over we were tighter than thieves. Leroy started teaching Henry the secret to making the tonic, and I knew then that Henry was a keeper."

I notice my tea has gone cold. "Whew, Avery," I say. "We better get to bed. It's past midnight."

"You're right, it is late," she says. Her eyelids are drooping and she yawns. "Promise me you'll tell me more stories about you and Henry and Miss Sally?" she asks.

"Sure, honey," I answer. "If it's stories you want, I've got plenty of those."

I crawl into bed and turn out the light, but sleep evades me. Sharing my memories with Avery is a double-edged sword: comforting on the one hand and painful on the other. I saw so much of myself in Avery ten years ago. Her scheme resulted in a painful change in multiple lives. My own childish plot—what I thought was an adventure—had similar results. Can either of us forgive ourselves? She has a chance to make things right with Aaron. My chance has passed, buried with the man I loved. In spite of spending years trying to honor Henry's memory by advocating for the black community, I still live every day with the guilt over my part in losing him.

Chapter 12

Avery

After a late morning trip down to the dock to eat cereal with Celi and look out over the water, I head out for a run on the path around the lake, and Celi joins Will in the garden to pick peas. The motion of my body and the impact of my feet striking the ground give me a welcome opportunity to sort through last evening's events. Each time Will tells me a story, I feel a tiny bit closer to understanding my history. But so far each story raises more questions.

I contemplate how I'm going to go about getting an answer to the number one question that's eating me up. Now that I'm here, I would like to come out and ask Will whether there are any black people in our family. But how can I do that? *Oh, by the way, Will, my child has sickle-cell disease, but she inherited it by having a black father and a black mother. Do you know how that could have happened?* Maybe it's as simple as that, and she'll answer me, and I'll be done with this wondering—wondering who and when and how. So let's say I get my answer. What difference will it make? What will I do with that information?

It's not simple. If I reveal that the Pritchett or the Reynolds family lineage includes blacks, then I'll be compelled to reveal the reason I need to know—Celi's disease. I have personally been the object of secrets kept and I know the emotional pain of that role.

How many people will be caught in the wake of destruction left by my newfound obsession with the truth? Just because I've decided to open up all of our secrets and illuminate every dark corner doesn't mean that everyone else in this family is ready to stand in the glare.

Maybe I could start by looking into the Reynolds family history. Maybe it's someone on Grandpa Jacob's side of the family. I know very little about him. But Will was always the nonconformist in the family. It seems more likely that the secret lies with her.

I wonder about getting Mark involved in this search. But then, why would it matter to him? He's marrying a white—very white—girl. I smile at the thought of how Mason and Laura Elise Collier would react to having blacks in their family trees. Especially since they like to trace the Collier ancestry back to some Civil War general.

So I'm stumped about where to begin. As I head back up the sloping lawn to Oak Knoll, I decide I'll keep listening to Will's stories and piecing things together. I stride up to the back porch door and stop. Sally Monroe is with Will and Celi. I peer through the screen door; none of them has heard me walk up. They're all three in rocking chairs, with small washtubs full of purple-hull peas in their laps. An afternoon soap opera is blaring from an old TV set in the corner. The old women are both drinking iced tea, and Celi has a big glass of Kool-Aid and several of what look like homemade peanut butter cookies on a plate beside her. Will is telling her about one of the characters on the show.

"So then Lisa had the nerve to leave him after all that," she's saying, as if my daughter is an old friend and they're gossiping about a mutual acquaintance.

Sally nods. "That's right, she did. And it like to broke his heart. That's the very time he turned to that Mallory for comfort," she says.

Celi is looking back and forth between the two women, apparently enthralled. I'm certain this is the first time she's ever watched a daytime TV soap opera, and I'm not too happy about it. I remember how Mother used to complain that the world stopped when it was time for Will's "programs."

"It might be called *As the World Turns*," she'd say, "but as far as Willadean is concerned it should be *When the World Stops*."

I open the screen door, and Celi, whose hearing is keen, looks around and smiles at me. She has a bright pink mustache, obviously from the Kool-Aid, and looks completely content shelling peas and watching soap operas with two old women. I start to worry about the amount of sugar she's ingesting, hoping it won't put her into a crisis. Then I'm mad at myself for being silly.

"Mom! Look!" she says, and holds up her hands for my inspection. Her fingertips are stained a deep purple from the pea hulls. "Grandma Will says you have to use lemon juice to get it off. Isn't it cool?"

I walk into the room, feeling Sally's and Will's eyes on me.

"And look at this," Celi says, holding her pan up. "Grandma Will and Miss Sally taught me how to shell peas. I've got almost half a pan full. Grandma says I'm fast!" She looks so proud of herself. I smile and reach down to give her a kiss.

"Hello again, Avery," Miss Sally says, and I reach down to take her outstretched hand. She takes hold of my fingers and doesn't release them when I try to pull away, forcing me to look into her eyes. "I'm sure enjoying this spunky little girl of yours. She's sharp as a tack, and pretty as can be," she says, smiling and looking over at Celi, who is practically beaming.

I still don't know how to handle being around Sally. Celi doesn't know anything about her father, much less the fact that this woman is her paternal great-grandmother. Aaron looks so much like Miss Sally—same eyes, same deep brown velvety skin color. Why couldn't things have turned out differently? What if Sally Monroe was my grandmother-in-law?

. . .

April 1991

I could tell from his breathing that he was fast asleep. Since those first tentative kisses, our physical relationship, along with our emotional connection, had continued to grow. Aaron's touch was tender but confident and ignited my body with a passion I hadn't known before. Sex with Aaron was so unlike the fumbling backseat fiascos I had attempted with other boys.

The knowledge that our relationship was taboo, my growing love for him, and the irresistible physical attraction between us lent a sense of urgency to the time we spent together. Unfortunately, it also made us reckless. How many young girls have said to themselves when having unprotected sex, *It's only once.* I was one of those girls. And even though Aaron and I admitted to each other that we were playing with fire and started using a condom, we didn't know then that Celi had already been conceived.

We'd been lying on a blanket on the bank of the lake, staring up through the branches of the old willow that draped around us in a canopy of green. I turned on my side and propped myself up on my elbow so I could look at him. My fingers ached to touch his face and chest, but I didn't want to wake him, so I contented myself with watching him sleep. He never looked as relaxed when he was awake. He always had worry in his eyes. Once again, I told myself that I should be the one to put an end to our relationship. But it was 1991 and people needed to get over their bigotry. What was wrong with Aaron and me being a couple? In places like New York and California there were tons of mixed-race couples. Why not in Greendale?

Then I thought about what my parents would say if they knew about us and the reason they would give for ripping us apart. They would say it was wrong. I had heard Mother and Mrs. Collier talking one day after seeing a mixed-race couple on the television news.

"God didn't mean for the races to mix," Mrs. Collier said. "If those people had a godly bone in their body, they'd know that. God separated the races at the Tower of Babel and he didn't mean for them to mix after that. Just causes trouble. People need to keep themselves separate."

Of course, Mother jumped right in. "I know it. Why, I wonder about the children. Little high-yellow half blacks that don't fit in anywhere. It's not right."

I got so angry remembering those ignorant comments that I plopped down hard on my back and woke up Aaron. He turned toward me and put his arm across me. I pressed the muscles in his forearm.

"What's up?" he asked me.

"Oh, nothing. I was thinking about some stuff Mother and Mrs. Collier said the other day and I got mad all over again."

"Mmm." I could tell he was drifting off again. I sat up suddenly and he jerked awake, rubbing his eyes.

"Aaron, I need to talk to you about something," I said, and I started to tremble with the sheer audacity of the idea that had started to germinate a few days before and hadn't let go of me since.

"What's that?"

"You have to go to the black debutante ball, right?"

"Yeah?" he said suspiciously. I knew he was wondering what I was getting at. Aaron's family had nowhere near the status of the elite group of blacks who hosted the annual black debutante ball. But since he was so smart and handsome, not to mention the fact that he was the star basketball player on the Greendale high school team, he had been chosen as an escort for Lacretia Brandon, a daughter of the wealthy black funeral home director. Aaron had already told me that he was only doing it because of pressure from Lacretia, whom I was sure had a crush on him. He and I agreed that the debutante rite of passage was an antiquated pain-in-the-ass tradition.

"What if we went to each other's debutante balls?" I asked, playing with the tail of my shirt, afraid to look at him just yet. "It would be a great way to make a statement, you know? To show them all that we're not going to hide anymore. That we want to be together and they can't stop us. We'll 'come out' just like the debs!" I was getting more and more worked up as I thought about how daring it would be. I turned to look at him, but his expression wasn't readable.

Aaron sat up and leaned back on his arms, stretching his long legs out in front of him. He tapped the air with his right foot. He was obviously not as excited as I was. Why did he have to think about everything so much? Maybe he needed more convincing.

"It'll be a social statement. We'll show them all that blacks and whites can mix and get along great. We'll change how things are done around here. Wouldn't that be cool?"

He turned to me, and I could tell he would reject the idea.

"Look. Please don't take this wrong, Avery, but I don't think Greendale is ready for a mixed-race couple. Especially not at the debutante ball. Besides, I think my people like it that they have a separate event. You know, it makes it their own. They don't have to play second fiddle to whites. . . ."

His people? Since when were they *his people* and *my people*? I was getting angrier. Was he actually siding with my mother? How could he lie here on this blanket, make love to me, share his deepest secrets, and then not want to go with me to a stupid debutante ball? "How will things ever change if someone doesn't do something, Aaron?" I asked.

"I know, I know, but . . ."

"What are we afraid of, anyway? So people talk. I say, let them talk. I'm tired of hiding and sneaking around." I was so frustrated I couldn't stand it anymore. I started to roll up the blanket we'd been lying on. "Let's go. I need to get home."

A big cloud hung between us as we walked to Aaron's truck and he drove me to the end of Will's driveway, where I always left my car tucked into a space under the trees sheltered from the road. He leaned over and kissed me good-bye. As I got in my car I said to him, "Think about it, okay?"

"Okay," he said, and raised his hand to wave as he drove away.

Sally releases my hand and I sit quietly with the three of them while the soap opera drones on. Sally and Will cluck like hens over the antics of the heroine, and Celi munches contentedly on her cookies between rounds of pea shelling. At this moment, I can imagine them as Celi's great-grandmothers, drawing her into their lives, nurturing her the way old Southern women do best—with food and family. But Will's house has always been a sanctuary for me, isolated from the real world, where Celi will be an oddity and at risk. Maybe not at risk from the danger Aaron experienced, but at risk for the pain of being politely ignored. Around here, people who don't fit in are made invisible.

Sally seems to have let go of her anger toward me. But now that Celi is getting to know Sally, I'm imagining my daughter's anger at me when she finds out I've kept this part of her family from her. Instead of making things clearer by coming here, I seem to be making them progressively more complicated. And the potential for a blowup seems to be multiplying with each passing day.

Chapter 13

Marion

"Yes, I have all of the details under control," I say into the receiver, trying to keep the irritation out of my voice.

"Very well. But you know how featherbrained Marjory Dean can be," Laura Elise says in her most oh-so-helpful tone.

"Laura Elise, the woman has been planning weddings and rehearsal dinners for forty years," I say, louder than I intend. Right at that moment, Leona walks in with a hamper of laundry and raises her eyebrows. I turn my back to her and lower my voice.

"Everything will be fine," I finish quietly.

We say our good-byes and I hang up the phone, annoyed. It seems that each interaction with Laura Elise leaves me more out of sorts than the last. What has happened to me? For so many years, I accepted our friendship as it was. I let go of my resentment toward her long ago. We've been through most of the major life events together. For some reason this one, our children marrying each other, has sent me into a storm of memories and is bringing up old jealousies and hurts that I thought were long calmed.

Maybe it's because Mason Collier was my first love, and a first love carves out a space in your heart that can never be filled by anyone or anything else. I'm convinced of it, yet I thought I'd made my peace with it. I believe that Mark and Nicki are each other's first loves—at least I believe that's true for Mark. He has all the signs. That look in his eyes—it's almost painful at times, the way he beams when he watches her. I hope it lasts. Mason wrapped a string around my heart when we were in high school and reeled me in like a fallen kite.

May 1959

"I don't like it," Mother said.

"It's only a church social, Willa," Daddy said. "What harm can that do?"

"He drives that fast car, he's rude to us, and I think he's shaping up to be just like his father and grandfather."

I sat on the edge of my chair in the living room, looking back and forth between my parents, trying to decide whether it was more to my advantage to jump into the conversation or let them work it out. Mason Collier and I had been going around together at school for weeks, but I'd finally passed my sixteenth birthday and now he'd asked me to the dance at the First Presbyterian Church.

I thought then of Mason's dreamy smile, his handsome face, wavy blond hair, and sky blue eyes; the way he opened the car door for me that day the four of us went to the drive-in together. I hadn't asked permission that day. When Laura Elise and I agreed to go to Rudy's Drive-In with Mason and her boyfriend, Woody Cole, we felt so adventurous. Riding in Mason's yellow Thunderbird with the top down was the most exhilarating thing I'd ever done. And when he reached for my hand, I knew Laura Elise and Woody saw. Laura Elise and I talked about it later. "I think he really likes you," she whispered. "I bet he asks you to the dance."

I didn't dare dream it, but it had happened. And Mother and Daddy had already said that when I turned sixteen, I could date. So now, rather than risk being seen out with Mason without permission, I knew I'd better ask. Rumors spread like lightning in Greendale.

"Marion, do you understand that Mason's father is a member of the Citizens' Council?" Mother asked, looking at me like I had done something horribly wrong. "Did you know that? Does that matter to you? And his grandfather . . ." She stopped and looked at Daddy, who shook his head. "Don't even get me started on him." She got up from her chair and walked across the room to stand by Daddy. She never could sit still when she got excited about her cause. I was so weary of it creeping into every single part of my life that I wanted to scream. Other mothers didn't make their daughters form their whole lives around who went to some stupid meeting and who didn't; around whether colored people got to vote or go to the library or attend a university.

"Now, Marion," Daddy said, chuckling. "That Citizens' Council includes just about every white businessman around here, except me."

"You think this is funny, Jacob?" she asked, her eyes flashing. "You think it's funny that your only daughter is going on a date with the son of a man who is probably in the Klan? Do I need to remind you what happened just last week?" *Oh, please, dear God, not another horror story.* I wanted to have a normal life. To be like the other girls, carefree and silly. It was all so hopeless. I felt the tears start to well up in my eyes.

"Now look what you've done, Willa," Daddy said. "Come over here, baby girl." He held his arm out to me.

I went to stand beside his armchair and let him wrap his arm around my waist. Mother rolled her eyes and looked disgusted.

"I tell you what, Marion," Daddy said, giving my waist a squeeze. "How about you have this boy come by and have a talk with me this week."

"Okay, Daddy," I said, carefully wiping a tear so my mascara wouldn't smear.

"Jacob, do you promise you'll find out where he stands on things?" Mother asked.

Daddy promised, and even though I didn't mean to use tears, I was thrilled that they had worked.

Mason was due to pick me up for the dance. My first date and Mother chose that night of all nights to tutor three Negro sharecroppers in our kitchen. They were gathered around the table with their Big Chief writing tablets and fat yellow pencils, learning to write the alphabet. My only saving grace was that they stayed in the kitchen. Mother had tried to get them to sit in the front parlor, but they were so jumpy and uncomfortable there that she finally gave up and moved her schoolroom. Thank the Lord. Even so, I never had guests. The idea that one of my girlfriends would visit and find my mother sitting around the table, laughing and talking with Negro men, horrified me so much that I almost broke out in hives considering it.

When Grandma Reynolds was alive, Mother would never have brought Negroes into our house. Until she died when I was ten, Grandma was a constant civilizing force at Oak Knoll. My grandfather died the year Mother and Daddy married, so after Daddy came back from the war, they agreed to live at Oak Knoll and care for Grandma Reynolds. During those last years of Grandma's life I could remember lovely afternoon teas with finger sandwiches and lemon snap cookies, or her Garden Club meetings with fresh flowers on the dining room table and a white linen tablecloth. Grandma would call me into the parlor to play the piano, and all the sweet-smelling ladies in their flowered dresses and hats patted me on the head and told Grandma what a lovely young lady I was.

When Grandma was alive, Clarice Johnson was our cook and Trixie Smith was our maid. There were always cookies in the wide-mouthed glass jar on the sideboard and delicious meals every evening. After Grandma Reynolds died and Clarice left us, Mother refused to hire any more colored help. How I missed Clarice's cooking and how I hated taking over Trixie's chores.

Laura Elise and every other girl in our circle had cooks, maids, and gardeners. Not us. Mother herself managed the household, and although her cooking was passable, it was nothing like Clarice's had been. Laura Elise could grow her nails out long and her hands were smooth. My hands were rough from washing dishes and cleaning floors.

"Stop your whining," Mother would say when I complained

that no one else I knew had to do their own housecleaning. "It doesn't matter what everyone else does. No daughter of mine is going to grow up thinking that she has to have a colored woman clean her toilets and raise her children." But it mattered to me. I didn't want to be that girl who was different from everyone else. I wanted desperately to fit in, and part of fitting in was having a maid—and, of course, all maids were colored. That's just how it was.

I appealed to Daddy, but he was like a mule wearing blinders when it came to Mother. Nothing she did or said was wrong in his eyes. It was as if he couldn't see how ostracized she was from other white women. Daddy moved through life with one purpose, and that was to save Oak Knoll from ruin. I'd heard people say what an impressive businessman he was to be able to turn around the plantation like he did. Even though he dressed plain and didn't join the gentlemen's club downtown with the other fathers, he was quiet, soft-spoken, and loved by everyone. I never worried that Daddy would say something embarrassing.

Since Grandma Reynolds's death, Mother's Negro causes had escalated. And Daddy didn't stop her. Whenever she went on a tear about the injustice done to Negroes or rampant maltreatment in the sharecropping system or literacy tests and poll taxes, Daddy would nod his head and agree with whatever she said. I could never decide if he supported what she did or simply tolerated it. Whatever his motivation with Mother, when it came to me, there couldn't have been a better father. Indulging me was the closest he came to disagreeing with Mother.

"You're encouraging her idea that she's privileged," she would say.

And Daddy would shake his head. "Now, Willadean, she's a young girl. Let her have her day."

It was Daddy who gave me the money to shop in Memphis for the new dress I was wearing. "Is your mama going shopping with you?" he asked, looking hopeful.

"No, sir," I said quickly. "She has a class, I think."

Daddy nodded, pressed a roll of bills into my hand, and said, "Have a good time, baby girl. Buy something pretty."

What I didn't want to tell Daddy was that although Laura Elise's mother had me protectively under her fashion wing, her kindness did not extend to Mother.

When I told Mother that I was going to Memphis with Laura Elise and her mother to shop, she said, "Again? Child, don't you have enough dresses?"

It was useless to remind her about the dance and my first date with Mason Collier.

Upstairs in my bedroom, I gazed in the mirror and turned to check my profile. My breasts had gotten full and round in the past year and filled out my fitted bodice nicely. My narrow waist was cinched by a wide pink belt. My dress was a pink floral on a white background. It had a swing skirt with sheer, full, puffed sleeves and a square neck, cut low in the back underneath my shoulder blades. Mrs. Reed had said it was perfect with my dark brown hair and eyes. I was pleased with the way the creamy skin of my back peeked out below my hair. The dress came from the little dress shop in Memphis called Louisa's, where Laura Elise and her mother always shopped. Laura Elise had gotten the blue taffeta and we both bought new three-quarter-length gloves. I styled my hair in the new chin-length cut with soft waves, just like Elizabeth Taylor's.

Through the open window I heard Mason's Thunderbird emerge from the trees. I looked out and saw the car prowling up the driveway like a big yellow cat. Oh dear, the top was down. I quickly held my breath, buried myself in another cloud of Aqua Net, and reached for a pink scarf to tie around my hair. I had spent hours with my hair in rollers, and since I had finally tamed my coarse waves into smooth submission, I didn't want anything to ruin it now. Besides, I always had to compete with Laura Elise's blond good looks.

I debated briefly about slipping down the back staircase and into the kitchen to show Mother my dress. The other girls were probably having their parents take their photographs right about now with their Brownie cameras. But then I remembered the three men and thought better of it. Besides, I might end up smelling like whatever horrid thing Mother had on the stove. Her pupils always brought some kind of food offering from their wives in appreciation for Mother's teaching them, and this time was no exception. Poor colored people ate the most disgusting things. Mother always said that in her youth, someone named Leroy had taught her to love all kinds of food, so she sat down readily at our table to feast on whatever the current offering was—pigs' feet, chitterlings, or head cheese.

I knew that Daddy was in the front parlor, reading, smoking his pipe, and waiting to answer the door. When the lion-head knocker resounded, a little thrill rippled through me. I prayed that Mother wouldn't surface from the kitchen. I heard Daddy open the door and greet Mason. They discussed the weather and the current crop Daddy had planted. Mason was polite and deferential. Daddy was playing his part perfectly.

I made it a point to descend the stairs slowly, exactly like I'd practiced at Laura Elise's house. I practiced there instead of at home, because the one time I tried it at my own house, Mother came through the front hall and said, "What in the world are you doing, Marion? Are you hurt? Is there something wrong with your back?" She was hopeless, absolutely hopeless.

When I reached the bottom of the stairs, Mason was waiting for me with a grin on his face. He looked so handsome. His hair was combed rakishly to the side, with one small curl kissing the sharp line of his bold dark eyebrows. His blue eyes sparkled as he glanced my way.

I loved that Mason never looked nervous. He carried himself with such confidence, even a little bit of a swagger. He knew who he was in the world and wasn't ashamed of showing it. Consequently, people deferred to him everywhere he went. Even the teachers at school would blush sometimes when he was especially sweet to them. Tonight he dipped into a suave bow as I took in his gray sport coat and flashy yellow tie. I felt like Elizabeth Taylor with Paul Newman.

I was getting excited that Mason and I would make our exit without a hitch. Daddy and I had already talked about what my curfew should be. Laura Elise said boys thought that girls with curfews later than ten o'clock were easy. So when Daddy asked me what he should say, I suggested ten.

I hurried to offer Mason my hand, and he pulled an adorable wrist corsage from behind his back and slid it on my wrist. Just as I thought that we would make it out the door, Mother surfaced from the back of the house. I was mortified. She was wearing a dowdy old housedress with an apron tied around her waist like a maid. She had to wipe her hands off on the apron before she could shake Mason's hand. I was sure then we'd never have another date. Mason frowned, and although he covered his surprise at her appearance, I saw his eyebrows shoot up when she entered the front hall.

I practically pushed Mason out the door to avoid any conversation with Mother. When the door closed behind us and he took my arm to guide me to the car, I immediately started to prattle on about his car and the dance, hoping that my chatter would forestall any conversation about what Mason had witnessed in my home. Why did she have to pick right then to come out of the kitchen? I finally took a breath long enough to notice that Mason had gone silent. He pulled the car into the grass alongside the church and turned to me, his expression serious. "So, Marion," he said, looking down at the gearshift, "is it true what they say about your mother? That she teaches niggers how to read so they can pass the literacy test?"

I immediately panicked. Had Mason known that there were three men in the kitchen? Had he seen one of them? "Oh, my goodness, where did you get such a silly idea?" I said in the lightest voice I could muster. "Of course not. Why would she want to do that?"

Mason smiled and looked relieved. "I don't know. My mother . . . Oh, anyway, it doesn't matter now. You know how parents can be."

"Do I ever," I said. "Oh, look. There are Laura Elise and Woody going in. Let's go catch up with them," I said, tugging Mason toward the hall's entrance. He came along agreeably but paused as we stepped inside the door.

"I was wondering—how come your daddy doesn't belong to the Citizens' Council?"

Before I could answer, Laura Elise swooped in, grabbed my arm, and pulled me off toward the ladies' room with promises of a brand-new cherry lipstick and a juicy bit of gossip. We left the boys to go in search of punch, and much relieved, I put the dismal situation at home out of my mind. That night I told myself that I would tell however many lies I had to, to hold on to Mason Collier.

My first official date with Mason turned out as perfectly as I'd hoped it would. And when he suggested we park at Alligator Lake to look at the stars, I didn't argue. After all, I had Mother's reputation to overcome. I knew that allowing Mason just the right amount of free rein with his hands would keep him interested in me and his mind off my mother's foolish antics—until I could garner a proposal. Before the end of the summer, we were going steady and I was hopelessly in love with the idea of myself as Mrs. Mason Collier. Having Mason as a boyfriend gave me the legitimacy among the other girls that I craved.

I stop myself, realizing I've been caught up in memories that are best left behind. I need to focus now on my family and on what it will take to pull us together. This evening I'll get to spend time with Celi while Avery goes out with Mark and Nicki. I'm surprised that I've discovered this fierceness within myself: a will to protect my own family. I'm not sure when it happened, but I'm not going to hide behind my self-created image of perfection anymore. Things are a little awkward between Avery and me, but I'm hopeful. And that's more than I thought I'd be able to say at this point.

I walk into the dining room in search of the guest list for the rehearsal dinner. I've been working on this dinner with Marjory Dean, Greendale's oldest wedding planner, since the day I found out that the kids were engaged. I was completely surprised when Nicki did not choose to use Marjory Dean to plan the wedding. She's the best. But Nicki has strong opinions. Laura Elise has had to step back and relinquish control—a lesson I've been learning.

I certainly know what it means to have a strong-willed daughter. I feel a touch of pride in Avery. She's grown into a confident, independent woman. Did she learn any of that from me? It seems that most of my life has been about working to maintain my standing in this community—Holt's, too. I locate the guest list on the mantel of the dining room fireplace. Leona must have moved it when she was dusting. I see Avery's debutante photo there, right next to mine. My own coming out was lovely, in spite of Willadean. Daddy's money meant no one in Greendale could openly refuse to include me. It was what they said behind my back that kept me feeling insecure.

I shopped in Memphis for a dress that no other girl could match. I chose my parents' clothes for the debutante ball, and all they had to do was show up. I rehearsed with Willadean what to say when she talked to the other ladies. I knew Daddy would be fine because men always talk about business.

And now here we are planning my son's wedding. Where did the years go? After all that business with Avery and Aaron Monroe, I wonder if Avery will ever have a chance at romantic happiness. It breaks my heart to think that she'll end up a single mother and alone. I'm wondering about Celi when the doorbell rings. That little girl is sweet, and she seems very smart, but I worry that her life is going to be really hard.

"Leona," I call. "Could you get that, please?"

I step into the foyer as Leona is showing Avery and Celi in. Avery is hugging Leona and introducing Celi. I'm suddenly intensely self-conscious about having a black maid. I probably shouldn't have had her answer the door, but it's such a habit. I can see Leona staring at Celi, and I hurry to get her back to her cleaning. "Thank you, Leona," I say, stepping between her and my granddaughter. "I've got them."

"Yes, ma'am," she says, walking slowly away but glancing over her shoulder at Celi.

"Hey, Mother," Avery says, looking a little nervous. Not surprising, since she hasn't set foot in her own home in ten years.

"Wow!" says Cecelia, gazing up at the staircase. It is beautiful.

It's one of the reasons I chose the house. It makes such a grand initial impression. I'm pleased that Celi appreciates it—Avery never did.

"Um . . . well . . . how are you two?" I ask, cursing myself for feeling so awkward in my own home. "Come on in. Celi, you can set your backpack at the foot of the stairs, and we'll take it up later when I show you your room." She sets the pack down on the last step and runs her hand over the railing. "We'll sit in the sunroom and visit for a little bit," I say. "Would y'all like a glass of tea? Lemonade?"

They both murmur, "No, thank you," saying something about still being stuffed from lunch.

"The house looks great, Mother," Avery says as we walk down the long center hall. "Looks like you've changed the colors in here," she says, poking her head into the dining room.

"Why, yes, I have. Thank you for noticing." Celi makes a beeline to the mantel and begins to examine the photographs.

"Mom, is this you?" she asks, pointing to Avery's debutante portrait.

"Yep," Avery says. "That's me."

"And who's that?"

Avery walks over to stand beside Celi as they look at the picture. Avery frowns. "That's Seth, Miss Nicki's brother."

As I watch them together, I'm still having a hard time believing this moment is real. When Avery left this house, she was a young girl barely out of high school, full of angry rebelliousness. And now she's a grown woman, still slender, but not as bone thin as she was then. I wonder what she looked like pregnant, if she enjoyed her pregnancy, if Celi was an easy baby. . . . I've missed so much. And now they're here and I don't know how to act. I can sense how uncomfortable Avery is around me, but the child seems at home. I find that strange.

"You look beautiful, Mom," Celi says, running her small fingers around the edge of the frame. "Why were you all dressed up?"

"Um . . . that was for my debutante ball," Avery says. "Mother, maybe we'll have some iced tea after all."

Avery is obviously trying to get the child off the subject of her debutante ball. I can't say I blame her. What a disaster that was. Avery is steering her toward the sunroom. "Anyway, Celi, Leona makes these wonderful lemon cookies. You are going to love them."

"Okay, Mom, sounds great," Celi says, but she will not be deterred and she is apparently wise to her mother's tactics. "Grandma," she says, turning to me, "what is a debutante ball?"

I look at Avery, and she shrugs. "Oh, go ahead and tell her. I've got to pee. I'll meet y'all out in the sunroom." Avery heads off toward the downstairs powder room.

"Your mother was never one for formal affairs and dressing up," I say to Celi.

"I know," she says, looking very wise for her age. "She hates getting dressed up for anything. She'd rather be in scrubs or sweatpants."

"And what about you?" I ask.

"Oh, I love beautiful dresses!" There's an adorable twinkle in her eyes. "The new dress you and Grandpa gave me fits perfectly. And on Friday, we get to go and be fitted for our dresses for the wedding!"

I have to smile as she tells me all about her and Avery's dresses. She really is a beautiful child—straight white teeth, adorable little nose and full lips, flawless skin. I've never seen skin the color of hers. Of course, she would never pass as white, but she doesn't look like the dark blacks around here, either. I've seen one or two mixed-race children in town, but it's rare. This child is prettier, of course, than any in Greendale. Her hair is kinky like a black person's. I wonder how Avery deals with that. She never even dealt with her own hair. Today, Cecelia has her hair plaited in a pretty braid with little clips on each side.

She seems to be a happy child; she smiles a lot. And I can tell she's smart—her grammar is certainly better than that of most of the children I've met. And she's persistent. She asks again about the debutante ball, so I find myself telling her about the coming-out process and all of the events that go along with it. Unlike her mother, she is fascinated. Her interest touches me. I buried my hopes for a girl whom I could share such things with long ago—right about the time Avery started choosing her own clothes. Of course, even if Celi grew up here, she couldn't be part of the Delta Debutante Club. I wonder if the blacks would take her.

When Avery comes out to the sunroom, Cecelia and I are still discussing the Greendale debutante ball, so she wanders out of the room again in search of Leona's lemon cookies and iced tea.

"Do you still have any of the dresses?" Cecelia asks me.

I have to think for a minute. "You know, as a matter of fact, I think I do. I have mine stored, along with my wedding dress. Um . . . Avery's dress, we don't have anymore. It was . . . not something she wanted to keep," I say, thinking how utterly that dress was destroyed on the night of her ball. But I'm certainly not going to tell her daughter that story.

"Ooh, could I please see them?" Celi asks. She's so sincere and so thrilled at the prospect of seeing those old dresses, how can I refuse?

"I suppose we could do that," I say. "We'll have to go upstairs."

Soon we are in the guest room buried in a sea of taffeta and lace. We are so absorbed in the dresses that neither one of us hears Avery enter the room. Celi is asking one question after another, and when I look up and see Avery, I know she is worried that I'll try to turn Celi into a Southern girly girl. I almost laugh at the irony.

Chapter 14

Avery

As I drive downtown to meet Mark and Nicki at Desiree's, I pass the Southern Belle Dress Shop where I got fitted for my debutante dress and where Celi and I will go for the fitting on Friday. I notice the current version of the prom gown displayed in the window, some garish lime green chiffon thing that, unbelievably, comes in two pieces. Visions of Jasmine in Disney's *Aladdin* pass through my mind.

Downtown hasn't changed much over the years. Still the same tall live oaks lining the streets, the same colorful storefronts, the same imposing brick First National Bank on the corner. The First Baptist, First Presbyterian, First Methodist, and St. Elizabeth Catholic churches anchor the city's five primary blocks. I pass through the central business district and cross the old railroad tracks before turning north.

Fourth Street still looks sketchy; at this time of day, just before dark, it's easy to see how old and dilapidated the buildings are. As I spot the neon sign flashing *Desiree's* on what most people would consider a run-down shack, and start searching for a parking place, I remember how Aaron and I talked about going here together so long ago. Watching Celi with my mother today, so enthralled by the debutante dresses, and passing the Southern Belle Dress Shop have brought back so many memories of my debutante experience. The only thing that got me through it was my excitement about the possibility of sneaking Aaron into the ball.

May 1991

Eleven giggling debs and their overly made-up, barracuda mothers were packed into the parlor of Mrs. Ladmeyer's antebellum home on Gardner Street. I was seated at a table with four other girls and I thought I might explode out of my miserably uncomfortable sundress. I looked around, hoping for some escape. Maybe the house would burn down, or fat Mrs. Ladmeyer would have a heart attack or choke on a shrimp. But she was sipping a Bloody Mary and breathing just fine. Could I go out to the kitchen and accidentally leave a dishcloth on the stove? But the fire department would blame the fire on the catering company. Mrs. Ladmeyer would make sure they never worked in Greendale again. I couldn't do that to them.

"I'm so tired," Alicia Randall complained, covering her mouth with her pink-tipped fingers. "And we still have to be fitted this afternoon."

Can't wait for that, I thought, picking at my shrimp and grits and wondering for the gazillionth time who had come up with all of this debutante nonsense. Brunches, lunches, dress fittings, rehearsals. All for what? Mother's words floated through my cotillion-addled brain. . . .

"A young girl must have a proper introduction to society. . . ." As far as I was concerned I'd met Greendale society and no, thank you.

Lorna Deason snorted—a very undeb-like response. "Alicia, if you hadn't been out so late last night with Landon, you might not be so tired."

Alicia giggled and whispered, "Yeah, I've got to stop coming home with my panties in my purse. Pretty soon, Mama's going to catch on and I'll be absolute toast!"

All the girls at my table laughed and I thought I would throw up. Landon Hornsby—or Horny Toad, as I liked to refer to him—was the most obnoxious boy at Greendale Prep. A football player, he thought he was God's gift to girls. And Alicia? Size four dress and a size nine thousand ego. For her, this whole deb thing was perfect. So many ways to be the center of attention.

Lorna leaned forward and looked around before whispering, "Did y'all hear about Farley Cole and Seth Collier?" The other girls tilted their heads to hear over the chatter in the room. I leaned in, too, not wanting to let them know that I couldn't give a rat's ass about their conversation.

"They went down to the coast for spring break, you know." She paused as the other girls nodded; I was obviously out of the loop. Who kept up with where these morons went for spring break? Lorna continued, "Anyway, they were slumming in Biloxi and Farley got arrested!"

They all gasped. I imagined pretty little Farley Cole, with his oh-so-perfect polo shirts, perfectly pressed khaki shorts, and expensive Cole Haan loafers—no socks, of course—slumming in Biloxi. I hoped the police officer who arrested him was black.

"What did he do?" asked Alicia.

"Rumor has it he tried to pick up a black girl, and when she wouldn't go with him, he got in a fight with her boyfriend."

My stomach turned and I pushed my food away. Slumming was a disgusting custom of the boys who were deb escorts—and usually members of the Delta Bachelor's Club. Every year, they went into the black nightclub area of Biloxi and dared each other to pick up black girls and have sex with them. The ones who scored wore an extra flower in their boutonnieres at the ball. It made me sick.

"Is he still in jail?" asked Merilee Waverly, pushing her glasses up on her nose. Merilee would probably be our valedictorian. She was the closest I had to a real friend in this group. But she was as docile as a kitten without its eyes open. Merilee had absolutely no backbone. But look at me; I wasn't saying anything, either. Neither one of us fit in with these girls. But thanks to our mothers, not to mention our families' money, there we were.

"No, he didn't stay in jail. His daddy drove over and bailed him out. He said he and his daddy laughed and joked all the way home. His daddy told him stories about his own slumming and all." Lorna smiled as if this was the cutest thing a boy could do. "That Farley—he's such a cad."

"Is he still going to be your escort?" asked Alicia.

"Of course," Lorna said, waving her hand dismissively. "He knows I'm mad at him, so he'll probably try to make it up to me somehow." A round of giggles followed.

"I can't believe those boys think it's such an adventure to go down there and pick up black girls. Why do they think that's such an exciting thing to do?" asked Alicia. I could tell from the way she was asking the question that she didn't really care about the black girls those boys tried to force themselves on. She was simply making conversation. Of course Merilee, Miss Nerd Queen of the Universe, had an answer.

"My mother told me it goes way back to the days when our families owned slaves. . . . You know—the master and the slave girl kind of thing. . . ." The other girls nodded knowingly as if this made perfect sense to them. I was wondering about that kitchen fire again.

Alicia leaned forward. "Have y'all ever wondered what it would be like to have sex with a black boy?" The other girls sat back instantly, making noises of disgust and disbelief.

"Oh my God, Alicia!" said Lorna. "That's sick. How could you even think such a thing?"

"Excuse me," I said, getting up too quickly and knocking my chair over. "Oh, sorry," I said, mortified as my mother looked up from her conversation with Laura Elise Collier and frowned. One of the white-coated waiters, a black man, hurried over and picked up my chair. I escaped to Mrs. Ladmeyer's perfectly appointed powder room, wondering if they'd miss me if I stayed in there until the brunch was over.

The dresses were lined up on racks with their big poufy skirts sticking out and their tiny bodices hidden on hangers straining under the weight of sequins, lace, netting, and ribbon. All the girls were squealing like piglets running from a barnyard dog, and I was in hell. That seemed to be a theme those days. I kept asking myself how I could avoid the debutante ritual and still live at home, at least until I graduated from high school. Maybe that was the answer—leave home. I could go and live with Will. But Mother would blow a gasket. Funny how when you didn't fit the mold around here, you were crazy, or else you were white trash, or there was always Alicia's favorite: "Bless her heart, she doesn't know any better."

Alicia was trying to stuff her size four body into a size two dress—such a dilemma—and complaining to Miss Esther that the dress didn't fit right. Miss Esther was the German Jewish lady who owned the Southern Belle Dress Shop and had been fitting girls for this shindig since Alicia's grandmother was a deb in 1952. God, Miss Esther must be tired. But she smiled and patted Alicia and told her how stunning she looked, while Alicia primped and turned and all the other girls oohed and aahed until I thought I was going to gag.

Lorna emerged from the dressing room and I had to cover my mouth and pretend to cough to keep from laughing out loud. Lorna was a big girl—generous proportions, Miss Esther called it—and her breasts filled up half of any room she occupied and got almost all of the attention. They were phenomenal. Once when Merilee was drunk, I had heard her calculate that each of them must weigh twenty pounds—a shocking statement if only because Merilee was usually so mealymouthed.

Right now, Lorna was looking down at her "girls" and trying to push them back into the neckline of the dress Miss Esther had recommended for her. "This one is usually perfect for our better-endowed debs," Miss Esther said, but even she looked at a loss right now. She joined Lorna in the attempt to shift her boobs around, but they were not having any luck. All the other girls, including me, were watching, awestruck by the sheer magnitude of Lorna's dilemma. Of course, Alicia, who didn't like the attention to leave her for an instant, had the first suggestion.

"Now, Lorna darling, I have an idea," Alicia crooned.

"What?" Lorna asked, choking back tears. Miss Esther had already told us that she had to have all alteration decisions by today and that this dress selection was the best she'd had in years. I felt sorry for Lorna.

"I've heard that Landry's dress shop has more dresses for . . . well . . . fuller figures. Maybe you could try there." Alicia smoothed the front of her gown and pushed her blond curls from her shoulders in her favorite oh-so-deb gesture. Miss Esther looked horrified, and all the other girls were holding their breath. Merilee pushed her glasses up on her nose to see Lorna better. Big fat tears were falling onto Lorna's overly exposed chest.

"I can't go to Landry's dress shop, Alicia!" she blubbered. "The *black* debs go there. What would people say?"

Everyone nodded in agreement and the whispering and murmuring began as Miss Esther shuttled Lorna back into the dressing room, clucking like a hen and telling her, "Not to worry, we'll have your mother get something custom made. I'll see to everything. . . ."

Alicia had a wicked smile on her face the whole time. She didn't miss any opportunity to embarrass Lorna. Crazy thing was, no one seemed to notice it but me. Well, maybe Merilee, but she never said boo.

The black debutante ball was the weekend after ours. Mother was always complaining that the blacks could at least wait until a different month to have their ball. I don't know what she was so worried about. It was not like we were ever going to be at the same functions, or even at the same venues. Most of our functions were held at the all-white Greendale Country Club, except the grand ball, which was held at Rosewood Plantation. I was probably crazy to think any of it would ever change.

I cringed because it was time for my fitting. I hated poufy white dresses, and my body was about as curvy as a Popsicle stick. What was Miss Esther going to pull out for me? Something for the "flat figured," no doubt. I hated that we had to do this all together, like a herd. Why couldn't we suffer through it alone, in silence? But no! Tradition said we all had to do our fittings in a group and then go to tea at the club with our mothers. As if anyone would have an appetite.

Miss Esther was coming at me with a dress that looked like the bodice was stuffed with tissue paper to hold it in place. I was thinking she should leave it in there if she expected me to wear that thing. The skirt was voluminous and it looked really scratchy.

In the dressing room I stripped out of my sundress so she could pull the white gown over my head. My yellow sports bra was obviously not working with the look of the dress because Miss Esther pushed it underneath as best she could and clucked and poked, her mouth full of pins. I jumped when she reached under my breasts from behind and gave them a quick lift. Unfortunately, not much happened, and she shook her head.

"Out you go!" she said, motioning me out of the dressing room to the huge three-way mirror, where all the other girls were waiting. When I hesitated she gave me a little shove. "Out. You must show other girls."

They were all really quiet, even Alicia, when I stepped from behind the curtain. Maybe because my gnarly old flip-flops were showing. Or maybe because my hair was hanging in my eyes, looking like peed-on hay. They all seemed about to burst. Miss Esther sighed and said in her thick German accent, "Well, we might have to take a little dart or two. . . ."

Merilee let out a little squeak and then the rest of them exploded into gales of laughter, slapping one another and pinching one another's "dart" areas. Now I was the one about to cry. Then I looked in the mirror and the sight before me was so hilarious, I dissolved into laughter, too.

I smile at the memory of the laughter that day. I finally find a parking place and walk the two blocks to the nightclub. I can't help but notice that every person I meet on the sidewalk is black—such a contrast to where I've spent the last ten years. Most of the men and women I meet look at me with mild curiosity and smile. They probably think I'm a stranger in town, maybe a tourist interested in the origins of blues music. Little do they know that I was born here.

Mark and Nicki are waiting for me outside, and after our greetings, we step inside the darkened club. The aromas of cigarette smoke, stale grease, and crawfish spices hit my nose. Several old black men at the bar turn slowly to watch our entrance and then turn back to their beer and conversation.

We settle into a table near the stage, where the musicians are setting up, and order beer and a round of boiled crawfish. The icy cold beer arrives accompanied by a huge plate of the bright red prehistoric-looking creatures that taste so good. We laugh as we crack the shells over their plump bodies and pull the tiny bits of succulent meat from their tails. Of course, Mark has to put the heads on his fingers and make them dance. Nicki rolls her eyes and proceeds to suck the head of the crawfish in her hands.

"Oh, I can't believe you're doing that," I say. "I don't care how many crawfish I eat; I cannot bring myself to suck their heads."

"Girl, you don't know what you're missing," Nicki says, licking her fingers. "Scrumptious."

I'm having such a good time, eating, drinking, and looking around at all the ancient autographed eight-by-ten photographs of blues musicians who've played here over the years, that I'm oblivious to anyone else in the club until a voice from my past comes screeching across the room over the noise of the jukebox playing B. B. King. I peer through the dim light to see the familiar face of Merilee Waverly twisting and turning through the crowded tables and chairs, making her way toward me.

And suddenly my heart is pounding and I want to disappear into the floor.

Chapter 15

Marion

When Holt comes in from work, he finds Celi and me out in the rose garden. She runs to hug him.

"Hi, Grandpa," she says. "Grandma is showing me her roses."

"She's got a lot of them, doesn't she?" he says. Being a grandfather suits Holt, as does being a father. When Avery and Mark were young, it seemed so easy for him to allow them to be whatever it was they needed to be. He never seemed concerned about their future, or the long-term consequences of their decisions. I was always the worrier. I suppose I still am. He steps over to me and gives me a kiss.

"Celi has made my brain work overtime today," I say, enjoying, as always, the feeling of Holt's arm wrapped around my waist. "She's had me name every rose out here."

"They're so beautiful," Celi says. "I want a rose garden when I grow up."

I laugh. "I was telling Celi about visiting the rose garden in Memphis belonging to Laura Elise's aunt when I was a child and how it inspired me."

"Is that how you got interested in roses?" he asks. "I never knew that." It occurs to me that there is a lot about me that Holt doesn't know. When he and I met, I chose to make him my new beginning. I deliberately reframed everything about Laura Elise and Mason. I had to; otherwise the pain would have been too great. I realize now, watching Celi lead him from rose to rose, identifying their names with remarkable accuracy, how thankful I am for Holt.

"Maybe you will have your own rose garden someday," Holt says as they finish a full circle of the garden. "I think I'll get out of this tie," he says, pulling at the knot, "and grill us some steaks. Celi, do you like steak?"

"I don't know. We never eat it," she answers.

"I have some hot dogs, too," I say, glad that I thought about Laura Elise saying her grandsons always prefer hot dogs.

She purses her lips. "I think I'd rather have a hot dog."

"A hot dog it is," Holt says, and Celi and I head for the kitchen to make drinks and start preparations for dinner while Holt goes upstairs to change.

"Grandma?" Celi asks, sitting on a kitchen stool and swinging her legs. "Do you have any movies?"

This is something I haven't thought of—movies for a nine-year-old. "No, Celi, I'm sorry, but I don't. We do have the Disney Channel. Do you like that?"

I get an enthusiastic response. After I've settled her in the den with the television, Holt and I head out to our usual chairs on the terrace for drinks.

"Seems like she's having a good time," he says.

"I think she is," I answer. "She's an easily entertained child, fascinated by everything." I laugh. "We must have spent an hour earlier looking at my old dresses—including my debutante dress and wedding gown. She had to hear a story about each one of them. Then she wanted to see every room in the house, asked about all the photographs. She's full of questions. You know, I've been thinking of things she and I could do together. I'd like to take her to the club to swim, but I don't know if it would be a good idea."

"Why not?" he asks.

I find myself a little irritated by his nonchalance. "Think about it, Holt. She's black. There are no blacks in the club."

He shakes his head. This is an old aggravation for him. Five years ago he did some legal work for a black building contractor who had recently moved to Greendale. Apparently he and Holt became friends. He talked about the man very favorably, recounting his military service and his forthright business dealings. When Holt recommended him for the club, it caused an uproar. Laura Elise and the other women associate members—we ourselves are not true members—were appalled. That was the first time Holt had done anything to rock Greendale's racial boat. I stayed out of it and kept my mouth shut.

Of course, the nominating committee never voted on the man's application. Every time it was presented, they tabled it for the next year's election, effectively denying the man entrance. Now, a few years later, I am confronting our exclusivity head-on in the form of my own granddaughter. Of course, it crossed my mind then to wonder what I would do if Avery ever brought the child home, but I didn't let myself worry about it. What was the point? Avery was never coming back to Greendale, never going to force me to face the prospect of being the only grandmother in my circle whose grandchild was mixed race—which, in this town, meant she might as well be all black.

"So, what are you thinking you'll do?" asked Holt.

"I don't know," I answer. "I just don't know." He leaves the subject alone, knowing better than to patronize me by telling me that everything will be fine or to suggest I go against club policy and take her anyway.

"And how are you doing playing grandmother?" he asks, looking at me with his steady gaze.

"I have to admit, I was worried," I say. "But I'm actually more comfortable around Celi than I am around Avery. Celi is an open book, innocent and curious. She isn't at all self-conscious."

"Avery's done a good job with her, then," Holt says.

I'm instantly defensive. Could I have done a better job with Avery? "Maybe it's the other way around. Maybe it's Celi who has finally softened Avery up," I say. "There's still a wall between Avery and me, probably because of the past. I don't think she's let that go yet."

"And have *you*?" he asks.

"I'm trying," I answer, absorbed in thoughts of that summer, ten years ago, when Avery and I reached our impasse.

May 1991

The presentation of the debutantes went beautifully, and Avery dutifully participated in the traditional father-daughter dance with Holt. I was so pleased watching them. Holt was an excellent dancer; he even made Avery appear graceful. And she looked so pretty in her white gown, not at all the awkward tomboy I had grown accustomed to seeing. Afterward, as dinner was ending, I was distracted by some silly conversation with Merilee Waverly, and when I looked around, Avery had disappeared. Many of the parents typically left before the band started playing all of the teenage favorites, the girls started pulling off their shoes, and the boys removed their ties. Holt stopped talking to Mason, and we both looked around for Avery.

"Oh, you know kids," Mason said, winking at me. "Avery and Seth are probably out doing what we wish we were still doing." He smirked as he put his arm around Laura Elise.

Holt and I exchanged looks. We knew it was highly unlikely that Avery was fooling around with Seth Collier, since she had made it clear to us that she couldn't stand him. What I couldn't stop myself from thinking was that she had sneaked out to meet Aaron Monroe. I couldn't explain it, but I had had a constant, nagging suspicion since the day I heard the rumor about them.

I was beginning to regret having shared my concern about Avery and Aaron with Mason. At the time, I had thought I was doing the right thing—especially since Holt wouldn't take it seriously. Now I was beginning to wonder what Mason might have done. Did the fact that Avery and Seth were both missing have anything to do with what I had told him?

"Holt," I whispered, "maybe you should go outside and look for Avery. I'm worried about her."

"She's fine, I'm sure," he answered. "You know how she hates this formal stuff. She's probably already gone home to change into blue jeans."

I insisted on checking the ladies' lounge, but Avery wasn't there. Holt and I waited around a few more minutes after Mason and Laura Elise left, but neither Avery nor Seth returned. I found Merilee in a group of girls and pulled her aside. "Have you seen Avery?" I asked. "I wanted to tell her good-bye."

"Oh, my goodness, is she not back yet?" she said. "She and Seth must have gone somewhere. Don't you worry, Mrs. Pritchett. I'm sure they'll be back. You want me to have her call you? How about I do that? Then you won't be worried." Merilee patted me on the arm and I felt like a worrying old biddy. Holt convinced me that we needed to leave so the young people could get on with their fun.

Just as we were leaving, I caught a glimpse of two boys coming in the rear door of the ballroom, the entrance usually reserved for caterers and other service people. The boys looked a little disheveled and they had already removed their ties. I looked to see if Seth was with them, but he wasn't.

When I commented to Holt on their appearance, he laughed. "Probably sneaking out back for a smoke and a beer. Come on, honey. Let's go home."

I worried all the way home. I could not get rid of the bad feeling that something was terribly wrong. I was removing my makeup and Holt was taking a shower when the phone rang. I rushed from the bathroom to the bedside table and snatched up the receiver. "Avery?"

"Hello, Marion," my mother's voice clattered through the line. "Avery is with me, and she's not hurt, just badly shaken up."

"What's happened?" I asked in a panic. Willadean's answer confirmed all of my worst fears. Avery had not been very forthcoming about the details with Willadean, but apparently she had had some kind of plan with the Monroe boy that went awry. And now he was in the hospital, badly injured from an alleged beating, and no one knew who the perpetrators were. Avery had shown up at the hospital to see him, but thankfully his grandmother would not allow it.

"We'll be right out to get her," I said, as Holt, wrapped in his bathrobe, came to stand beside me.

"She wants to stay here tonight," Willadean said.

"What? Stay there? But, why?"

My mother hedged. "I think it's probably for the best. She's had quite a shock. I'll take good care of her, and y'all can come get her in the morning."

I hung up the phone in a daze. I explained what little I knew to Holt. Once he was assured that Avery wasn't hurt, he asked what I knew about Aaron Monroe's condition.

"Nothing," I snapped. "Why should it concern me what that boy has gotten himself into?" I was already placing the blame squarely on Aaron Monroe's shoulders.

"He's just a boy, Marion. And whoever the creeps are that beat him up should be punished."

Holt's reply fell on deaf ears. I ignored him and started for the door. "I'm going downstairs. I'll be back up later," I said. For most of the remainder of that night I sat staring into the darkness of the back lawn, wondering where I had gone wrong as a mother and vacillating between fear and anger at Avery for her behavior. Mostly, I contemplated what damage control I would need to do in order to preserve her reputation in the community, as well as ours. No telling how many people had seen her traipsing into that hospital in a debutante ball gown. Rumors would be all over town by sunrise. I was certain that our friends and neighbors would rehearse our humiliation over their morning coffee.

I remained completely confused over what happened the night of the ball. Laura Elise called to say that Seth confessed he saw Avery in the garden behind the ballroom and tried to stop her from doing anything foolish. After that, she ran away, and he didn't know what became of her. I didn't know how Seth knew what Avery was planning, but I was so grateful to him for trying to intervene. After our conversation the next day, Avery hadn't spoken more than two words to me, and she'd spent most of her time either in her room or at Willadean's house.

"Avery, what have you done?" I asked that morning she returned from Will's. It was as if the words came unbidden. My anger with her behavior consumed me and acted as a shield against my fear.

"I haven't done *anything*, Mother," she said, daggers in her eyes, "except try to be with the boy I love. It's pretty crazy, you standing here asking me what I've done, when Aaron Monroe is lying in a hospital right now because of idiots who think just like you do. You should be asking what *they* have done!"

"But, Avery." I struggled to find words. "You just can't do this. . . . Your future . . . your reputation. It's one thing to have a friendship, but you don't . . . *date* black boys."

She raged at me then, calling me bigoted and racist, screaming that I had no idea how she felt or what mattered to her. I seemed to become the target for all her anger. After her fury, she distanced herself from me even more, scarcely speaking to either Holt or me. Other than attending her graduation ceremony, she saw no one. She refused phone calls and did not spend any time with her girlfriends.

Willadean and I discussed Avery only once. She actually defended her, saying she was young and in love, stressing how Avery called the hospital every day and tried to get information about Aaron but received it only secondhand from what Sally passed on to Will. I had no interest in what happened to that boy. As far as I was concerned, he was not part of our lives and never would be.

Avery moped around for weeks, listless and morose. She came to the table for meals in the evening but didn't participate in the conversation. Her hair was oily and unwashed and she was pale and ghostlike. When I passed by her door one morning and heard her retching, I wondered if she had caught some kind of virus. She had refused to allow Leona in her room, so it hadn't been cleaned in weeks.

I finally couldn't take it anymore. I knocked and pushed the door open, finding her stretched across her bed, staring at the ceiling. Clothes and blankets were scattered everywhere, empty drinking glasses on her nightstand, and the room smelled stale and musty. I decided that it was time to take charge. Leona followed me into the room.

"Avery, get up and take a shower," I said, raising the blinds and opening the window. "Leona is going to clean up this mess and change your sheets." Avery slowly shifted her blank gaze to me. I was surprised when she complied and rolled on her side to push herself off the bed. The minute her feet touched the floor, she was retching again and she barely made it to the bathroom before vomiting. Leona and I looked at each other. The possibility seemed to dawn on both of us in the same moment. My knees buckled under me and I collapsed onto the side of Avery's bed.

"Leona, how about you go get some sheets from the linen closet," I said. "I need a little time alone with Avery." Leona patiently followed my instructions. She looked toward the bathroom as she was leaving the room and shook her head.

When Avery emerged, she was paler than ever and so weak she could scarcely stand. She wiped her mouth and face with a washcloth and dropped to the floor, leaning against the frame of the open bathroom door.

"Avery, I'm taking you to the doctor today. This is no stomach flu. Something else is going on," I said. I couldn't bring myself to state the possibility that she might be pregnant. I could barely let myself think it.

When Dr. Boggess confirmed what I had suspected, Avery remained silent and withdrawn. We didn't speak during the ride home. When we walked in, Holt was just arriving home from work and I told him what we had learned.

"Avery, we need to talk about this," I said. As had become her pattern, she attempted to walk past me and ignore me. I stepped in front of the stairs and took her arm. "No. Not this time, you don't," I said. "You will go into the den and you will sit down and talk to your father and me." To my surprise, she turned toward the den, and Holt and I followed her. Holt looked at me, and now that I had her ear, I panicked, searching for the right words. She sat on the sofa, staring straight ahead, refusing to make eye contact with me.

"Avery, there's still an opportunity to put this horrible experience behind us," I said, trying to remain calm. "Dr. Boggess said that you're only a few weeks along. He knows a doctor in Jackson who can take care of this quietly and safely right in his office. No one from around here ever has to know." I stopped and coughed. Holt raised his eyebrows as if to question me, but I ignored him. "Then you can get registered at Ole Miss and get on with your life." I tried to get her to look at me. She seemed so broken, and I sensed that I had an opportunity to get through to her. "Wouldn't that be good . . . to get on with your life?" I asked.

What happened then remained fixed in my memory for years—the dead coldness of her eyes when she tilted her chin and looked into mine; the way she rose slowly, walked over to Holt, and dropped a kiss on his cheek. She walked out of the room, packed her suitcase, threw it into her car, and drove away. Before I could do anything to stop it, Willadean had hatched a plan to send her to Colorado to live with Aunt Lizzie. I sat by helplessly and watched my daughter throw her life away.

"I think that I might as well let the past go," I finally answer, feeling Holt's gaze.

What good will it do anybody for me to dwell on what happened? I'm still worried that Celi will feel rejected. I mean, what must it be like for her when she looks different from her entire family? And what about her black family? Avery hasn't even brought them up—other than seeing Sally out at Willadean's. As far as I know, the child doesn't know that Sally Monroe is her great-grandmother.

"Holt, did you know that Aaron Monroe has moved back to Greendale to practice with Dr. Boggess?" I ask.

"I think I did read something about that last week."

"Why didn't you tell me? I had to hear it from Laura Elise, who couldn't wait to get over here and show me the newspaper article." I'm getting annoyed all over again, remembering Laura Elise's attitude.

"I'm sorry, Marion," he says. "It must have slipped my mind in all of the excitement about Avery and Celi coming home. You seem especially irritable with Laura Elise lately. Have y'all had a falling out?"

How can I explain to Holt? I never told him what happened all those years ago. He assumes that Mason and Laura Elise and I are simply childhood friends; he knows that Laura Elise and I were college sorority sisters. He doesn't know how I've struggled all of these years. Back then I didn't believe he should know. It was too humiliating, and it might have made him hate Mason. And we needed Mason's influence to succeed. I thought I needed Laura Elise. Now I'm beginning to wonder.

"We'd better get those steaks and hot dogs on," I say, standing. "You get the steaks, and I'll check on Celi."

Holt prepares to light the grill, and I go inside and poke my head into the den. Celi is curled up in Holt's leather recliner, giggling at a Disney program. "You doing okay?" I ask.

"Yes, ma'am."

"We're outside on the terrace if you need us," I say. She nods and turns her attention back to the screen. I can understand why the women at the club say they have to pry their grandchildren away from the television.

When I step out onto the terrace, Holt has already started the grill and has placed a CD in the player. His favorite Duke Ellington collection wafts through the outdoor speakers and across the garden. I turn on the outdoor ceiling fan to circulate the cooling evening air and take a seat near the grill. The peppery-rich scent of the steaks makes my mouth water and I notice how hungry I am.

"It's not that Laura Elise and I have argued or anything," I say, trying to find words, knowing Holt's waiting patiently for my response. "Since this wedding was announced she has been consumed with it. Then, when she found out that Avery was coming home, there was something about her attitude. . . . It's difficult to explain. . . ." I look up at Holt, and he's watching me closely, the grill tongs poised in midair. I sigh, frustrated with how to express what I don't understand. "Let me put it this way," I say, lowering my voice and glancing back through the French doors. "I think Laura Elise and Mason are going to have a difficult time with Celi."

Holt frowns and pokes at the steak as if he's angry with it. "She's just a little girl, Marion," he says. "How can they take issue with an innocent little girl?"

"I've thought about this . . . a lot," I answer slowly. "I think it's what Celi represents. That our two families are joining because of Mark and Nicki's marriage, and Laura Elise and Mason can no longer make Avery's history exclusively our problem. . . ."

He interrupts, slamming the tongs down on the grill. "Avery is not a *problem*, Marion. She's our daughter, and Celi is our granddaughter. Mason and Laura Elise Collier be damned. This is our family we're talking about."

I'm surprised by the intensity of his response, and also surprised to find myself bolstered by it. The small kernel of hope that's been forming inside me starts to grow. Yes, *our* family, mine and Holt's. We have a chance—or I have a chance—to pull together around Celi and Avery. Maybe the Colliers *aren't* so important.

"I agree with you, honey," I say. "I don't know where to go from here. . . ." I wonder if that makes any sense to him. He's so confident, so clear about who he is. And I'm still struggling. "I'm going in to get everything ready for supper," I say. "Would you like another beer?"

"Yes. Come here for a minute," he says, holding his arm out toward me. I allow him to pull me into his embrace. He kisses the top of my head in the familiar, comforting gesture that never fails to reassure me. "We're going to figure this out," he says. I want to believe him, but I can't seem to stay positive.

In the kitchen I place three potatoes in the microwave to bake, then pull out lettuce, tomatoes, and carrots and begin preparing a salad. The ache in my chest is so heavy that I almost can't breathe.

Thoughts of my younger years and Mason Collier come unbidden at unexpected times. Have I never really let go of Mason? How can the memories of losing him still be so painful? Was this how it was for Avery? Does she blame me for ruining her chance at happiness with a man she loved like I blame Willadean?

May 1961

I fell asleep to the sound of the katydids. The nights had not melted into the sticky, oppressive heat that June was certain to bring, so the breeze coming in my upstairs window was balmy and smelled of Alligator Lake. I was drifting into a dream of a summer wedding. Now that Mason and I were finished with high school and headed to Ole Miss, what was there to stop us from getting engaged? Sleep came in a soft, billowy cloud, but somewhere in the recesses of my consciousness a harsh noise awakened me. I sat up in bed and shook myself slightly, trying to determine what was wrong. Was it a difference in the light? What was that smell?

As I looked around my bedroom I noticed a flickering light on the wall across from my bed. The smell of wood smoke, typically a winter scent, drifted into my window. Something was burning! Fear gripped my belly. We had to get out! I had to wake Mother. Daddy was gone to Jackson on business and we were alone at Oak Knoll. Had she left the stove on? Had someone set fire to the house?

I flung myself out of bed, leaving my slippers behind, and ran from my room. Mother and Daddy's bedroom was at the end of the hall. I screeched to a stop at the open door of their room and found it empty, the sheets and bedspread in disarray. Would Mother leave me in a burning house and not wake me up? In my bleary haze, I was confused. How could she? I rushed down the stairs toward the front hallway. I saw the flicker of flames in the darkness framed by the open front door, and the smell of smoke was even stronger in the entrance hall. As I rushed toward the door I heard Mother's voice coming from the front yard.

"Get the hell off my property!"

Fear raced across my heart like sheet lightning, and I stopped dead in my tracks. The house wasn't on fire. The fire was somewhere outside. I cautiously approached the front door, forcing myself to drag one foot in front of the other, horrified at the prospect of what was happening. I heard another sound, the loud click of metal against metal. At first I didn't know what it was, and then I recognized it: a shotgun being cocked. My mother was outside with a shotgun? I envisioned wild animals baring wicked fangs and lunging at Mother to tear her apart.

What if whatever it was that she was threatening to shoot came into the house? How would I protect myself? I had no clue how to use a gun. I thought of other possible weapons—a knife from the kitchen? A shovel from the shed out back? But what if the beasts were out there, too? I was paralyzed with panic.

That's when I heard the other voice. A man's voice. This was even worse than I'd feared. Mother could shoot a rabbit or squirrel at thirty feet. I'd heard Daddy say so. But would she shoot a man?

The cold, sick knowledge that Mother and I could be raped, robbed, or killed ripped through my consciousness. Crazily, my next thought was that I would never get to be that beautiful bride I had fallen asleep dreaming about a little while ago. I could hide. My mind went quickly through possible places—the attic? The root cellar? The kitchen pantry? I was seized with the shame of my cowardice, for not running out to stand beside my mother and protect our home with her.

"Willadean Reynolds, you are a disgrace to the white race," the man yelled. The voice was vaguely familiar, but in my terrified state I couldn't place it. "Let this serve as a warning," he continued. "Stop your nigger-loving Communist ways, or next time it will be worse!"

"Get off my property, or I'll show you worse!" Mother shouted, and the crack of the shotgun filled the smoky air. An engine roared to life and the twin headlights of a large vehicle filled the doorway. The crunch of tires on the gravel in our drive signaled what I desperately hoped was the man's departure.

Finally getting my feet to move, I crept to the sidelight window and looked out. I stood carefully to the side of the window, making sure to prevent my profile from showing. What I saw then became permanently etched in my mind, hammered into my memory. Mother stood on the front walk of the house, her bare feet planted in a defiant stance, her long loose white nightgown billowing around her when the gentle breeze suddenly turned to a strong wind that would surely bring a storm. Her thin hair, undone from its usual braid, whipped across her face. She held the shotgun leveled at the large farm truck that looked as if it could barely contain the group of at least six men dressed in white robes with pointed hoods who hung over the slatted wooden sides and careened forward from the force of the driver's hasty retreat. They were laughing.

I turned my gaze past Mother to the source of the flame. On the front lawn, in the center of the new rose garden Daddy had planted for Mother just a week ago on Mother's Day, stood a six-foot-tall burning cross. I began to shake; the trembling started in my hands and moved rapidly through my body. My knees collapsed under me, and I sank to the floor as the gut-wrenching fear turned to cold anger. Mother's attention to her causes, the way she worked to help the colored, even going so far as to travel to Jackson with Sally Monroe to support those reckless Freedom Riders, was never going to stop. And now her relentless striving for colored rights had brought these threatening men in white robes—the Ku Klux Klan—to our home. Was nothing sacred? I started to retch, the taste of bile bitter in my throat.

The sensation of fear mixed with anger was something that I would associate with my mother for many years to come.

Mason picked me up the next night for our date, but something was different about him. We had a silly argument because I wanted to see *Return to Peyton Place* and he wanted to see *The Alamo*—again. I won, but instead of giving in easily like he usually did, he was sullen. At the drive-in for milk shakes afterward, when we met Laura Elise and her date, he barely spoke to me.

"What's wrong with Mason?" Laura Elise asked when the boys left to get cigarettes.

"I don't know. He's been really quiet all night." Even then I had a sinking feeling in my chest, and Mother's words to Daddy echoed through my mind: *"Your only daughter is going on a date with the son of a man who is probably in the Klan."* I hadn't said anything to anyone about the night before. I was too ashamed. I was trying to go on pretending everything was fine, but I knew it wasn't. We got through the rest of the evening. Mason talked mostly with the other boys, and Laura Elise and I plotted about which sorority to pledge in the fall.

When we drove home, instead of taking the usual route to my house, Mason headed down to the bank of Alligator Lake. He parked the car and we sat in silence for a long time. He didn't put his arm around me. I still remember how the moonlight reflected off the lake that night. Under other circumstances it would have been so romantic. I tried to tell myself I had it all wrong. His awkwardness was because he was planning to propose. He was nervous.

When he turned to me and said, "Baby, we need to talk," I tucked my hair behind my ear the way he liked it and gave him my most winsome smile.

He stammered and stuttered before finally getting the words out that shattered my dreams and laid waste to my future. "I can't see you anymore. . . . It's not going to work out, you and me. . . . I'm sorry." He couldn't even look at me.

At first I thought I could change his mind. "But why? What have I done? I don't understand," I said.

"It's not you, baby. My daddy . . . well . . . you know how my parents are. . . . And your mother . . ." I watched him struggling to tell me what I already knew. "She's so public about niggers' rights and all, and Daddy can't afford to lose business, and you know how bad I want to go to medical school. Who knows? Maybe things will calm down and it'll work out when we get to Ole Miss. . . ." He looked back at me then, his eyes pleading with me to understand. I stopped him and made him take me home.

My life was over. Once again, Willadean had destroyed my happiness.

As I stand in my kitchen now, in the home that Holt and I have created together over the past thirty-six years, my perspective on what makes for happiness is completely different. I know now that what I share with Holt I could never have experienced with Mason Collier. Mason's primary interest in life is collecting possessions and flaunting his wealth. Why did it take me so long to grasp that? Why have I spent all these years believing that Holt and I had to measure up to some imagined standard set by the Colliers? Why did I risk losing my daughter because of the same fears that have driven me apart from my mother? I don't have any answers right now, and I'm exhausted from thinking about it.

I pull the potatoes out of the microwave, wrap them in foil, and place them in the warming oven. I set the condiments and steak sauce on a tray with the salad and head outside with another beer for Holt and a white wine for me, trying to leave the past in my kitchen.

"Where was it again that Mark and Nicki took Avery?" Holt asks, taking a sip of his beer and expertly turning the steak.

"Desiree's," I answer.

"I don't remember ever going there."

"That's because you and I have never been," I say. "It's in the black part of town, in a seedy area. Now, apparently, it's getting popular among young people who want to hear original blues and jazz."

"Maybe you and I should try it sometime," he says. "We could still swing, don't you think?" At this, he grasps my hand and twirls me around, laughing as I attempt the steps I've almost forgotten. How long has it been since we danced together?

Celi surfaces from her television show and giggles at our feeble attempts. She helps set the table while I bring out the rest of the dinner, and we enjoy listening to her stories about her school and activities in Denver, while the sun sets and the perfume of my rose garden scents the humid night air.

I want so much to fully experience the peacefulness of these moments. But it's too much for me at once—what to do about the club, how to deal with Mason and Laura Elise, memories of the past, how I'll salvage my relationship with Avery. I shrink into my worry shell as Holt gives Celi a taste of his steak and her eyes light up. I'm filled with yearning to be the grandmother I've always wanted to be. I thought I might have to wait for Mark's children. But here in front of me sits a beautiful granddaughter whose only request of me is that I love her. She's certainly placing no conditions on her regard for me. Why must I be saddled with all of the fears that my upbringing has placed on me? Who am I protecting by keeping Celi safe in my rose garden, hidden from my day-to-day world like a princess in a tower?

And yet, I'm not sure I have the courage to become this new person I want to be.

Chapter 16

Avery

Merilee Waverly is practically turning over chairs in her haste to get to our table. I've plastered a smile on my face because I'm trapped. There is no getting out of this situation. I'm as captive as a caged bird right now.

"Is that you, Avery Pritchett?" she asks. Merilee looks almost exactly like she did the last time I saw her, which would have been the night of our graduation. She was pulling on my arm then, saying "Come on, Avery, let's go to the party down at the lake. I can't go without you." And I was begging off, completely disinterested in anybody or anything to do with my senior class. All I wanted to do then was hide. I felt totally defeated, I was buried in guilt over what had happened to Aaron, and although I didn't realize then what it was, I was starting to get morning sickness.

"It's me," I say, standing to greet her as she throws her arms around me, almost knocking me backward into the table.

"I can't believe it. I thought I'd never see you again," she says, turning briefly to nod hello to Mark and Nicki before pulling out a chair and turning it to face me knee to knee as we both sit down. "Where have you been? What have you been doing?" she asks, pushing her ever-present glasses up on her nose. She's updated the frames, but she still has the same straight dark hair, styled in the same way, with bangs. She's definitely filled out and gotten a little less frumpy since high school. The jeans she's wearing are tastefully tight, and her top reveals a little bit of cleavage—something I never thought I'd see.

I try to encapsulate a decade in a few words, wondering what she's heard about me and also feeling guilty for so completely disconnecting from the one girl I considered a friend—not enough of a friend to reveal my pregnancy to her, but still, she did try to help me out that night.

"I moved to Colorado after graduation. We have a relative there, and I wanted a change of scene," I say.

Merilee nods. "I can understand that."

What does she know? Should I tell her about Celi? Am I wrong to leave out her part of my history?

"Are you still out there? What are you doing?"

"I'm a nurse, and yes, I still live there. I'm home for Mark and Nicki's wedding," I say, turning to them, hoping that Merilee will take the hint and change the subject to them.

"A nurse? That's terrific, Avery," she says. Looking at Mark and Nicki, she says, "You know, I think I saw y'all's announcement in the paper."

The waitress comes by to check on our drinks and I feel compelled to ask Merilee to join us. I'm relieved when she says, "I can only stay another minute. My fiancé is waiting for me." She turns and waves at an Asian man seated at a table near the back of the bar. He waves back, bows his head slightly, and we all smile.

"The Asian guy?" asks Mark. The incredulity is obvious in his voice. I glare at Mark, who instantly apologizes. "I'm sorry, Merilee," he says, while Nicki glowers at him. "I was just surprised."

"It's okay," she says. "We get that a lot." She turns to me and taps my knee lightly. "I was that girl who thought she'd never marry, you know, Avery?" I nod, remembering how she cried on my shoulder in high school because she was never asked on a date. "I thought I would be old maid Merilee," she says, laughing and putting quotation marks around her words with her fingers. "But after college I got this great job with an import-export company doing their software training. I met Kenji on one of my business trips to Japan. He was traveling there with another American company. His parents live in New Jersey—they emigrated from Japan. He's terrific, and he loves the blues. So I promised him I'd bring him here the next time we were in town." She barely takes a breath before continuing. "Remember this place when we were in high school, Avery? It was dangerous to even come down to this part of town then. And look at us now, two white girls partying at Desiree's." She motions around the room.

"Yeah, here we are," I say, laughing weakly. What a strange world I had returned to. I'm about to ask Merilee more about her work when she starts again.

"Are you married?" She looks down at my left hand.

"Nope," I say. "Not married." She nods, and then her eyes light up as if she's thought of something really important.

"Oh! So, I guess you must know that Aaron Monroe is back in town. Did you guys stay in touch after that fiasco?" She says this so casually, with no idea that she has just sent my world careening into anxiety and fear. I pick up my glass of beer while shaking my head and bring it to my lips. Mark and Nicki had been talking quietly to each other, trying to stay out of our conversation, but Mark must have overheard Merilee's last question and he jumps to my rescue.

"No kidding? What's Aaron doing back here?" he asks, as if he and Aaron are old friends. He hardly knew him.

"He's going into practice with Dr. Boggess. According to the paper, he finished Tulane medical school not long ago," she says, studying her engagement ring and glancing back over to wink at Kenji.

I finally find my voice. "Really? How about that."

"Yeah, the article said he has a wife and two sons," Merilee continues. "You know what's crazy?" she asks. I shake my head, wondering what's coming next. "There was a wild rumor going around here for a while that you left in a hurry because you were pregnant with Aaron Monroe's baby." She laughs then, so hard that I can smell the beer on her breath. I smile like an idiot and search my addled brain for an answer. The band starts to tune up with loud groans and squeaks of the instruments, and Merilee shouts to be heard over the din. "I've got to get back to Kenji, but promise me you'll call so that we can get together while you're in town, okay?"

I nod dumbly, grateful for the interruption. Merilee reaches over and gives me a squeeze and a peck on the cheek and makes her way back to her table. I can tell that Mark has a question on his lips. I hold up my hand and shake my head. "Not now." The music starts and as much as I try to lose myself in the soulful bluesy rhythms, I'm completely preoccupied with the thought that Aaron Monroe is here in Greendale again, married with two sons.

Merilee was the only person I told about my and Aaron's plan that night. She wouldn't have talked to Seth Collier. No, I still believe it was my mother who betrayed me. But how did she know? What did she suspect?

Even though Aaron always promised that he was coming back to Greendale to practice medicine, I never believed that he would. The humiliation I experienced on the night of the debutante ball was enough to make me never want to see any of the people I grew up with again, and I assumed he would feel the same way. I still don't know exactly who was responsible for what happened, but I've always suspected that Mother heard a rumor and had Mason Collier send Seth after me. Right or wrong, Mother has always been the target of my anger.

May 1991

It took a lot of whining and pleading, but I finally convinced Aaron to go along with my plan. He was so cautious. I think if it had been up to him we would have gone on seeing each other in secret until we both went away to college and . . . and then what? He was planning on premed at Tulane and Mother said I would go to Ole Miss or she and Daddy wouldn't pay. Would we ever see each other again? My parents thought that by going the debutante route I would hook up with one of the local boys in the Bachelor's Club and carry on the family tradition by staying right here, getting married, having babies, and never leaving Mississippi except for an annual ski trip to Colorado or a cruise to Mexico.

I wandered out of my bathroom and over to my bedroom window, toweling my hair and thinking about Aaron. It was going to be a beautiful evening for the debutante ball. It was still early enough in May for the night to be balmy. The magnolia in our front yard was covered with creamy white blooms that I could almost reach from my window. I was aching to see Aaron, but I reminded myself that I didn't have to wait much longer. I just had to make it through the getting-ready part and the ceremony. I had practiced that stupid St. James bow until I was blue in the face and I was still not sure I had it right. But once the individual presentations and dinner were over, the dance would start and that's when I would sneak Aaron in.

It occurred to me that Aaron and I might have to leave this state entirely to be together, which would be fine with me. I didn't have any attachment to anybody or anything in Greendale, Mississippi. I could easily leave Mother. It would be harder to leave Daddy, but he might come to visit us. Aaron, on the other hand, was very close to his family. He said he could never leave his grandmother. She had raised him since his mother died, and he had promised her that he'd come back to be a doctor here.

I decided to put all of those worries out of my mind. Tonight was my and Aaron's night and I was not going to let anyone or anything spoil it. I felt a little quiver of excitement in my stomach. We would show them all. I wished he could have been my escort for the coming out, but that would have required going through the committee. There wasn't a snowball's chance in hell of me having a black boy as an escort, so I had settled for meeting Aaron after dinner for the dance. Mother and Daddy had somehow arranged for Seth Collier to be my escort, which was interesting considering that Seth and I couldn't stand each other.

The ball was being held at the old Rosewood Plantation.

Mother had made me work there as a tour guide during the summer after my freshman year of high school. She said I needed exposure to the "finer arts of Southern culture." I had to stuff myself into a hoopskirt for eight hours a day and talk to Yankee tourists and their snot-nosed kids about the grand old plantation days of Rosewood. I had to admit, it was a beautiful house—with tall white columns and big old live oak trees, set on a huge tract of land on the north side of Alligator Lake. There was a garden in the back with tons of flowers and a gazebo. I imagined Aaron kissing me in that gazebo. He would be in his black tuxedo, and I would be in . . . I was having a hard time picturing myself in my imaginary scene. I looked over at the white dress hanging on the hook on the closet door and sighed.

I almost started to doubt the plan when I remembered my conversation with Aaron the previous night. I was telling him about Rosewood's layout to be sure that we had everything straight.

"There's a service entrance in the back where the slaves used to bring in food from the detached kitchen," I said. "That's where I'll sneak you in."

"Great," Aaron said. "You want to make some big social statement, and you're sneaking me in through the slave entrance?"

At first, I got really defensive. "It's the best place to come in without being seen. . . ." Then I realized he was laughing, trying to make a joke. I tried to laugh, too, but there was a lump of fear in my throat and I got quiet. The reality of what we were planning must have hit me.

"What's wrong?" Aaron asked, putting his arm around me. "You know I was kidding around. It's just some old slave entrance. Most of the big houses around here still have those. Believe me, I'm used to it. You wouldn't believe how many of the white folks in this town make me use the back door when I'm making pizza deliveries."

My fear turned to anger when he said that, and I dug in with more determination. "Okay, Aaron, here's what I'm thinking. An old service road runs along the back of the property down near the woods, and you can hide your truck in the trees back there. Then walk up the road—it's not far—and across the back lawn. There's an old garden shed right before you get to the kitchen garden. I'll meet you there."

He nodded, looking thoughtful. "What's your plan once we're inside?"

This was the part that I was most uncertain of, but he was watching me closely so I tried to sound confident. "We'll slip into the ballroom," I said. "I figure once you're already in the building with me, what's anyone going to do? They're all too well-mannered to throw you off the dance floor."

His eyes changed then, and for the first time I saw something that looked like fear. I tried to be strong for both of us, enjoying the thought of how we'd shock everyone. "And at your debutante ball next weekend we'll do the same thing! I really think things will change around here after this," I said, snuggling into his embrace. "We'll show them that this is no big deal—at least in other places besides here. Maybe everything won't be so separate anymore. Maybe other couples like us will be able to date in the open."

If there were any other couples like us. I paused with my comb in the air over my head. Had I ever seen a black-and-white couple in Greendale? Then I remembered Larry Owen and Ruby Westcott, who owned Owen's Market. Miss Ruby was white and Larry was black. I thought about the stories I'd heard off and on all my life: how Ruby was always getting beaten up by her daddy and how Larry took her in and protected her. People around here seemed to overlook Larry and Ruby, probably because they thought of her as white trash and Larry was so big and strong, nobody messed with him. Anyway, they were old—probably in their forties.

I started to feel like I was going to throw up. I kept going back and forth between excitement and fretfulness. I wished I had someone to talk to, but the only person I had told about my plan was Merilee Waverly. I had to get her help to make sure my parents were distracted when I sneaked out the back door of the ballroom. When I told her, she had looked worried, but then, she always looks worried.

"But, Avery," she said, "what if someone gets hurt?"

"Hurt? Why would anyone get hurt?" I responded, irritated with her for always thinking the worst. "Someone might ask Aaron to leave because he has no invitation, but what are the chances of that?"

"I don't know. It sounds risky to me." She started twisting her hair around her finger.

"Do you remember last year, when you and I were assistants at the deb ball, and Lonnie Thurgood brought that girl to the dance who was actually dressed in pink?" I asked.

Merilee giggled. "Yes, I still remember the look on his mother's face when they came in together. I thought she was going to faint."

"Well, see there. That turned out okay, didn't it? I've even heard they're engaged."

"But, Avery . . . she's white."

"Her family is dirt poor! They live in a trailer behind the Piggly Wiggly, Merilee! Aaron is a star athlete and the valedictorian of his class. That's got to count for something."

"But he's still black."

It was always that way. It was either "She's black, but . . ." or "Even though he's black." Why couldn't people be good at something or smart without the "but he's black" clause?

I took my dress off the hook. I still thought it looked like an upside-down snow cone before the syrup, but it was the best Miss Esther could do considering what she had to work with—me. I stuffed the dress into its bag and threw my tote over my shoulder. It was filled with the push-up bra Mother had made me buy, the silly shoes, panty hose, and of course the white gloves. We were all getting ready at Alicia Randall's house. Her mother had hired a hairdresser to do all of our hair. I was dreading it. The best thing was that Lorna Deason had promised to sneak in a bottle of vodka to spike the tea punch. And the Randalls' cook, Jezebel, made the best cheese straws and ham biscuits in the world.

I heard a honk outside and looked out the window. Merilee was parked in our driveway looking impatient in her new red Volvo, a graduation present from her daddy. Poor Merilee. She was smart and had a great car and tons of money, but no boyfriend. Her daddy had had to convince another one of the fathers to force his son to be her escort.

At least she was not in love with a boy who had absolutely no chance of ever being accepted by her parents.

I passed Mother as I was running down the stairs. She frowned, as usual, when she saw me.

"Why don't you have your hair rolled yet, Avery? You know how long it takes it to curl."

"Heat rollers, Mother," I said as I pushed past her, trying to manage the huge dress. She backed up to let me by and called after me.

"Be sure you have that woman tease your hair. Otherwise it will look flat. And be sure . . ."

I ignored whatever else she was saying and called, "Yes, ma'am," over my shoulder before slamming the front door behind me.

Chapter 17

Avery

It's close to two a.m. when I get back to Oak Knoll. I spent the rest of the evening trying to ignore my worry over running into Aaron, and ultimately drinking a little too much. I wonder how Mother and Daddy managed with Celi's sleepover. When I called earlier in the evening, Mother said they were settling her into bed, getting ready to read together. I was taken aback by Mother's attentiveness. I still don't know how Celi is going to fit into my mother's all-white life here. Maybe that's what she meant about us being allies. Could it be that my mother is more accepting than I expected?

After a shower, I stretch out on the smooth worn cotton sheets of the four-poster bed, feeling the gentle breeze of the ceiling fan cool my body. So, Aaron is in town and he's married with two sons. Since I refused to allow Will to talk to me about him over the years, I was able to stay in denial about him moving on with his life. Now here we both are again in Greendale, and I can no longer pretend our lives are completely separate. And that's because of a little girl who is probably sleeping peacefully right now in her grandmother's giant guest-room feather tester bed, complete with new pink sheets and bedspread, dreaming of dresses and weddings.

Coming back here, I knew I might have to face Aaron. And I know it's only right to tell Celi about him. But what if he's not willing to see her or make her part of his life? What if he's angry? What if his wife rejects Celi? How can I possibly make the leap across the chasm of distance I've created?

I wonder why Will hasn't mentioned Aaron—probably because I so vehemently resisted knowing anything about him. I'm not surprised that Sally wouldn't mention him. Her words from that awful night still ring in my mind: *"Don't you think you've done enough?"*

May 1991

I was so nervous I could feel the sweat in my armpits and dripping down between my breasts, which were crammed into that damn push-up bra Mother insisted I wear. I stooped down, no easy task in my dress, to put a folded-up program in the service entrance door, so it wouldn't lock behind me. No one really used that door anymore; the caterers were around the other side of the house. I picked up my skirt and headed across the brick pathway through the kitchen garden toward the potting shed where Aaron was supposed to meet me, hoping no one saw me leave. Merilee had done exactly as I had asked her to and distracted Mother and Daddy. When I left, she was carrying on some inane conversation with Mother about compact versus loose face powder. She had been a good friend to me.

Conscious of every little sound, I stopped to listen, but all I could hear was the muffled squeaks of the band cranking up in the ballroom behind me and the usual night sounds of frogs and crickets. The moon was beautiful, and I thought for a second that maybe Aaron and I should run away right then. We could elope! I was already wearing a white dress. But he would never go for that. Besides, we had a plan.

It took three tries to open the little gate at the back of the garden since my hands didn't seem to operate properly. Finally, I got it open. All I had to do then was take the short path to the shed. The brick pavers ended, and I was walking in gravel—not so easy in those shoes. It was silly, but I was excited for Aaron to see me all dressed up. Of course, I was also terrified he would think I looked stupid. Thinking about dancing with him at an all-white debutante ball was not nearly as scary as the thought that he might laugh at me.

It was a lot darker here. The old shed was wrapped in shadows, and I could smell fresh-turned dirt and the rusty scent of the old tools propped against the walls. I thought I detected a whiff of cigarette smoke, but that couldn't be right. Aaron didn't smoke. I looked back to make sure no one was following me. All clear. I told myself to breathe; maybe I'd had too much of Alicia's spiked tea punch—or maybe not enough.

As I rounded the corner of the shed, I was surprised to find that Aaron wasn't there yet. I waited nervously, trying to keep my white dress off the ground. I decided to venture a little way onto the lawn toward the trees and look to see if I could see his truck coming up the service road. Nothing. I started to get angry. He agreed to this. How could he abandon me? Chickening out at the last minute and never even letting me know. I paced back and forth for another five minutes. He wasn't coming, I told myself, but then I argued that he was simply a little late. I was getting worried that I'd be missed soon and someone would come looking for me.

Finally, I couldn't wait any longer. My chest felt as if a big gaping sinkhole had opened up in my heart. All my plans were ruined. How could I go back in there and face all those people now? This was our chance; this was a way for me to be with the boy I loved. As I passed the front of the shed, a hand reached out and grabbed my arm. My scream was short as I was jerked around to find myself looking into the blue eyes of Seth Collier. I lost my balance and fell against his wide chest, close enough to smell the whiskey and cigarettes on his breath.

"Well, hello there, Avery," he said in his usual sluggish drawl.

My voice was caught in my throat and I tried to pull my arm away from him, but his grip was too strong. He tugged me into the darkness of the shed's overhang and pinned me against the wall with his body.

"What are you doing back here in the garden all alone, Avery Pritchett?" he slurred. He stepped back and held my shoulders as I tried to squirm away.

"Nothing," I said, my voice a squeak. "I needed some air." I tried to move my shoulders out from under his hands. "Let me go, Seth," I insisted, anger boiling up inside me.

He gripped me tighter, sliding his hands down my bare arms until I felt the splintered wood siding of the shed pricking my skin. "Coming out here to meet your nigger boyfriend, maybe?"

Fear clenched my stomach. How did he know about Aaron? I instantly thought of my parents and their closeness with the Colliers. Did Mother find out somehow? Maybe Seth didn't know anything. Maybe he was bluffing to see what I would say. I decided to play ignorant.

"What are you talking about?" I asked. "If you don't let me go, I'm going to scream like hell. I don't think your mama will be too happy with you, taking advantage of a deb in the garden shed."

Seth pressed his big body into me, pinning me against the wall again. "And I don't think your mama and daddy would be too happy to know you're sneaking out back planning to stir up all kinds of trouble for those nice folks who've planned your coming out." He looked at me with disgust. "Did your boyfriend stand you up, Avery?"

"What boyfriend?" I asked, starting to panic and trying to keep my breathing even. "I told you, I was hot in there and needed some air. Why don't we both go back and pretend we didn't see each other?" Seth loosened his grip slightly and ran his finger down my chest and between my breasts. I shuddered at his touch.

"How about you giving me a kiss first, Avery? After all, I saved you from the embarrassment of ruining your debutante ball by bringing a nigger to the dance, didn't I?"

Now I was certain he knew something. And suddenly a horrible thought occurred to me. What had happened to Aaron? I was afraid to ask—it would have been the same as admitting our plan—but wasn't I planning to show them all tonight anyway? Mostly, I was afraid for Aaron.

"Where's Aaron? Did you see him? Have you done something to him?"

"I don't have time to run around after your black boyfriend, Avery," he said with an arrogant grin. "Not when I have to keep up with you."

I fought him then, trying to pull away, trying not to scream. I had to get away from him and find out what had happened to Aaron. He leaned down close to my face and I could feel his breath on me.

"Don't you know you don't mix with niggers, Avery? It's not right. We've got to keep the white race clean." He brought his lips over mine, forcing his tongue into my mouth. All I could taste was sour whiskey and cigarettes, and a wave of nausea brought tea punch to the back of my throat. I sunk my teeth into his lip and bit down hard. He shouted with pain and pulled away from me to grab his bleeding lip. Bright red drops of blood fell onto his white tuxedo shirt. I was frozen by what I'd done, ignorant of what to do next.

"You nigger-loving bitch," he growled, and slapped me hard across the face.

Instantly my eyes filled up with tears and I was running, running away from the shed and across the wide lawn behind it. I threw myself wildly into the woods near the lake; the underbrush tore at my dress as I tripped over tree roots and pushed blindly past low branches. I reached the service road and looked back and forth, trying to decide which way to go, when a new sight halted my steps. Aaron's truck was parked a little ways down the road, pulled off onto the narrow shoulder. Panicked, I ran over to the truck and looked in the windows, expecting to see him there, fearing the worst. But he wasn't there. His tuxedo jacket lay neatly across the seat, and the truck was empty. I ran around behind the truck and stopped abruptly before stepping into a dark pool of what looked like blood in the red gravel of the road below the bumper.

I never made it back to the ball that night. In a daze, I walked the two miles through the woods to Owen's Market, ignoring the scratches on my arms, and my dress tearing as I yanked it loose from the clinging undergrowth. I emerged into the streetlight over the store and stopped, checking for cars. Thank God the store was deserted. I crashed through the door and called for Ruby, praying she would be there. It was Larry instead. He didn't voice any questions when I asked for a ride to the hospital.

"I'll take you," he said. I stuffed myself into his truck and he sped along the back roads to Greendale Regional Hospital. I didn't know what he knew, if anything. We rode in silence all the way there. I was afraid to speak. Larry dropped me off at the emergency room entrance. "You all right?" he asked. I thanked him and assured him that someone would come for me, not knowing or caring at the time who that would be.

I hurried to the desk and asked the dour-looking black nurse if an Aaron Monroe had been admitted. She jerked her thumb behind her toward a curtained area. "Bed three," she said.

Sally Monroe stood vigil outside of Aaron's space. When she saw me approaching, she held up her hand and shook her head.

"Don't you think you've done enough?" she said. "Now, get on out of here and let me take care of this mess you created."

"But can't I see him just for a minute? I need to know what happened . . . how he is," I pleaded with her.

"He's hurt; that's how he is. He's been beaten badly by somebody, and I imagine you have a pretty good idea who. He'll be lucky if he doesn't lose an eye," she said, looking at me as if I were the devil himself.

I was crying by then, my bedraggled updo and my torn and dirty white dress making me a curiosity among the doctors and nurses who kept stepping over and around my skirts. That was when Will showed up. She came walking down the corridor in her blue jeans and high-tops, a natty old sweater clutched around her shoulders. Miss Sally had probably called her first. Will convinced me to sit with her in the waiting room and give Sally some time to change her mind, but to no avail. Sally would not let me see Aaron. Much later Will convinced me to go back with her to Oak Knoll. There was nothing else I could do.

It's always haunted me that I should have done more to help Aaron. Lying here in the dark in Will's sunporch, I feel hot tears on my face for what happened ten years ago. I've been trying to sort these feelings out for a long time. Shame is an elusive ghost that follows me around. I know that my mother was ashamed of me for even considering dating a black boy, much less getting pregnant. And Seth Collier's treatment of me that night certainly was an attempt to shame me for being a traitor to the white race.

But the shame I feel is from having run away, for refusing to stand my ground and persist until Sally let me see Aaron. Most of all, I'm ashamed of the pain that my foolish naïveté brought upon him. My greatest fear is that Celi will sense this shame in me and take it on as her own. I want her to experience joy in who she is, in both her families. But that seems impossible now.

From my distance in Denver I was beginning to tell myself that my past was a series of events brought on by my rebellious teenage ideas and that I had put it behind me. I told myself that the details of what happened didn't matter. Now that I'm here in my grandmother's house, in the town where I grew up, surrounded by people and places that trigger all of my memories, the unanswered questions are swirling in my mind like a tornado.

How did Seth Collier know about our plan that night? Who was responsible for beating Aaron up? Exactly what did they do to him? And how is he able to come back here to face meeting those same people on the street or in the grocery store?

That question brings up even more questions. How am I going to tell Celi about her father? Will Sally tell Aaron that she's seen us? Will he want to meet Celi? And what about Celi's sickle-cell disease? There's still the unanswered mystery of how I contributed the trait.

Exhaustion finally overtakes me and I fall into a restless sleep, unable to come up with an answer to a single question in my troubled mind.

Chapter 18

Willadean

Avery comes into the kitchen looking like something the cat left on the doorstep. Hair all every which way and big bags under her eyes. She looks like she either had too much to drink last night or was up crying for hours, and maybe both.

"What time is it?" she asks, squinting at the clock over the refrigerator.

"It's ten after ten," I say. "You don't look so good, young lady. Was Desiree's too much for you?" I chuckle, but she doesn't laugh.

A pained expression crosses her face. "Has Mother called? I need to check on Celi." She stumbles toward the kitchen phone, and I hand her a cup of coffee as she punches in the number. I act like I'm focused on snapping some string beans I picked this morning, while I listen to her short conversation with Marion. She hangs up and collapses into a chair at the table.

"Okay, here's one for you," she says, and the look on her face says she can't believe what she's heard. "Mother wants me to meet her and Celi at the club for lunch. She says to bring our suits so we can go for a swim afterward." She shakes her head.

I take this as the best news I've heard in a long time. If my Marion is going to take her black grandchild and her daughter to that country club of theirs, then something important is happening here. Wait till I tell Sally. But Avery doesn't look as happy as I would expect her to be.

"Honey, this is good news," I say. "You do see what this means for your mama, don't you?" Avery looks lost in thought, like she hasn't even heard me. "Avery?"

She jerks her focus back to me. "Yes . . . I mean, I guess so. . . . I'm kind of shocked, you know? I wasn't expecting her to be this way. To be trying so hard." She looks down into her coffee. "All I really want to do right now is hide out here. I don't want to face Greendale again."

She tells me then about seeing Merilee Waverly last night, the news about Aaron, and the rumor about her pregnancy. "Not much can be kept secret in a town this small, honey," I say.

"You must have known about Aaron coming back here," she says, looking at me. "I'm assuming Miss Sally told you." She gets up to pour more coffee. "How come you didn't mention it?" Her voice sounds accusing, edgy.

"I was waiting for the right time. Sally wanted to tell you right away. As a matter of fact, she wanted to tell Aaron that you were coming home, but I stopped her. I figured you needed to sort this out in your own way, in your own time."

"I appreciate that, Will," she says, softening her tone. "I really do." She sighs heavily. "I'm pretty confused right now about the best way to handle the situation. Do I call him up and say 'Hey, it's Avery. I know I've refused to let you see your daughter for, oh, nine and a half years, but here we are!' I mean, really, how do I do it? What about his wife?"

"I don't know, honey," I say. "I reckon you have to make up your own mind about how to proceed. There's no easy way." I wish I could ease her hurt and fear, but I can't.

"I want to stay right here until time for the wedding, get that over with, and then go back home to Denver as quickly as I can," she repeats. She looks around the kitchen. "I know I have to face this, and I'm acting like a whiny brat right now." She rubs her hands over her face and pulls down on her mouth as she looks up at me. "Sorry."

I smile. At least she's able to hear how she sounds. "Try not to fret so much, hon. You'll figure it out."

"Will, do you know that Oak Knoll is the only place I've ever really felt safe? When I was coming out here those last couple of summers before I left, I never wanted to go home."

"How about that," I say. This is such a contrast to Marion, who couldn't seem to get away fast enough. But then, Marion's experience was at a very different time in my life.

"This old place has always been a haven for me, too," I say.

"You said that Sally's mother worked here, right?" Avery asks.

"Yes, Miss Clarice was the Reynoldses' cook."

"So how did you meet Grandpa Jacob? Did you two go to school together?"

"Oh, no. I went to Greendale High School. Your Grandpa Jacob and his sister Jerrilyn were sent off to boarding school. Your grandpa said that he and his twin sister were change-of-life babies for your great-grandmother, Beatrice. She must have been around forty-two years old when those twins were born."

"I didn't know Granddaddy had a twin," Avery interrupts. "How come I never heard of her?"

"She died young," I say, and quickly change the subject. "I remember the first time I ever saw Oak Knoll. I certainly had no idea that night what this house would come to mean to me. That was the first time I met your great-grandmother."

I think of how enamored I was of the Reynolds family. I was so curious about this big old house, the twins, even that sick old man. Maybe if I hadn't been so intrigued by the secondhand stories I had gotten from Sally and Henry, maybe if I had never been so envious of Jerrilyn's independence, or so excited about being on an adventure with Henry—everything might have turned out differently—especially for Henry.

July 1941

"Willadean," Daddy called as he burst through to the front of the store. He'd been working late in his compounding room.

"Right here, Daddy," I answered. I was restocking the lady's lipstick and perfume shelf behind the counter and talking to

Henry while he mopped the floor. We were discussing the new Ernest Hemingway novel he and Sally and I were passing around.

"Beatrice Reynolds called," Daddy said, pushing his glasses up on his head. "Says Mr. Reynolds is hurting something fierce. I need you and Henry to deliver this medicine to him tonight," he said, holding out a package wrapped in brown paper. "I can't leave the store right now because I'm expecting a late delivery." Henry and I looked at each other. We both knew what delivery Daddy was talking about. Gus Pinkus, who made the moonshine for Daddy's tonic in a still down in the woods behind Alligator Lake, delivered a case of it once a month.

"Willadean, I want you to go along with Henry and bring the medicine to the door so Miss Beatrice won't be scared," Daddy said.

Henry stepped up then, still holding the mop. "Mr. Franklin, sir, Miss Beatrice, she knows me. My mama's been working for her for near about ten years now, sir. No need to make Miss Willie here go out in the night."

"I understand that, Henry," Daddy said. "But I know Beatrice Reynolds, and I think it's best if Willie is the one to bring the medicine to the door and collect the money, it being this late and all."

Henry nodded like he immediately understood what Daddy was getting at without him having to say it. "Yes, sir."

Henry put the mop away and I closed the perfume case. I took the package from Daddy, and Henry and I climbed into Daddy's old Ford pickup. This was Henry's first actual experience driving Daddy's truck, and he laughed at himself as we jerked along the already bumpy and deeply rutted road out to the Reynolds house.

"Driving this old truck is a little bit different from a tractor, but I'll get the hang of it," he said, and it wasn't long before he was shifting smoothly. I was considering this an adventure because I'd been on this road lots of times before with Daddy when he drove us to his favorite fishing spot on Alligator Lake, but I'd never been as far as the Reynolds house.

"You know much about the Reynoldses?" I asked, thinking Henry's mama had probably told some stories.

"It's just the two of them out there now," Henry said. "They got twins, a boy and a girl, Mr. Jacob and Miss Jerrilyn, but you don't ever see them."

"Why is that?" I asked.

"They both got shipped off to boarding school when they were little. They only come home a few days out of the year."

"I saw Jerrilyn once. She came into the store with Mr. Reynolds." I remembered noticing how beautiful she was and how much nicer to me than most of the local girls. Jerrilyn treated me with friendliness and respect. She didn't look down her nose at me. And even though everyone's head, both men's and women's, turned when she came in the store, she never put on airs.

"Mrs. Reynolds, she takes care of Mr. Reynolds since he's been sick," Henry continued. "Mama says he won't let nobody else near him. She said that place smells awful bad some mornings when she gets to work. She's glad she's not Trixie—that's Trixie Smith. She comes in to clean twice a week. Mama says Trixie'll come in the kitchen complaining something fierce about cleaning up after that old man." I imagined then how awful it would be, to have to take care of a sick husband. I didn't think I was cut out for it.

It was a bright, clear night. I rolled the window down on my side and let the breeze cool my face. Henry and I continued our conversation about *For Whom the Bell Tolls.* Henry liked to read about war and adventure in faraway places. He said if there was ever another war, he'd like to be a soldier. It occurred to me to wonder why Mrs. Reynolds would be afraid of Henry Johnson like Daddy had implied. I thought Henry was as courteous and smart as my own daddy, and that was saying a lot.

When Henry turned off the main road, it got a lot darker, and I leaned out to look at the trees arching toward the truck from either side, completely obstructing the sky. I could have reached out and touched the Spanish moss dripping down so close to us as we passed by. "Henry, are you sure we're going the right way?"

"Yep, this is the road to Oak Knoll."

"Can you imagine living in a house that has a fancy name?" I asked.

"No, I surely can't," Henry said. "My people been working for the Reynoldses since this house was built. That must be about a hundred years now."

I thought about Henry's family. He'd already told me his grandparents had been born slaves on the Oak Knoll plantation. I'd never met his mama, Clarice. "A lot's changed, huh?" I asked. "Things are better now?"

"Not that much, Miss Willie," he said. "Daddy used to say sharecropping wasn't much better than being a slave. The white man still owned everything. Made it real hard for a black man to get ahead. Only thing is, if my daddy had been a sharecropper instead of Mr. Reynolds's man, he wouldn'ta been on a tractor. Ain't no sharecropper owns a tractor. Mr. Olan Reynolds, he was like all the rest of them. Miserly old son-of-a-bitch. Most of his croppers got tired of getting further behind every year and caught the Illinois Central up north to Chicago. That's when Reynolds fell on some hard times. Word is Mr. Jacob fixing to have his hands full when he comes back from school next year. Can't say as I feel too sorry for Mr. Reynolds now. That's why I'm glad to be working for your daddy. Sharecropping ain't for me."

"I remember Mr. Reynolds coming into Daddy's store a couple of times before he got sick," I said. "He was an ornery old man, even then. He didn't have very good manners with Miss Inez, our clerk, either, but she acted like that didn't bother her. Daddy would have taken a switch to me if I acted so rude to somebody."

"Yeah. Look like money take the place of manners most times," Henry said. "Especially for white folks." I didn't take offense because I knew Henry was right.

We cleared the trees, and the big white house with its tall, eight-sided cupola loomed ghostlike over us. The house was completely dark except for the dim glow of a lamp in the front window. Daddy said that Mrs. Reynolds was expecting us, but she sure didn't bother to leave the porch light on.

"I reckon I'd best stay in the truck," Henry said, turning off the engine and killing the lights.

I peered through the windshield at the dark front steps. It looked like the porch was screened in. Right then that porch looked as dark as a cave. Surely Mrs. Reynolds had heard the truck.

"You suppose I should go through the screen door and knock on the main door?"

"I ain't never been to the front door," Henry said. "But Mama says Miss Beatrice don't hear too good. So yeah, that's what you need to do. Knock real loud."

I wasn't sure what made me so nervous about approaching that house. It didn't help that when I got out of the truck, the wind picked up and the house groaned like it was in pain. I eased open the screen door and it let out a loud creak. The planks of the porch floor squealed under my feet as I neared the wide front door. There was a door knocker shaped like a lion's head, and I lifted the knocker and rapped it against its base three times hard. Then I waited. I looked back and tried to see Henry watching out for me to bolster my courage, but I could only see the outline of the truck through the screen.

I waited there by the door for what seemed like forever before I heard footsteps, and a quavery voice asked from the other side of the door, "Who is it?"

"It's Willadean Franklin, Mrs. Reynolds," I said, remembering to talk loudly. "I'm J. W. Franklin's daughter. I'm delivering the medicine you ordered."

"Where's your daddy?" she asked. The door didn't budge.

"He had to stay in town because of business," I said.

"How'd you get out here?" she asked, still through the door.

"Henry Johnson drove me in Daddy's truck," I said. "He works for Daddy."

"Clarice's boy?"

"Yes, ma'am."

I heard the sound of a key rattling in the lock and the door opened and Mrs. Reynolds's head appeared. She glared up at me through thick glasses, and as if she was satisfied that I was who I said I was, she opened the door wider. She was at least three inches shorter than me and about twice as wide. She had her hair in a tight bun with a hairnet over it, and she was wearing a plain housedress and a tattered old sweater. She didn't look like a rich lady right then. I could barely see into the house behind her, it was so dim, but I could sure smell it. I had to swallow hard to keep from gagging. I figured that must be what dying smelled like.

"Come on in," she said, stepping aside as I entered. She immediately closed the door tight and turned the key. She glared at me in the wan light of the only lamp in the high-ceilinged entrance hall. "Your daddy shouldn't be letting you ride in a truck at night with a nigger," she said. "Has he lost his mind?"

I didn't know what to say to this. Daddy wouldn't let me learn to drive the truck until I turned sixteen next year. I wanted to argue with her, but I knew it was pointless.

"Here's the medicine, Mrs. Reynolds," I said, thrusting the package toward her and wanting to get this over with.

"Yes, yes, follow me, and I'll get your daddy's money."

I was afraid I might lose my dinner, going farther into the house, the way it smelled. It was the stench of human sickness, so intense that my eyes were burning. But Mrs. Reynolds was already headed toward a room at the end of the entry hall. I followed her obediently. That's when I heard the other sound coming from the open door of a dark room we passed on my left. It was the sound of breathing. Each breath was ragged and long, like it was being drawn through water, and every few breaths were followed by a whining groan. It reminded me of the way our horse Daisy sounded when she foundered. That was right before Daddy shot her so she wouldn't suffer any more.

I must've stopped in my tracks because Mrs. Reynolds turned and said over her shoulder, "That's my husband you're hearing. Best if you come on now. This way."

I followed Mrs. Reynolds into a small room. She reached over and turned on the light. My eyes had to adjust to the sudden brightness. All that was in the room was a desk and a large wingback chair and hassock. I could tell that was where she spent a lot of her time because of the deep round indention in the chair from her behind. You could still hear that breathing from in there, but the smell was much better.

Mrs. Reynolds lowered herself into her chair with a loud whoosh and reached into the sack and pulled out the medicine Daddy had sent. She studied it for a while and I stood there looking around, trying to disappear, not sure what I should do—especially when she pulled a tissue out of her pocket and wiped at her eyes. I felt sorry for her then. How lonely it must be for her out here in this big old house, listening to nothing but that terrible breathing all night. There wasn't much to look at in the room: a large collection of books on shelves that went all the way from the floor to the ceiling, and some framed photographs over the mantel. I drifted over toward the pictures.

One of them looked like it was taken when the Reynoldses were young. Mr. Reynolds was all dressed up in an old-fashioned-looking suit, and she was all plump with swept-up hair and wearing what must have been a wedding dress. Then I spied a picture of a couple of children next to it. They looked almost exactly alike except one of them was a girl and one was a boy. I remembered that Daddy said people like it when you admire their photographs, so I said, "These are nice pictures, Mrs. Reynolds. Are these your twins?"

"Yes, that's my Jacob and Jerrilyn," she said proudly. "Jacob is studying at Chamberlain Hunt military school over in Port Gibson, and Jerrilyn attends St. Mary's up in Raleigh, North Carolina, the very same school where I matriculated." She reached down into the crevice between the cushion and the chair and pulled out a large brown envelope. Opening it, she sorted through what looked like a large sum of money. "They will both graduate next spring. I hope their father lives to see it," she said as she handed me a dollar.

I thanked her and headed toward the front door as quickly as I could without appearing rude. As I was fixing to open the front door, I heard Mr. Reynolds holler out to her, "Beatrice! I've messed my bed again." I had never been so glad to get out in the fresh air as I was then.

. . .

"I bet she was lonely," Avery says.

"She was," I agree. "She nursed her husband, Mr. Olan Reynolds, until the day he died."

"When was that?"

"He lasted until that next summer. Long enough to see Jacob graduate from Chamberlain Hunt, but he died before Jacob and I married in September 1942." I get up to stir the beans. I finished snapping them while we were talking and put them on the stove for dinner. I've had about enough of bringing out old memories for today. Avery is bound to ask me eventually what happened to Jerrilyn. I'm not sure I'm ready to tell that story. I'll never forgive myself for that night. Sally has always said that I was only doing what Jerrilyn wanted, but I could have said no. Then everything might have turned out differently for all of us.

Avery yawns and glances up at the clock. "Oh, my gosh!" she says, pushing back from the table and hurriedly placing her cup in the sink. "It's almost eleven thirty! I'm going to be late meeting Mother and Celi at the club. Sorry, Will," she says, kissing my cheek. As she rushes to her room, she says over her shoulder, "I have more questions for later."

"That's fine," I call. "No hurry," I murmur to myself. I haven't dusted off these old memories in so long that it suits me to take them out slowly, one at a time, or maybe not at all.

Chapter 19

Avery

My head is still full of thoughts about Will and Henry in 1941 as I drive to meet Mother and Celi at the Greendale Country Club. I think of Will riding in the truck with Henry and taking flak about it from my own great-grandmother, and how fifty years later, Aaron and I were still worried about someone seeing us together. What a world this is.

A lot of Will's stories involve Henry. Could Will and Henry be the link that brought the sickle-cell trait into our family? But that would mean . . . My thoughts jump to Mother, who is probably waiting impatiently for me at the club. I wonder what Celi will think of the Greendale Country Club.

My memories of when I was her age mostly involve swimming in the club pool with Mark until we were both sunburned and pruney, then going to the clubhouse at the end of the day, changing into dry clothes, and shivering in the dim, air-conditioned restaurant, eating giant cheeseburgers and drinking cherry Cokes. I stopped going to the club in high school, except for when Merilee convinced me to attend some party or another. After I met Aaron, I completely lost interest.

At the clubhouse entrance I give my name to the attendant and walk into the restaurant looking for Mother and Celi. They're waiting at a table near the windows overlooking the pool. I recognize it as Mother and Daddy's usual table. A grinning Celi rushes into my arms.

"Hey, Mom," she says.

"Hey, sweet pea. I missed you. Did you have a good time with Grandma and Grandpa?"

Celi assures me that it was "great" and proceeds to fill me in on her activities, while Mother looks on smiling.

"Did she behave herself, Grandma?" I ask.

"Yes, she did. She was a perfect little lady."

Mother, Celi, and I enjoy lunch together, and I get a chance to introduce Celi to the double cheeseburger and cherry Coke that taste almost as good as I remember. Mother seems relaxed. I tell her about seeing Merilee Waverly last night, and she raises her eyebrows when I tell her about Merilee's fiancé.

"He's Japanese?" she asks, looking as incredulous as I felt.

"Yep, sure is," I say. "Well . . . Japanese-American. His parents emigrated here." I'm shocked when she laughs. Not a polite titter, but a belly laugh that shakes her shoulders. I find myself laughing along with her, as Celi looks at both of us quizzically.

"What's so funny?" she asks.

"Oh, nothing, sweetheart," Mother says, gasping for air and wiping her eyes with her napkin. "It's a strange world sometimes, that's all."

"Can we go swimming now, please?" Celi asks.

"Of course," Mother says. She signs the tab, and we walk out of the restaurant toward the pool house and dressing room.

"The club seems deserted today," I observe. "I'm surprised there weren't more people in the restaurant."

"Most of the women are probably at Garden Club," Mother says.

"Do you go to that club, too, Grandma?" asked Celi. The world of country clubs and garden clubs is completely new to her. I'm still wondering if she noticed that she is the only person of color in sight today, except for the staff.

"I do, but I decided I'd rather spend time with you two today," she says.

I can't help it. My first thought is: *How convenient. Bring us to the club when you know all of your friends will be somewhere else.* Celi and I head for the women's dressing room to don our swimsuits, and Mother says she'll find a table near the pool and wait for us. "I don't often go out in public without most of my body covered these days," she says.

When Celi and I are ready, we meet Mother, who has found a table with an umbrella near the shallow end of the pool. Several children are already splashing in the water, and Celi immediately plops down on the side to watch them. I'm pleased to see that it isn't long before she's busily playing with two little girls who look about her age.

"Well, if it isn't Avery Louise Pritchett," says a high-pitched voice. I look up into the plump face of Mabel Waverly, Merilee's mother. "Marion, why didn't you tell us Avery was coming home? We could have had a little welcome get-together."

My mother looks a little nonplussed, but she recovers with her usual finesse. "Mabel, how are you today? You're not at Garden Club?"

"No, not today—babysitting," she says, setting her bag of corn chips on our table so that she can hitch up the voluminous yellow tote on her shoulder.

I cringe, thanking my lucky stars and my mother that Mabel didn't know I was in town. I know what those little get-togethers are like, and no, thanks. Mother looks at me, then up at Mabel, and without batting an eye says, "Well, Mabel, you know how busy we've been, planning Mark's wedding and all. Avery's arrival slipped up on me." She's smooth, so smooth.

Mabel pulls up a chair without being asked and squeezes her broad derriere into it. "Now, Avery," she says, pulling her incongruous white glam sunglasses from her face, "I have to hear about what you've been doing with yourself out there in Colorado all this time. Your mother told us you're a nurse."

"Yes, ma'am, that's right," I answer, not sure how to continue. But Mabel barrels on.

"You know my Charles's wife is a nurse," she says, and tells me all about Merilee's sister-in-law. I wonder what she thinks of Merilee's new fiancé. If I ever get a word in edgewise, I might ask her. However, she's really not the least bit interested in me, I'm relieved to note. "She works the night shift, so I bring the girls swimming in the afternoons while she sleeps. It's so hot out here, isn't it?" she asks, fanning herself with her hand. "I'm too old to stand this heat, I tell you," she says, patting sweat from her forehead with a hand towel she pulls from her bag. "Those girls are like fish. They don't ever want to get out of the water." As she says this, the lifeguard blows his whistle for the hourly break.

"Oh, well, there you have it. Now they'll have to get out for five minutes."

I notice that Mabel keeps darting glances at the pool. I follow her gaze to see two little girls sitting happily on the side, chatting energetically with Celi between them.

I watch the scene unfold as if I'm in some sort of dream state. It's as if Mabel Waverly's words grow protracted and distant and everything goes into slow motion.

"Marion," she says, not taking her eyes from what I'm assuming are her granddaughters, "did that black family finally get voted into the club?" She leans forward at the waist, attempting to slide up in the chair, which is a feat given her girth. "I was sure Jefferson told me that man's application was tabled again this year." Without looking at my mother for an answer, she leans back with a huff. "Oh, well." She laughs wryly, looking at me. "There goes the neighborhood."

I'm unable to respond. All of the comments that come into my mind, most of which include profanity and something about Mabel's fat white ass, are stuck in my throat. The last thing I expect happens. Mother speaks.

"Mabel," she says, and her voice commands attention. Mabel tears her gaze from her happily color-blind grandchildren and looks at my mother blankly.

"Yes, dear?"

"That little girl you're examining is Cecelia Louise Pritchett. My granddaughter."

Did I hear my mother correctly? No, she didn't say "Avery's daughter"; she said "my granddaughter." My mother has suddenly become my hero. Where did she get this courage? And when did she develop a sense of humor?

Mabel is speechless. She looks from Mother to me and back again. Finally finding her voice, she splutters, "Oh . . . well, then . . . You know, Avery, I was being silly when I said that about the neighborhood. I mean . . . it's inevitable, isn't it? Everything these days is integrated." She blushes a bright pink, realizing she's digging herself deeper. "Not that I personally have any issue with it . . . I . . . Well, you know how these men are with their ideas. . . ." Seeing that neither Mother nor I will rescue her from her senseless gibberish, she stops. I know that she is desperately curious about Celi's father, but in her current state of embarrassment, she will not dare ask. So, in splendid Southern female form, she deftly changes the subject.

"Marion," she says, with such sweetness that I think I'll gag, "you must be so busy with the wedding. When is it again?"

I am now taking mental notes on my mother's amazing ability to remain calm. Mother relays minor, unimportant details about the wedding, letting Mabel think that she's successfully recovered from her faux pas. I watch Mabel begin to fidget and make small withdrawal statements and actions. She yawns, says she needs a nap herself, says she'd better gather up the girls. I haven't been able to speak. How does Mother do it? More important, why? But then, I remind myself, Mabel is one of her people. Mother has cultivated this group for years. Will they turn against her now?

Mother nods and smiles as Mabel makes feeble attempts to graciously withdraw. As she calls the girls, who look back at her only briefly before ignoring her, Mother clears her throat.

"Mabel, Avery tells me that she ran into Merilee last night at Desiree's." Mabel turns toward Mother, a wary expression in her eyes.

"Well, how about that?" she says. "I'm sure you two enjoyed seeing each other." She turns again toward the pool. "Girls, I mean it. Come on, right now."

Mother looks at me while Mabel's broad back is turned, lowers her chin, and pulling her sunglasses down from her eyes, gives me the go-ahead.

"Yes, that's right," I say. "I met Merilee's fiancé, Kenji." I speak loud enough to be heard over her whiny, dripping granddaughters, who have finally ceded defeat. "It sounds like you'll be having a wedding soon, too."

Mabel opens her mouth, closes it, and opens it again. "Yes, we're thrilled," she finally says with a complete lack of sincerity. "Got to go. Talk soon," she says as she waddles away.

Mother and I are watching the hasty retreat of Mabel's generous backside, granddaughters in tow, when Celi joins us at the table.

"How's the water, kiddo?" I ask, reaching over to push a wayward curl from Celi's eye.

"It's great. You should come in with me," she says, pulling on my arm as the rest break comes to an end and the children scurry to jump back into the water.

"Okay, but let me sit on the edge first and get used to the water." As I lower my feet, I realize the water isn't much cooler than the hot air surrounding us. Celi and I sit side by side, watching our toes rise and sink.

"Did you have fun playing with the girls you met?" I ask.

"Yeah," she says, sounding a little glum. I look over at her. She's pulled her knees up to her chin and is studying her toes. "Mom," she says in that way she does when she's about to ask one of her impossible questions, "did you know that they don't allow black people to swim here?"

I feel an instant tightness in my chest, that familiar mix of anger and helplessness. This is the very thing I wanted to protect her from, the very thing I've feared might happen. I feel guilty for hedging, but I answer with a question while I try to calm my breathing and decide how to respond. "What makes you say that?"

"Those girls," Celi says. "They said they'd never seen a black kid here before. They asked who I came with." She turns to look up at me, shading her eyes from the sun. "When I pointed over at the table and told them that was my grandmother, they didn't believe me."

I'm amazed at her calm and I attempt to match it, though I want to hit something right now. "And what did you say then?" I ask.

Celi sighs and shrugs her shoulders, looking exhausted, and it occurs to me that today might be too much for her—the sun, the water, and now this. The last thing I want is for her to go into crisis. "I said that yes, she was, and that you are my mother and you used to live here. Then we started playing." She slips off the side of the pool into the water, floating in place while she holds onto the side. "But is it true? Do they really not allow black people in this pool?"

"It's true, Celi, that this country club has no black members. So those little girls have never seen a child your color in this pool," I say, feeling an ache in my chest.

"Did Grandma know that?"

"Yes," I say, thinking about this as I lower myself slowly into the water beside her. "She knows that. Why do you ask?"

"I guess it doesn't matter to her," Celi says, looking toward my mother, who sits at the table, still appearing a little agitated as she sips her favorite diet soda and leafs through a *Veranda* magazine.

"I guess not," I say, and it begins to dawn on me how important that simple fact is to Celi. And as quickly as the conversation began, it's over. Celi insists I watch her do underwater flips and, ever mindful of her fatigue level, I allow exactly six flips before I insist it's time for ice cream and the trip back to the safety of Oak Knoll.

Chapter 20

Avery

Celi promptly falls asleep on the return drive to Will's house. Her cheeks look flushed and I reach over to lay the back of my hand against the soft side of her face, feeling for the familiar clammy sensation that heralds a fever. She doesn't stir and I'm relieved that I feel only normal warmth. I decide that I'll convince her to do something calm and quiet this evening—to be sure she's getting enough rest.

Will is waiting for us on the back porch and Celi happily accepts her invitation to play Chinese checkers. Still processing my frustration over the country club experience, I decide that I'll go for a run. I leave Celi and Will poring over the same colorful metal Chinese checkerboard that I remember from my own childhood, throw on my running clothes and shoes, and strike out, taking a different route today.

As I run down the long driveway and head for the road, I try to breathe out the anger and frustration I'm feeling. I need to get myself and my daughter away from here as soon as possible. We need to return to civilization, where the color of Celi's skin is not an issue. The sun is sinking over the long straight rows of soybeans in the field to my right, and pink-tinged clouds hang low above the horizon in the balmy evening air. It is beautiful here. I think again of Aaron being back in Greendale. I remember his promise to Sally that he would return here to practice, and I wonder again: How can he live here after being beaten to unconsciousness by men who are probably now considered pillars of the community?

I find myself remembering Aaron's brilliant smile, his lean, muscular body, the graceful way he moved. I remember being fascinated with his skin—the warm deep brown color, the smooth texture. We used to laugh that if I could push all of my freckles together we would match. But we didn't match and there was nothing I could do about that—just as there was nothing I could do about loving him. I didn't intend to. It was one of those helpless loves that a young girl falls into before she even knows she's tripped. We weren't blind—of course we saw the differences race made in our lives—but I wanted to deny that. The pull I felt to Aaron was about our sameness, about being more true to myself when I was with him. On some level in my stubborn mind I knew that if anyone saw us together, the soft shell I had built encasing our relationship would crack, and my delusion that we could overcome our differences would vanish.

So we found ourselves hiding. I was caught up in the terrible thrill of doing something that I knew would be condemned, while at the same time pushing against the conformity that was expected of me. My friends joked about dating black men as something they would do to humiliate their mothers or to get their fathers' attention. Every conversation ended with, "But I could never do that!" I would sit, listening to them giggle and speculate, wondering if what I was feeling for Aaron was written all over me.

Loving Aaron brought everything about the culture in which I was raised into sharp relief. I can see that now, from the perspective ten years has given me. Back then, I lived in anticipation of the next time I would see him. I lived all day, every day, for the short time we spent together.

Then it ended. I never saw him after the night he was taken to the ER, and I've never known what really happened to him. I always suspected that Mother knew. There was something suspicious about the way she acted toward me after the debutante ball. I was already past caring. With Aaron gone, nothing mattered. I fled to Colorado and never looked back.

As I turn onto the main paved road into town, I try to shut down the flood of memories. Even the trees seem to be steeped in my childhood, waving to me like roadside banners: Remember this? Remember that? Each piece of dripping Spanish moss seems to carry a memory reaching toward me. The crepe myrtles are in bloom and the road is lined with pink and white blossoms. I feel the warm, humid air creep across my skin and smell the red dirt drifting up from the gravel on the side of the road.

Alligator Lake spreads out in front of me as still as a mirror reflecting the now orange-streaked sky in the early evening heat. I can smell the earthy, fishy scent of the water and the mud on the banks. The moss from the trees dips into the water and I glimpse a small boat tied to a tree near the bank as I run past. Aaron and I used a boat like that. Only we put it in the lake on the opposite side—away from the prying eyes of people passing by on the road.

Before long, I've gone past where the lake is visible and run about a mile up the paved road. I begin to relax a little, looking out over the pastures and barns of my childhood. It's all so unchanged. The limited growth that Greendale has experienced is on the other side of town. That's where the big discount store is and a couple of new subdivisions.

Out in this direction, it's still mostly farms and the occasional shack or trailer near the road. I pass one of the house trailers that I remember from years ago. Aaron and I always laughed at the outdoor décor. The short driveway is still lined in tires that have been cut in half and painted white to form a sort of scalloped fence. The trunks of the trees surrounding the yard are painted white from the ground to about four feet up. Poor man's yard art.

I remember Aaron's laughter when he labeled this place nouveau white trash. We were having one of our many conversations about the similarities and differences between whites and blacks—me arguing that people weren't that different and him trying to convince me otherwise.

"At least black folks have more color," he said. We passed by the next trailer down the road and he smiled and pointed. "See, look at that." Sure enough, the yard of the black family's home was studded with bright yellow spinning flowers that twirled in the wind. I ended up agreeing with him. He was usually right. How I hated and loved that about him.

The summer evening really is glorious. Rows of ripening soybeans stretch as far as I can see on one side, and corn reaches toward the sky on the other. The land rolls and dips in wavy hills and the occasional live oak spreads out like a giant spider hovering over the ground. I slow down as a huge combine approaches, taking up two-thirds of the road. I move over as far as I can without going into the deep ditch and wave as the driver nods and touches the tip of his John Deere cap—always polite, these Southern men.

As I approach the place where I plan to turn around, I'm surprised to see that Owen's Market is still open. Owen's has been out here since even Will was young. It's where she'd go back in the thirties to buy bologna and crackers for her father when he owned the town pharmacy. When I was a teenager, I loved stopping by here after school on my way to Will's. Larry and Ruby always had the coldest Cokes. He still kept them in one of those deep box coolers that you reached down into. You'd pop the top off with the opener on the side of the box, drink two or three icy-cold swigs, and then pour in a bag of peanuts. So good. My mouth is watering at the memory and I decide to go in for a minute for old time's sake.

The store doesn't look much different than it did when I came here. I could swear the dog lying near the bench outside the front door is the same dog. But I know that's impossible. The one Larry owned was also a reddish brown bloodhound. I think his name was Duke. I used to pet him every time I stopped in. This one is also brown and barely raises his head as I walk past. The doors are different. Instead of the creaking screen doors with cigarette ads painted on the wood across the middle, the doors are now made of clear glass, pasted with all the usual credit card signs.

The interior is different, too. I try to determine what has

changed. I spot the familiar meat case in the back and the baked goods area. The café has grown. There are actual tables and chairs now where previously there was only a counter with stools. The biggest difference, I finally figure out, is the air. It has that consistent dry coolness of air-conditioning. Gone are the one tired air-conditioning unit in the window near the café and the big fan in the back. On really hot days, with my Coke and piece of fried chicken in hand, I'd stand near the air conditioner and let the cold air chill my sweat. It was heaven.

I look around for the Coke cooler, knowing it's probably been replaced by a tall glass case with doors. My attention gets distracted by a rack of postcards showing Alligator Lake, the Collier and Rosewood plantations, and other local landmarks. When I look up, I'm elated to spot the old cooler over near the window. Who knew I could get so excited over a cold Coke? I reach in and plunge my hand down in the icy water, savoring the feeling. The coke bottles are much smaller now than I remembered.

As I pop the top off, I'm contemplating where the peanuts are located when a voice behind me says, "Avery Pritchett, is that you?"

I turn and almost fall into the open arms of the short, round woman standing right behind me.

"It *is* you! I can't believe it, and as pretty as ever! What are you doing back in your old stomping grounds?" she asks as she wraps her arms around me and gives me a squeeze. I have to hold on to my Coke so I don't spill it while I return her hug, turning my head to keep her piled-up red bouffant hair out of my nose.

"Miss Ruby?" I ask, instantly taken back to when Ruby Westcott was one of the few people in the world who understood and accepted me in all of my adolescent fury. I'm having difficulty believing she's still here.

"When did you get into town?" she asks, and then her hand flies to her mouth. "Didn't nothing happen to Miss Willadean, did it? I'll be fit to be tied if she's done got sick and I ain't been out there to check on her. Why, I told Larry—"

"Wait, wait, Miss Ruby," I interrupt before she has Grandma

Will dead and buried. "Will is fine. As a matter of fact, I'm staying with her. I was out for a run, and I couldn't believe y'all are still here. So I had to come in."

Ruby looks instantly relieved. "Well, what's brought you back to Greendale after all these years? Let me see. . . ." She puts her stubby finger with its almost equally long red fingernail on her chin and looks up into the distance. "The last time I saw you was the summer after you graduated from high school. You stopped by here to tell me good-bye. You were on your way somewhere. . . . Where was it? Somewhere far . . ."

"Colorado," I answer. Miss Ruby was one of the few people who knew about Aaron and me, but even she didn't know about Celi.

"That's right," she says, as pleased as if she'd remembered it herself. Then her face drops into a powdery frown. Her red lips purse and she shakes her head. "That wasn't a very good time for you. I remember wondering if you'd ever come back."

"Um . . . yes . . . Well . . . I have a question for you, Miss Ruby," I say, intent on changing the subject. "Do you have any peanuts? I'm dying for a Coke with peanuts in it."

Ruby smiles and pats my back. I could always count on her to let me talk when I was ready and not insist if I wasn't.

"Sure, hon. We got all the peanuts you need." She walks over to a rack and pulls off a tube of salty nuts. "Here you go, on the house," she says, handing them to me. "Now, tell me you've got time to come sit a minute and talk to me. I've got to get back to the counter, but I would love to hear all about Colorado and what you've been doing."

I look down at my watch. Habit, I guess. What else do I have to do right now? Maybe talking with Miss Ruby will help me get this lead weight out of my belly.

"Well, maybe for a few minutes . . . if you're not too busy," I answer.

"Oh, hon, I'm never too busy to catch up on gossip with a youngster," Ruby says, and waddles toward the counter to squeeze through the small door barring the public from entering. She motions me in and points to a stool beside her. "Now, tell me, what have you been doing with yourself for ten years?"

As I'm opening my mouth to speak, the back door opens and Larry comes in carrying a case of Cokes. Sweat glistens on his dark face. Ruby smiles the way she does only for him and jumps up to open the cooler for him.

"Larry, you ain't going to believe who's here," she says, barely able to contain her excitement.

"Who?" he asks, as he pulls out bottles and drops them down into the cooler. He obviously hasn't noticed me perched on the stool behind the counter like a cake on a pedestal.

"It's little ole Avery Pritchett. Can you believe it?"

"Where?"

"Right over there behind the counter."

Larry looks at me from across the store, frowns, sets down the case of Cokes, and pulls a pair of glasses out of his shirt pocket, puts them on, and looks again, frowning more. Ruby watches him with a big grin on her face.

I've never seen a couple so in love for so long against such incredible odds.

Ruby always said if Larry hadn't pulled her out of Alligator Lake when she was fifteen, she'd be with Jesus and the angels right now. I never knew the whole story, but once when I was complaining about my parents, Ruby told me I should be glad I had parents who loved me like they did. Rumors about Ruby's life included incest and regular beatings until the day she tried to end it all in the lake.

Larry was the star football player on the Greendale High School team. Still a tall, heavy man now, back then Larry had a reputation for being the meanest, blackest linebacker this side of the Mississippi River. Larry pulled Ruby out of the water that day and fell instantly in love with her. All of Greendale frowned on it, of course. Larry even lost his opportunity for a scholarship to Mississippi State because he wouldn't give Ruby up. They never married because those were the days before it was legal for mixed-race couples to marry in Mississippi. And when the law finally changed in 1987, Ruby said she didn't need a piece of paper to prove anything. By then, she and Larry had already been together for twenty years.

"I'll be damned! If it ain't Avery Pritchett. Girl, where you been keeping yourself all these years?" Larry strides over and wraps me up in the best hug I've had since I left Mississippi. I feel the tears starting and scold myself for being so silly. "It's so good to see you," he says, and steps back to put his arm around Ruby, who fits under it like a baby chick under a hen's wing.

"She's been out there in Colorado, Larry," says Ruby. "She still ain't had a chance to tell me what she's doing here. . . ."

"Miss Willie?"

"No, her grandma ain't sick. Same thing I thought . . ." The cowbell on the door of the store clanks as a customer enters and walks to the counter to pay for gas. Larry steps aside and finishes filling the drink case while Ruby rings her up. After she leaves, they both turn back to me.

"Where should I start?" I say with a sigh. "First of all, I'm here for my brother Mark's wedding."

"Oh, that's right," Ruby says. "I saw their announcement in the paper. He's marrying that Collier girl, right?"

"That's right," I say.

"Well, honey, that Nicki, she's a sweet girl, but I am so sorry that you have to be in the same family with Seth Collier. That man is the biggest prick I ever laid eyes on."

I laugh with relief to finally be around someone who tells it like it is. Ruby has always had a mouth on her.

"Now, Ruby, don't go getting your back up about Seth Collier," Larry chides.

"You know it's true, Larry," Ruby says. "He is the most racist, sexist man in Greendale. Hasn't changed a bit since high school when he and those boys—"

"Ruby!" Larry says with a warning in his voice.

Ruby stops and takes a deep breath. "Well, anyway, forget about him. Tell us what you've been doing with yourself, Avery," she says.

"I went to nursing school in Denver," I say. "I'm an RN now—a pediatric surgical nurse."

Larry and Ruby look at each other, beaming with pride as if I were their own daughter. They never had children of their own. Ruby couldn't. In her words, "the door to my little oven got too much of a pounding on before my time. It don't work right now."

"A nurse! That's fine, Avery. Ain't that just fine, Ruby? She's gone and made a nurse."

"I think that's wonderful, Avery. Do you wear one of those pretty white uniforms with the white hose and shoes? I always thought nurses looked like angels."

Ruby has obviously not been in a hospital in several years. It's all scrubs now. All colors, all patterns. And as near as I can tell, we're not angels.

We chat for a bit longer about my nursing work and Colorado. I tell them good-bye and promise to come again before I leave town, and as I walk out the glass door I realize that I haven't told them about Celi. That's weird. Why didn't I feel comfortable talking about my daughter? And not only that—there was that comment Ruby made before Larry cut her off. The one about Seth Collier and his friends and something they did in high school. Could she have been referring to the night of our debutante ball? I make a mental note to ask her. I'll also introduce her to Celi. She'll love my daughter.

Larry and Ruby live on the fringe of the community and mostly keep to themselves. My own grandmother defied what was expected of her when she became friends with Sally and her brother, Henry. I'm suddenly struck with a shocking thought; I can't believe I haven't considered it before. If Henry Johnson was my real grandfather, then that would make Aaron my first cousin. I feel sick inside. I don't think I want to know any more. But if I don't see this through now, I'll spend the rest of my life wondering.

I stop outside the store and stoop to the bloodhound stretched out in the shade. I pull his collar tag into view and note that his name is Duke II, which makes me smile. Totally preoccupied with my thoughts, I scratch Duke behind the ears. He lifts his head slowly in response to the affection, and watching him relish it, I'm barely aware of the crunch of gravel as a car pulls into the lot behind me. I rise to go, and when I turn, murmuring good-bye to Duke, I find myself looking squarely at Aaron Monroe.

Duke raises his head at my sharp intake of air. Aaron is turned away from me, pointing his key fob at his truck to lock it, but his tall lean frame is unmistakable. I consider bolting, turning my back quickly toward him and escaping around the side of the building. I glance around for something to hide behind, but nothing is in sight and I'm frozen in place. Aaron is only ten feet away from me when he looks up and sees me. The slide show of expressions on his face goes from surprise, to something that looks like pleasure, to confusion, and finally ends in a cautious watchfulness.

"Avery?" he asks, as if I'm an apparition instead of a sloppy woman in mismatched running clothes. I'm instantly self-conscious. His inquisitive frown deepens the crease of the scar that runs diagonally from the left side of his forehead, disappears in his left eye, and resurfaces, like a road out of a tunnel, across his left cheek. I feel hot tears filling my eyes as I'm confronted for the first time with the physical evidence of what he endured because of me.

I search for something to say, something to fill the awkwardness created by ten years of silence, ten years of running following the few months of happiness we shared together. Finally all that comes out is "Hi."

Questions tumble from him as he chooses one to ask. "What are . . . When . . . How are you?" he finally asks. He flips the keys he's holding over a couple of times and then shoves them into his pocket along with his hands. Other than the scar, the ten years have only made him more handsome. He's dressed casually in a white button-down shirt with the sleeves rolled up, loose jeans, and leather flip-flops. His hair is cut close and the shadow of a perfectly clipped beard covers his strong jaw.

"I'm good," I answer, self-conscious of my sweaty ponytail

and running clothes. I can't believe it's been ten years since I looked into his eyes. I'm having a difficult time not staring at the scar on his face and I'm still fighting tears. Me dissolving into a puddle of emotion right now won't help this situation. I take a deep breath to calm myself and attempt to explain my presence in Greendale. "I'm here for Mark's wedding. I'm not sure if you remember him. He's a couple of years younger. . . ."

"Yes, I remember Mark. Played baseball, right?"

"Right. Anyway, he's marrying Nicki Collier, and he talked me into coming back for the wedding."

"Is she related to Seth Collier?" he asks, and the name sounds sour on his lips.

"Yeah," I answer, wondering what barriers Seth's name will place between us. Is Aaron still angry? I want to tell him that Nicki is different from her brother. I want to say a lot of things, but where do I begin to tear down the wall that separates us—the one I created? I find myself struggling to maintain eye contact with him. Duke pulls himself up and wanders over to Aaron to sniff his feet. I sense what Aaron's next question will be. How can he avoid asking about Celi? He wouldn't be the Aaron Monroe I loved all those years ago if he didn't.

"And Celi?" he asks. I notice a change in his tone, a wariness that thinly covers the tension that sets into his jaw and mouth. There's definitely anger there. How could there not be? How could I expect anything different?

For a split second I consider lying and saying that she didn't come. Wouldn't that make it easier for him? He has two other children now, not to mention a wife. Will Celi matter as much to him now that he has his own family? But when I look up into his eyes, I see pain coupled with something else—vulnerability. He's taking a much greater risk here than I am. The guilt of keeping them apart washes over me.

"She's here, too. She's actually in the wedding—we both are." The set of his lips softens, then tenses again, and his eyebrows dip down in a frown, as if he's preparing for an argument. "Aaron, I . . ."

"I really want to . . ." he says.

We each stop, knowing what the unspoken words were. We've each made a small step toward each other, but the distance of several feet remains—a space filled with fear and uncertainty, and for me, loss. Loss of that girl I was then, for the mix of reckless abandon and excitement I felt when I was with him, for what I'll never be able to share with him now.

"I want you to see her," I say hurriedly before I can talk myself out of it. The hopeful expression in his eyes pulls at my heart and suddenly I'm asking myself why I waited all these years. Why didn't I let him into her life, when he's standing here, flesh and blood, the man who fathered my beautiful daughter, and the yearning to meet his daughter is written all over his face?

"Aaron, I'm sorry," I say, brushing away tears that won't stay in check. "I had this idea in my head that the way I was handling things was for the best." I rub my hands across my face, trying to clear my mind. "I thought that we could get on with our lives, that it would be better for Celi. . . ." I glance up at him then and see that his eyes are filled with tears, too. "But I know now that I was wrong. She wants to know you . . . but it's so complicated. I don't even know where to begin."

Before he can speak, two cars pull into the gravel lot almost simultaneously. One, an aging Buick, is driven by an elderly white-haired woman who carefully parks, slowly pushes her door open, and emerges straightening her dress. She closes the car door, locks it with the key, and proceeds toward the store, looking warily at Aaron and me. The second car, a low-slung Cadillac, pulls in on the other side of the lot. Rap music blares from the open windows. Three young black men spill from the car. They nod to Aaron and me as they sidle past us, walking like crabs to keep their sagging pants from falling down around their knees. Baseball caps sit cocked to the side on their heads. Two of them wear muscle shirts and gold chains, while the third sports a knee-length athletic jersey. They mumble to one another in imperceptible syllables, using a language of their own. They reach the door at the same time as the elderly white woman and she stops, eyeing them suspiciously. The first of the three opens the door and motions for her to enter.

"Thank you, young man," she says, and the youth smiles and nods as he and his friends file in behind her. Aaron and I watch them, and I wonder if he's thinking about the clash of cultures, as I am.

Aaron looks at me and grins. The gleam of humor in his eyes reminds me so much of the boy I knew. I find myself smiling back, relief washing over me like a baptism.

Aaron takes another step toward me. "Do you have time to sit for a minute?" he asks, and he points toward a beat-up picnic table under trees shading the end of the store. I think of Celi and Will, happily playing Chinese checkers, and probably eating cereal—Will's favorite evening meal. Briefly I contemplate walking in the door with Aaron in tow, greeting Celi with "Hi, honey. This is your father . . ." but the image vanishes as soon as it arrives. I haven't brought my phone but decide that, since Will is not a worrier, it will be fine to linger a little longer.

"Yes," I say, swallowing hard to quell the surge of my heart rate as we start for the table. Looking around to see who might be watching is so automatic that I don't even notice I've done it until Aaron reaches out and lightly touches the back of my arm.

"Hey, no more hiding, okay?" he says. I hear strength in his voice, and when he looks at me for confirmation, I see in his eyes that, unlike me, he has thought about how we would approach seeing each other again. I see resolve in his scarred face and I nod in agreement as I throw my leg over the picnic table bench to sit across from him. I prop my elbows on the table and rest my hands on its splintered surface, wondering how many years and how many conversations it has weathered.

The scene has a surreal quality to it. What do I share? Where do we start?

Aaron lays his hands flat on the table and I watch as his familiar fingers stretch and curve as if he's using them to form his thoughts. Finally, his hands come to rest in gentle curves as he says, "Maybe it doesn't have to be so complicated. You know, if we take things slowly . . ."

"I know you have a family and a whole life of your own," I say, and I decide to ask the question that's been troubling me since I found out about his wife and sons. "Does she know? I mean . . . about us . . . about Celi?"

He looks away then, and I know the answer. He hasn't told his wife about the high school girlfriend he got pregnant. Unbidden anger clenches my jaw and I'm aware of the edges of the shame I've carried around for so long. He's telling *me* no more hiding? But why am I feeling this way? What right do I have to be in his life?

He looks down at the table. "No, Lacretia doesn't know." I must be wearing more of my anger than I know, because when he looks up at me he says, "Look, Avery, as far as I knew, you were never coming back here and you were never going to let me see Celi. So I never got around to telling her. I always planned to, but it never seemed like the right time."

I know I'm at fault for creating this situation and that my anger is unreasonable, but I don't want to be reasonable right now. Maybe we should go our separate ways and pretend we didn't see each other. But then the image of Celi floats through my mind, and anger leaks out of me through the hole punctured by Celi's unanswered questions: *"What's my dad like? Will I ever get to meet him?"*

"I get it," I say, managing to maintain eye contact with him. "So, what now?" I know, even as I ask the question, that I will fight to control the situation, that my protectiveness toward Celi will probably make me do or say something stupid.

"Hey," he says, gently laying his hand on mine. "How about we start over? Tell me about your life and Celi. I'll tell you about med school and my family. Maybe how we should handle this will become clear." His eyes are warm and I wonder again how he's able to be so wise, so calm. His confidence quiets my fears. I've fast-forwarded past ten years as if we could cancel them out.

"I went to nursing school," I say, chastising myself for feeling so inhibited.

"Really?" he asks. "I would never have guessed that."

"I know. Surprised me, too," I say. Our conversation is careful and light; each of us reveals only what will paint a favorable picture of ourselves. I share anecdotes about Celi and tidbits about Colorado; he describes the accelerated med school program he completed at Tulane, talks about his boys and his plans for a Greendale medical practice. When we pause, I observe that the sky has darkened to slate blue and decide that even Will might become concerned at the lateness of my return.

Aaron looks around and asks, "How did you get here?"

"I was out for a run. I really should get back. Will might be worried."

"It's too dark now to run. Let me give you a ride."

I tense at the prospect of being questioned about who dropped me off. I can't tolerate the thought of more explanations tonight. Aaron must see my dilemma because he says, "I tell you what. I'll drop you at the end of the driveway, okay?"

I nod with relief. "That sounds good."

The ride in his truck is awkward. There are child safety seats in the backseat, and the lingering scent of a woman's perfume—reminders of the life he has built. Fortunately, the ride is short and at the end of Will's driveway we part with my promise to call the cell phone number he's given me. We agree to set up a time for him to meet Celi, but only after I've had a chance to tell her about him.

"We'll figure it out," he assures me as I'm closing the truck door. I wave as he drives away, the déjà vu experience making me feel like that teenager again who watched him drive away from this exact spot so many times before. Only we're not those kids anymore.

I turn and make my way down the tunnel of trees that hover over the darkened driveway, and I feel as if my life has taken a turn into a shadowy and unknown place.

He said "we" and I believe him—each of us has work to do. Aaron has to figure out how to tell Lacretia about Celi and me, and I have to talk to Celi. I'm learning that there's no sense building up to these conversations. You either have them or you don't. For a long time I've chosen avoidance, but it's time to plunge in. As I emerge from the trees, Oak Knoll glows softly like one of Celi's lightning bugs. Will has left the porch light on for me, and I want to run to her for advice, to pour out my fears and have her tell me what to do, especially how to handle the secret of Celi's disease, which I continue to keep from all of them.

Chapter 21

Willadean

I'm relieved when Avery comes in the door. It's close to dark and I was getting worried. But when she spies Sally, she stops so suddenly that the screen door slaps her in the behind. I reckon she might as well get used to seeing Sally. She's over here nearly every other day—and, of course, more since Celi got here.

"You feel better?" I ask.

"Yes, ma'am," she says, although she still looks a little jumpy to me. "A good run always helps me get my head straightened out." I'm not sure I believe her. She looks a little shell-shocked if you ask me. She nods to Sally. "Hey, Miss Sally. How are you this evening?"

"I'm doing fine," Sally says. "Still enjoying that great-grandbaby of mine." I can tell from the way Sally says this and peers over her glasses at Avery that she's dropping a big hint. She is beside herself for Avery to tell that child about her black family. I keep telling her Avery has to do that when she's good and ready, but Sally doesn't want to hear it.

Avery looks a little funny. "Um . . . well . . . good," she says. "Where is Celi, anyway?"

"That child was so tired she was fixing to fall asleep right here on the Chinese checkerboard," I say. "We sent her off to get a bath and get in bed with a book. She's in y'all's room reading."

"I reckon all that swimming tired her out," says Sally, putting emphasis on the word "swimming." I watch Avery's face fall.

"I guess Will told you what happened," she says.

"Yes, and I'm sorry to hear that, sugar," says Sally. "There are some mighty ignorant folks in this world."

"Yeah, and a whole lot of assholes, too," Avery says as she flops down onto the glider.

"They's some good ones, too," says Sally. "Your daddy is a good man; so was your granddaddy."

Avery looks at me and then at Sally for several seconds, like she wants to ask us something but she can't figure out how to do it. Then, all of a sudden, she pops up and says, "I better go kiss Celi good night before she goes to sleep. Can I bring y'all anything from the kitchen?" We both shake our heads "no, thank you," and watch her leave.

"Reckon when she's going to let Aaron see Celi?" Sally asks me after a while, as we rock and watch the stars start to sparkle over the lake.

"I don't rightly know. It seems to me she's scared of something," I say, shaking my head.

"You don't think she's still carrying a torch for that boy, do you? Why, she's the one who pushed him away," Sally says, getting stirred up. "After he found out about that baby, I could hardly keep him from giving up his scholarship and moving out there to Colorado."

"Shhh," I say to her. "Keep your voice down. I know. You're right. But, still. She's having enough trouble trying to deal with her family. She's probably not ready to deal with Aaron and y'all's family, too."

"Well, at least with my family she won't risk getting kicked out of places," Sally says with an edge to her voice.

"Now, hold on there a minute, Sally," I say, starting to get a little riled up myself. "That was a terrible thing Mabel Waverly said. She's following right along in the footsteps of everyone else in that club. But do you mean to tell me it's going to be all sweetness and light when Aaron brings home his half-white child to meet his wife and kids? What has Lacretia said about Celi?"

Sally's quiet then, doesn't answer me right away. For a minute I'm wondering if she heard me and I look over at her ear to see if she's got her hearing aid in.

"It's in there," she says. "I heard you." She shifts in her chair, pulls a tissue from her dress pocket, and blows her nose. "To tell you the truth, Aaron's never told Lacretia about Celi."

I'm fixing to react when I hear Avery's step. She comes out wrapped in a bathrobe, toweling her wet hair, and carrying a drink. "Decided to take a quick shower," she says. "I feel so much better!" She sits down on the glider, sets her drink on the table, props up her feet, and looks at us.

"Miss Sally," she says, without a how-do-you-do, "Will was telling me about your brother, Henry, last night. I didn't remember that you had a brother."

Aaron meeting his daughter is a big old elephant in the room, but all you need to do to distract Sally Monroe is to ask her about Henry. She loved that brother of hers more than life itself. Of course, I loved him, too. He was a fine man, and we had us some adventures, Sally and Henry and me. Before you know it, Avery is fixing Sally one of her nightcaps and the stories are flowing.

I'm a little surprised at Avery's interest. But Sally's family is her family now, even if she hasn't told Celi. I find myself tensing, as usual, when we talk about Henry. I was lucky to have two men in my life who loved me. Jacob always said to me, *"Willa, I have loved you from the minute I laid eyes on that freckled face of yours the night you came spilling out of your hiding place on the floorboard of that truck—all piss and vinegar."*

"I suppose Willie done told you about how we first met her?" Sally asks.

"Yes, ma'am," Avery says. "And she told me that your mother worked for the Reynolds family."

"Yes, she sure did. Beatrice Reynolds was a sour old woman, but she loved my mama, Miss Clarice. I think that's why she got old Dr. Collier to write Mama a prescription for pain medicine."

Hearing the Collier name, Avery looks surprised. "Did you say Dr. Collier?" she asks. "As in the Mason Colliers?"

"That's right," I answer, trying to keep the bitterness from my voice. "The Dr. Collier who Sally is talking about was Mason's grandfather. He was the only doctor around these parts back then. He delivered most of the white children in Greendale." Sally and I exchange a look of disgust. I wouldn't give two cents for any of those Collier men. It seems like hate and violence must flow in their blood.

"So did y'all know Grandpa Jacob when you were little, too?" Avery asks Sally.

"No, not in those early years," Sally answers, looking at me for support. "Since your great-grandma shipped him and his sister off to boarding school, we only got an occasional glimpse of him and Jerrilyn when they were home for short visits."

"Beautiful girl, that Jerrilyn," I say.

"She was," Sally agrees.

"And Will said that your mother was sick a lot," Avery says.

"Oh, yes. We know now that she had sickle-cell disease. There wasn't much you could do for it back then. We didn't even know what it was, really. We thought it was something else the black folks had to struggle with." Sally shakes her head sadly. "Lots of folks died young."

"Yes, ma'am," Avery says, looking thoughtful. "It wasn't until the late 1940s that they figured out what was happening to the red blood cells of people with sickle-cell anemia. That was when they discovered that the red blood cells can't carry oxygen because they change into a sickle shape. They didn't start testing newborns routinely until the seventies."

"You mean there's a test to see if you have it?" I ask.

"The test tells whether you have the trait or the disease," Avery answers.

"What do you mean, trait?" asks Sally.

"You can inherit just the trait, which means you don't have the disease or any symptoms, or you can inherit the disease, which means that both your parents had the trait. So, if one person has the trait, and one doesn't, there's a fifty percent chance that one of their kids will inherit the trait. If both parents have the trait, there's a one in four chance that one of their kids will have the disease, and a fifty percent chance that their kids will have the trait."

"Now, that is too complicated for my old brain to follow," says Sally. "But I reckon my Cleome, Aaron's mama, must have got the disease, because the doctor said that's what killed her."

"I remember Aaron saying his mother died right after he was born," Avery says, looking sad.

"You certainly are well versed in this, Avery," I say. A question tickles at the back of my mind, one that I don't ask.

"Well, I was a pediatric oncology nurse before I went into surgical nursing," she says, too quickly, I think. "We had lots of kids with sickle-cell disease on our unit."

Sally and I both nod.

"Will, do you remember the time we took Mama to the root doctor?" Sally asks.

"Oh, Lord, yes," I say with a shiver. "That old woman liked to scare me to death."

"What's a root doctor?" Avery asks.

"That was the only kind of doctoring the black folks had in those days, honey," Sally says.

"There was that Mississippi Health Project that came through here for a few summers," I say.

"That's true," Sally says. "Do you know, Avery, that Dr. Ferebee herself gave Henry and me our shots," Sally says, smiling proudly at the memory.

"Who is Dr. Ferebee?" Avery asks.

"Oh, she was an important black doctor. We had never seen a black doctor before—especially a female one. Dr. Ferebee was sponsored by a black sorority called Alpha Kappa Alpha to bring a mobile health clinic to the small communities out here in the delta and provide some basic care for the black folks. A lot of smallpox and diphtheria immunizations, teaching about healthy eating, brushing your teeth, that kind of thing. It was only for a few weeks each summer—called the Mississippi Health Project. Lasted for six summers. Dr. Ferebee was one of the people that got the Knights and Daughters of Tabor to build that hospital over at Mound Bayou—the Taborian Hospital—in 1942," Sally says.

"But your mama still wouldn't go over there," I remind her.

"Yes, that's true. Mama didn't put much store in modern medicine. You see, her mama was born a slave over on the Collier plantation and they used the root doctor for all kinds of ailments. After the War between the States ended and my grandmother's family started sharecropping, there still wasn't medical care for the black folks. So when Mama came along in the early 1900s, they were still using the root doctor. Mama had known and trusted Granny Mathis all her life. She wasn't about to stop going to her because the Knights built a hospital."

"Was the root doctor using voodoo?" Avery asks, looking suspicious.

Sally sips her drink and thinks. "No, not voodoo, but there is another African religion they called hoodoo. During the slave times it became a sort of mix of the old African ways with the Christian ones. If a person had a sickness, then the root doctor believed they were out of balance between their body, their mind, and their spirit."

"Wow, that sounds like the philosophy nurses operate from," Avery says, looking surprised.

"I still think Granny Mathis was some kind of witch doctor," I say.

"Mama sure depended on her," Sally confirms.

"I remember that evening you came to the back of the drugstore, looking for Henry," I say.

"That's right," Sally says. "I had never seen Mama that bad off. . . ."

· · ·

October 1941

It had just turned dark and a there was a damp chill in the air from the rain earlier that day. A big orange harvest moon was coming up over the horizon. I could see it through the trees behind the store as I was leaving. It was fall and the tang of wood smoke was in the air from folks building the first fires of the year. Henry was finishing mopping up and planning to walk home as usual, so I was surprised when the Johnson's old mule appeared around the corner pulling their wagon with Sally at the reins. The only time they hitched up that old mule anymore was to plow the garden in the spring.

I paused to watch as Sally brought the mule to a halt. She looked scared. That's when I noticed what appeared to be a person wrapped in quilts and lying in the back of the wagon. A low moan carried across the yard, reaching my ears at the same time Sally jumped down from the wagon seat.

"Where's Henry?" she asked, already rushing past me toward the door.

"He's inside closing up," I answered, turning to follow her. "What's wrong?"

"It's Mama," she said. "She's real bad. Willie, I've never seen her this bad." I saw the tears in her eyes then and pushed ahead of her, opening the door and calling for Henry. As soon as he saw Sally, he propped the broom against the wall and came to her, steadying her with his strong hands on each of her shoulders.

"Mama's real sick, Henry," Sally said. "She says we've got to get her to Granny Mathis tonight or she's going to die." Sally was crying then, fat tears trailing down her cheeks. I stood helplessly by, but Henry bolted into action.

"You bring the wagon?" he asked.

"Yes, Mama's wrapped up in quilts in the back. I was afraid to leave her." Sally followed Henry as he grabbed his hat, shoved it onto his head, and pushed his arms into his jacket. I trailed behind them and almost ran into him as he stopped abruptly and turned to me.

"Miss Willie," he said, his face creased in worry, "I was almost done here. I'll come back later and finish up. Right now, I got to take care of my mama." He finished pulling on his jacket and slid his arm around Sally. "Come on, now. It's going to be all right." I followed the two of them out the door and watched as Henry whispered something comforting to his mother and then climbed up on the wagon seat. Before Sally got into the back of the wagon, she turned back to me.

"Bye, Willie," she said. "I'll see you soon."

I couldn't stay silent. My intense curiosity about Granny Mathis and my affection for Sally and Henry took over. "Can I come with you?" I asked, forgetting all about my promise to Daddy to come right home for supper.

Sally looked at Henry and he nodded. "Come on," she said, and we hoisted ourselves into the back of the wagon on either side of her mother, whose low moans filled the air around us. Sally drew the quilts tighter as Henry clucked to the mule and we started down Main Street, headed out of town. It wasn't long before we were on the old gravel road leading toward Alligator Lake.

"Mama, look at the moon," Sally said, trying to soothe her mother by pointing to the orange ball that reflected off the lake's surface, as if it had caught fire. Miss Clarice quieted and opened her eyes. She stared at the moon for several seconds and then looked at me, her eyes glassy and confused. Sally said, "It's Wil-ladean Franklin, Mama. You remember. She's a friend of ours." Miss Clarice nodded as she closed her eyes again.

We soon left behind the deep glow of the night sky, the hoarse croaking of the bullfrogs around the lake, and the gravel crunching under the wagon's wheels, and turned onto a narrow dirt wagon track that disappeared into the woods. The lake scents were replaced by the earthy smell of rotting leaves, and the sky overhead darkened as cypress boughs blocked out the light. I had never been on this road before and I didn't understand how Henry could see two feet in front of him.

"Where are we going?" I whispered to Sally. All sound was

tamped down in these deep woods, as if the night creatures were holding their collective breath, waiting for the wagon to pass.

"Granny Mathis's place is down near the swamp," Sally answered in a low voice. She glanced down at Clarice, who appeared to have fallen into a fitful sleep. "She's a root doctor. She helps Mama with her pain and . . ." Sally stopped then. It seemed she'd decided not to say what else this Granny Mathis person did for Miss Clarice. "I almost forgot," she said, and turned toward her brother. "Henry, we have to stop by the old cemetery."

I saw Henry's shoulders drop and his head lift as if he were looking up at the sky for help. "What? Why we have to do that?" he asked.

"You know why," Sally said, glancing at me. "We got to get the dirt."

"What dirt?" I asked. The wagon continued to creak slowly along the narrow road. I felt a tree limb graze my hair, and a spider's night web clung to my face. I brushed it quickly aside and shivered, hoping the spider hadn't come along for a ride in my hair.

"Granny Mathis has to have some dirt from my grandmother's grave," Sally said. "It's part of the conjure she does that helps Mama's pain." Sally must have sensed my reaction, even though we could barely make out each other's faces in the dark. "I know it probably sounds strange to you, but Mama's been seeing Granny all her life for her pain, and my grandmother did before her."

"Is your grandmother buried in these woods?" I asked.

"Yes, there's a colored cemetery out here. It was a slave cemetery. No one uses it anymore, but my grandmother insisted on being buried here near her parents."

"What's wrong with your mother?" I asked. "Why does she have so much pain?"

Sally shook her head and reached down to smooth her mother's forehead as Clarice turned on her side and moaned again. "We don't know. She gets these spells and her joints swell up so she can barely move. Sometimes, like tonight, the pain is agonizing. I hate it," Sally said. "I'll do whatever she wants to help her feel better."

But why hadn't Sally's mother gone to a medical doctor? I was fixing to ask when something descended from above us with a flapping sound and a shriek that made my blood run cold. Sally threw herself across her mother and I dove to make myself flat in the bottom of the wagon. Whatever it was swooped over us so closely that I felt the air around me stir.

"What was that?" I asked, forgetting to be quiet. Sally sat up, looking around and then back at her mother, and up on the wagon seat. Henry sat there chuckling.

"That's old Mr. Owl thinking y'all is something good to eat," Henry said. "I reckon he figured out you wasn't."

Considering the darkness, the spiders, the owls, and the prospect of visiting a cemetery at night, I was beginning to wonder if I should have stayed home safe in my own bed. I scrunched down lower in the wagon bed and pulled my jacket up around my ears. The wagon slowed and Henry called softly to the mule, "Whoa, girl." When I sat up to look around, I saw Henry pulling a kerosene lantern out from behind the wagon seat. In the eerie quiet of the woods I heard the scratch of the match against the paper. The yellow flame from the lantern cast a ghostly glow, and all I could see were the whites of Henry's and Sally's eyes as they looked at each other.

"You got to do it," Henry said. "You know it won't work otherwise."

Sally shrugged and started to climb out.

"I'll go with you," I said, not wanting to miss any part, now that I'd come this far. "How come you have to go?" I asked.

I joined Sally at the end of the wagon as she said, "Granny says the conjure works best when it's the first-born girl who collects the graveyard dirt." Sally sighed and reached into the wagon for a small Mason jar and a long-handled spoon. "Thank goodness, it doesn't take much."

Henry handed Sally the lantern. "I'll stay here with Mama," he said. "Y'all okay?"

Sally peered into the woods. I didn't see anything but more trees and tangled underbrush. The night sounds had gotten louder and I could hear the scuttling noises the nocturnal creatures made as they hunted in the dense undergrowth. *Please, Lord, let there be a path.* Sally nodded and started toward the woods. I followed close behind her. The last thing I wanted was to be lost out here alone. The lantern cast a short span of light at our feet and I could see that there was a narrow one-person trail leading into the woods.

We walked about thirty yards along the winding path, the ground soft and squishy under our feet. Sally trudged on with a determined set to her shoulders as we ascended a gentle slope and reached a clearing. Out of the glow of the lantern appeared a weathered wooden picket fence about three feet tall that dipped and turned with the uneven terrain on which it was built.

Following along the fence with the lantern, Sally located a small gate that creaked open in response to her push, and we found ourselves in the graveyard. In the glow of the now risen moon, my eyes adjusted and I could see small plain headstones peeking haphazardly from the swamp-soft ground. What a contrast to the elaborate headstones, perfectly placed flowers, and neatly mown grass in the cemetery where Mama was buried.

The dates I glimpsed as we wove our way among the headstones, trying not to tread on the graves, were early 1800s. Finally, in the back of the cemetery, under what looked like a dogwood tree, Sally stopped and knelt before a simple stone, which read *Sally Ann Collier, 1864 to 1936.* I gasped involuntarily. "Your grandmother was a Collier?"

Sally frowned, the light of the lantern making her dark face glow. "When they were freed, they took the name of their owners, the Colliers. I've always wished they'd picked something else. I hate the Colliers." I had never heard such passion from Sally before.

"How come?" I asked. I knew of Dr. George Collier. My daddy often filled prescriptions for his patients. His nurse would call the drugstore to talk to Daddy about patients and their medications. George and Mamie Collier also had a son, Ralph, who was a year or two older than Sally and me. He was the one who tried to get the job that Henry got, the one Daddy thought was worthless when it came to work.

Sally set the lantern down near the headstone, pulled the spoon out of her coat pocket and the jar out of the other pocket, and leaned back to rest her bottom on her feet. "The Colliers treated my people bad, Willie," she said, looking up at me. "I've heard stories from my grandmother that would break your heart. And once, Mama tried to get some help for her spells from Dr. Collier. She went over to the white folks' hospital. They made her go down in the basement. She said she felt bad asking for help, what with all those poor black folks down there in that gloomy basement, hollering in pain and stinking from bedsores, one black nurse trying to take care of them all. That nurse was so tired, she took one look at Mama and said, 'Honey, if you ain't dying, you don't want to be here. We don't ever know when the doctor might come, and when he do, he only here for ten or fifteen minutes to drug up the ones that's hurting the most.' Mama was so disgusted, she left there and ain't ever been back. Dr. Collier don't treat colored in his office, neither."

I felt so sad for Sally and her family, so bad they had this mysterious disease that grabbed hold of her mother like it did. I knelt down then, not worrying about the damp ground soaking through the bottom of my skirt, and watched in fascination as Sally turned her attention toward the headstone and began to talk to her grandmother.

"Old Mama," she said softly, her warm voice blocking out the frightening rustling in the underbrush. "Mama needs your help. She's hurting something fierce, and I'm afraid she can't bear up under this pain." As she spoke Sally took the spoon and gently loosed a clump of grass and weeds that covered the grave. "I've brought Mama's spoon to take some of your healing power to her." Sally turned the clump over and brought the jar beside it. "Please help her now, Old Mama," she said, and she grasped the dirt on the underside of the clump and broke off pieces and crumbled them into the jar. When she had what looked like a couple of tablespoons' worth, she screwed the lid on the jar and put it back in her pocket. "Thank you, Old Mama," she said as she replaced the grass clump and patted it down. I shivered, as at that moment a cold wind rustled past my skirt and rippled through the cemetery.

Sally didn't seem to notice as she picked up the lantern and rose to leave. As we made our way back down the path, I tried not to think about the snakes that were still roaming the woods at this time of year. We were halfway to the wagon when a scream coming from the direction we were facing pierced the darkness and Henry's face appeared before us. His eyes were wide and he was panting with fear. The scream had come from Miss Clarice.

"What's taking y'all so long?" he asked. "We got to get going, Sally. It's bad. It's real bad this time."

I was shaking then, trembling with fear of what might happen to Miss Clarice and angry because all she could do was go see some strange root doctor in the middle of the night with a spoonful of dirt. What was that going to do? It even crossed my mind to talk to Daddy. Was there anything he could give her? What about some of his tonic? Would she accept it?

Sally held her mother's head in her lap and stroked her brow as we bumped along through the blackness. After not too much longer, the trees opened up into a small clearing and ahead I saw one window glowing in a cabin that seemed to appear out of the woods like a ghost house. Fog from the swamp surrounded the house and the air had turned dank and wet. I had a creepy sensation that this was a dream and I was going to wake up any minute in my own bed. My ears were filled again with the sounds of the woods and the swamp, of the night critters croaking and screaming. Henry brought the wagon to a stop and Sally leaned over her mother and said, "Mama, we're at Granny Mathis's now. We're fixing to get you inside." Miss Clarice groaned and we helped her sit up.

"You got Old Mama with you?" she asked, her voice barely a whisper.

"Yes, ma'am. We got her," Sally answered as we focused on helping her move to the back of the wagon, where Henry waited to help her out.

Miss Clarice sat on the edge of the wagon, bracing herself with her hands, as weak as a kitten. Sally continued to reassure her while Henry attempted to help her stand. I noticed then that her knees were swollen like fat gourds and her fingers looked like sausages. I turned to see how far she would have to walk, and before I could stop it, a scream escaped my throat. I clamped a hand over my mouth as I found myself facing the biggest, blackest man I had ever seen. My eyes were even with the clasps of the overalls covering his massive chest, and I was a tall girl. He was so dark skinned that his face was hidden in shadow as he stood silently watching us.

Henry's look of relief calmed me as he said, "Big Jack, I don't think Mama can walk tonight. Looks like you and me might need to carry her." Before Henry could say more, Big Jack gently scooped Miss Clarice into his arms. Her head fell across the hard pillow of his upper arm as he stopped to look over our group. He paused and studied me, a frown of curiosity briefly crossing his face. When he spoke, his voice rumbled like thunder and I jumped again, reaching for Sally's hand. "You," he said, nodding at Sally, "come with me. You other two, stay here."

I wanted to protest, my natural curiosity once again overruling my fear, but Henry took my arm firmly, while Sally followed along behind Big Jack as he carried her mother up the rickety steps onto the cabin's dark porch. I admired Sally's bravery when she didn't pause until she was illuminated by the open cabin door. When she looked back at Henry and me, I saw the briefest look of fear in her eyes. Then she turned toward the door, where against the interior glow of the cabin I saw a very small stooped woman holding a rope. I followed the rope to its end. The leashed animal at her side was an alligator.

I sat on the back of the wagon with Henry and waited. When I shivered at the dampness of the cold night air, Henry took off his coat and draped it around my shoulders.

"Thanks," I said, unexpectedly conscious of his warm presence. "Henry, what is all of this? I mean, what does a root doctor do?"

"Granny Mathis uses the old ways the slaves brought over from Africa," Henry said, sounding older and wiser than his years. "I've seen her put the root on people who need protection from somebody who's out to get them, and I've seen her find the evil root that's making somebody sick and destroy it. Sometimes, even white folks come see Granny Mathis," he said, searching for my reaction in the dim light cast by the cabin window.

"They do?" I asked, surprised that I'd never heard of Granny Mathis.

"Yep," he answered. "Granny Mathis, she uses whatever she thinks is going to get a person's problem worked out. Might be graveyard dirt, like Mama's, might be fingernails, might be spiders or plants. Granny can tell you when to plant in the spring, when it's going to rain. She knows all kinds of things."

"But how does it work?" I asked, thinking of how scientific Daddy was about his medicines; how he carefully measured each amount of a compound—which usually consisted of white powders or benign-looking liquids.

"I don't know exactly," said Henry. "But folks believe in Granny Mathis. Mama wears the root around her neck in a little leather bag. She swears it helps with the pain. But tonight she said something done happened to take the root off. She wouldn't tell Sally what, just told her to get her to Granny Mathis quick. So here we are," he said as he stood up and looked toward the cabin door. I noticed how much colder it was when he moved away from me.

"And you believe it, too?" I asked.

Henry let out a breath and pushed his lips up toward his nose, causing his mouth to turn down as he creased his brow. "Well, I've seen it work for Mama when nothing else will. And I can't get her to try something like your Daddy's tonic. She can't get medicine from Dr. Collier, so"—he paused and appeared to be weighing his decision—"I reckon I do believe in it." He reached up and pulled off his hat to scratch his head, then replaced it as he added, "Some of the white folks say Granny Mathis has herself some sort of deal with the devil. But Mama doesn't see it that way.

Mama goes to the Missionary Baptist Church every Sunday. She says Jesus doesn't contradict conjure any more than those white folks going to see Dr. Collier contradict going to see their preacher—there's always a little of the spirit that is sick along with the body, she says."

I was thinking how close I felt to Henry and how glad I was that I got to share this night with him and Sally, when a bloodcurdling scream from the cabin sliced into the canopy of night sounds around us and I jumped to my feet. We both started for the cabin when the door opened and Sally stepped out holding her hand up to stop us. "It's all right," she mouthed, as Henry and I stood immobile, side by side, and I wondered if we should believe her. Then Big Jack appeared in the doorway, carrying Miss Clarice. This time, instead of nestling against his chest, her body was limp and draped across his arms like he was carrying a folded tablecloth.

Big Jack carried Miss Clarice to the wagon and Henry and Sally hurried to pad the back with quilts, and I stood transfixed, watching the cabin's open doorway. The small woman appeared again in the rectangle of illumination. The light settled around her head and crept into the deep wrinkles that twisted her features and drew her toothless mouth into a catfish-like pout. She wore a simple cotton dress covered by an apron so white that it glowed. She held a corncob pipe in the corner of her mouth with one hand and with the other she reached down to stroke the head of the alligator that waddled up beside her. When I noticed that the alligator was no longer attached to a rope, I decided it was time for me to get myself back in the wagon for the return trip to Greendale.

"So why did your mother scream like that?" Avery asks Sally.

"When Granny put the root on her . . ." Sally stops at Avery's look of confusion. "When Granny put the little bag around her neck, the only thing I can think is that must have been when that pain spirit came out of her, because that's when she screamed. Then she went limp as a rag doll. But it didn't look like a faint to me. She was as peaceful as a baby rocked to sleep in a cradle.

"Anyway," Sally continues, "we got Mama loaded in the wagon. Then Big Jack handed me a small brown cloth pouch and said in that big deep voice of his, 'Granny say put this under her bed when you get home.' I looked at Henry, and he said 'Yes, sir,' paid the man two dollars, and we got out of there as fast as we could."

"Daddy liked to taken a switch to me when I got back home so late," I say. "He was worried sick when he went back to the store and found both me and Henry gone. He calmed down a little bit when I told him about my adventure with the root doctor. 'Yes, I know better than to interfere with anything Granny Mathis does,' he said. That was the last time I was at Granny Mathis's place until that night in forty-two," I say, exchanging looks with Sally.

"You mean 1942?" Avery asks, ready for another story.

I could kick myself for bringing up that other night, but, thankfully, Sally gets up, stretches, and says, "I got to go home, y'all. It's way past my bedtime. We'll have to tell that story another night."

"You're right," I say. "I think it's time we were getting to bed. Avery and Celi are going into town tomorrow to get fitted for their dresses, and I need my beauty sleep." I unfold my body from my chair.

"Miss Sally, it's late," Avery says. "How about you let me follow you home in my car?"

"No, no, don't you trouble yourself," she says. "I'm fine. I'll let myself out. Willie, I'll see you tomorrow," she says as she steps out into the night. I turn the outside light on for her to see her way to her old Ford. As soon as she's in and has the engine cranked, we head for bed. I fall asleep and my dreams are filled with root doctors, screaming barn owls, and alligators on the porch.

Chapter 22

Marion

Today Avery and I are having lunch at the Randolph with Laura Elise and Nicki. There was a time when the prospect of lunch at Greendale's finest restaurant would have been a pleasing one. But now everything seems to have shifted, and the thought of listening to Laura Elise drone on about the wedding for two hours has no appeal. Plus, I have a headache—probably from tension.

Yesterday's events at the country club left me drained. If I read Avery's expression correctly, she seems to believe I was some kind of champion for desegregation. She even hugged me before she left for Willadean's—something she hasn't done since she was ten. But we've both always been a little awkward when it comes to physical affection. Avery doesn't have any idea what it took out of me to stand up to Mabel Waverly. She doesn't know how close I came to denying my own grandchild. My heart was racing and my mouth went dry when Mabel scrutinized Celi at the pool yesterday. I knew what was coming. I could read Mabel's thoughts as if they were a movie marquee. Once, I might have had the same thoughts, had I been in her place. But I'm not in her place anymore.

Unless I want to lose my daughter and my granddaughter, I am no longer a member of the exclusive club that remains intent on keeping blacks and whites apart. I must admit to a small amount of wicked glee in finding out that Mabel's daughter has gotten herself engaged to an Asian. I wonder what Mabel's husband, Jefferson Davis Waverly, is saying about that one. I picture him stewing from behind his massive desk at the bank. He'll sit and puff on his fat cigar, rub his vast belly, and probably determine, like I have, that there's not much he can do about it.

I suppose we all have to accept that things have changed. I find myself vacillating this morning between exhilaration in my newfound strength and a desire to run and hide. The Mabel Waverlys of the world are not going away, but neither are my daughter and granddaughter. Most important, I don't want them to.

I think of my own young adulthood. So much of my time and energy were spent avoiding my mother and my home. I pick up my coffee cup and walk into the den, searching for the visual evidence of how my world has changed. I find what I'm looking for on one of the shelves flanking the fireplace. The Ole Miss yearbooks are lined up according to year, beginning with my own freshman year, 1961–1962, and extending through my graduation year, 1965, then beginning again with Mark's Ole Miss years—1993 through 1997. Thirty-two years in between. I have never looked closely at Mark's senior yearbook.

I pull two of the albums from the shelf, mine from 1962 and his from 1997, and carry them back to the kitchen, lay them on the table, and pour more coffee. I choose Mark's album first, flipping through the pages, noticing the colorful pictures—spring tulips and dogwoods blooming, fall leaves in oranges and yellows, rebel flags in bright blue and red. I'm not sure what I'm looking for.

I notice the scattering of black faces among the others, and the yearbook falls open to the "Distinction" section—what we would have called "Features" in the sixties. I find myself gazing at the picture of Miss University 1997, a beautiful black girl, the first African-American Miss University in the history of Ole Miss. Looking at her dark eyes, softly curling black hair, and serene smile, I find myself wondering what the Ole Miss experience was like for her and I'm seized with the realization of how different my children's world was from my own.

I reach for the 1962 album and turn pages of photographs of lily-white beauties smiling coyly from brocade chairs or while posed on grand staircases in antebellum homes. I fail to find a single black face. I've never thought about these photographs from any perspective other than my own experience, which was all about trying to avoid integration. What my children take for granted, I found frightening and threatening.

My first year of college offered a welcome escape from the unrelenting persistence of my mother's fervor for black rights. My heart was still broken over losing Mason, and I was filled with rage at my mother. Escaping to Ole Miss meant being surrounded with other young whites who believed that college, sororities, fraternities, and football were our birthright; it was our duty to uphold the traditions of the South. All of it—the rebel yell, the pep rallies, the way we thrilled when the band played "Dixie"—was heaven for me.

I dared not tell anyone that my own mother supported the Freedom Riders and was working every day to help educate poor blacks so that they could pass the literacy test. Ole Miss was the home of Miss America in 1959 and 1960, the rebel flag, and passionate Southerners who liked to talk about the Civil War heroes in their families. My future sorority sisters were not interested in a race of people who, in their experience, were invisible.

I threw myself into rush, pledging Delta Gamma along with Laura Elise. There were parties, ball games, late-night food runs—anything to take my mind off Mason. The crazy thing was, when he saw me getting attention from the other fraternity boys, he came around looking hangdog and convinced me to see him—but only in secret, when he could be sure his parents wouldn't find out.

"Marion, you know I would be with you if I could," he said, pressing his body against mine as we hid behind the sorority house.

"I know," I said, allowing him to kiss my neck and fondle my breasts. I hated myself for doing it, but I wanted so much for him to love me, to see that I was nothing like my mother.

"Maybe your mother will give up on all that stuff with the niggers and we can be together," he said, unbuttoning my blouse and pulling back my bra. What would Mother and Daddy say now if they could see me? I still didn't understand why they hated the Colliers so much, but I knew then that I would go as far as Mason wanted if it meant I might have a chance with him. But that chance never materialized. Just when I thought he might come back around, he would stop calling, stop seeking me out, and I would see him around campus with another coed. And again, when I was certain he had found the "one," he would surface again, find me on the way to class, convince me to meet him. Looking back, I can't believe I let it go on as long as it did.

Ole Miss became my safe haven that first year. I spent the summer working as a counselor for the Presbyterian children's camps in Oxford. The only time I went home was for a couple of weeks before each semester started and during the Christmas holidays. For the few short weeks I was home, I managed to avoid Mother's activism. But then, in the fall of 1962, the beginning of my sophomore year, what I thought I had escaped followed me, and my sanctuary was violated once again because of a black man.

September 1962

Early that September I heard about James Meredith trying to register to attend Ole Miss and how Governor Barnett turned him away. We girls were in the common room of the sorority house putting one another's hair in curlers and waiting for *The Red Skelton Show* when Governor Barnett came on the news. He said: "And in order to preserve the truth, and in order to maintain and perpetuate the dignity and tranquility of the brave and tall State of Mississippi, under such proclamation I do hereby, now and finally, deny you admission to the University of Mississippi."

Governor Barnett was smart. He wanted to prevent violence. He even said that his decision was for James Meredith's own safety.

"I'm thankful that our governor is so strong," cooed Frannie

Lipswich, holding a mirror to her face and applying the new shade of pink lipstick we were passing around.

"Yes," said Laura Elise. "It would be awful if that colored man got in. Can you imagine?"

"Everything would be ruined," I said, wanting to join the conversation.

We moved on to our favorite topic—boys—and were soon rolling on the floor with laughter at the antics of Red Skelton, the threat of any change coming into our sheltered world forgotten.

That fall our football team was preparing to play Kentucky and we were all terribly excited. The September night brought a touch of cool air. Twelve girls from our sorority piled into two cars and traveled to Memorial Stadium in Jackson for the game. It was thrilling to be with my friends among a crowd of forty-one thousand people, waving our Confederate flags and cheering our team. At halftime the score was seven to zero, our favor. The band marched onto the field carrying our huge rebel flag, and "Dixie" resounded through the packed stadium. The crowd was wild. Rebel yells filled my ears and people began calling for Governor Barnett to speak. It was eerie the way the crowd quieted as he stepped to the microphone at the center of the field. He took a look around at the quiet crowd, threw out his arms, and shouted, "I love Mississippi!"

His words brought the crowd to its feet in a fever pitch. Everyone around me was caught up in the fervor of support for our school. As long as Governor Ross Barnett was in charge, we were safe.

"I love her people!" he continued, and we screamed even louder. And finally, "I love her customs!" The roar was deafening. I felt cold chills creep down my spine and I wasn't sure why, but I had a sneaking suspicion even then that something was about to change. The governor returned to his seat, and as I was sitting down, the boy behind me tapped my shoulder and handed me a leaflet with the words to a song printed on it.

"New song," he slurred, and I could smell the whiskey on his breath. "Join in!"

I looked down at the words thinking how exciting it was to be part of something new—maybe a new Ole Miss tradition. I heard snippets of the words being sung around me, and I started to catch the tune as I sang the first few:

> *Never, never, never, never*
> *No, never, never, never*
> *We will not yield an inch of any field.*

I thought then of our brave boys on the football team and how exciting the second half of the game was going to be. The song continued:

> *Fix us another toddy, ain't yielding to nobody.*
> *Ross is standing like Gibraltar; he shall never falter.*
> *Ask us what we say, it's to hell with Bobby K.*

That was when I realized we weren't singing about football. We were singing about James Meredith. My voice dropped as I spoke the final words. Everyone else seemed so carefree. Why did I have to be such a worrywart?

> *Never shall our emblems go*
> *From Colonel Reb to Old Black Joe.*

As halftime ended and the team fought for victory, I fought to maintain the college spirit that had buoyed me during the first half. I laughed and yelled and even had a few sips of toddy from the girl next to me. But the sense of foreboding wouldn't leave me. As had become my habit, I mentally blamed my mother for ruining my college pride with tales of beatings and murder. As the second half progressed, I pushed the thoughts away and immersed myself in doing my part to cheer our boys to victory.

Glynn Griffing was amazing. There was absolutely no stopping him. We went on to beat Kentucky and we cheered, sang, and waved our flags all the way to our cars. The laughing and singing continued as we inched along the road leading away from the stadium, where cars were lined up bumper to bumper. Little did we know that during our revelry, the president of the United States was in the process of signing a federal order that would change our lives forever.

We spent that night at a hotel in Jackson, falling into our beds by threes in a state of exhaustion. On Sunday morning, we began our trek back through the delta toward Oxford. One of the girls was from Yazoo City, and we stopped at her house because her mother had insisted on making us lunch. We arrived on campus in the late afternoon. As we drove down University Avenue and neared the Grove, we noticed that a lot of kids were already back and there was a buzzing in the air, like a disturbed beehive. Through the open car windows, we heard chanting:

Two, four, six, eight . . . hell, no, we won't integrate.

Laura Elise and I were in the backseat and we strained to see what was going on as we approached the Lyceum. That's when we saw them.

"Oh, my God," exclaimed Laura Elise. "What's happening?" Men in white helmets with white bands around their arms and something strapped to their chests were lined up in front of the Lyceum.

"Those are federal marshals," said Jane Hubert, the driver of the car and one of our smartest girls.

"But why are they here?" another girl asked. No one had an answer, but I had a heavy feeling that it had to do with James Meredith. Why couldn't he attend a black university? There was Jackson State. This standoff felt intensely personal for me. Why did he have to ruin my Ole Miss experience?

Jane pulled over and we piled out of the car. Students were lined up three and four deep, facing the federal marshals. The air had the exciting, electric feel of a pep rally. Another chant rose from the gathering crowd and we melted into the group and joined in:

Hotty Toddy
Gosh Almighty
Who the hell are we?
Flim-flam
Bim-bam
White folks, by damn!

At first it was exhilarating, being part of the crowd. I was finally taking a stand against the loss of our traditions. With every "white folks, by damn" that crossed my lips, I saw my mother's face and felt my anger against her hurling out through my vocal cords. I looked across the sea of faces and saw Mason surrounded by his fraternity brothers, his strong arms raised in protest. His blond hair glowed in the late afternoon light and a ripple of excitement gripped my stomach as I watched his tanned face and dazzling smile. He turned my way, caught my eye, and winked. My heart soared and I cheered louder.

Someone pushed against me from behind. "Hey, watch it," I said as I turned. Looking behind the crowd, I saw that vans marked with the logos of the major news networks had arrived. Reporters with cameras were everywhere. Flashes from cameras blinked in the twilight like lightning bugs.

I gasped as I saw a boy I recognized as one of the football players draw back his fist and slam it into the face of a reporter. The man fell to the ground, his nose bleeding profusely. Another boy standing nearby shouted, "Kill the bastards!" A third boy saw the reporter fall and quickly picked up the camera that had been knocked from his hands and smashed it into the ground. The students standing nearby cheered.

I felt sickened by the expressions of hatred I saw on their faces. Images of white-sheeted men laughing and pointing at my wild-eyed mother as they drove away from our house filled my mind. I was frightened. Maybe if I could find Mason, I thought, he would make me feel safe.

I looked back, but I had lost track of him. Finally, after searching the crowd for what seemed like an eternity, I caught sight of his blue-and-white-striped shirt, but my gaze faltered. Mason's arm was raised and in his hand he clenched a lead pipe. Gone was his flirtatious smile, replaced by a snarl of hatred that twisted his face into one I didn't even recognize. It prickled the hairs on the back of my neck. Before I could see where Mason was going, Laura Elise's voice rang in my ear.

"Marion, come on," she yelled frantically. "We're getting out of here."

Jane barely got the car off University Avenue and onto Sorority Row before the crowd closed in behind it. Several passersby slammed their hands onto the hood, causing us to jump in fright with each impact. Students I recognized as well as strangers were lining the streets and moving toward the Lyceum, their eyes wild, their mouths contorted, their fists raised. "Two, one, four, three, we hate Kennedy," they shouted. Jane maneuvered us slowly through the crowd. Federal marshals were patrolling the sidewalks in front of the dorms as we passed them, and girls were actually leaning out of the windows and throwing books at them. The ground below the windows was littered with thrown items—books, lamps, even hairbrushes.

As we rounded the corner and finally turned into the lot behind our Delta Gamma house, I glimpsed older people that I didn't recognize parking cars and trucks on the grass at the back of the campus. They emerged from their cars looking as if they were about to do battle. I glanced at the license plate on the beaten-up truck of one particularly greasy-looking man in overalls: Alabama. Was this an issue for the whole South? Fear rippled through my chest again, and I walked faster. As we passed the tall white columns and comfortable rocking chairs of our front porch and entered the cool stillness of our sorority house, I breathed a sigh of relief. Laura Elise and I looked at each other after closing the door to our shared room.

"Do you want to go back out?" she asked.

"No, I don't," I said, realizing as I answered that I no longer wanted to be part of the growing mob.

"Me, either," she said. Other girls must have felt the same, since when Laura Elise and I ventured down to the common room, we found all of our friends there huddled around Jane's transistor radio.

"Let's turn on the television," one of the girls suggested, and we all piled onto the sofas and pulled up chairs. I held my breath as we watched images of a crazed mob assaulting the federal marshals, overturning and setting fire to cars, and hurling bricks at reporters. I prayed I wouldn't see Mason's face. Jane held her transistor radio close to the side of her head, while she popped her gum and listened for more reports.

The noise outside got louder and louder. A girl came rushing in with the remnants of a broken egg dripping down her back.

"This is nothing." She laughed excitedly, as if it were all a silly college prank. "I saw some boys getting ready to set off Molotov cocktails!"

I shuddered. Jane spoke up then. "Hey, y'all. It's Governor Barnett." We all listened as his voice, scratchy on the radio, informed us that James Meredith had been brought to the state of Mississippi under federal order to register for classes tomorrow.

"Gentlemen, you are trampling on the sovereignty of this great state and depriving it of every vestige of honor and respect as a member of the United States. You are destroying the Constitution of the United States. May God have mercy on your souls!"

I thought of my mother then. She would be in the kitchen, glued to the radio as she stomped angrily from sink to table. All of the excitement seeped out of me, replaced by a deep sadness. The screaming outside escalated. Later we learned that several of the marshals were assaulted by students. One of the boys bragged about "getting one" by hitting him on the head with a lead pipe. Someone in the crowd yelled, "Let 'em have it!" and the federal marshals opened tear gas on the crowd. We slammed the windows shut in the common room, but not before enough of the gas seeped through to leave our eyes stinging. We fled to our rooms and stuffed towels under the doors.

We pulled the curtains tightly together but couldn't resist peeping out. A heavy haze hung over the campus, and I could still see the flickering lights around the Lyceum. Lights I knew were from firebombs. And then we began to hear gunshots.

"Oh my God!" Laura Elise said. "Someone's going to get killed."

All the girls lined up in the hall to call their parents to let them know they were safe. I wasn't going to call, but Laura Elise made such a big deal of it that I thought I should at least make a show. I prayed that Daddy would answer. But Mother's loud voice stung my ear on the first ring.

"Hello. Willadean Reynolds here."

"Mother, it's me, Marion," I said.

"Marion, you're not out there throwing things at those federal marshals, are you?" she asked, dashing my hopes for any sympathy. "You know they're doing what they have to do. It's ridiculous that they won't let that boy into Ole Miss."

Argument was useless. How could I explain to her what it had been like to live in the sheltered domain that was Ole Miss? How could I convince her that a way of life was rapidly being destroyed? I heard her muttering, and Daddy's voice rang clear and gentle through the line.

"How you doing, baby girl? You need us to come get you? You scared?"

Tears stung my cheeks. "No, Daddy, I'm fine. We're staying inside."

"Good. I'm glad to hear it. Y'all stay safe, now." I could hear Mother in the background telling him some new instruction I should be given, but he must have ignored her, because when I begged off, saying that other girls needed the phone, he said, "We love you, sugar. Call us again soon."

The next morning, as we picked our way through broken bottles, empty tear-gas containers, and bricks, we learned that the worst of Laura Elise's fears had come true. Two people had died in the riot and almost four hundred were injured. Overturned, still smoldering cars littered the once lush green lawn around the Lyceum. Shattered windows gaped like empty eyes surveying the carnage. We wept for our loss. We weren't sure exactly what was gone, but we knew that nothing would be the same. That morning, October 1, 1962, under President Kennedy's orders, James Meredith was allowed to register for classes at our university.

I am so deep in reverie over my Ole Miss days that I'm startled when Holt comes into the kitchen.

"Good morning," he says. "What you got there?" He leans in from behind me and kisses my cheek, looking over my shoulder at the still open 1962 yearbook.

"Oh, just an old college yearbook," I answer, a little embarrassed to be caught looking back.

"And Mark's, I see," he says, sliding the more recent yearbook toward him as he sits down with his coffee.

I watch Holt as he absently flips through the pages of Mark's yearbook, wondering what he sees when he looks at the photographs, envying his detachment. Unlike me, who stopped on the picture of the African-American Miss University, Holt moves right to the sports section and studies the football team. He closes the yearbook, looks up at me, and smiles. "So what's gotten you looking at these?" he asks.

"Oh, I don't know," I answer, sighing in frustration. Will he understand the inner conflict I'm experiencing? Do I dare share it with him? Holt is ten years older than I am; it was part of his appeal when I met him, but it also means that he didn't experience the tumult of being in college in the sixties. By the time we met that December of my senior year, he was already on the way to becoming a successful attorney. "Change, I guess," I answer vaguely as I get up and pull cereal bowls out of the cabinet.

"You mean between your college experience and Mark's?" he asks, looking puzzled.

"Yes . . ." I hesitate, facing him with a box of Cheerios as a shield. Who else am I going to talk to about this? "The whole integration thing . . . There was so much violence and anger around it when I was in college. And, Holt . . ." He waits patiently for me to speak. "I might not have been throwing bricks, but I was as opposed to integration as everyone else. I mean, I was actually frightened. . . ." I bring the cereal to the table and go back to the refrigerator for the milk. I'm so preoccupied I can't remember whether Holt drinks two percent or skim. I finally grab them both, closing the refrigerator door with my hip. Holt is still watching me, calmly sipping his coffee. I plunk the milk cartons down on the table. "Now, looking back, I don't know what I was so afraid of." I sit quietly while he pours cereal into our bowls.

"I mean, there couldn't have been a more polite and quiet young man than James Meredith. Holt, do you know that one of the white girls . . . I can't remember her name now . . . anyway, she sat next to him one day during class. She was so harassed after that—they painted ugly words on her wall, said things behind her back. It was terrible. She must have been so humiliated. Anyway, she finally left school and I heard that she and her family even left the state. That's how bad it was." I shake my head, pouring milk onto my cereal.

When I look up at Holt, he has a strange expression on his face. I can't tell if it's anger or sadness or both. We've never talked about race. Holt has always seemed so comfortable in his relationships with blacks. Yet, he's managed to keep his separateness, too. And that's never been difficult here in Greendale—well, until now.

"People went to great lengths to stay segregated, that's for sure," he says. I'm wondering what he's thinking, but he doesn't elaborate.

I continue with my story. "And then there was Loretta Hodges, my junior year at Ole Miss. I was twenty years old. Loretta was a freshman, had pledged our sorority, Delta Gamma, and was going through rush. She was a beautiful girl with long smooth brown hair—I remember envying her hair—and she had these catlike hazel eyes, and the most beautiful figure. We all liked her. She was friendly and smart, and she had already started to date one of the fraternity boys—a football player, I think. Anyway, Mavis Greenburg, one of our sorority sisters, happened to see Loretta coming out of a black church one Sunday when she was driving through the country with her boyfriend. Mavis came back to school and told all of us. It spread like wildfire through the sorority, and before you knew it, Loretta was asked to withdraw from rush. Turned out she had a light-skinned black mother and a white father, and she was trying to pass. It was horrible. She tried to deceive us all, and that boy she dated was the most embarrassed of all. His daddy almost pulled him out of school."

At that point in my life, Loretta's exclusion from Ole Miss made sense to me. She was perpetrating a lie, and she experienced the consequences. But now, close to forty years later, I'm struck with the awareness that, if things hadn't changed, my own granddaughter would be one of the excluded. Segregation looks much more reasonable when it's happening to someone else's family. What a hypocrite I am.

Holt shakes his head and looks away from me. He pulls the newspaper toward him and opens it to the business section, probably hoping I'll stop talking. Maybe he'd rather not hear it, but for some reason I can't stop myself.

"Loretta, of course, left Ole Miss," I continue. "How could she stay after that? What humiliation! But then, how long did she think she could carry off such a ruse? We all thought she got what she deserved. At the time I remember thinking that you can't pretend to be what you're not."

He looks up at me then as if he's about to say something. But his expression changes. "Let's hope things will be a lot different for Celi," he says. I nod in agreement.

We eat our cereal in silence, each lost in our own thoughts. I wonder if he's moved on in his mind to his workday—probably—while I continue to ruminate on a past that I can't seem to let go of. At the edge of my awareness is a troubling thought. The very thing that we've experienced in our family—our daughter getting involved with a black man, having a black child—was what so many whites in the sixties were so afraid of, and are still afraid of even now.

Why was my mother never saddled with those fears? In our years of attempting to tolerate each other, we've never discussed my experiences or hers. I'm sure she's not struggling with having a black child as a member of the family—especially since the other great-grandmother is her best friend. My best friend, on the other hand, is Laura Elise Collier. I think again about the upcoming lunch and sigh. Laura Elise is starting to feel more and more like part of my past and less and less like a good fit in my present. It's the strangest thing. I kiss Holt good-bye and head out to the rose garden to get some work done.

I pull into the circular drive of the old Randolph mansion turned restaurant. Holt and I have been coming here for so long, I feel I know every inch of this place. It's the only decent restaurant in Greendale, in my opinion. The Randolph was built by Alistair Randolph in 1832 and stayed in the Randolph family for a hundred and thirty years, until the last remaining Randolph left Mississippi to seek his fortune in New York City as an actor. He became wildly successful in the seventies and decided to return to Mississippi to restore his ancestral home, choosing to open an elegant restaurant and bed-and-breakfast and convert the former detached kitchen into his living quarters.

Perfectly restored and maintained, the Randolph has tall white columns that flank wide front steps. Comfortable wicker furniture with deep, soft cushions is arranged around the large porch. For all the memories I've deliberately made here with Holt over the years—birthdays, anniversaries—I'm appalled that my memory of Mason has to come up now. When I first saw this place as a young girl, even before it was restored, I dreamed of a wedding reception here, and for years it was Mason Collier beside me in my fantasy. I shrug off these thoughts. Everything that's happening has me too caught up in the past.

I step out of my car and hand the keys to the valet, a young black man with a polite smile. I look up and see Gunter waiting for me at the top of the steps. The Randolph's gracious maître d', Gunter was new to his post when Holt and I started coming here.

"Afternoon, Miz Pritchett. I've got yo table ready," Gunter says. Up until about two years ago, he'd come down and open the car door. But he's gotten so old, he can't get up and down the stairs like he used to.

I stop to admire the deep red Don Juan roses climbing up the iron trellis beside the steps and study the combination of caladiums and asparagus fern that Mo Creekmore has set in the six stone urns that grace the steps. The colors are breathtaking. Mo is a genius with containers. He's been doing the flowers for the Randolph forever. I wish Laura Elise would get him to do the flowers for the wedding, but they're using somebody over in Grenada.

"Afternoon, Gunter," I say. "Looks like I'm a little early."

"You want me to bring you a glass of tea? You could sit out here on the porch. It's a fine day."

"No, thank you, Gunter. I'll go on in to the table." Gunter always walks me over, in his courtly way. It's one of my small indulgences. Always makes me feel a touch royal, as do the floor-to-ceiling windows sparkling in the afternoon light and the brilliant white linen tablecloths on tables set with roses, silver, and crystal water goblets. As soon as Gunter has me seated and has gone back to the entrance, I head for the ladies' room. Maybe if I dawdle in there, fix my lipstick and put on a little powder, I can meet them coming in.

I feel a little guilty that I'd rather be the mother of the bride. I tell myself how proud I am—and I really am—of Mark. But Nicki's mother gets to be involved with all the choices: the dress, the bridesmaids' dresses, the flowers, the cake. They've been at the final fitting for her dress. I know for a fact that Laura Elise wanted to take her to New Orleans; the selection is so much better there. But Nicki insisted on buying her dress from Miss Esther.

That old woman can barely see now, and her hands are so crippled up with arthritis, I don't know how she does alterations. But apparently Nicki was adamant; she has a soft spot for Esther, or so Laura Elise says. Seems like everyone around here is getting old.

As I'm coming out of the ladies' room, I can't help but feel a little pang of jealousy when Laura Elise and Nicki walk in, arm in arm, all smiles. Nicki is a beautiful girl. Dressed casually for the Randolph—in jeans and a long loose blouse and sandals—she reminds me of a young Michelle Phillips. Nicki seems to be so calm and confident for her age, with beauty, wealth, education—all of the things a mother wants in the girl who'll marry her son.

"Marion, honey, how are you today?" Laura Elise says, as she swoops in and practically smothers me as usual with her silicone breasts and her excessive use of White Diamonds perfume. Her hair is done up in a chignon, and she's gone a new shade of blond, I notice. It's becoming, of course. Laura Elise would never be caught with a hair color that wasn't perfect. Nicki is trailing behind her now, still talking to Gunter.

"I'm fine," I answer. "You're looking lovely today."

"We have had the best time this morning," she says, and then takes my arm and pulls me close. "You wouldn't believe how hard it is to watch your beautiful daughter parading around in her wedding dress," she whispers. "Between you and me, it made me feel a little old."

"Oh, shush now. You barely look older than Nicki," I say. I adjust my jacket—Laura Elise has this way of pulling on my clothes that I have always found particularly annoying—and prepare to greet Nicki.

"Hey, Mrs. Pritchett," she says, giving me a warm hug.

We settle into our chairs, and Emily, a young black woman, brings the menus. She and Nicki exchange a few words. Turns out they graduated from Ole Miss together, and Emily will be attending the wedding. Laura Elise raises her eyebrows ever so slightly. I pretend not to notice.

We decide to order drinks while we wait for Avery, and Laura Elise starts to tell me all about Nicki's dress. I smile and nod, trying to show interest and fight the sad little feeling in the pit of my stomach. My mind is wandering; I can't help it. Ten years ago, I stood in that same dress shop, trying to convince my daughter that she looked fine in a white dress—a debutante dress. That was before everything changed. Now my neatly repackaged world feels as if it's breaking apart again—especially when I'm in an environment like the Randolph, and with Laura Elise. I find myself unable to reconcile the disparate pieces. And I despise the thought of going through another scene like the one with Mabel at the country club. What was I thinking? I keep watching out of the corner of my eye, and finally Gunter approaches with my own daughter, the person who seems to trigger more conflict within me than anyone else.

Avery comes rushing over to the table, Gunter at her heels. "Sorry I'm late," she says. "How is everyone?" Laura Elise frowns as we all watch Avery bump the chair, drop her purse, knock her napkin off the table, and finally plop noisily into a chair and tuck her hands under her legs, as if she's trying to keep them still. I try to distract Laura Elise from Avery's nervousness by calling Emily over. We've all ordered iced tea, but Avery orders a gin and tonic.

Laura Elise frowns again, but Nicki says, "You know, that sounds good. I'll have one too, Emily."

Laura Elise lays her long, elegant hand on the table in Avery's direction. "It's so good to see you again, Avery. How have you been?"

"Fine, thanks . . . busy, you know . . . my job, and being a mom and all," Avery answers, fidgeting with her napkin.

"And Nicki tells me that you are a nurse," Laura Elise says, as her gaze travels over Avery's clipped-back hair, her freckled face without makeup or lipstick, and her nondescript sleeveless shirt and khaki pants.

"Yes—a pediatric nurse."

"That must be handy when it comes to taking care of your child," Laura Elise says, and I tense, wondering where this is headed.

I'm not sure why, but Avery seems instantly defensive. "What do you mean?" she asks.

"Just that you have a lot of knowledge about children . . . you know, what to do if they get sick . . . things that most mothers worry about."

"Yes, I guess that's true," Avery says. Emily arrives with our drinks, and Avery takes a long sip.

We're temporarily distracted with ordering lunch, and I decide to steer the conversation away from Avery. "So, Nicki, tell us where you and Mark are going for your honeymoon," I say.

Nicki describes their plans for a trip to Jamaica, and we all express our envy for an island vacation. But it doesn't take long for Laura Elise to return her attention to Avery. "Avery, do we hear wedding bells in your future, dear?" she asks.

Avery crosses and recrosses her legs. "Um . . . nope. No prospect of that any time soon," she says with a weak smile. "Gotta have a groom, you know."

Laura Elise smiles wanly. "Well, I'm sure you'll want some help raising your daughter, won't you?"

"Actually, I'm doing just fine so far," Avery responds, and I can hear her voice tightening.

"Celi is an adorable little girl," Nicki says, jumping into the conversation as if she senses Avery's discomfort.

"I'm sure she is," Laura Elise says. "Does she look much like her father?"

Everyone freezes, except Laura Elise, of course, who calmly sips her iced tea, pats her lips with her napkin, and continues to gaze at Avery, who stares back at her.

I can't stop myself from jumping in. "I tell you, Celi is just fascinated with formal dresses. Why, the other day, she even asked to see my wedding dress—"

"Actually, she does look like her father," Avery says. "And she's dark skinned, if that's what you're asking."

"Oh, Avery, I don't think—" I start to say.

Avery turns on me then, as if I'm once again the enemy. How do we always end up in this same place? Me saying the wrong thing, her angry with me. "There's no need to try to sidestep this, Mother," she says, glaring at me. She turns back to Laura Elise, as if awaiting her next question. Laura Elise doesn't even flinch.

"It must be terribly hard for you, raising a mixed child," she says. "I'm sure you must have to deal with a lot of questions about her origins." I glance at Nicki, who seems to be petrified by her mother's audacity.

Avery is obviously shocked into silence. She looks at me as if I should come to her defense, but I dare not say anything for fear of it being exactly the wrong response. *Is it hard for her?* I wonder. *Does she deal with a lot of questions?* I realize that I don't know the answer to Laura Elise's observations, either. Only, unlike Laura Elise, I've been hesitant to ask.

Avery's response is flat and hard, as if she's struggling to maintain her composure. "No, it's not hard. Actually, raising Celi is the best thing that's ever happened to me. And people in Denver, unlike people in Mississippi, don't make a huge deal of Celi's color."

Just then, thank the Lord, we get a reprieve when Emily arrives to take our order, and Avery excuses herself to visit the ladies' room. I take the opportunity to ask Nicki about her work as a schoolteacher, and I think we're finally on a safe topic, but just as Avery returns to the table, Laura Elise says, "If only you would get out of that dreadful public school system, darling." She turns to me. "You know as well as I do, Marion, the blacks don't have any interest in education. They just want to get pregnant as soon as possible, drop out of school, and get on welfare, just like their mothers."

I can feel Avery glaring at me as I nod helplessly in response to Laura Elise. What am I going to say? I'm no expert on social issues. Laura Elise has a point. Our county has the highest teenage pregnancy rate in the state, and most of those are black girls. But will Avery see this conversation as a direct affront to her child?

"Let's talk about a less heavy topic, shall we?" I ask, looking pleadingly at Laura Elise, hoping she'll get the huge hint that I'm dropping, hoping Avery's obvious discomfort and anger will matter to her.

Avery says with false flippancy, "Yes, Mother always finds that a polite change of subject is the solution for any uncomfortable conversation." Nicki laughs nervously, Laura Elise raises her penciled brows at me, and I push on, ignoring Avery's sarcasm.

"Let's talk about my plans for the rehearsal dinner, shall we?" I say.

Chapter 23

Avery

Through the remainder of the lunch I keep a polite smile plastered on my face. I can feel Mother examining me like she used to at the dinner table, scrutinizing my hair, my nails, even my teeth. I've never thought much about how different we look. I told myself that I ended up looking more like Will, and Mark got her and Daddy's looks. But today I notice how smooth and creamy her skin is, almost the same tones as Celi's, but more pale. Her lips are still full, even though she's starting to get wrinkles on either side of her mouth, and when she removes her reading glasses and places them carefully beside her plate, I can see the resemblance between her hands and Celi's—long, elegant fingers with oval nails. Of course, hers are perfectly manicured.

What would she think if she knew I was sitting here during the chatter about Nicki and Mark's upcoming engagement party, wondering if her biological father was black? I imagine myself bringing it up, the explosion it would cause. Simply for mentioning the possibility, she would probably never speak to me again. Of course she would deny it.

What would public knowledge that we have black family members do to my parents' standing in the community? Would they be ostracized? Would it create a giant rift between my parents, one they couldn't withstand? It's one thing for me to satisfy my own craving to know, but would the cost be too great? Today, I'm so frustrated with Mother and her lack of support for me, and for Celi, that I'm feeling vindictive—as if I want to punish her for not coming to my defense with Laura Elise, whose racism is so embedded she's not even conscious of it.

"Avery, I want you to be sure and bring your daughter," Laura Elise is saying. "Since Nicki and Mark announced this wedding so late, we're having a small get-together—to bring the families together, you know. And, of course, we want to be sure and have Willadean there, too," she says, turning to Mother. Is that a glint of wicked satisfaction I see in her eyes? Is Laura Elise enjoying my mother's obvious discomfort?

"Oh, yes," Nicki adds. "I love your grandmother, Avery," she says, reaching out and resting her hand on my arm. "She and I have had the best time getting to know each other."

Mother nods to the waiter for coffee and busies herself stirring in cream. "Laura Elise, I'm not sure that an engagement party is any place for a child. Why, she'll be bored witless. And you know how those men sometimes get to drinking and talking, and it's difficult to get my mother out of that house, you know."

I'm amazed at how smooth my mother is. If I didn't know her real motive, I might almost buy it. I might think it was best for me to leave Celi home with Will. Wouldn't that make it so much easier for everyone? Hide the misfits out at Oak Knoll, make sure to keep them away from the watchful eyes of Laura Elise Collier, whom I'm certain is itching to get a look at my daughter. *Over my dead body will I hide my daughter at Oak Knoll with her great-grandmother.* But I'm also struggling with the ball of shame that knots up in my stomach. I should take up for my daughter, resist my mother, come to Will's defense. But something silences me. And before I have a chance to figure out why I can't speak, Mother has handily moved the topic of conversation.

I'm still puzzling over my mother's behavior as I drive back to Oak Knoll to pick up Celi. Was Mother trying to protect Celi by suggesting that the party would not be a good place for her? Or was she attempting to put off the inevitable exposure? We didn't get a chance to talk after lunch. She hurried off, claiming that she had an appointment and that she'd meet us later.

Celi and I are going into Greendale for what I consider the dreaded dress fitting, but which for Celi is the height of excitement. I try to reframe the experience so as to appreciate her pleasure, but I'm having a hard time. My head is swirling with all of the history I've been gathering over the past week we've been here. So far, I've pieced together much of Aaron's side of the family puzzle, but I'm still no clearer on mine. And now that I've seen Aaron, I worry that I'll run into him again before I figure out how to talk to Celi.

We pull into the dress shop parking lot and Celi wiggles with anticipation. "What color is my dress again, Mom?" she asks.

"White," I say, bracing myself for the Miss Esther experience. I'm not sure I'm willing to be poked, prodded, and tucked now any more than I was ten years ago. But I love Mark and Nicki, and I remind myself that I'm doing this for them. Celi and I enter the shop and the little bell jingles over the door. It looks exactly as I remembered it. I don't think she's changed the silk flower arrangement in the window since 1980.

"Wow, Mom!" Celi exclaims. "Look at all of these beautiful dresses." She wanders toward the back wall, attracted like a bee to a flower to the fabrics, lace, and frills that her little fingers are itching to touch. I watch her react in awe to the dresses hanging above her head, and I feel a sense of inadequacy for the part of mothering that I don't do very well. Celi and I have never dressed up for anything. Sure, I take her hiking and snowshoeing; we've even been camping with friends a couple of times. But never tea at the Brown or a night at the ballet. I make a mental note to plan a different kind of mother-daughter outing with her. It seems like I've been making a lot of mental notes lately.

As Miss Esther walks in from the back room, dusting crumbs from her mouth, I notice how much older she looks. She's gotten thin. And she walks less like a German drill sergeant than she used to.

"Hallo," she says. "Please excuse, I was having a little luncheon. May I help you?"

"Yes," I say, thinking that her German accent is as strong as ever. "I'm Avery Pritchett, and this is my daughter, Celi." I motion for Celi to come over. "We need to get fitted for dresses for the Pritchett-Collier wedding." As Miss Esther studies Celi, I start to get that fearful feeling in my stomach. I know that Miss Esther still deals primarily with Greendale's white population. The wedding shops are still segregated.

Miss Esther frowns; then comprehension smoothes out her face. "Oh, yes, yes, yes. You are the sister from Colorado. I remember you, Avery Pritchett. You were the one for the debutante ball with the sporting bra and the stringy hair." She nods to herself in recognition while I blush miserably. Celi is grinning from ear to ear. Obviously, she thinks this is very funny. "Yes, I was expecting you girls. Come, come, let us go back and get started." Esther leads the way, then turns and looks at Celi. "Such a beautiful child," she says, holding out her hand, which Celi takes after a quick glance at me for my nod of approval. "Come along, *liebchen*, let's put you in a pretty, pretty dress, eh?"

Maybe this won't be so bad after all.

I've added a pushup bra to my wardrobe, and Miss Esther has made Celi feel like an absolute princess. All in all, it's been a successful experience. We set out to walk the two blocks to Daddy's office. We're visiting Daddy and Mark there today. I'm feeling a bit of nostalgia for the shops and businesses of my hometown. Celi is studying everything with her usual intensity.

"So what do you think of the thriving metropolis of downtown Greendale?" I ask playfully, swinging her arm.

"There are so many black people here," she says. "I never see this many black people at home."

"That's because about seventy percent of the people who live in Greendale are black—only thirty percent are white," I answer.

"Is that why some of the white people act like they do?" she asks. "Maybe they don't like that there's less of them?"

"What do you mean?" I ask.

"Like that lady at the pool, and . . . well . . . sometimes like Grandma. It seems like it's really important to them that they're white."

I laugh. *Out of the mouths of babes.* "Now that you put it that way, Celi," I answer, "I think you're right. I'd say it's especially important to people like Mrs. Waverly that they're white—absolutely essential, I'd say."

"Mom, can I tell you something?" she asks, stopping to look up at me.

"Of course, Celi. Anything."

"Sometimes I wish I were solid white, or solid black, but not both."

Her words pierce my heart. I swallow hard and ask, "Why is that, sweetie?"

She turns casually and starts walking again, still holding my hand, still swinging arms. I know she's thinking. I'm grateful for the walking so I can try to blink away the tears that sting my eyes.

"Well, I have this white family, but I don't exactly fit there. And I don't know my black family, so I don't know if I'd fit there. So it seems like it'd be easier to be one or the other, but I can't, you know?"

"Yes, baby, I know," I say, feeling the blade in my heart turn again.

"And people stare at me a lot here," she says as a middle-aged white woman passes us on the street, looking from me to Celi and back.

As we approach Daddy's office, I know that this would be a perfect moment for me to tell her about Aaron and Miss Sally, but there isn't time. We are interrupted by Daddy's voice.

"Hey, what's with the long faces?"

We've arrived in front of Daddy's office and he's walked outside to greet us. "We were having a little conversation about looking different in Greendale, Mississippi," I say, not attempting to hide the bitterness in my voice. Daddy looks at me with such sympathy as he embraces Celi and puts his arm around me that my heart melts.

"Y'all certainly are different," he says as Celi looks at him with surprise. "You're prettier than any of the girls in all of Washington County!"

Celi looks happy as we go inside and Daddy proudly introduces her to Merle and the other two women on his staff. I exchange fond greetings with these women who've been peripheral to my life for as long as I can remember. Mark returns from a meeting and joins us as we all sit in Daddy's conference room, sipping cold drinks and munching on Merle's famous cheese straws. I allow myself to relax and enjoy my daddy and brother, their wonderful Southern courtesy, and the way Celi seems to feel perfectly at home here, allowing Merle and the other ladies to spoil her rotten.

Chapter 24

Avery

This afternoon is the engagement party at the Collier Plantation. Regardless of Mother's perfectly placed cautions about Celi being too young and Will being too old for the party, we are all going. Given the Southern penchant for courtesy, maybe everything will go smoothly. No ripples, no uncomfortable questions—just polite, light conversation. The thought of having to spend time with Seth Collier is enough to make me want to go screaming back to Denver. But Mark and Nicki will be there as buffers. Celi is excited because Laura Elise and Mason have a swimming pool and they've invited everyone to bring their suits.

The Colliers own a huge piece of property outside of town that was once a family cotton plantation. Will has kept the Reynolds family home, Oak Knoll, almost exactly as it was when it was built in 1840. Nowadays it looks a little shabby around the edges. But the Collier house, which was built around the same time, has been completely renovated. I have to say, I am impressed as we follow the lengthy driveway past the immaculate green lawns and lush flower gardens. Even Will falls silent in appreciation, and Celi is amazed. I keep hearing "Wow!" from the backseat. When the black butler ushers us in the front door, I watch her carefully as she exchanges looks with him.

The butler shows Will, Celi, and me through a stunningly

furnished drawing room, replete with expensive-looking antiques and thick Oriental rugs. I think of my parents' house and wonder if Mother feels she has succeeded over the years in her ongoing quest to keep up with the Colliers. She and Laura Elise have an odd sort of friendship, if you ask me. Mother describes Laura Elise as her dearest friend, but I find it difficult to see genuine warmth between them. The competitive edge in their relationship was apparent to me during lunch at the Randolph.

As the butler opens the wide French doors leading to the stone patio, I spot Mother with Laura Elise, Nikki, and a woman who might be Seth's wife, Alicia Randall. I'm pretty sure he married the belle of our debutante ball. I wonder how she and Seth got together. I notice with guilty satisfaction that she's gotten fat. Today, wearing a clingy pink dress, she looks remarkably like Miss Piggy. The women are studying a designer's display of swatches and colors for the wedding, and I recognize Alicia's childlike voice from across the patio.

At first no one notices Celi, Will, and me. The men are gathered around a patio table examining a set of blueprints, probably for the house that Mark and Nicki are building—on Mason Collier's property, of course. Her daddy can't have his little sugarplum too far away, now, can he? Whew, where did that bitterness come from? My own daddy would have me right next door if I'd let him. And Nicki has been nothing but warm and welcoming. My guard is up mostly because of the man who turns toward us now.

If it wasn't for Mark, I don't think I could stand to be in the same space with Seth Collier. He doesn't look much different than he did in high school—a little taller and thicker, but with the same smug expression and the same obnoxious laugh. I shudder when Seth's the first to reach me and he wraps his arm around my shoulders. It's all I can do to keep from swatting his arm away. He smells of bourbon and cigarettes, just like he did the night of the debutante ball. Today, a salmon-colored Izod polo shirt is stretched across his wide chest, and plaid shorts and loafers complete his outfit.

No one could ever prove that it was Seth, along with Farley

Cole and Landon Hornsby, who beat up Aaron that night. Then again, no one ever tried. It was all swept under the rug. What I've never understood is why Sally Johnson didn't press charges, didn't even try to make those boys pay for what they did. It was 1991, not 1960; surely, the law would have ensured some small measure of justice. Even so, I admit how people like Seth Collier and his parents will never change. Why should they? What incentive do they have? Certainly not the presence of my daughter.

"Mama, would you look here?" Seth is calling, as I try to wriggle from his grip without anyone noticing. "Here's Avery and her little girl and Miss Willadean."

Suddenly there's a high-pitched squeal from across the patio and Alicia comes jiggling across to me and I'm smothered in pink nylon and a cloud of overpowering perfume.

"Avery Louise Pritchett, as I live and breathe! Girl, you look great! That Colorado air must agree with you. I can't believe it's been ten years. . . ."

"Now, baby, let her go," Seth says. "She's got to introduce us to this little girl of hers." Mark must see my plea for help because he immediately comes to stand between Celi and me. Nicki breaks away from a clump of women, including my mother, and joins us. Mother remains where she is, looking tense.

Mark throws his arms around Celi and me. "Y'all remember my big sister, Avery," he says with a grin. "And this beautiful young lady is my niece, Cecelia Louise Pritchett. We call her Celi for short. Celi, this bunch of reprobates and scoundrels is Nicki's family."

Celi giggles softly and murmurs, "Hello."

"Oh my God, Avery," Alicia coos, grabbing my arm and pulling me into her plump side. "She's so pretty!" Mark squeezes Celi gently and my heart aches a little as I watch her squirm at being the center of attention. I know how she hates it. Alicia drones on about having twin boys. "I want a little girl to dress up so bad I can't stand it. Don't get me wrong, I love my boys," she says, "but I would love to have a little girl to spoil." She motions toward the pool where two large identical boys, who look to be about Celi's age, are wrestling loudly under a manmade waterfall that fills the entire end of the natural rock pool. Seth is beaming as he looks at them.

Laura Elise offers us drinks. She shows Celi the pool house and Will offers to go with her to change into her suit, since I can't seem to extricate myself from Alicia. After a few minutes I see them emerge. Will wanders over to the small bar that is set up in the corner of the patio under the shade of a live oak. She strikes up a conversation with the black bartender, in her usual way not bothering to socialize with the *correct* people.

"How do you deal with her hair?" Alicia asks as she watches Celi take two tentative steps into the shallow end of the pool. "I mean, I know their hair is really different. Does she get it wet?"

I'm so taken aback by this bizarre question that I'm unable to speak for a few seconds. *Their* hair? Is my daughter part of some strange category of *them*? Even as I think this, I know that for Alicia she is.

I am not about to tell Alicia Collier that I was initially panicked myself at the thought of trying to fix my own daughter's hair. But I found a black nurse on staff at the hospital who gave me some tips.

"Oh, it's like everything else about parenting," I say, trying to sound nonchalant. "You learn as you go."

"Isn't that the God's honest truth," Alicia says, rolling her eyes and biting into a shrimp. "I sure never thought I'd be having twins." She leans closer, as if we're old friends, and whispers, "Seth and I got married because I got pregnant. It was definitely an accident. But things turned out just fine, don't you think?" she asks, looking around the Collier's lush property. Two young women dressed in white jackets are picking up empty glasses from the tables. I am actually surprised to see that one of them is white.

So Alicia landed Seth by getting pregnant, did she? Isn't that interesting? As I try to figure out how to disengage myself from her, I'm relieved to see Nicki walking over to where we've drifted to watch Celi in the pool. Celi loves to swim. I signed her up for lessons early because every time I'd take her to a pool when she was little, she'd jump immediately into the water. So far, Alicia's twin boys are too busy wrestling each other to take any notice of Celi at the shallow end.

"Alicia, can I borrow Avery for a minute?" Nicki asks, giving me a wink. "I've gotten my dress from Miss Esther and I want to show it to you."

I look again at Celi. She swims like a fish, but I still hate to leave her. Will looks up and sees my dilemma, ends her conversation with the bartender, and walks over to me. "I'll look after her," she says, pointing to a chaise lounge by the pool. "I'll sit right here and stretch out my legs. You go on, now; we'll be fine."

I'm hesitant, but I follow Nicki, Laura Elise, Alicia, and my mother up the stairs to an exquisitely decorated room with a huge four-poster rice bed, a delicate antique lady's writing desk, and a massive rococo armoire. Alicia plops onto the bed, making the whole thing groan like it's about to fall apart. I glance at Mother and notice she's frowning with disapproval at Alicia's bulk. Nicki opens the armoire and pulls out an antique white satin confection of a dress.

Mother comes to stand beside me and we're all admiring the dress when we hear a commotion outside. Mother, who is closest to a window overlooking the back patio and pool, leans over and looks out. "Oh my word!" she says. "What is Willadean doing now?"

I reach the window in time to see Will holding one of Alicia and Seth's chubby twins by the hair. His eyes are wide and he is staring into her face, which is about an inch from his. With her other hand, she is pointing a finger at his dripping chest and saying something that I can't hear.

"I'd better go see what's going on," I say, bolting for the stairs. Behind me I hear Mother's voice calling.

"Tell Willadean to leave those children alone."

I step out onto the patio as Will is dragging the twin by his arm toward Seth. Daddy, Mark, and Mason Collier stand watching. The boy is hollering, "Let me go, lady!" at the top of his lungs, while his brother trails behind, joining in with, "Yeah, you'd better let my brother go!" Beyond them, Celi, still in the water, glides to a stop and comes up to rest her arms on the side of the pool to watch.

I hurry over to where Seth has met up with Will, who has his son in tow. Will is confronting Seth, still holding on to the squirming boy. "Did you not teach these boys of yours any manners, Seth Collier?" she demands, and thrusts the child toward him.

"Boy, what did you do?" asks Seth, as his son stands in front of him, his brother right behind.

"I didn't do nothing, Daddy," he says.

"Ask him what he said," says Will, and I can tell from Seth's expression that he would love to defy my grandmother, but he won't.

"Trey Collier, what did you say? Did you say something rude to Miss Willadean?" Seth asks, taking his son's arm and squeezing it tightly.

"No, sir. I didn't know who that girl in the pool was," he whines. "Ow, Daddy, that hurts," he says, trying to free his arm.

"Your son insulted my great-granddaughter," Will says. "I'm not even going to repeat what Trey said, but he needs to apologize to her."

A look of comprehension comes over Seth's face, along with a patronizing smile. "Yes, ma'am." He turns Trey toward the pool and makes him walk over to the edge where Celi hovers awkwardly. "Go on, now," he prods. "Tell this little girl you're sorry."

"Sorry," he mumbles, barely looking at her.

"Now, y'all go on in the pool house and get dried off and dressed. We're fixing to have some ribs here in a little bit."

"Yes, sir," the boys say simultaneously and waddle toward the pool house with Alicia hustling to catch up to them. Seth returns to the group of men, shaking his head and laughing.

"Boys will be boys," he says, as his father claps him on the back and the men order more drinks from the bartender.

As Will and I stand there awkwardly, Alicia overtakes the twins. They're walking away when I overhear her ask, "Trey, honey, what happened?"

"Nothing, Mama. How come there's a nigger in our pool?"

Trey's words sear into my brain as if I've been burned with a hot iron. It's always there, right under the surface, waiting to rear its head like one of the alligators in the nearby swamp. But this isn't some random racist comment about some random black person. This is about my daughter. I know that Will is watching me and that she can tell I'm seething with anger.

"What did the kid say to her, Will?" I ask through a clenched jaw.

She shakes her head and glances over to see if Celi is listening. She's taken off again and is swimming across the pool.

Quietly, Will says, "He looked up and saw Celi swimming down here at the shallow end and said to his brother, 'Hey, Troy. There's a jig in our pool.' "

I shake my head in disgust, trying to put the boy's words out of my mind, wondering if Celi even knows what that term means. Mother appears at my side, fidgeting with a strand of beads around her neck. Behind us, Laura Elise is loudly giving orders to the waitstaff about serving dinner.

"What happened?" Mother asks, her voice low and apprehensive. Where is the brave woman who confronted Mabel Waverly yesterday at the country club pool?

"Seth Collier's children are simply showing their ignorance," Will replies. The three of us stand watching Celi, all of us at a loss for words.

"Can we just try to get through this?" Mother says, breaking the silence.

"Sure, Mother," I answer irritably. "God forbid we disrupt the Colliers' little soirée." I call to Celi, "How's the water, sweet pea?" and leave Mother and Will to deal with Laura Elise, who descends on us with breathless animation.

"Seth told me what happened," she blurts out. "Is your granddaughter upset, Marion?" I overhear her ask. Am I hearing things, or does she sound like she would like nothing better?

Chapter 25

Avery

When we're back in the safety of our bedroom at Oak Knoll, I decide that it's time for a talk.

"How about you rest for a while, sweet pea," I say. "Swimming is pretty tiring, you know."

"Okay," she says, and I'm surprised at how easily she agrees. I wrap my arms around her and pull her close, surreptitiously checking to see if she feels feverish. I glance down at her hands, looking for swelling.

"You doing okay?" I ask.

She nods and looks contemplative. "Mom, what's a jig?" she asks, and I feel my stomach drop. It breaks my heart to have to answer the question.

"'Jig' is a mean word for a person who's black, kind of like 'nigger,'" I answer, feeling the pain of saying these words out loud to my daughter. I want to strip them of their power. I want to rage at the world, while at the same time teaching her and myself to ignore racism. What's the right way to handle it? Ignore it? Confront it? Is it my job to do that for her since I'm her mother? Or is this her burden to bear—a burden I've saddled her with?

"I've never been called that before," Celi says.

"I know, honey," I answer. "Things are really different here, huh?"

To my amazement, Celi smiles. "Boy, you were really steamed. And I thought Grandma Will was going to pull that boy's arm off. It was kind of funny, actually, him all flabby and drippy, stumbling along behind her while she held on to his arm. He was yelling like he was dying, and his brother yelling, too." Celi giggles at the memory of Trey and Troy.

"I'm glad you can laugh about it," I say, with a wry smile. "Hopefully, they'll learn how inappropriate they were."

"Whatever," she says, shrugging her shoulders. I wonder if she really feels that nonchalant or if she's covering up her hurt. "Everything was kind of awkward after that happened, wasn't it?" she says.

"Yeah, sort of," I answer, remembering how Mark and Nicki tried to smooth over the incident by getting everyone another drink and starting a conversation about their house plans. Daddy and Dr. Collier disappeared into the den. And Laura Elise started talking about her troubles with the caterer for the bridesmaids' luncheon. I could tell Mother was trying to act interested, but she was distracted. Will sat back down in her chaise near the pool and watched Celi, who swam for a little while, demonstrated some of her underwater tricks, and then headed for the pool house to change back into her clothes.

Now Celi stretches out on her bed and I sit beside her. "When I was in the pool house changing back into my clothes," she says, "I heard the sliding glass door open, and when I peeped out I saw that big man named Seth looking for something in the refrigerator. Nicki followed him in, and I don't think they knew I was in the next room changing. I heard Nicki say, 'Seth, you need to teach those boys not to use that language. They're acting like rednecks.' "

"And what did Seth say?" I ask, wanting to hug Nicki and strangle her brother.

Celi yawns, then deepens her voice to sound like Seth. "He said, 'What do you expect? Ain't nobody they know got a high-yellow kid in an all-white family.' Mom, why did he call me high yellow? I'm not yellow, am I?"

"No, honey, you're not." *Dammit! I hate Seth Collier!* I get up from the bed and go in search of the book she's left on the chair, trying to brush back my angry tears without her noticing. "High yellow is another one of those names for people who are mixed race like you. It's old, old stuff, Celi. I'm really sorry you're having to hear it." I clear my throat. "So what did Nicki say?"

"She sounded pretty disgusted with him," Celi says. "She said, 'You're as bad as they are.' I could hear her open the sliding door to leave. And then Seth laughed and said, 'Aw, come on, now, Nick. I'm just kidding. You know I ain't prejudiced. Hell, we hired ourselves a black secretary down at the office.'" Celi mimics Seth's Southern drawl so well that I can't help but laugh. Celi laughs, too, and the tension and fear I was feeling begin to melt a little.

I hand Celi her book, and she takes it and lays it on her stomach. She looks pensive and I can tell there's another question coming. I brace myself. But it's not a question this time.

"I wonder what it would be like to be around the black part of my family," she says, yawning again and closing her eyes.

Now is the time. Tell her now. I open my mouth to explain about Aaron, but before I do, she changes the subject. "Mom, do you think I get called names at home and I just don't know about it?"

"I guess it's possible," I answer with a sigh, deciding I can't do it. I can't talk about Aaron right now. I can't handle anything else today. "There are people like Trey and Seth Collier everywhere."

Celi turns on her side, holding her book out to me. "Will you read to me?"

"Sure," I answer, grateful to lose myself in the Trixie Belden book Celi has discovered on Will's bookshelf. Tomorrow. I'll figure out how to tell her tomorrow.

But tomorrow turns into the next day and the next, and I find myself getting lulled into lazy days spent with Celi and Will, hiding out at Oak Knoll, swimming in the lake, eating wonderful food from Will's garden, and sharing the country life with Celi. Mother calls each day, issuing halfhearted invitations but not putting up much of an argument when I decline, giving some excuse related to what Celi and I are doing. She and Daddy come out to Will's twice for dinner, during which we make small talk, and then we distract ourselves afterward playing Chinese checkers and cards. It is as if all of us are conspiring together to enjoy one another's company and avoid confronting any tough subjects.

Will starts teaching Celi and me to "put up" vegetables, as she calls it. We cut sweet corn off the cob with Will's special corn cutter and make cream corn, pick long rows of purple-hull peas and butter beans, and bring dozens of ripe red tomatoes in from the garden. The cream corn is ladled into serving-size plastic bags and stored in the freezer, along with the peas and butter beans we shell while watching either Will and Sally's soap operas or movies that I rent from Larry and Ruby's limited selection. The tomatoes are stewed and canned in large Mason jars and lined up along the shelves in Will's cool, dark pantry. We fall into our beds at night exhausted and happy from hard work and good food.

Celi is fascinated by everything. She moves from one project to the next, Rufus faithfully following, as if she was born to the country life. To my amazement, she never once complains of being bored or wanting a video or computer game. She is also enthralled with the vintage collection of Nancy Drew and Trixie Belden books that Will keeps on shelves in the front parlor. We read them together, and on Friday evening after Celi falls asleep I'm returning *The Gatehouse Mystery* to the shelf when I notice a small black album, about eight inches square, that has gotten pushed to the back of the shelf and turned sideways.

I take the small scrapbook down, and it opens with a crack of the aging spine to reveal thick yellowed pages. Held inside with old-fashioned "corners" are just three black-and-white photos. The first is of a small group in front of what appears to be a store with an overhead sign saying FRANKLIN DRUGS. I recognize Will's lanky figure in a shirtwaist dress, bobby socks, and plain brown lace-up shoes. To her right stands a man who could only be her father, judging from the thick dark-framed glasses I remember her describing and the white pharmacist's jacket he wears. On her left is a short elderly woman who must be the infamous Miss Inez. Behind the three of them, two young men peek between Will's and her father's heads: one white, one black. They must be Beau Waverly and Henry Johnson.

The second photograph is of Willadean and Sally. I smile at the joy in their young faces. They are seated on the branch of a tree that dips so low it almost touches the ground. This must be the favorite tree that Will always refers to. The third photograph is of a young man in a military uniform who looks like my grandfather, posing with a beautiful raven-haired girl who looks very much like him—probably Jacob and Jerrilyn.

The rest of the pages appear to be blank, but as I'm about to close the album I notice a small corner protruding from the back two pages. When I turn there, a picture that must have become detached flutters to the floor. I stoop to pick it up and gasp as Aaron's face looks back at me. He's wearing a formal military uniform, complete with hat and white gloves. Only it can't be Aaron, because when I look at the back, I find written in Will's familiar scrawl: *Henry Johnson, Camp Lejeune, North Carolina, 1942.*

I tuck the picture back into the album and go in search of Will. I find her at the kitchen table in her housecoat, working a crossword puzzle. She looks up at me over the top of her glasses.

"What you got there?" she asks.

"I found it behind the Trixie Belden books," I say. "It's a photo album."

"Oh, yes," she says, reaching to take it from me. "I remember this. A long time ago I thought I'd start a memory album." She shakes her head as she turns the few pages. "I reckon I didn't get very far, did I?"

"There was one more stuck in the back. It must have come loose," I say, handing her the picture of Henry. I watch her for a reaction.

She runs her fingers across the face in the portrait, pausing on his chest. "Henry, Henry," she says with a sigh. She seems to have forgotten I'm there. I hesitate to break her reverie and wait while she remains lost in her thoughts. After a few seconds, I can't stand the suspense any more.

"Is that Miss Sally's brother?" I ask.

She looks up at me as if she's having a difficult time registering my face. Her eyes are filled with tears and the depth of her grief. Then she smiles through her tears. A soft smile; the smile of a woman with a particularly bittersweet memory. "Yes, it is," she says. "It was taken in the summer of 1942, just a month before he died." Will's expression hardens. "I wish he'd never gone to that training camp."

I can hear the sorrow in her voice. "What happened?" I ask gently, feeling a tremor of excitement that maybe I will finally get answers to my questions.

"It's a long story," she says, sighing, "and the end is not a good one."

"I love your stories, and I want to hear this one . . . if that's okay," I say, sitting down and getting comfortable in a kitchen chair.

Will stares at Henry's picture for a long time, and I'm beginning to think she's forgotten all about me. Her voice, when she first speaks, is uncharacteristically soft, and I find myself straining to hear her, but it's not long before I'm hanging on her every word.

Chapter 26

Willadean

May 1942

"Mama says Mr. Jacob and Miss Jerrilyn are both back home this summer," Henry said as he pushed a case of milk of magnesia onto the storeroom shelf. It was just the two of us in the store. Daddy had gone over to Mound Bayou to consult with the black pharmacist at the new Taborian Hospital. We'd had a delivery truck come in that afternoon, and Henry was stocking while I finished counting money for the bank deposit. I stopped counting, my hands full of dollar bills. I had lost count and would have to start over—again.

"I was beginning to think those two had disappeared," I replied, leaving the stack of money on the counter and sticking my head through the storeroom door to watch Henry. I'd not seen either one of the twins in months.

"Nope, they're back. Mama says Mr. Jacob wants to go over to England and fight the Germans, but his mama doesn't want him to leave on account of his daddy being so sick. Says she needs him on the plantation."

"What about Jerrilyn?" I ask, thinking of the stories I'd overheard Adda Jenkins telling Beau Waverly and the other girls at the soda fountain. I tried not to listen, but sometimes when I was working the counter, I couldn't help but overhear. According to Adda, Jerrilyn had not come back from boarding school quite the lady her mama thought she should be.

"She's downright wild," Adda whispered. "I heard somebody saw her coming out of the Top Hat the other night." The girls were scandalized. The Top Hat was a nightclub down on Walnut Street. Nice girls didn't go there. "When she came out, she was tipsy, and she was wearing . . ." Adda leaned over to whisper and I couldn't hear the rest of the story.

"I reckon she's not too happy being back in Greendale," Henry said. "Mama says she mopes around the house, coming in the kitchen all hours of the day wanting something to eat, or talking on and on about nothing in particular. Mama said she must be bored." Henry stopped to reach into his pocket and pull out a bandana to wipe his sweating face.

I turned back to my counting, saying over my shoulder, "Wouldn't you be bored if you had to be cooped up in that big house with nobody to keep you company but a sick daddy and an old worrywart like Beatrice Reynolds?"

Henry laughed. "I reckon I would."

We fell silent, focusing on our tasks, but I felt a ripple of anticipation at the prospect of meeting Jerrilyn on my next delivery. Since I'd turned sixteen and Henry had taught me to drive, Daddy had started letting me make deliveries on my own during the day. I was due to deliver medicine to Oak Knoll the next morning. As I pushed the wad of money into the bank bag, I imagined striking up a conversation with Jerrilyn Reynolds. I knew she was different from the Adda Jenkinses of Greendale—and so was I. Maybe we could be friends.

It turned out I was to be disappointed. Jacob and Jerrilyn came home in May, but I rarely saw either one of them except from a distance through all of June and July. Once or twice I glimpsed Jacob talking with a group of men outside the courthouse. Jerrilyn came in to the soda fountain twice for chocolate malts. Beau Waverly stumbled all over himself to wait on her. She was a beautiful girl with long wavy dark hair and dark brown eyes. She dressed more like one of those models on the cover of *Harper's Bazaar* than like any of the girls in Greendale. She looked like the picture I'd seen of Ava Gardner, the movie star.

Each time, she would say hello to the other girls who were at the counter as she plunked herself down on a stool. She wasn't very graceful. I admired the way she threw her body around like a young colt learning its legs. Best of all, she wore pants, like Katherine Hepburn, one of my favorite movie stars. Sally and I went to the movies every Saturday; sometimes Henry would join us. I had to sit up in the colored section with them, but I didn't mind. Adda Jenkins kept reminding me that I'd never get a husband if I kept running around with coloreds, but I didn't care. What I liked most about Jerrilyn Reynolds was that she didn't seem to care what people thought, either. When the girls snubbed her at the soda fountain counter, she spent her time charming any boy who happened to be seated nearby, making them green with envy.

Once, I watched her from the corner of my eye while I was waiting on Mrs. Collier and Mrs. Waverly, who openly glared at her, clucking to each other about her unseemly manner of dress. When Jerrilyn looked my way, I smiled, hoping she would see that I was at least a friendly face. But both times she came into the store, I was busy with customers, and she left before I could talk to her.

It was my August delivery before I saw Jerrilyn again. It was sweltering hot and sticky, one of those days when Alligator Lake was so still it made the turtles sunning on the cypress knees look like they were moving fast. I rolled down both windows of the truck, hoping to catch a small breeze, but mostly I caught the red clay of the road in my nostrils. I made my delivery to Miss Beatrice, and as had become my habit, I sneaked around to the kitchen to say hello to Miss Clarice. If I was lucky, she saved a piece of pie or a biscuit for me. As I was fixing to get back in the truck, I heard a sound coming from the hydrangea bushes beside the house, like somebody whispering my name.

I walked closer, and there, tucked in the space between the

shrub and the porch steps, was Jerrilyn Reynolds. She popped her head out and motioned toward me. "Willadean, come over here," she whispered, looking back over her shoulder at the front windows. I was shocked, since she had never said two words to me before. I found myself looking around to see whom she was hiding from.

"Willadean, I need your help!" she said. Now I was wondering how she knew my name and what I could possibly do to help a rich girl like her.

"What's wrong?" I asked, crouching down so that I was eye level with her. She stood abruptly, and I tilted back on my heels and caught myself to keep from falling into the hydrangea. I stood and she emerged then, quickly, grasping my arm and pulling me around the side of the house toward the old dovecote out back. I followed along, struggling to keep up with her and walking awkwardly since she hadn't let go of my arm. She was dressed in high-waisted navy slacks with a narrow red belt. Tucked into her slacks was a prim white shirt with a Peter Pan collar and pearl buttons down the back. I wondered how she got it buttoned. She was wearing red sandals. Feeling overwhelmingly dowdy in her presence, I wondered if I would ever have the nerve to wear clothes like she was wearing.

When we were safely ensconced behind the dovecote, she peeked around the corner once more, then turned to me and said, "I'm in trouble—real bad trouble. And if Mama and Daddy find out, they'll kill me—or worse, they'll send me away somewhere."

"What kind of trouble?" I asked, and I couldn't help feeling excited knowing it was me she had chosen to confide in.

"I'm pregnant," she said, and my heart sank. This was the last thing I had expected her to say. There wasn't anything I could do about that. Did she want to run away? Did she want me to take her somewhere to hide?

"Who is the father?" I asked, but she shook her head, refusing to tell me.

"It doesn't matter," she said, and this shocked me, too. How could it not matter?

"He can never know about it," she said. She spoke of the baby she was carrying as if it was a loathsome thing. "I want to get rid of it," she said breathlessly. "And I need your help."

I was temporarily speechless. I must have looked like I didn't understand because she repeated herself, taking both my upper arms in her hands and shaking me slightly. Her eyes were intense and flashing with anger. "I don't want it. I want it out of me. I hate him. I hate him!" Her eyes filled with tears then, and she let go of me and turned away long enough to wipe her arm across her eyes.

"You hate the baby?" I asked stupidly, not knowing how anyone could hate a little baby.

"No, I don't care about the baby, either, but I hate him for what he did to me." She grasped my hand in hers. "Your father is a druggist. You can get me some kind of medicine from him, right?" Her dark eyes were pleading. "Something to make it come out. I've heard of other girls at boarding school who, you know . . . take something."

I instinctively pulled away from her, horrified and out of my depth. I wanted so much to help her, but at sixteen, I had no idea what she was talking about.

"I'm sorry, Miss Jerrilyn," I said, "but I can't do this."

"Please help me," she begged, and she was crying in earnest now. "My life will be ruined. My parents already think I'm crazy. They'll put me over at Whitfield and I'll die there—I promise I will. Please help me." My heart was breaking for her, and I felt a surge of anger for whoever the man was who had done this to her.

"What about your colored friend, Sally, Clarice's daughter?" she asked. "I've heard that the colored people go to the root doctor when they want to get rid of a baby. Could you ask her?"

I shook my head. A cold chill ran through me thinking of our trip last fall with Miss Clarice to Granny Mathis. "No, no, I can't. Sally can't do something like that," I said. "What about Jacob? Can't he help you?" I asked.

She shook her head, using the back of her hand to wipe her dripping nose. Black mascara streaks ran down her face and my heart ached for her. I had heard of girls being sent away to homes for unwed mothers. But mostly it was gossip, and mostly it came from Adda Jenkins, so I didn't pay much attention. There was that girl last year whose father decided that she was hysterical. Her parents did send her to Whitfield and she never came back.

I heard the creak of the back screen door then, and when I looked around the side of the dovecote, I could see Miss Beatrice standing out in the backyard, shielding her eyes from the sun. "Jerrilyn," she called. "Where've you gone?"

"I'm sorry, Jerrilyn," I said again, feeling horrible for leaving her and utterly disappointed that any chance we may have had for friendship was ruined. "I have to go."

She nodded mutely, her shoulders slumped as if she was resigned to her fate. As I turned to leave, she reached out again, her fingers not quite brushing my arm. She pulled her hand back quickly, as if she was ashamed of begging. "If there's anything . . . You're my only hope."

I ran then. Ran to the truck, threw it in gear, and drove away as fast as I could. Jerrilyn's sad brown eyes possessed me all the way back to Greendale. They haunted me all night and all the next day. On Saturday afternoon Sally and I were sitting on my tree limb facing each other, drinking root beer, and since no one else was around I found myself telling her about Jerrilyn.

"She even asked me about Granny Mathis," I said, watching Sally carefully.

Sally's eyebrows shot up, but then she nodded knowingly. "I heard my mama and her friend Mrs. Elmore talking one day. They were out on the porch and they didn't know I was listening. Mary Elmore, Mrs. Elmore's girl, she's about our age, maybe a year younger. Mary cleaned for a white family over in Indianola. The father was a big-shot lawyer, got her pregnant—I heard her own mother say she was a stupid girl. He promised her all kinds of things to get in her drawers. Then when she came up pregnant he fired her. Granny Mathis got rid of her baby somehow."

"What does she do?" I asked. "Is it an herb or a root? Jerrilyn seemed to think Daddy has some kind of drug."

"I'm not sure," Sally answered. "I'm pretty sure she mixes a potion to make the baby come out." Sally looked at me then and started shaking her head. "No, Willie, no," she said, turning away from me and setting her bare feet firmly in the cool dirt underneath the tree limb. "I know that look you get when you're bound and determined to do something. But this ain't something you need to get mixed up in. And I sure don't need to, either. My mama works for Mrs. Reynolds. If she found out, Mama could lose her job."

"But, Sally," I said, "nobody's going to find out. All's we have to do is wait until nighttime when Daddy's sleeping and we'll take the truck. It'll be quicker that way. You, me, and Henry. We'll take her out to Granny Mathis and she can give her the potion, and we'll bring her back and we'll be done."

"Are you crazy? Do you know what could happen if we get caught?" Sally asked, looking at me like I'd lost my mind. "How come you're so worried about this girl?"

I shrugged and shook my head. "I can't really tell you, Sally. She was so desperate . . . and scared, too. From what little I've seen of old Mr. Reynolds, I could see him putting her away somewhere. That would be so sad." I looked up at Sally and I could see the slightest bit of softening around her eyes. She was still trying to hold her mouth in a tight line, but I knew she was thinking about things.

"I don't think Henry will agree to it," she said.

"Maybe if you tell him it's for me?" I said, and I didn't even comprehend that I was acknowledging something that had been growing between Henry and me. Something that would make him want to do something dangerous just because I needed him to. "You know, I really can't see us braving Big Jack without Henry," I added.

"That's the truth," Sally said, smiling then. "He was gentle with Mama, but I'd hate to surprise him—especially at night." Sally's expression turned anxious again. "Willie, I don't think we should do this. I'm scared."

In the end I talked her into it, and she talked Henry into it. All

I had to do then was figure out how to tell Jerrilyn. I got lucky the next week when she came into the drugstore and sat down on a stool. She looked utterly dejected. Her usually shiny rippling hair was caught up in a ponytail, she wasn't wearing any lipstick, and her clothes were rumpled as if she'd slept in them. Despite Jerrilyn's disheveled appearance, Beau was all eyes. I had to seize my opportunity.

"Beau," I said, speaking firmly to get his attention away from Jerrilyn, who was staring at the menu board as if it was written in Greek, "Daddy needs you out back to help with something."

"Help with what?" he asked, treating me with the surliness I had come to expect since I had refused his advances so often.

"I don't know," I said sharply. "Go see what he needs. I'll help this customer." Beau dragged his heels but trudged obediently toward the back door. I immediately jumped into action.

"Jerrilyn," I said, trying to get her attention. Her eyes were frightening. She seemed to exist outside of herself, and it took several seconds for her to focus.

"Hi, Willadean," she said listlessly. "I'll just have a Coke today." She propped her elbows on the counter and put her head in her hands. "I'm so sick all the time. I can't keep anything down," she whispered. "Mama thinks I've got a nervous stomach, but it won't be long before she learns the truth."

"Listen, Jerrilyn," I said in a low voice, looking around to make sure Beau was still occupied, hoping that Henry could stall him outside for a little while. "You remember the root doctor you asked me about?" Her head jerked up and she looked at me with an eagerness that brightened her features and reassured me so that I could press on. "Meet us tonight at the big willow tree down by the cutoff road from Alligator Lake. Ten o'clock." That was all that I had time to say, as Beau came charging back in.

"Your daddy wasn't even back there, Willadean." He slammed the gate to the soda fountain closed behind him, reaching for his apron and tying it behind his back, then turning to Jerrilyn with dripping courtesy. "Now, how can I help you, Jerrilyn?"

I ignored Beau's stomping around and slid a Coke across the

counter to Jerrilyn, who nodded ever so slightly at me. "Sorry, Beau," I said, turning my attention toward a customer who had come in the door. "I must have heard him wrong."

That night after Daddy was asleep I snuck out the back door, closing it quietly behind me. Henry pushed the truck out onto the road with Sally and me helping. Then he cranked it and Sally and I piled into the cab. Nobody said a word. Henry drove with the lights off until we got through town; then he turned them on so we could see our way out to the lake and the old willow where we were meeting Jerrilyn. I wasn't sure how she was going to get herself there. She'd have to figure out that part.

The truck's lights barely punctured the fog coming off Alligator Lake. Henry stopped the truck at the turnoff and I jumped out. "Jerrilyn," I called softly. "Are you here?" I startled when she appeared out of the fog like a ghost.

"Here I am," she said, grabbing on to my arm like something was after her.

"Are you sure you want to do this?" I asked.

"Yes . . . yes, I'm sure. Let's go." She nodded to Henry and Sally, who remained silent as we turned into the woods. By the time we reached Granny's house, my heart was beating out of my chest. There had been no way to contact Granny Mathis in advance, and I was counting on her letting us in when she recognized Sally. Henry waited for us in the truck.

"This is women's business," he said. "I'm just the driver."

I noticed details I hadn't seen when we were there last time—like the way the Spanish moss hung from the trees, almost touching the leaf-covered ground, and how the air was filled with scents from the swamp water, decaying things, and the smoke coming from Granny's chimney.

The cabin was tiny, but the porch was scrubbed clean. As we approached the door, I noticed a long row of animal skulls hanging along the cabin's outer wall. I looked at Sally, whose eyes were glowing white in her face, and then at Jerrilyn, who was ghostly pale and gripping my hand until I thought my fingers would break.

We had agreed that Sally would be the one to knock. We figured whoever answered the door—Granny or Big Jack—would be friendlier to a colored face. Sally raised her hand and I stood right behind her, with Jerrilyn hovering close to me. Suddenly, the door was jerked open and Big Jack loomed in the open doorway, almost blocking the light from inside. In his hand he clutched a sawed-off shotgun. Sally gasped and stepped backward into me, trodding on my toe. I let out a small scream of fear and pain. Jerrilyn allowed herself to be buffeted by my movement and didn't utter a sound. Her gaze was glued to Big Jack.

"What you want?" he asked as a look of recognition came over his face.

Sally squared her shoulders. I could tell she was trying to be brave. "Miss Willadean Reynolds here has someone who needs to see Granny," she said, her voice trembling.

"Granny sleeping," he barked. "What business y'all got needs to be done at this hour of the night? Can't be nothing good." He turned then, in response to something behind him, and Granny Mathis's small, white-kerchiefed head appeared from under his arm. He stepped back as she moved in front of him.

She was even smaller than I remembered, barely five feet. She wore a simple faded red cotton dress and could have been one of the teachers at the black school, she looked so prim. "What y'all need?" she asked. When she looked over Sally's shoulder and saw Jerrilyn and me, she adopted a suspicious expression.

Sally looked up at Big Jack and then leaned in and whispered to Granny. I caught the words "family way." Granny's eyes got wide for an instant, and then she motioned for us to come in. When we were all inside the cabin, she peered out into the dark and saw the outline of Henry sitting in the truck.

"That the daddy?" she asked, looking at Jerrilyn.

Jerrilyn seemed to have completely lost her voice. Her gaze was darting around the cabin, as mine had been. The front door opened into what appeared to be the main room. In the fireplace, low embers glowed, even though the night was hot and muggy, filling the room with a slight haze of wood smoke. The walls on either side of the fireplace were lined with shelves filled with all manner of glass jars and clay bowls. In the dim light, I couldn't tell what kinds of creatures floated in some of them, and didn't think I wanted to know. The room contained two rocking chairs near the fireplace and a battered wooden table and chairs near a woodstove and dry sink. A door on the right wall must open into a bedroom. Another door, almost hidden among the shelves on the back wall, looked like it led outside. Big Jack disappeared through that portal, shaking his head and muttering, slamming the door behind him.

"No, ma'am," Sally was saying. "That's my brother, Henry." She looked at Jerrilyn, who still hadn't made a sound and was standing so close to me I could feel her trembling. "The daddy is a white man in town. She won't tell us who it is."

Sally and I jumped when Jerrilyn, as if waking from a dream, finally spoke. "Please, ma'am," she begged. "I've heard you've got herbs and such that will make me cramp up and lose this baby. . . ." She stepped forward then and collapsed to her knees in front of Granny. "Please help me. I'll pay you whatever you want."

I was surprised by how gently Granny reached over and laid her hand on Jerrilyn's head. "Get up, child," she said. "Y'all get her into this room," she said, motioning toward the door to our right. It led into a small, immaculate bedroom. The tiny bed was covered with a handmade quilt. Beside it stood a small table holding a kerosene lamp, which was already lit.

Granny had Jerrilyn stretch out on the bed, and she pressed on her belly, while Sally and I stood by, uncertain what to do.

"Child," she said to Jerrilyn, "I'm going to ask you this once, so you need to be sure of your answer."

"Yes, ma'am," Jerrilyn said, her teeth rattling so loudly I could hear them.

"I can see that you're about four months gone, and this baby is a boy," Granny said. I wondered how she knew that by pressing her hands on Jerrilyn's belly, but she seemed absolutely certain. "Are you dead sure you don't want to bring this child into the world?"

Jerrilyn nodded her head vigorously up and down.

"Does the daddy of this baby know that you're killing his child?" Granny asked.

I think we all shivered then. No matter how much she hated the man who'd done this to her, I could see the agony in her eyes when Granny referred to the baby. Jerrilyn got a hard look on her face then, and she spoke so quietly we had to lean in to hear her. "The father of this baby will never admit that it's his, and I'm the one who will die, because if my mama and daddy find out, my life will be over." Jerrilyn was crying; fat tears rolled down the sides of her face into her ears.

"All right, then," Granny said. She reached under the bed and pulled out a large canvas bag. I couldn't see what was in it, but it looked like a tool bag. Cold fear gripped my belly. What was she going to do?

"You girls need to step out," she said.

"No," Jerrilyn begged through her tears. "Please let them stay. Please!"

But Granny refused, pushing us out the door and closing it firmly behind her. "Out on the porch, both of you," she said. "Big Jack," she called, and I heard bedsprings creak from the back porch and footsteps as Jack came back into the room. "See that these girls stay out on the porch," she said. It took only one look from Jack for us to file obediently out of the cabin. The key clicked in the door, locking us out.

Sally and I sat together on the porch steps. As the minutes passed, I kept looking around, wondering where that alligator was I had seen last time we were there, also wondering if I'd dreamed it. The hypnotic music of cicadas and the eerie groans of the swamp filled my ears, and my knees were knocking together, I was so scared. I tried to tell myself that I was doing the right thing, helping Jerrilyn. And that's when she started to scream.

Sally and I reached the door at the same time. We pounded on it, hollering for Granny to tell us what was going on. Big Jack opened the door and blocked us with the wall of his body. He grabbed my arm and his hand swallowed it up like it was a stick. "Y'all need to calm yourselves," he said. "Granny ain't gone hurt that girl."

Henry must've heard the screams from the truck, because I heard him coming up the steps behind us. But we all had to stop, helplessly, in the face of Big Jack's ominous glare.

And then, as abruptly as the screaming started, it stopped. Granny emerged a few minutes later, wiping her gnarled hands on a towel, and I was horrified to see that it was stained with bright red blood. "What happened?" I asked frantically.

"She was too far along for the root to work quick as she wanted," Granny said, shaking her head. "Begged me to use the hook." Sally and Henry and I looked at each other, afraid to ask what that meant. "Y'all can come in now."

"I'll wait in the truck," Henry said, escaping to the safety of the yard.

Jerrilyn was stretched out on the bed, looking as pale and still as a corpse. Granny Mathis handed me a bottle containing some kind of liquid and took us both aside. "I've given her this to make her sleep," she said. "But y'all got to make sure she takes this other one brewed in a tea every few hours." And she shoved a cloth bag full of something dried and crackly into my hands. Sally and I exchanged looks. We knew we were in trouble, because we thought we'd be taking her home that night, not looking out for her. This had gone all wrong. We didn't have any idea what we'd gotten ourselves into.

"She's going to bleed for two or three days. If the bleeding gets bad, she needs to go to the white doctor in town. Sometimes they bleed; sometimes they die. You girls have bought yourselves a lot of trouble. Y'all need to get her home and stay out of this." Granny bent down and picked up a stack of quilts, piling them into Sally's arms. "Go make her a bed in the back of that truck," she ordered. "Big Jack will bring her out."

"But, but . . ." I panicked. "Couldn't she stay here until she's better?" I asked, terrified at the prospect of being responsible for Jerrilyn.

"No," Granny said firmly. "She can't stay here. Now, I've done what I can. Y'all gone have to take over from here."

Sally and I argued over what to do with her and finally decided we'd have to take her back to my house. I had no idea how I was going to explain her presence to my daddy. We placed Granny's quilts in the back of the truck and loaded her in there, bundling her up tight based on Granny's advice to keep her warm. I didn't see how anyone could be cold in this heat, but I believed Granny knew best. We started back down the dirt road, and we'd just pulled onto the main road back to town when lights shone in the mirror from a car behind us.

My blood ran cold when Henry said, "Uh-oh, we got trouble now." I could hear the fear in his voice.

"What do we do?" Sally and I asked simultaneously.

Henry kept his eyes focused on the road. I was amazed at how calm he was. "Sally, you need to sit still and let me do the talking. Willie," he said, glancing over at me, "you need to get down on the floorboard."

"I will do no such thing," I insisted. "I'm not scared."

Henry growled in frustration. "Willie, if that's white men and they see a white girl in the cab of this truck, what you think they going to do?" I knew he was right, so I ducked down as the other car pulled up beside us.

From my position on the floorboard I couldn't see anything. I felt Henry pulling the car over and I whispered, "What's going on, Sally?" She kicked at me with the toe of her shoe and placed her finger over her mouth for me to be quiet. I could see the sweat dripping from Henry's chin, and he was gripping the steering wheel so tight his knuckles looked almost as white as mine in the glow of the headlights of that other car. I saw Sally turn to look in the back and make sure Miss Jerrilyn wasn't moving around. Please God, let her stay asleep.

I heard a car door open and shut. Henry let out a breath then. "Oh, sweet Jesus," he said. "That there is Jacob Reynolds." I wasn't sure whether to be relieved or more frightened. I knew nothing about Jacob Reynolds. Sally had said that he was a quiet boy who didn't have much to do with her or Henry, but Miss Clarice said he was always polite to her. Henry rolled down the window.

I could hear the gravel under Jacob's feet as he walked to the truck window. I didn't know whether to stay down in the floorboard or get up. I wanted to be sure that he didn't blame Henry or Sally for my doing. I heard him say to Henry in a quiet voice, "Evening."

"Evening, Mr. Jacob," Henry answered.

"Y'all haven't seen my sister, Jerrilyn, out around these parts, have you?" Jacob asked. "She's disappeared from the house. She's not at some of her usual spots in town, and I'm worried about her. She hasn't been acting right lately." I could see Sally and Henry look at each other, and in that split second when they were trying to figure out how to answer him, Jerrilyn awakened, moaning in pain.

I couldn't stand it anymore. I came spilling out from the truck and ran around to where Jacob stood. I must have scared him, because he jumped back. "What the hell?" he asked. After he quickly assessed that I was no threat, he started for the back of the truck. Before he could reach over and pull the quilt back from Jerrilyn's face, I grabbed his arm.

He turned on me. "Who the hell are you, and where'd you come from?" he demanded. "What are y'all up to out here?" He looked suspiciously at Henry and Sally, then wrenched his arm away from me.

"Jacob, this has nothing to do with Henry and Sally. This is something your sister talked me into," I said. He looked at me then, and I could see the panic in his eyes.

"My sister? You mean that's Jerrilyn under there?" And before I could stop him, he pulled back the quilt from her face.

She opened her eyes, blinking wearily, and slurred, "Jacob? What are you doing here?" She was out of her head. Before he could answer her, she was begging him not to tell her mama and daddy. She kept saying, "They'll put me away, Jacob. They'll put me away."

Jacob grabbed me by the shoulders and shook me. "What's happened?" he hollered.

I was trembling all over, realizing how much trouble I had caused by giving in to that girl, and pulling Henry and Sally in, too. I had no idea what this man was going to do to us or to his sister. I mustered up every bit of courage I could find and I got right back in his face and said, "Your sister is in bad trouble, Jacob Reynolds. She couldn't get any help from her own family, so she came to me—a perfect stranger—for help! I'm only doing what she begged me to do, and Henry and Sally are only here because I convinced them to help me."

He backed off a little bit then, and dropped his hands from my shoulders. He looked over at Jerrilyn. She had closed her eyes again and she continued to whimper in pain, sounding like an injured wild dog. I climbed into the back of the truck, gripping the bottle Granny had given me. "She was pregnant," I said, spitting out the words. "She begged us to take her to Granny Mathis."

"You took her to a root doctor?" he exploded.

"She wouldn't go to Dr. Collier," I yelled back at him. "She was afraid your mother and daddy would put her away somewhere." I was angry with him now. It didn't make any sense, but I took out all my pent-up fear on him. "Whoever it was got her pregnant, she hated him. I don't know what happened, but she desperately wanted to get rid of this baby." I knelt beside Jerrilyn and picked up her head, intending to pour more of the murky brown sleeping liquid down her throat. Jacob, looking frightened, climbed into the truck on her other side.

It was then that I noticed the wetness through my skirt. When I looked down, I could see the black outline of two wide patches of blood covering my knees. Jerrilyn's bleeding had soaked through to the quilts underneath her. My voice caught in my throat, and all I could do was point at my skirt. "She's . . ."

Jacob saw it first. "We've got to get her to King's Daughters," he said. He knelt and began to search for the edges of the quilt to pick his sister up.

Realizing what had happened, Henry stopped him. "Wait," he said. "Don't move her. I'll drive."

Jerrilyn must have been more awake than we thought because she screamed in anguish. "No! You can't take me there! Mama and Daddy will find out!"

"It doesn't matter," Jacob argued. "Jerri, you're bleeding bad. We've got to get you to a doctor." She was crazy then, swearing and screaming. She sat bolt upright and glowered at Jacob. All the blood had drained from her face, her hair was loosened from its clip and fell halfway across her face, and the black circles under her eyes made her face look as hollow as a skull. "Jacob Reynolds," she said. "If you let Dr. Collier touch me again, my blood is on your hands. This was his baby I got rid of. I'll die before I go near any hospital where he is!"

As all of us went statue still in disbelief, all the strength left Jerrilyn and she fell back in a dead faint. It was Henry who suggested we take her to the new Taborian colored hospital over in Mound Bayou. That was nearly forty miles away, but we didn't know what else to do. So Sally and I got in the back with Jerrilyn, and Jacob got in the cab with Henry, and Henry drove as fast as he could to Mound Bayou. Henry knew those roads like the back of his hand. He got us there in around forty-five minutes.

But it was too late. The black doctor did his best to save her, but she'd lost too much blood. Henry, Sally, and I were numb with shock and grief. She was such a beautiful girl, so young. Jacob broke down and cried in my arms like a baby.

Henry and Sally waited outside in the hallway, unsure what to do. Sally told me later that she and Henry were certain that Jacob was going to blame them. They were thinking they may have cost their mama her job. But it wasn't like that at all. Jacob Reynolds was a fine man.

After he got hold of himself, he shook Henry's hand and patted Sally on the shoulder, and he said, "I know y'all were trying to help her, and I appreciate it. She was a stubborn thing, couldn't nobody tame her. And when she got her mind set on something, there wasn't anything could stop her. She'd have found a way to do this, no matter what."

I feel that old heavy sadness come over me, thinking about that summer so long ago. Avery is listening quietly. All we can hear now are the squeaks and groans of this old house settling in for the night. I sigh, looking down at the yellowed photograph of Henry in his uniform. How proud he was to be a marine—even with the way he left town. I'd never seen my daddy so angry. I look over at Avery and realize she's spoken.

"What was that, honey?" I ask.

"I said what a horribly sad story. What did Grandpa Jacob do?"

"That night when we left the hospital, Henry talked Jacob out of finding Dr. George Collier and killing him on the spot. He convinced Jacob to go home, tell his mother what had happened, and try to deal with Collier in the morning, when he had a clearer head."

"I hope Collier got what was coming to him," Avery says angrily.

"No, honey," I say, "it didn't work that way in Greendale. It was Jerrilyn's word against Dr. Collier's, and Jerrilyn was dead. Miss Beatrice wouldn't believe a word of it. She just wanted to make sure that the pregnancy and abortion stayed hushed up. She insisted that Jacob tell the undertaker that Jerrilyn had suffered a terrible illness while visiting a friend in New Orleans and had died suddenly. This was to be the story in the community. Since Beatrice was essentially useless and had to remain with Mr. Reynolds, I ended up helping Jacob get all of her arrangements made.

"The most difficult thing was when Jacob asked me to accompany him to confront Collier. He said that he knew I could keep my wits about me and help him be civil. Me, imagine that," I say, shaking my head. "Dr. Collier ushered us into his office; he was full of condolences and sympathy, asking us what he could do for us. Jacob got right to the point and described what happened, including Jerrilyn's accusation. I still remember what Collier said in response. 'Now, Jacob, we both know that your sister was, shall we say, a little loose with her favors. I was probably the first one who came to mind when she was desperate. It would break your mother's heart if this kind of thing got out around town, now, wouldn't it?'

"Jacob was so torn that it ate him up inside. He knew he could never prove anything about Collier, but he believed his sister's story. He sat silently for several seconds staring at the floor; then he looked up at Collier and said in a low, steely voice, 'You know that I can't prove anything, you lying bastard, but mark my words, I will be watching and listening. If you so much as mention anything disparaging about my sister in this town, or if you ever lay your filthy hands on another innocent girl, and I find out about it, I'll find a way to make you suffer.' Collier sat back then, obviously intimidated by the power of Jacob's threat. He didn't respond. We got up to leave, and as we were walking out the door, Collier said, 'Willadean Franklin, I suggest you consider carefully the kind of people you keep company with. And I am not referring to our good man Jacob, here.' I was the one scared then, afraid of what he might do to Sally or Henry.

"Jacob and Henry got to be friends after that. And when Collier threatened Henry, it was Jacob who told Henry about the marines taking colored soldiers up at Camp Lejeune. By the end of the summer Henry had signed up."

"Wait a minute," Avery says. From her confused expression, I figure I must have left something out. "Why did George Collier threaten Henry? Because he knew about Jerrilyn?"

"That's right," I say. "I still don't know how he found out, but Dr. Collier knew that the three of us had tried to help Jerrilyn. Old Collier knew he couldn't do anything to me or Jacob, and he knew no one would listen to Sally since she was a black woman, but he could make accusations against Henry that he knew would get him lynched."

"What kind of accusations?" she asks, leaning forward.

"He came to see my daddy late one night not long after Jerrilyn was buried. I could hear them talking through my bedroom door. At first he was all friendly, acting like he and Daddy were colleagues, them both being in medicine and all—"

"Had you told your father what had happened to Jerrilyn?"

I think back to that night, remembering Daddy's stern face as he stood waiting when I came rolling into the yard early that next morning. "Yes, I did," I answer. "I was so exhausted and heartbroken, I fell into Daddy's arms and confessed the whole thing. I remember the look of cold anger that came over him when I told him about Dr. Collier. He was silent for a long time. And then he said, 'That young girl died, and her story died with her. Now that bastard will be able to do the same thing again.' He slammed his fist down so hard onto the hood of the truck that he left a dent in it. He grabbed me by the shoulders and I was terrified. My daddy had never hit me, but he was so angry, angrier than I'd ever seen him. But he didn't hit me. He pulled me close to him and hugged me hard. 'Willie, don't you ever let yourself be alone with that son-of-a-bitch. And if he ever so much as gives a hint of laying a hand on you, you got to tell me.' He squeezed me harder. 'Right away, you hear?'

"I promised him I would. He and Leroy cleaned the blood out of the truck and burned the quilts. And we went on with our lives. We attended Jerrilyn's funeral. I was shocked to see Dr. Collier there with his wife, acting all sympathetic toward Miss Beatrice. Mr. Reynolds was too sick to attend his own daughter's burial. Jacob spent all of his time watching out for his mother, which was probably a good thing, because he was boiling with hatred toward George Collier."

"So you said that Dr. Collier came to visit your father?" Avery asks, reminding me that I've gotten sidetracked.

"Yes. Yes, he did. But Daddy wasn't having any of it. When Collier found out he couldn't find an ally in Daddy, that's when he threatened Henry. I could hear him through the wall and I still get chills thinking about what he said. 'That girl of yours is awfully cozy with niggers,' he said. 'Be a shame if some of the boys took it in their minds to teach that Henry Johnson a lesson about spending so much time around a white girl.' Daddy threw him out then. Demanded he leave our house. And I prayed that would be the end of it."

"But it wasn't?" Avery asks.

"No. I guess the threat was real, because Jacob and Daddy talked Henry into joining the marines. It didn't take much talking. Henry had always wanted to see the world. He thought this might be his chance."

"Did he go overseas?"

"No, he died before he ever got out of that training camp," I answer, remembering the day Sally came to tell me that a soldier had shown up at their door with a death notice. I thought Miss Clarice was going to die herself that day.

"What happened?" Avery asks.

"They said it was heat exhaustion. Said his heart just stopped. They were doing some hard training, and it was hot, real hot. He came in from training that day, and he was still breathing hard, said he wanted to sit down on his cot for a minute before he got in the shower. And when his buddy got out of the shower, Henry didn't respond. He never even got to wear his uniform except for this picture," I say, feeling the tears forming.

Avery shakes her head and mumbles something about the sickle-cell trait.

"What's that you say?" I ask.

"I think it was sickle cell, Will," she says. "Do you remember a few years back that boy died right after football practice at Ole Miss?"

"Yes, seems like I do recollect that. He was a healthy boy and died all of a sudden."

"That's right. What they think now is that some of these guys have the sickle-cell trait, though not the disease like Henry's mother had. But if they get severely stressed—like with extreme heat and workouts—then they have the same problems with their blood carrying enough oxygen as a person with sickle-cell disease does. And their bodies can't handle it and they have a severe crisis and sometimes die."

"Do you think there's any way we could have known that?" I ask.

"No, ma'am, I don't," she says. "We've only recently begun to figure this stuff out. In 1942, we didn't know any of it. Not even about him carrying the trait."

I'm surprised to feel warm tears running down my wrinkled old cheeks. I reach in my pocket for my handkerchief and wipe them away. "I reckon that's enough storytelling for one night, young lady," I say, trying to sound perkier than I feel.

"You loved him, huh?" Avery asks, looking at me with compassion.

I sniff and blow my nose. "Yes, I did. Henry was a fine man. I'll never forgive myself for involving him in that ordeal with Jerrilyn." I get up and place my crossword pencil in the chipped cup where I keep it on the table. I tuck my handkerchief back in my pocket and drop a kiss on Avery's head. "Now, I've got to get some sleep, and I suggest you do the same."

I look back as I leave the kitchen and she's still sitting at the table looking lost in thought.

Chapter 27

Avery

My arms are full of towels, sunscreen, and my and Celi's hats. Every day after breakfast on the porch and some work in the vegetable or flower gardens, Celi and I head down to the dock to cool off in Alligator Lake. The wedding is only nine days away, and so far this week I've managed to avoid any more major confrontations. Of course, that I haven't left Oak Knoll helps, but I keep telling myself it's good for Celi. And look at all the information I've gleaned from Will. I'm certain now that she and Henry were lovers. That has to have been what happened. It's obvious to me how much she loved him. She as much as admitted it. She must have been pregnant when he died, and then she married Jacob because she didn't know what else to do. If only I could figure out the right way to ask that question—to confirm my theory.

I think of Mother and wonder again how she would feel if she learned that Henry Johnson is her biological father. No one would ever guess from her appearance that Mother is half black. If there's anything I've learned about inheriting skin color, it's that it's unpredictable. Celi inherited more African-American features, but not every mixed-race child does; hair, eyes, skin tone—they all depend on what that dancing spiral of DNA decides to reveal. I suppose Will never had to explain she was carrying Henry's baby because Mother was born looking as if she could easily be Jacob's child. I wonder who knew. Maybe Sally? Maybe Grandpa?

The ringing of my cell phone is an incongruous sound among the splashing made by Celi's and Rufus's bodies hitting the lake. They've established a ritual of diving off the dock together every morning. She throws in his toy and then jumps in after it at the same time he does. She paddles in place while he retrieves the toy.

"Stay where I can see you," I say, digging for my phone in my bag, while still keeping my eyes on Celi.

I don't stop to check who's calling, just flip the phone open and answer a little out of breath. "Hello?"

"Hey, Avery. . . . It's Aaron," says a warm, familiar voice.

"Oh. Hey."

I drop onto the wooden planks of the dock beside my bag. I glance up to be sure that Celi is safe. She's climbing up the ladder now, preparing to throw Rufus's toy for him again. Rufus sits perched on the edge of the dock, trembling with anticipation. He makes a whining noise—something between a whimper and a low growl—while he's waiting for her. His tail thumps against the dock in excitement. As many times as they repeat this process, it never ceases to make Celi laugh. Her laugh is like Aaron's, rich and deep, coming from low in her belly.

"Is this a bad time?" he asks. "Sounds like someone's having fun."

I hear the pain in his voice. He knows who that "someone" is. Immediately my guilt over procrastinating in telling Celi grips me and turns to irritation. Why is he rushing me? Doesn't he know how difficult this is?

"Um . . . no . . . I mean, it's okay." I search for something to say. "How are you?"

"I'm doing okay. Busy, you know, with new patients and being on call and all . . . You?"

"Doing well. Busy, too." I wave at Celi, who is jumping into the lake once again. I wonder vaguely if she's overdoing it. I also debate whether to ask her to be quieter.

"So, what's all the commotion?" he asks.

"That's Celi and Will's dog, Rufus, you're hearing. They like to jump into the lake together," I reply, feeling strange talking to him about his own daughter.

"Oh, okay. I thought it was probably something like that. Sounds like my boys. When it comes to water, all they want to do is jump—in and out, in and out." He laughs and I laugh nervously with him, wondering where we're going with this conversation. We're both quiet for several seconds, each waiting on the other to talk. Then we speak at the same time.

"So, did you tell—" I start to ask.

"Did you talk to—" he asks.

"Uh, sorry, go ahead," I say, knowing what he's going to ask me, and how my answer will disappoint him again.

"I was going to ask if you had a chance to talk to Celi."

My heart is racing now with the fear of angering or hurting him, yet again. Why can't I be stronger? Why can't I make myself bring him up with her? "Um . . . not yet. But I am going to have a conversation soon." I look up and Celi has stopped playing with Rufus. She must see that my expression is apprehensive because she drops his toy and starts toward me.

"Mom, is everything okay?"

I hear Aaron start to say something, but I'm too busy figuring out how to respond to Celi. I only catch the words "really want to" before I say, "Could you hold on for a second?"

"Sure," he says with a sigh.

I pull the cell phone down beside my hip, as if Celi can see Aaron through it, and say, "Yep, everything's fine. I'll be off the phone in just a minute, okay?" Celi nods and heads for the ladder, and I have an idea. "Celi," I whisper, and she turns toward me. "Could you go up to the house and get us a grape soda?" I feel really bad now, plying my child with bribes of soda when I'm always fussing at her about drinking too much of it. But the ruse works. She nods eagerly, slides on her flip-flops, and with Rufus trailing, heads up the slope to the house.

"Sorry about that," I say, putting the phone back to my ear.

"It's okay," he says. "Look, Avery, I know this is hard, but y'all aren't going to be here that much longer and I really want to spend some time with Celi. . . . That is, if she's willing once she meets us."

The "us" catches my attention. "So you've talked to Lacretia about her?" I ask.

"Yep," he answers.

"And?"

"It went as well as could be expected, I guess. She's pretty upset, but we'll get through it." He clears his throat. "Haven't told the boys yet, though. Lacretia says she's not ready for that, and, well . . . I guess I feel it should be her call."

I consider how Lacretia must feel to learn her husband has not only an old lover, but also a child he's never met. Celi's impact on our lives—through no fault of her own—hits me, and my irritability is replaced by a deep despondence.

"Yes . . . that makes sense," I say, at a loss for words now. I'm half grateful when Aaron takes the lead.

"I was thinking that we should plan a time for Celi and me to meet each other. There's really no way to do this gradually. I'm on call Friday and Saturday at the hospital, but I was thinking we might meet on Sunday afternoon? You could talk to her between now and then." He pauses and then adds quickly, "I don't want to rush you, Avery, but . . . I've been waiting almost ten years. . . ." When I don't respond immediately, he continues, "What do you think?"

So often in my life I've taken charge, done what I needed to do, been the caretaker, made the decisions. But now? Now I find myself so fraught with conflict that I'm completely weary. At least Aaron is taking action, trying to move us forward—toward what I'm not sure, but at least I'll get past this damnable eddy of emotion that I'm swirling in.

"Sounds good," I say, trying to convey an enthusiasm I don't feel. "You name the place, and we'll be there."

"Great," he says, sounding vastly relieved. "I want you to know that I've thought about this a lot—where to meet, that is. Playground, the lake, restaurant . . . none of them sound right.

So . . ." He pauses. "I think we should meet over at my grandmother's house."

"But—" I start to say.

"Now, let me finish," he says gently. "Celi's already met Sally and likes her a lot, right?"

"Right," I answer.

"And she's already familiar with Sally's place?"

"Yes—we didn't go inside, but generally, yes."

"That's why I think it would be a good place. No prying curious eyes. Just us and Sally, and we know that Celi's already comfortable with her. And, Avery, this will make my grandmother so happy. It would mean so much to me. It's hard to explain, but . . ." His voice breaks and my heart is aching for him and for the family we missed having together. I hear his breath catch as he controls his emotions. "Anyway, it feels like the right way to do it."

I brush away tears as I look up and see Celi approaching with a wide grin on her face and a frosty grape soda in each hand. I hurry to respond, wishing I had better words for all that I'm feeling. "That makes sense to me. Oh, look! Here comes Celi," I say, feeling horrible for cutting off this conversation and praying he'll forgive me for my callousness.

"Right," he says, acknowledging my dilemma. "How about two o'clock, Sunday afternoon? Meet you there?"

"That sounds fine," I say cheerfully. "See you then."

Before I flip my phone closed he stops me. "And, Avery . . ."

"Yes?" I say, reaching to take the soda Celi thrusts toward me.

"Thanks."

"Bye," is all I can manage, and we each hang up. I shift my attention immediately to Celi, but the whole time we're pulling our floats into the lake, climbing on top of them, and paddling around while Celi pretends we're pirates exploring a hidden cove, I'm distracted with trying to figure out the best way to tell her that in three days she will meet her father.

Chapter 28

Avery

I'm driving home feeling proud of myself for having survived yet another wedding event—this one, the bridesmaids' luncheon. It was held at the club, of course. Nicki is a great girl and I've enjoyed getting to know her better, but I'm also glad I don't have to judge her by her friends: a classic collection of coy young Southern women. If I heard "Y'all look so cute" one more time, I might have had to leave the room.

Celi stayed out at Oak Knoll with Will today. She would have loved the luncheon, but Nicki specifically said that it was a "big girl" event. That meant lots of alcohol. Those girls sure can put away the booze. Their mamas must have trained them well. The poor waiter kept bringing round after round of a drink called the Southern Belle. I'm not sure what was in it, but there was plenty of rum and peach schnapps. I had to stop after one since I was driving. But the girls had rented a stretch white limousine and they were still at it when I left.

I need to get back to Oak Knoll because today is the day I tell Celi about her father. I promised myself that. As soon as I get home, we're going swimming. And while we're sitting out on the dock, I'm going to tell her that tomorrow afternoon she will meet her father. There's no getting around it anymore.

As I drive up to the house, I don't see Will or Celi outside.

Maybe they're out in the garden, but I don't find them there. The house seems awfully quiet when I enter.

"Hey, Will. Where's Celi?" I ask, walking into the kitchen. Will's at the sink washing dishes. She turns to me with a frown.

"She wasn't feeling too good this afternoon. I told her she'd best lie down for a while. She's in y'all's room, and I gave her another old book from my shelf to read. She didn't want to start it without you, but I told her I didn't think you'd mind."

I try to keep the panic out of my eyes so Will doesn't see it. Celi being willing to lie down in the middle of the day usually means one thing—she's going into crisis.

"I'll go check on her," I say.

Our room is dim in the afternoon light. Will has closed the curtains, and it's quiet except for the low drone of the ceiling fan. Celi is lying on her back, sleeping, a Trixie Belden book propped on her chest. Rufus is curled up on the rug beside the bed. He looks up when I enter, sees me, and immediately puts his head back down. I debate whether to touch her. I don't want to wake her, but I need to know if the fever has started.

While I'm agonizing over what to do, she stirs, and her eyes flutter open. She squints in the weak light and sits up, rubbing her eyes. The book falls from her chest and tumbles down onto Rufus.

"I'm sorry, Rufus," she says, and I can hear a scratchiness in her voice—that husky tone I've come to associate with an impending respiratory infection. Damn! "Hi, Mom," she says, and we exchange a look—the one that says she knows what I'm going to ask.

I move over to her and sit down on the side of the bed, immediately reaching for her forehead, pushing the hair from her eyes. Her skin is hot and clammy, and as I take her hands in mine, I can feel the familiar puffiness in her fingers. Apprehension fills my stomach with acid. This is how it always starts.

"Hey, sweet pea," I say. "How long have you been feeling like this?"

"It started this afternoon. Grandma Will is really worried

about me. I told her I'm okay; I just need to rest," she says. Her eyes look watery and lack their usual sparkle.

I go into nurse mode; I can't help it. When Celi is at risk for a full-blown sickle-cell crisis, it automatically kicks in. Even though my attention irritates her and makes her feel like a sick patient, I have to do it—it's the only sense of control I can gain over this shitty disease.

"I'm going to get you some Tylenol, and I want you to drink the whole glass of water with it," I say, getting up. "Is the pain really bad?"

"Not yet," she says with a sigh. "I was trying to be really still, like you said to do when I start to feel it coming, and I drank lots of tea today, so I'm not dehydrated."

I notice the half-full glass of tea on the nightstand and pick it up, forcing myself not to scold Celi. She doesn't understand that Will's tea is caffeinated and full of sugar, which will only dehydrate her more. I wonder how much she's had today, in her zeal to follow my constant reminders to drink lots of fluids in this Mississippi heat. "I'll be right back," I say, heading for the kitchen.

"How's she doing?" Will asks. "Do you think she's getting a cold?"

Why can't I bring myself to tell my own grandmother the truth?

My mother's words echo through my mind: *"They're different from us, Avery,"* she said the day she found out I was pregnant with Aaron's baby. *"White people were not meant to mix with black."* Even though I know that Will would never say anything like that, the fear of my mother's "I told you so" has caused me to protect Celi for so long that it's become a habit.

"She might be," I say as I reach for a glass from the cabinet. "I'm going to give her some Tylenol and see if that helps her feel a little better. I think I'll keep her in bed this evening."

"That sounds good," she says, still looking worried. "Seems like it came on so sudden. We were out in the garden, and I found some hornworms on one of my tomato plants. I was surprised that she was fascinated with them, so different from when we found those earworms on the corn. I was having to convince her that we had to kill them or they'd eat my tomatoes. All of a sudden she got real flushed and it seemed she was breathing faster. She didn't say anything, though. It was almost like she hoped I wouldn't notice. The spark went out of her eyes, and I asked her if she'd like to go in the house and have a glass of tea. Well, she took to that right away, and then she took me up on my suggestion for a nap." Will nods knowingly. "That's when I knew she wasn't feeling good."

I inwardly cringe as I listen to Will relay the familiar pattern of responses that typically precede Celi's sickle-cell crises. Should I explain? Will she notice how worried I am?

"I'll take her this Tylenol, and maybe she'll feel like coming to the table for supper," I say, hurrying out of the kitchen before Will can ask any more questions.

Chapter 29

Willadean

I have a sick, sad feeling in my bones. I've seen this before and it's all too familiar. Surely Avery knows that little girl's got that awful disease. For some reason, neither one of us is talking about it. I wonder how long Celi's been sick. I want to ask Avery, but I'll wait until she's ready to tell me. Maybe she's protecting Celi. That child is a spunky one. I'm sure she doesn't want folks treating her like she's an invalid.

I remember when Sally and I finally understood about Cleome, Aaron's mama, who died so young giving birth to him. It was sickle cell that killed her. Avery seems to think having the trait is what killed Henry. My heart still weeps when I think of him, so young, so strong. The last time I saw him he was headed off to Camp Lejeune in North Carolina. He was so proud to be one of the first black men to train for the marines. Whenever I see Celi, I'm reminded of Henry. What would have happened if he hadn't died? I'll never know.

Telling Celi and Avery stories of those long-ago years has brought back so many memories of Henry. It's not that Jacob and I didn't have a good life together. We did. I loved him and I believe I was a good wife to him. But Henry . . . No one, not even Sally, knows how much I loved Henry. I didn't admit it even to myself for a very long time. But when that hole in my heart was never quite filled up, even by the birth of my beautiful baby, Marion, I finally understood it was because of losing Henry. Maybe it was seeing his mama in constant pain that made Henry so sensitive. Clarice barely outlived him. It was as if Henry was born old. He didn't want me to drag him into that trouble with Jacob's sister, Jerrilyn, but what was I to do?

February 1942

Henry had just returned from making the last delivery of the day. It was early evening, still chilly in the deep shade when winter's last pockets of coolness seeped out of the corners of the back lot. I pulled my sweater closer as I walked out to greet him.

"How'd it go?" I asked.

"Oh, well as could be expected, I reckon," Henry replied.

The last delivery was for Miss Inez, who'd fallen sick right after Christmas. The doctor said there was nothing they could do. The poor old woman was dying alone in her little house on Washington Avenue—with no family to care for her. Leroy fixed her supper every evening and Henry delivered it. Henry and I took turns helping her eat it. At first she wouldn't let Henry come in the door, but he was so kind and so persistent that he wore her down. Now she let him feed her same as me.

"How's she feeling today?" I asked.

"Not too good, Miss Willie," he said. "I could scarcely get her to eat a bite." The look of concern on his face touched my heart. Since we'd all been working together to help Miss Inez, I'd begun to be aware of my changing feelings for Henry—more than the excitement of sharing a new novel and more than the camaraderie of laughing with him and Sally over the silliness of the girls' gossip at the soda fountain. Watching Henry unload the delivery crates from the truck, I was moved by the strength of an emotion I couldn't name. He stopped and looked at me, still holding the box.

"You all right, Miss Willie?" he asked.

"I'm fine," I answered, suddenly shy. He handed me one of the crates and our hands touched. There was a tingling sensation in my fingers and I dropped the crate. Henry stooped to pick it up. He stood slowly, studying me intently.

"You got a strange look on your face," he said. "You sure you're all right?"

"Henry," I said, with a surge of recklessness, "do you ever think about us? I mean . . . as more than friends?"

Henry's expression changed from concerned to something I couldn't identify, but it looked a little like fear. "I'm not sure what you're getting at, Miss Willie," he answered, turning away from me to place the crate on the back steps.

I pushed on, knowing that if I stopped now I'd never get the courage to ask again. "I mean you and me . . . as . . . well . . . a couple."

Henry turned back to me and looked around the quiet, empty lot before reaching down and taking my hand. He drew me into the deep shadow between the drugstore and the live oak tree. I found myself trembling with anticipation, wondering if he would kiss me. But he didn't. Instead he took my other hand and stood holding both of them. His features in the dark were indistinct, but I could hear the distress in his voice.

"Miss Willie, I think you're just about the finest girl I've ever met, and I would be honored to court you. But you and I both know that can't happen."

"But, Henry," I argued, "I don't care about all those bossy white women who think they know what's best for me. I love you. I think I have for a long time. I finally let myself admit it to myself."

I could see him shaking his head in the gathering darkness.

"I reckon I love you, too, Miss Willie," he said, making my heart soar. "But there can't be nothing more between us than friendship."

"But, Henry . . ."

"No, you need to get this idea out of your head," he said sternly. "It just can't be. I think if you stop and give it some thought, you'll see why. I'm sorry, Miss Willie. Believe me I am." He let go of my hands and shrugged. "Now, I got to get the rest of that load put away."

That was the last we spoke of our feelings for each other until the night Henry was getting ready to leave for Camp Lejeune the next August. It was as if everything we'd been feeling—our young love for each other, sadness over what had happened to Jerrilyn, fear of Dr. Collier's threats against Henry, Henry's excitement over joining the military, my grief over saying good-bye to him—all of it came together in that one night, hidden in the hayloft of the Johnsons' barn. I never regretted one minute of that sweet time with Henry. I never dreamed I'd be attending his funeral just one month later.

I hear the bedroom door slam, and here comes Avery carrying Celi. That child looks as floppy as an old rag doll, and I can tell Avery is fighting to stay calm. Her voice is low as she says, "I'm going to take Celi to the emergency room. She might have an infection. Her fever's pretty high."

"I'll go with you," I say, and hurry to grab my purse and sweater. By the time I get out the door, she's already behind the wheel of the car with Celi buckled in the back, ready to go.

Chapter 30

Avery

When we arrive at the hospital and are shuttled from the emergency room to a hospital room on one of the hospital units, I have to resist my usual urge to take over Celi's care. But I have learned that it's better to let the nurses do their jobs. Still, I'm unable to resist showing them the best place to start her IV, suggesting that they ask for an antibiotic and, of course, advising them about the drugs that best control her pain. I know they see people with sickle cell all the time here. I try to remind myself of that. But this is my baby.

Finally, they get us settled in a room, and after the nurse leaves saying, "The doctor will be in soon," I pace the floor. I left Will out in the waiting room for now. I think she knows more than she's letting on, especially since she's spent so much time around Sally and her family. She recognizes these symptoms as well as I do. After the doctor visits and we get Celi's pain under control, I'll let Will know how she's doing. There's a cursory knock on the door. When I glance up from checking that Celi's blood transfusion is dripping at the correct rate, I find myself face-to-face again . . . with Dr. Aaron Monroe.

My breath catches in my throat and it feels as if my heart has stopped. In his crisp white lab coat, dark gray slacks, blue oxford cloth shirt, and navy striped tie, he looks the consummate professional. Typically, I would have been reaching out right now, shaking the new doctor's hand, getting ready to launch into a summary of Celi's medical history. But I'm frozen in place.

Aaron looks equally dismayed. He stands as if rooted to the floor, taking in Celi's features for several seconds, and I know what he is seeing: her small frame, which always looks lost in hospital beds; the slight frown she wears when she's in pain. In the instant he sees her, I know I have made a terrible mistake in keeping them apart. Then he turns to me and the anguish in his eyes is almost more than I can bear. We are both about to speak when the hospital nurse hurries in behind him and stands waiting to discuss Celi's status with him.

He immediately tears his gaze from me and begins studying Celi's chart. This gives us both a chance to regain our self-control. My mind is screaming, *Not this way! I didn't want him to meet her this way!* while at the same time I am chastising myself for all the years I kept him from his daughter.

What should I do now? How can I move on from this moment?

Whatever composure he lost, he has regained. He extends his hand toward me, and as I take it and look up at him I am impressed by the confident medical expert who regards me with such calm detachment that it shakes me to my core. After introducing himself, he asks the usual questions regarding patient history, which I answer as if I am quoting from a script. I'm beginning to feel as if we are two actors in a play.

He approaches Celi tentatively, touching her arm and saying her name. My heart breaks a little more when she opens her eyes, attempts to focus her drugged attention on him, and smiles weakly.

"Hi, Cecelia," he says. "How are you doing?"

"Not too great," she whispers.

I can see the struggle he's having. Waves of emotion are crossing his beautiful face as he pulls his stethoscope out of his pocket. "I'm going to listen to you breathe now, okay?" he asks as she nods and begins to take the deep breaths that she knows from experience will be expected of her. As he finishes his assessment and asks me a few more questions, Celi closes her eyes again and dozes off.

Turning to the nurse, he asks, "Do we have the chest X-ray back yet?"

"I'll go check," she says, and quickly leaves the room.

He walks away from Celi's bedside toward the far side of the room. I follow, wondering how long we'll keep up this charade. His tone is accusing as he demands in a low voice, "Why didn't you tell me?"

I examine the tiles in the dull gray floor. I can't look at him. I know now how wrong I've been, and I have no excuse. I mumble helplessly, "I guess I thought it would worry you. There was nothing you could do. I thought it would be easier if—"

Aaron's words punch out through clenched teeth. "Easier? Why is it, Avery, that you always assume that keeping me away will make it easier? Easier for you, maybe?"

"I . . . I'm sorry. I . . ."

Aaron holds up his hand, stopping my feeble apology. "I've got to get out of here," he says, not bothering to whisper now. "I'll see that Celi gets assigned to another doctor."

The door closes behind him and I collapse into the chair, trying to choke back my sobs.

I jump from the chair when Celi says, "Mom?" I reach up and wipe the tears from my face, trying desperately to assume a calm expression.

"Hey, sweet pea. I thought you were asleep," I say, barely able to get the words out. I reach for one of the tissues in the box beside her bed. "Whew, I must be getting a cold."

"Mom, I know you were crying," Celi says, tuning in immediately as she always does to my emotional state. "What's wrong?"

"Oh, I think I'm just tired," I answer, fussing with her sheets and trying to sound nonchalant. But she's not buying it. Something obviously feels different to her, and I know how much she likes to know what's going on. She grabs for my hand and squeezes it hard. I stop. "Okay, okay, I know. Don't fuss with the sheets.

Sorry." I sit on the edge of her bed and look out the window, willing the tears to stop.

"Mom?" Celi says again, and I turn slowly toward her. It's as if I'm looking at her through a fog.

"Yes?"

"Am I dying?"

I'm instantly alert and suck in practically all the air in the room with my gasp. I reach down and grab both her arms. "Good God, no, Celi! Why would you think that?"

"The way you and the doctor were talking. I . . . I wasn't asleep. I heard you tell him that you didn't want to worry him . . . and then he got mad and left. I thought maybe—"

"Cecelia Louise Pritchett," I say in my sternest voice, "you are not going to die. I don't know where you get these crazy ideas, but you're stuck with me for a long time. So I don't want to hear that again, you got that?" My breath has quickened and my anxiety level is so high I have to move. I get up from the bed, check her arm where the needle enters her vein, straighten the items on the bedside table, all of the things that give me order and structure—neither of which my life seems to have right now.

"Mom, stop!" Celi demands, mustering her strength. I freeze, set down the water pitcher, and stare blankly at her. "Why did the doctor ask you that?"

"What do you mean?"

Celi is so frustrated with me that she growls. "Stop trying to act like you don't know what I'm talking about, Mom. How come there was something you didn't tell him, and why did you say you didn't want to worry him?" Before I can say anything, she continues. "And why did he leave like that, saying he was going to get another doctor to take care of me?" All I can do is stand dumbly in front of my daughter with my mouth open. "Tell me, Mom," she says. "Tell me the truth."

My daughter wants honesty. She and Aaron both want honesty. I can't avoid this moment any longer.

I've thought about how I would tell her so many times, but I feel completely unprepared. She is patient, and I see the growing comprehension in her eyes as I work my way through the story of meeting a boy in high school and falling in love with him. She listens carefully, interrupting with only a few questions as I tell her that when I learned I was pregnant with her, I thought leaving for Colorado was for the best. I believed then that it would be too much to ask Aaron to be a long-distance father to her. I didn't tell her about our plans to integrate the debutante ball or the assault on him and his hospitalization.

"I've seen him only once since we got to Greendale," I say, "and that was unintentional. I was trying to figure out how to tell you when you got sick."

She's sitting up in bed now, piercing me with her intense glare. Her eyes are hollow with the exhaustion caused by the pain and anemia. Her little arms are crossed across her chest and she frowns thoughtfully. "So he didn't know about my sickle cell? Is that why he was so mad?"

"He's angry with me, Celi, not you," I hurry to reassure her. I'm sitting on the side of her bed and I reach for her arm, but she pulls it away. "I should have told him. . . . I realize now I should have done a lot of things differently. . . ." I stop talking. None of what I should have done matters now.

Celi scoots down into the bed and turns to face the wall. "I'm tired," she says.

Her coldness is worse than any anger could be. "Celi, I'm so sorry," I say, restraining myself from reaching out to rub her back. "Could we maybe talk about this some more later when you're feeling better?" I ask, trying not to sound as desperate as I feel.

"I don't want to talk anymore," she mumbles into the pillow. "I want to sleep now."

The distance she puts between us bears down on me like an anvil on my heart. "Okay, I'll go out and talk to Grandma Will. I'll come back and check on you in a little while." I lean over to kiss her cheek and she doesn't move.

"Whatever," she says.

Chapter 31

Willadean

It's been so long since I heard any news, I sure hope that child doesn't have something serious. The way her color got so ashy, and her eyes looked sunken, reminded me of Sally's Cleome. That girl should never have gotten pregnant. She wasn't strong like Clarice. Of course, they didn't have all the treatments then that they do today. Cleome's pregnancy took everything she had left. And then that sorry excuse for a man who got Cleome pregnant in the first place ran off, leaving Sally to raise Aaron.

Sally's done a fine job with that boy. I haven't seen him since he's been back in town. One of those volunteer ladies in the pink coat brought me some bad hospital coffee, and I wonder as I'm sipping it if Aaron ever works here at the hospital. I remember old Dr. Boggess used to see patients here. I should warn Avery that she might run into him. I'm sure she hasn't thought about that, she's so worried about Celi.

It's a bad situation. Here that child is sick like this and Mark's wedding only a week away. And once word gets out, which it's bound to do, a lot of talk and trouble is going to get stirred up.

There's no lonelier place than a hospital waiting room. I've been watching the fish swim around in the big aquarium they have for what seems like hours. So I'm so relieved when Sally bustles in. She's walking behind a young man with a name tag that says *Escort* and she looks flustered.

"Thank you, son," she says to the boy as he nods and heads off down the hall. "What's going on, Willie?" she demands, turning to me.

"How did you know we were here?"

"I called over to your house to check on Celi and y'all weren't there. I had a bad feeling; don't ask me why. So I called up here to the hospital, and they wouldn't tell me a thing. I got in my car and drove up here, and sure enough, here you are," she says as we sit down in the corner.

"By the time Avery got home from that bridesmaids' lunch, Celi was a lot worse," I tell Sally. "She decided she'd better bring her in. I don't know anything yet. I been waiting to hear something."

Sally shakes her head. "Reminds me of being here with Cleome." She's pulling a tissue from her purse when suddenly she stops.. "You don't think that child—"

"Yes, I do, I'm sorry to say. I do."

"Why didn't her mama say anything? Reckon how long she's known?" Sally asks, tucking the tissue in her pocket and setting her purse on the floor.

"That's the part I can't figure out. Near as I can tell, maybe she's trying to protect Celi."

"Cleome must have passed it down to her. It looks like it skipped Aaron, and I was hoping . . . You know Aaron and me talked about sickle cell when Lacretia got pregnant. He had all kinds of questions then about his mama. He wanted to know if she'd ever had something he called a 'definitive diagnosis.' I told him I didn't rightly know about that, but the doctor said she had the sickle cell and that she probably got it from the way mine and Louis's blood mixed. Lord, I don't understand all this."

"Do you think Aaron's boys have it?" I ask, wondering how much more suffering her family is going to have to endure.

"Aaron tells me there's a test now. I reckon all babies got to get the test for sickle cell when they're born. And he and Lacretia both got themselves tested before she got pregnant." She shakes her head. "You know these young folks, they got all this information now—you remember all that stuff Avery was saying the other day about sickle cell?"

"You mean about the trait and the disease, and all those percentages, and the like?" I ask. She nods. "Yes, I remember. I didn't follow all of that very well, either."

"After she talked to us about it, I got to thinking. And now I'm remembering Aaron told me that he ended up with the trait, and Lacretia doesn't have it. So Brandon is like her—doesn't have it, and the little one, Louis, does."

"Will Louis get sick like Celi?" I ask.

"Aaron says no, thank the Lord. He says the mama and the daddy both got to have the trait, and that's what makes the disease."

I'm pondering all of this and trying to piece together what must have happened when Aaron and Avery's blood combined, and a thought is nagging at the corner of my mind about that when Sally clasps my arm, saying, "Uh-oh, Willie, look here."

Sally and I both stand to meet Avery coming into the waiting room. I haven't seen her look this bad since that night ten years ago when she came to this same hospital to try to see Aaron. She looks like she's weighed down with so much sadness and pain that she can barely walk. She searches the waiting room with a sort of desperation in her eyes. I reach her first, and although I'm not much of a hugger, I can tell this child needs some bearing up. I put my arms around her and that well of sadness erupts from her into deep, quiet sobs. She can't even talk. I've never seen her like this before. I'm so worried about Celi that I think I'm going to burst if she doesn't tell us something. I'm also wondering if Avery goes through this every time Celi gets sick. How often is that? And what has happened now?

Sally and I guide her over to the chairs and sit down on either side of her. Sally gives her a tissue, and I lay my hand on her back. I reckon Sally can't stand it anymore, so she asks, "How is she? She has sickle cell, doesn't she?"

Avery works to calm herself and blows her nose. "Yes, Miss Sally, she does. She's in a lot of pain and her blood count was really low, but I think we caught it in time." Sally and I look at each other and we're both breathing a big sigh of relief. "They got an IV in her, so she's getting some fluids, and they started antibiotics, and I think the pain medicine might be helping. . . ." She shudders with more sobs and can't talk. Sally and I look at each other again. I know Sally's as worried as I am.

"I didn't know . . ." she starts to say. "She overheard. . . ." Finally, she takes a deep breath, wipes her nose, and looks from one to the other of us, then back down at her hands in her lap, and she gets out what she's been trying to say. "Aaron was the doctor on call today. Celi was one of his patients."

Chapter 32

Avery

Will and Sally have gone in to see Celi. Neither one of them knew what to say after I told them what happened with Aaron and then with Celi. I know they're hurting for me; they were both so kind. I can also see in their eyes that they're not surprised by Celi's reaction.

Have I done anything *right* in the past ten years? I thought I was protecting her from pain. I thought I was taking responsibility for my mistake. I know that it took Aaron and me both to conceive Celi, but I've always felt responsible—that if I hadn't been such a risk taker . . .

But none of that matters now. Celi knows and she hates me for keeping Aaron's identity from her. And Aaron has met his daughter under terrible circumstances and learned she has sickle-cell disease. I can blame only myself for making it worse for them.

As long as I've worked in hospitals, I still hate the smell of waiting rooms. They remind me of all the times I've stood by while a doctor has delivered devastating news to an exhausted family or the times I've urged the parents of a child with cancer back to a hospital room because the end was near.

I can't stand it anymore. I have to get out, so I head down the hallway, through the lobby, and out the automatic doors into the early evening light. I breathe in the thick, humid air of the early

Mississippi summer. I resume pacing for a while and finally drop onto a concrete bench placed under the trees in the parklike outdoor seating area in front of the hospital, but my nerves are still jumping. The tension of Celi's situation and all the colliding revelations have left me ready to explode.

Hearing the clicking of heels on concrete, I look up to see my mother approaching. The hospital valet behind her is pocketing her car keys. Her Mercedes sits in a long row of cars waiting to be parked. She looks flawless, as usual. Her expertly cut gray slacks and jacket contrast with a pink silk blouse and expensive-looking printed scarf. How is it that she never looks ruffled or flustered? And what is she doing here? Silly question. This is Greendale. I'm sure someone at this hospital who knows Will or Sally called someone who knows someone else, and as usual, within a couple of hours the news has reached Mother.

She sits down beside me on the bench, looking worried. "I got word from one of the girls at your father's office that someone saw you and Will going into the hospital emergency room with Celi this afternoon. Is she sick?" Before I can answer, she continues, "Why didn't y'all call me?" The pain in her voice adds another layer of guilt to the load I'm already carrying.

"Yes, Celi's in the hospital," I answer tersely.

"What happened? What's wrong?" Her expression of surprise coupled with intense concern touches me.

I take a deep breath. "She has sickle-cell anemia and she went into sickle-cell crisis. She probably got dehydrated from the heat and drinking too much caffeinated tea. Anyway, she's having a lot of joint pain, and she might be getting a respiratory infection—she has a low-grade fever—and of course, she's anemic."

Mother looks completely confused. "Avery, slow down. I don't understand half of what you just said. What is . . . What did you say? Sickle-cell crisis?" she asks.

It occurs to me that my own mother doesn't know that she herself probably carries the sickle-cell trait. She's never had any reason to know what the disease involves. "Celi has sickle-cell disease, Mother. The crises happen when Celi's body gets really stressed. Her blood cells can't carry enough oxygen because they're sickle shaped, and she gets really bad joint and abdominal pain."

She sits quietly for several seconds, as if she's trying to capture a memory. "I remember hearing Willadean talk about this," she says. Then recognition dawns in her expression. "This runs in Sally's family, doesn't it?"

I nod and start to respond, "Yes, but—"

"Oh, Avery," she sighs. She looks away from me, pursing her lips and shaking her head. "This is a disease the blacks get. And now that little girl has it." She opens her purse, pulls out her compact and lipstick, and begins to reapply what for some insane reason I recognize as the same shade of Estée Lauder lipstick she's been wearing my entire life. She's completely unconscious of this ritual activity as she examines her lips and face, snaps her compact closed, and drops it and the lipstick in her purse. "Should I go in to see her?" she asks, without waiting for my answer. "I suppose Willadean is in there now."

"Yes," I answer tiredly. "Will and Sally are in visiting her."

"Poor thing," she says, shaking her head and looking across the flower-filled brick patio. Her voice and expression convey sympathy, but my deeply entrenched suspicion won't let me believe that she's being genuine. "This is what I was so worried about, all those years ago, Avery. When whites mix with blacks, everyone suffers. Now you have a half-black child and all of the problems that will cause in her life and yours, and she's inherited this awful disease from his family." She reaches over and pats my leg. "I'm so sorry, honey, so, so sorry."

All I can see sitting beside me is the condescending, imperious, self-righteous whiteness of my mother. I stand up thinking that maybe I can simply walk away, but all the tensions and frustrations of the last hours coalesce inside me. Something inside me snaps and my mother becomes the object of my rage. When I turn to face her, I descend on her with all my pent-up fury. Right now all I want to do is wipe that superior look off her face and make her suffer. And I know just the way to do that.

"Mother, who the hell do you think you are? I am so completely sick of your self-righteous, racist, bigoted, holier-than-thou attitude!" I say, louder than I intend. She's obviously shocked by my outburst and looks around to see if anyone else is within earshot.

"But, Avery, I didn't mean . . . I was just . . ." she splutters.

"For your information, our lily-white family is as much to blame as Aaron's family is for what you call Celi's *black* disease."

"Oh, now, Avery," she replies, looking at me with disbelief.

"Sickle-cell disease takes two parents with the trait—not just one, two. Aaron and me. Guess what that means, Mother?" I say, feeling a wicked satisfaction at the horror of comprehension that is descending over her face.

"But . . . but . . . that can't be. My mother and daddy are white. . . . We're all white. . . . There are no—"

I choose my next words deliberately to deliver the harshest blow possible. "Oh, but it's true. The illustrious Reynolds family of Greendale, Mississippi, has black blood in our family tree."

The look of pain and confusion on her face is almost enough to make me regret what I've done. She stands up and steps away from me, then turns back toward her car. I start to go after her, but shock at my own outburst stops me. The valet is just getting to her car as she hurries toward him, waving and calling, "Wait, stop!" She grabs the keys out of his hand, gets into her car, and pulls away as fast as she can through the busy hospital driveway.

Chapter 33

Willadean

Sally and I venture out in search of Celi's room. I go in first, with Sally close on my heels. When I see that Celi is sleeping, I turn to Sally and put my finger up to my lips to shush her. We try to tiptoe in quietly, but I'm so busy studying Celi that my foot bumps the chair and I start to lose my balance. Sally flings her arm out to grab me, but her other hand with her handbag in it flails out and hits a metal pole holding what looks like a bag of blood and one of some kind of clear liquid. The pole starts to sway back and forth like it's about to fall over. I reach to hold on to Sally, who's trying to catch the pole, and we end up making a terrible racket. When we finally get ourselves straightened out, Celi is awake and giggling at our clumsiness.

"Now look what you've gone and done, Willie," Sally says. "You woke the child up."

"You banged that big old purse of yours into this piece of equipment," I say, pointing to the blinking blue machine mounted on the pole.

"I was trying to keep you from falling over, you old coot."

I stop myself from arguing back, clamp my lips together, and walk over to Celi's bedside. "Hey there, darlin', how you feeling?" I ask. Sally comes up behind me and peers around my shoulder. Her smile crinkles up her wrinkly old face.

"Yes, you doing okay, baby?" she asks.

"I'm okay, I guess," Celi answers. She looks pale, and there are dark circles under her eyes.

"We thought we'd keep you company for a spell while your mama's out getting some air," says Sally.

"That's right," I say. I turn and try to pull a chair up to the side of the bed, but the thing is so heavy, I can scarcely move it.

"Here, let me help you with that," says Sally, but I push her away.

"I got it. Give a body time!" I say. I finally get the chair like I want it and sit down, while Sally takes the chair on the other side.

"Now, baby, if you need to sleep, you go on ahead. We'll sit here and be quiet for a while," Sally says.

"Okay," Celi answers. We're all silent for a little bit; then Celi pushes back her covers. "I think I'll sit up now."

Sally gets a twinkle in her eye. "Are you hungry?" she asks, and she reaches down in her big red purse and pulls out a plastic box. She hands it to Celi. As soon as Celi cracks the lid I know it's Sally's homemade peanut butter cookies.

"Thanks," Celi says, and for some reason, the child starts to cry. Poor little thing. Bless her heart, she's lying in a strange hospital, suffering a heap of pain, and us two old women are not sure how to help her. Of course, we both stand up, hovering over her and handing her tissues and patting her arms.

After a little bit, she calms down and sadly takes a bite of a cookie. I look across the bed at Sally and I can tell she's making her mind up about something. She says, "I reckon this has been a hard day all around for you, Celi." Celi nods. Sally continues, "Your mama told us that you found out about your daddy being Aaron Monroe."

I frown at Sally, because this starts the child to crying again. "Yes, ma'am," is all Celi can get out.

Sally won't look at me. She reaches over then, and takes Celi's hand in hers. I want to tell her to give the child a chance to take it all in, but she can't stand it anymore. "So, what did you think of your daddy? Aren't you glad you got to meet him?"

"I don't think I'll be seeing him again, Miss Sally," Celi says, and it looks like she's fighting back more tears.

"Why not, baby?" Sally asks. "Don't you want to?"

"Yes, ma'am. But he doesn't want me. He doesn't even want to be my doctor. He told Mom he would get me another doctor and he was real mad at her."

Sally now looks like she's the one who's going to cry. She's breathing fast and she puts her hand up to her heart like she's having palpitations.

I pat Sally's arm, trying to calm her. "It's all right, Sally," I say. "She misunderstood Aaron, that's all."

Celi looks from me to Sally with a confused expression. "Do you know him?" she asks.

Sally and I look at each other, and I nod to Sally.

"Celi," Sally says, "your daddy, Aaron Monroe, is my grandson. His own mama died when he was born, and I raised him myself. And I'm here to tell you, child, no man has ever wanted to know his baby girl more than your daddy wants to know you."

Celi's eyebrows shoot up, and a smile starts around the corners of her mouth, but then she frowns. "But why was he so mad?"

"There's been a lot that's happened over the past nine years of your life, little one," I say. "Your daddy was angry about things between him and your mama. It has nothing to do with you."

"That's right," says Sally. "He'll be around. You watch. Why, I wouldn't be surprised if you didn't see him later on this very night."

"Miss Sally—" she says.

"How about you call me Mama Sal, like my other grandchildren do?" Sally asks.

"Yes, ma'am, Mama Sal," Celi says, and she's smiling happily now. She thinks for a few seconds. "You mean my dad has other kids?"

"Yes, honey, he does," I say. "He's got a wife named Lacretia and two fine little boys named Brandon and Louis."

"That's right," says Sally. "Brandon will be five in August, and little Louis will turn a year next month." Celi contemplates this new piece of information.

We both breathe a sigh of relief when her next question is, "Mama Sal, could you tell me what my dad was like when he was a little boy?"

Chapter 34

Avery

I thought I'd feel relieved after all those years of pent-up anger were released—I fantasized that confronting Mother with the news that she is part black would provide me with sweet revenge against her for being willing to throw me away ten years ago. But I don't feel relieved and it wasn't sweet. I'm sinking into a pit of despair. I've managed to rip apart almost every important relationship in my life. Mother's devastated; Aaron's angry; Celi's angry. I feel sick inside, but I've got to stop wallowing in my own guilt, so I start to drag myself back into the hospital.

As I enter the hospital lobby, I hear my name being called and turn to see Nicki and Mark, who rush toward me. Mark is wearing running clothes, and Nicki has changed from her bridesmaids' luncheon outfit to workout tights and a T-shirt. Right now the luncheon seems like eons ago.

"We heard about Celi," says Mark, throwing his arms around me. "I was out for a run and when I got back, there was a message on the machine from Mama." Guilt over how I treated Mother preoccupies me. She really was worried about Celi. "Mama called Daddy and I left him a message, too. I think he's playing golf."

When Mark releases me, Nicki hugs me as well. "Sorry I look like this," she says. "I was at the gym. I didn't take time to change. How is she? Can we see her?"

I'm overwhelmed by this outpouring of support from my family. "Thanks for coming, y'all," I stammer. "She's in a lot of pain, but I think the medication is starting to help. Let's go in and see her. Will and Sally are in with her now."

"I hate to tell you this, Ave," says Mark with a smile, "but you look awful."

He gets a weak smile out of me as I accept the tissue Nicki pulls from her purse and blow my nose. "Yeah, I guess I do. I've made a royal mess of things today."

"What have you made a mess of?" Mark asks as we walk toward Celi's room. Nicki stops to speak to several of the nurses who recognize her and want to hear about wedding details. I pause to wait.

"Let's keep going," Mark says. "Nicki knows everybody. We could be here all day if we wait for her. What room is Celi in?"

"Uh . . ." I've forgotten the number. "End of the hall on the right."

Mark points toward the end of the hall and Nicki nods. We continue toward Celi's room. "So you were telling me about the mess you've made," he prompts.

I can't even begin to explain the afternoon's events in the few seconds we have before we reach Celi's room. "I'll explain it all later, but here's the short version. Aaron Monroe was Celi's doctor today and I blew up at Mother."

Mark looks confused, and then recognition seems to dawn on him and his eyebrows shoot up. "Oh . . . Aaron . . . Celi's father?" I nod. "Whoa, so does Celi know?

"Yes, and she's furious with me. And the thing with Mother—"

He waves his hand as if to negate my worry. "What's new about you and Mama having a fight?"

We've reached Celi's room and Mark opens the door for me. "This time, I think I may have gone too far," I say. He looks puzzled, but we stop our conversation as we enter the room. What I see makes me smile.

Celi is propped up on pillows, taking a bite of what looks like a peanut butter cookie. Her eyes are intent on Sally Monroe, who is sitting in a chair on the far side of the bed and appears to be telling her a story. Will is laughing and shaking her head. They all turn toward us as we enter the room. I instantly fixate on Celi, wondering if she's going to talk to me. She ignores me at first in favor of Mark, who heads directly to her.

"How's my favorite niece?" he asks, leaning over to kiss her cheek.

"Hi, Uncle Mark," she says shyly.

"I see that these ladies are trying the famous peanut butter cookie cure," he says, squeezing Will's outstretched hand and then circling the bed to hug Sally.

Will, Sally, and Celi laugh and I'm suddenly conscious of feeling left outside of this circle. Celi seems so at home right now. I approach her tentatively, looking for the telltale signs of fever in her eyes. "Hey, sweet pea," I say.

"Hi, Mom," she says, and I finally breathe again as she throws her little arms around my neck and whispers in my ear, "Mama Sal is my other great-grandmother."

At first I'm taken aback, and then I reassure myself that whatever conversation they've had, I don't have to worry anymore. There are no secrets here now. Well, at least not about Aaron and Sally and their relationship to Celi. What a huge relief! I sit down on the side of Celi's bed as I say, "That's right, she is. Pretty cool, huh?" Celi nods and grins.

"She's been telling me about my dad when he was little."

Her dad? That's a term I haven't often heard come out of my daughter's mouth. My mind is racing. Celi seems to be taking in her new family with such grace, and I'm freaking out. Why? Before I can figure that out, the door opens and Nicki walks in with her arm through Daddy's.

"Look who I found wandering around in the hallway," she says, smiling.

Daddy envelops me in a big hug. As he releases me, he takes my shoulders and asks, "Where's your mother? She left me a message to call, and then when I called her back on my way over here, she didn't answer. Has she been here?"

Shame for the way I treated her engulfs me, but I force myself to tell the truth. "She was here," I say. "It's all my fault, but we had words and she left the hospital without coming inside."

"Ah, that explains part of it." He gives me another hug. "Don't be too hard on yourself. But I do wonder where she's gone."

I find myself propped against the windowsill in the corner watching a roomful of people and it feels surreal. Instead of the bleak hospital experience that Celi and I always seek to put behind us as quickly as possible, this almost feels like a party. Nicki is deep in conversation with Celi. Sally is passing around peanut butter cookies as she and Mark bicker over the merits of crunchy versus smooth peanut butter, and Daddy and Will are discussing whether to put a window-unit air conditioner in mine and Celi's bedroom out at Oak Knoll. To say that this day has been strange would be a massive understatement. I feel myself going numb. There are more emotions going on inside me right now than I can process.

I'm jolted out of my frozen state by a knock on the door. I figure it's probably one of the nurses coming to run some of us out of the room. We're getting pretty noisy. I seem to be the only one to notice the knock, so I cross the room and open the door to find Aaron standing there. I open the door wide and step back as our eyes lock and I try to read him. His anger seems to have faded. The white lab coat and tie are gone, replaced by jeans, T-shirt, and tennis shoes. Conversation immediately falls silent as everyone turns to see who it is.

I'm still searching for words when Sally says, "Well, look what the cat dragged in," and everyone laughs. She hugs Aaron, and I notice that he looks over Sally's shoulder and grins at Celi. She shyly returns his smile. I see hope in her eyes. Everyone—Will, Daddy, Nicki, and Mark—greets Aaron and shakes his hand. They make small talk about how he's liking Greendale and the weather. I stand off to the side, unable to participate in these Southern niceties. Either I've lost my touch or I'm plain out of words.

Soon everyone begins to state reasons why they need to go. Daddy needs to go check on Mother. Mark and Nicki have dinner plans. And Will and Sally both say they're "worn-out." I've hugged everyone and I'm standing beside Celi's bed when I overhear Sally whisper to Celi, "See what I told you? Your daddy loves you, baby girl."

Once everyone's gone, leaving Aaron and me alone with Celi, I notice that he has the same nervous need to check the medical equipment and make a visual assessment of Celi that I do. He finally takes a deep breath.

"Celi," he says, clearing his throat and looking over at me, "and you, too, Avery . . . I'm sorry about earlier. I was just . . . really surprised. I'm sorry we had to meet here at the hospital." He pulls a chair up beside her bed. He sits on the very edge and I notice that one of his knees shakes up and down. Celi makes that same motion when she's anxious. "Anyway . . ." he continues, "your mom says she told you who I am, and I can't tell you how excited I am to finally get to meet you." He looks down at his feet, then back up at Celi. I can only imagine how difficult this must be for him. It hits me that he's probably worried that *she* will reject him—something that's never occurred to me before.

I don't often see Celi this quiet. The question she finally comes up with surprises me and makes me smile. "Mama Sal told me that you played basketball when you were in high school. Do you still play?" she asks. It's as if she instinctively knows how to put him at ease. A big smile crinkles up his whole face, and I'm struck by his and Celi's resemblance. Her skin is lighter, but her eyes and lips are shaped like his.

"Yeah, I do still play basketball. That's why I've got the sneaks on. Sometimes I play pickup basketball over at the Y on Saturday nights. Do you like basketball?" he asks. And from there their conversation is easy and light—about how much Celi loves basketball, how they'll play together when she's well. Then he tells her that she has two little half brothers who are too young to play much yet, but they're going to love meeting her. He asks her about school and what she likes to read. She's so engrossed in conversation with him that she barely notices when the lab tech comes in to draw blood.

I find myself inching closer to the two of them as they talk. I'm fascinated by the comfort they seem to find in each other. By the time a food service worker brings Celi's dinner tray, I'm sitting on the bed, laughing along with them at a story Aaron tells about fishing with Sally and Will. I've rarely seen Celi so happy. Despite the pain she must be feeling, despite her swollen hands and obvious fatigue, happiness pours out of her eyes each time she looks at Aaron. I notice her breathing get a little faster, and a slight flush starts to creep into her cheeks. When the nurse comes in with more pain medicine, I have to insist that it's time for her to settle down and try to sleep.

"You've had a big day," I say, pushing her hair back and kissing her forehead.

"I'm doing okay, Mom," she argues, though her voice sounds weak and scratchy.

"Yes, I know. But you want to be able to go home soon, right?"

"Yes," she says, pouting a little.

"Then we've got to get your swelling down and your pain under control. So you need to rest."

"Your mom's right, Celi," Aaron jumps in. "I'm off tomorrow, so I'll come back and visit you." He looks across at me. I nod in approval. How can I refuse? "Celi," he says, "could I borrow your mom for a little while? We've got a lot to catch up on." I'm caught off guard, not sure what he means.

"Sure," Celi says. I don't think she's really ready to share him yet, but she acquiesces a little bit grudgingly.

"Um . . . okay," I say, looking around for my purse. "I won't be gone long, right?" I ask. He shakes his head no. "And you can call my cell phone if you need me," I tell Celi.

"Mom, I'll be fine," she says. "I'm going to watch TV until I get sleepy."

We both kiss her good night, and I'm conscious of how strange this feels. In the almost ten years of her life, she's had only me. My feelings about sharing her are so mixed. As we leave the room and she raises a puffy hand to wave good-bye, I see a look of contentment in her eyes that should reassure me. But instead of feeling reassured, I find myself even more uncertain. Now that she's met Aaron and has made such an obvious connection with him, how will she feel when it's time to go home to Colorado?

Chapter 35

Avery

The windows of Aaron's truck are rolled down, and we ride in silence, watching the places of our childhoods drift past us, smelling the still familiar aromas of the local burger joint and the catfish house as we pass them. My stomach growls and I remember it's been hours since I've eaten. As soon as we pass Larry and Ruby's store, I guess where Aaron is headed. If he's feeling like I am, we're each still so full of questions that neither of us knows where to start.

When he suggested we go for a ride and talk, I was hesitant. Yet I knew we needed to get away from the prying eyes of the hospital staff. I can tell that many of the nurses are intrigued by the handsome new doctor. But the intimacy of riding in a truck with him stirs up such sweet memories within me for what we shared back when we traveled these roads together that I'm wondering if I did the right thing.

He pulls the truck into the road circling Alligator Lake, just as I thought he would, parks in a dimly lit, newly constructed picnic area, kills the engine, and turns to face me. I can see the shiny skin of the scar across his eye in the soft glow of the utility light high on a pole overhead. The irony that here we are, back where we started, Alligator Lake, is not lost on me.

He turns away from me again and stares out into the darkness. "How about we get out and walk?" he asks. "I need to move."

"Sure," I say, and we leave the truck, walking slowly toward the lake, surrounded by the soft whir of cicadas and the intermittent plop of fish jumping in the placid water. We approach the edge of the lake and turn onto the footpath that circles it.

"I've got to tell you, Avery . . ." he starts. There's a bitter edge to his voice now, and I struggle with an instant defensiveness as he continues. "I'm having a really hard time with you not letting me see Celi, and now that I know she's been dealing with sickle cell . . ."

"I know, I know," I answer, trying to tamp down the walls I always erect when I'm being chastised. "I thought I was doing the right thing; I really did. I thought it was best for you to go on with your life, you know? Finish school, find someone else, not be bogged down with a child . . ."

"Bogged down?" he says angrily. "Do you think Celi is some kind of weight to me? Don't you know how I feel about her, Avery? She's my daughter, not some irritation. I've spent ten years staying away because I thought you didn't want me to complicate *your* life. When Mama Sal finally told me the truth—that you had left for Denver and that you were pregnant—I had just gotten out of the hospital. I still had a patch over my eye, but I was feeling much stronger. I packed my suitcase, and I was ready to catch the first bus I could find headed west. But Mama Sal talked me into calling you first. I think she knew what you would say."

"I remember when you called," I say. "You begged me to let you come. You said you'd find a job, that we could get married. All I could see then was your dreams being crushed because of me. I couldn't forgive myself for pushing you into that crazy scheme of mine, and I couldn't face the possibility of what being in a relationship with you might mean. I'm so sorry, Aaron. I know I handled it all wrong."

"I'm sorry, too, Avery," he sighs. "After you refused me so many times during those first couple of months, I have to admit I gave up. I went on with my life. And when I found out from Mama Sal that we had a baby girl, even though it broke my heart, I told myself you didn't want me and that it would be best for the child if I stayed away. I thought that maybe you had found someone else to be her father. I don't think I've ever forgiven myself for not trying harder, for not taking some kind of action. But the last thing I wanted was a legal battle. And then I reconnected with Lacretia, and there was school, and the boys came along. . . ."

We walk in silence for a while, and when we come upon an old wooden picnic table, he reaches for my arm and says, "Let's sit for a few minutes." The sensation of his light touch on my arm yanks me from my rumination about my past mistakes into the present, in this place and time where I can feel the warmth of his body as we climb on top of an old wooden picnic table and sit, side by side, our feet resting on the bench seat.

"Tell me about her," he says. "What's it been like for her having sickle cell?"

I breathe in, allowing myself to feel a moment of connection, the tentative comfort of having Aaron as an ally, a possible person with whom to share the burden of my constant worry. Then I tell him the difficulty of the past five years—the moment I heard about her sickle-cell diagnosis, the multiple hospitalizations, her fight for normalcy, my puzzle over how I came to be a carrier of the trait, and my suspicion about Will and Henry. Aaron listens intently, asking questions now and then to clarify a point. He relays that he doesn't know anything about his uncle Henry and Will, especially since Henry died long before he was born.

"I never thought about sickle-cell disease in my family when I was growing up," he says. "We were just kids, you know?" I nod, thinking about the innocence of those days. "It wasn't until I studied sickle cell in medical school that I started to make the connections," he continues. "I started to think about my mother and my great-grandmother and the stories I had heard about how they suffered. And it occurred to me that the trait might be in my family and that I could pass it on to my own children. Lacretia and I got tested, and her hemoglobin is normal. Brandon tested negative on his newborn screening."

"And Louis?" I ask.

"He carries the trait," Aaron says sadly.

"Like you."

"Yes, like me," he replies, staring at the ground.

I tell myself I'm glad for him that Brandon is unaffected, Louis only carries the trait, and Lacretia doesn't share this legacy. He and Lacretia got lucky. So many couples have no idea that this disease lies waiting in their genetic code for the right combination that will unleash its power to destroy. "It's so sad, what your family has gone through," I say. "I can't imagine what it would be like if I couldn't get treatment for Celi—if all we had to offer her was pain medicine. If we couldn't treat the infections and the anemia . . ." I trail off, realizing that my sadness is weighing down on me like the night air coming off the lake, dense and heavy, making me feel vulnerable. I hate feeling vulnerable.

Aaron puts his arm around my shoulders, pulling me to him, "I know this must have been hard for you, Avery," he says. "I want you to know I'm sorry you've had to face it alone."

"I guess I set it up that way," I say, willing myself to sit still and not pull away from him. I want so badly to let him in, but I don't know how. What is left for us to share now? Can I allow myself to accept his friendship? His heart is so true, it makes me want to weep for losing him. But I tell myself it's time to open my heart to something new, to leave the past behind. I make myself sit up straight. It's time to ask the question that's been haunting me.

"Aaron, what happened to you that night?" I ask, confident he will know what night I mean. I wrestle with uncertainty, wondering if he'll be willing to tell me. Wondering if I want to know. He removes his arm and studies me carefully for several seconds; then he lets out a long sigh.

"Are you sure you want to talk about all of that?" he asks.

"Yes, I'm sure. You know I came to the hospital that night, don't you?"

He's surprised. "No, I didn't. . . . I thought . . . Well, I guess I thought you were scared . . . maybe regretted the whole thing." He looks puzzled.

I'm experiencing so many different emotions, I'm having a hard time sorting them out. Anger, for one, because Sally never told him I was there and he's thought badly of me all this time. Sadness for the happy-go-lucky kids we once were and are no longer.

"I found your truck parked out on the service road," I say. "I managed to walk to Owen's Market, and Larry brought me to the hospital. But Sally wouldn't let me see you. She said . . ." I feel the catch in my throat. "She said I'd done enough to hurt you already. She was so angry that night."

"Yeah," he says, "she was always like a mama bear—kind of like you are with Celi," he says, looking at me with a slight smile and those gentle eyes that always melted my heart. For a split second I wish . . . but I stop myself and work to focus on getting answers.

"I need to know what happened . . . if you're willing to talk about it," I say.

He rubs his hand across his face, his fingers lingering on the scar. He looks out toward the lake. "I parked my truck where you said—on the service road down near the woods behind the house. I was nervous, so I got out of the truck and I was pacing a little bit, trying to get up my courage to go to the house and meet you."

The knot of guilt in my gut tightens. If only I hadn't insisted on that crazy plan.

"I was standing at the back of the truck when a Dodge pickup came flying around the curve and pulled up right behind mine. Before I could get back around to the driver's side, two guys jumped out and pinned me against my tailgate. One of them was Farley Cole and the other one was that big guy . . . played football. . . . I think he ended up playing for Ole Miss. . . ."

"Landon Hornsby?" I ask, and he nods. "What about Seth?" I ask.

"Nope, Seth wasn't with them."

This is a revelation to me. All these years I've assumed it was Seth who beat up Aaron. Now everything looks different.

"I could smell the whiskey on them. I think they were pretty drunk by then. . . ." Aaron turns completely away from me and faces straight ahead. "Long story short, they made sure that I didn't make it to your dance." He seems completely closed off from me now, somewhere deep inside himself.

"Aaron, what did they do?"

"You know, Avery, I haven't talked about this . . . well, ever. I don't see the point in bringing it all up now."

"Please," I say. "I know it's hard, but you and I have to get this out and past us and . . . I can't believe I'm saying this, but I think I need to hear it."

He turns to me again, and I can't read his expression, but his eyes aren't soft anymore; they're hard and cold. "If you have to know, here's what happened. Hornsby grabbed my arm and twisted it behind my back, then pushed me down on my knees in the dirt. Then Farley bent over and got right up to my ear and said, 'We need to make sure you know your place, nigger. Rumor has it you're planning on busting in on our little dance, and maybe making a scene with that little nigger-loving bitch, Avery Pritchett. Is that true?'

"When I didn't say anything right away, Hornsby twisted my arm until I thought he was going to break it off, and then Farley shouted in my ear, 'Is it true, nigger?' At that point, I figured they were either going to kill me for talking or kill me for not talking. Part of me couldn't believe it was happening, you know?" He turns to me as he says this, and all I can do is nod, seeing the pain and shame in his eyes.

"I mean, I'd heard my kinfolks and Mama Sal talk about the old days and lynchings and shit like that, but I never thought . . ." He stops and takes a shuddering breath.

"Anyway, I told them yes, I was going to the dance, and yes, I was planning to meet you. Then Cole asked me where, and I told him the garden shed. He must have given Hornsby the nod, because he let up a little on my arm. I thought then that maybe they were done. Farley left and struck out walking toward the house, the way you had told me to go. Then Hornsby bent over me and said, 'You better not ever let us catch you around a white girl again, nigger, or there'll be hell to pay. Do you hear me?' I'm telling you, Avery, I was scared out of my mind, but something in me wouldn't let me say 'yes, sir' to that damn white asshole. But me not saying anything is what got me this." He points to the deep scar across his eye.

"What did he do?" I ask, horrified.

"Last thing I remember, Hornsby had his hand on the back of my head with his fingers gripping my hair so tight he had my eyes pulled back. I think I passed out after about the third time my head hit the back bumper of my truck. Later, the surgeon said there must have been a sharp edge that made the cut—maybe the license plate."

We sit quietly for a little while. I'm crying quietly, and he continues to stare at the lake. "Who found you?" I manage to ask. "I mean, how did you get to the hospital?"

"Mama Sal said it was Larry. Ruby overheard Farley Cole and his friends bragging to one another the night before the debutante ball about teaching a nigger a lesson, and she told Larry. I guess he must have gotten worried, because he was out driving around and he found me passed out behind my truck. He took me to the hospital and called Mama Sal. When I came to, I was in the emergency room and she was standing over me."

"I came out to meet you," I say, "and Seth was waiting for me at the garden shed. I still don't know how he found out what we were planning, but I've always suspected my mother because she was so close to the Colliers. Anyway, Seth was a complete jerk, and when I got away from him—"

"Wait a minute," Aaron interrupts. "Got away from him? Did he hurt you?"

I can see the anger building again in him. I remember Seth's thick hands pressing my body into the rough wood of the shed, the stink of his breath, and the sour taste of his mouth covering mine, the bright red blood dripping onto his shirt from my teeth piercing his lip, and the shame rises again in my throat. But I walked away unharmed. I wasn't shoved to the ground, my head slammed into the bumper of a truck, my body left bleeding and unconscious.

"No, not really," I say. Would Aaron understand that it wasn't the physical experience of Seth's brutality that hurt me? It was the death of my illusions—the devastating realization that I had no power. I want to reach out to him. I want him to hold me and tell me that what we tried to do didn't destroy something in both of us, but I don't. It's too late now. "Seth shook me up, mostly because he knew about our plan, and from the way he was talking, I was afraid for you. Anyway, I ran through the woods and out to the service road. I must have missed Farley and Landon somehow. When I found your truck there and it was empty, I panicked. And when I finally got to the ER, like I said before, Sally wouldn't let me in to see you."

"I'm sorry I never knew you came to the hospital that night." In the glint of moonlight creeping across the glassy water, I can see the sadness in his eyes.

"Yeah," I sigh. "I don't know what I thought I could do. It was probably best for you that Sally sent me away. When I called after you were transferred to the hospital in Jackson, she would only tell me that you were recovering, and then I found out I was pregnant. . . ."

"I guess we both know the rest," he says.

I turn to him, hoping he'll have the answers that I don't. "And now what?" I ask.

But the weight of the past and the unknown of our present seem to be too much for him, too. "I'm not sure, Avery," he says. "I'm just not sure."

I know it's too much for me to ask, for him to have a ready answer, a solution, a way to proceed, but I can't seem to stop myself. And now I find I'm feeling more vulnerable just when it's time for me to take charge again. "Wow! It's been almost two hours," I say. "I'd better get back to the hospital." I stand up and wipe my eyes on my shirtsleeve.

"Okay . . . yeah . . . you're right," he says, a little surprised by my abrupt change in demeanor. "I need to check in with the boys before it gets any later."

As we walk back toward the truck, I force myself to ask, "What about Lacretia? How is she doing with all of this?"

He shrugs. "Not good. But I have faith she'll come around." He stops, and the intensity in his eyes holds me in place. "I can't lose my family," he says. "Avery, I want you to know that I want to love that little girl, and if you'll let me, I want to be a father to her. But I can't lose my family."

My heart splits open, and I don't have any idea how we're going to resolve our conflicting needs, but I take a deep breath, and with a tiny inkling of my old stubbornness, I say, "I understand."

Chapter 36

Marion

Farms are hurtling past me and I'm not sure where I am. When I left the hospital I started driving and I don't know how many miles I've gone on Highway 61. How dare Avery make me the object of all that pent-up anger. I don't deserve it. Does she honestly believe that I haven't tried to deal with this situation? After all, she's the one who created it—and the rest of us have had to cope with the fallout. But this new information . . .

Is it possible that we have blacks in our family? I think of what I've experienced in just the past three weeks with Celi. If what Avery says is true, and the knowledge of it gets out into the community, I'll be the object of rumors and whispers, of invitations that don't come, of the subtle shift in topics of conversation when I draw near. Everything I've fought to avoid is happening all over again, but this time it's not by association; this time it's because I am one of *them*.

I don't have the first notion of how to deal with the *news* that Avery has dropped in my lap. All I know is that I hate myself for feeling this way. Why couldn't I have been supportive and strong for her? Just when I thought I was beginning to move past my irrational fear and I was beginning to accept Celi's difference, I learn that Celi is sick and that our family is not what I thought it was.

Is everything I've lived a lie? Of course, Willadean is comfortable with blacks, has friends who are black, but could she have become pregnant by a black man? I can't even imagine it. The road becomes blurred again and I miss reading the exit sign. I've got to pay more attention to the next one, or I'm going to end up in New Orleans. Maybe that's not such a bad idea.

Questions torment me as I stare out the windshield at the endless flat delta blacktop. Who could it have been? Since I was a little girl and I began to comprehend that I was never going to make anything of myself in Greendale if I acted like Willadean, I've avoided her association with blacks in every way. Are there people in Greendale who know this about my family? Have people been whispering behind my back all these years? If that's true, how can I ever face them again?

I think about that little girl back there in the hospital bed, my own granddaughter. It's obvious from our experiences already that Celi is treated differently here in the South. Celi and Avery apparently have a very different world in Denver, one that's not laden with the constant consciousness of race that we here in Mississippi seem unable to move past. The problem is that I've already begun to love that child. I didn't realize that I would, but I have to face it—I do. And the thought of having to keep my relationship with her confined to some other location, like Denver, is unacceptable to me. But I have no solution. Right now, I can't get past the shock of what I just heard.

I look at my hands on the steering wheel. I can't be part black, can I? My skin is creamy white. Granted, it's definitely not like Willadean's freckled and fair complexion, but I've always thought I looked like my father, Jacob. He had golden tanned skin from being outside constantly, and he had wavy dark brown hair, brown eyes—that's what I inherited. I reach up to touch my hair. There's no kinkiness there. It has always been difficult to manage, straight, wiry, and coarse. . . . Is that where it shows up in me? My hair? It's not my nose. Daddy had a kind of bulbous nose, and it got redder as he got older, but mine is long and thin like Willadean's.

Maybe it was Daddy. Or maybe old Beatrice, his mother. Daddy was one of a set of twins. His twin sister died. I don't remember the story very well. I know that Willadean and Sally sometimes talk about her death. Even Daddy would get involved in that conversation. Apparently Mother and Daddy met because of his sister. Maybe the black showed up more in her. Her name was Jerrilyn. I'll have to take a closer look at her picture if I can find one.

This is crazy! I can't make any sense of it. But where does it leave me? All I can feel right now is shame. No matter how far I've come in accepting my grandchild, I was only ever accepting *her* difference. I simply cannot tolerate the idea that *I'm* part black. The anger I feel for Willadean swells inside me, and I feel like I might have to pull over to vomit. Finally, I spot a road sign. Good God, I've almost driven to Vicksburg!

I take the Vicksburg exit and make my way downtown to my favorite coffee shop. I should probably call Holt to tell him where I am, but I can't bring myself to talk to him or anyone in my family, just yet. I change my mind about coffee and drive over to the Cedar Grove Inn instead. I'll sit in the garden room and have a glass of wine. Maybe that will calm my nerves. Maybe I can sort out how to handle this catastrophe. The cold, hard knowledge that my life will never be the same begins to settle around me like a shroud.

I tuck myself into a secluded corner table and order a glass of chardonnay. I can hear the buzz of my cell phone deep in the recesses of my purse. I try again to ignore my guilt over not taking Holt's calls. I'm too confused to articulate a thought even if I tried to talk to him right now. Holt, who is always strong and steady, who has never worried about family reputation. The twinkling overhead lights of the garden room remind me of the night I met him—at the Christmas formal, 1964. I thought then that my troubles were over, that I'd been given a special dispensation for all that I'd suffered when my mother's social activism destroyed my chance with Mason. I was so happy to meet Holt, who had no family and no ties to Greendale, Mississippi.

December 1964

My dress was a red velveteen sheath cut close to the body, with three-quarter-length fitted sleeves. Laura Elise said it was the perfect shade of cranberry for my dark hair and eyes. I was determined to look as beautiful as possible and to put my grief behind me. Laura Elise and Mason were engaged and that was final. While I was away at the Presbyterian summer camp the previous summer, dutifully playing counselor to a bunch of whiny children, Laura Elise had managed to get Mason to fall in love with her. Her letters over the summer had gotten sparse and vague, but I never saw it coming. When I returned for the fall term, I was greeted with a sobbing Laura Elise begging my forgiveness for stealing the man I loved.

"I promise you, Marion," she said, big fat tears falling from her eyes, "we didn't realize it was happening until it was too late. But I love him; what else could I do?"

What I had shared for those brief months with Mason obviously didn't mean anything—not to Mason, anyway. His on-again, off-again toying with my affection had been a game to him. The risk of losing Laura Elise's and Mason's friendships was too great for me to snub them. There were three important families in Greendale: the Colliers, the Reeds, and mine, the Reynoldses. So, keeping my future in mind, I dedicated myself to Laura Elise and Mason's happiness. I buried my own hurt in an endless series of conversations with Laura Elise about her wedding colors, her china pattern, her honeymoon plans, and the number of babies she planned to have.

By the time the Christmas dance rolled around, I was counting the days until Laura Elise's May wedding was over, and slowly accumulating a file of ideas to make my own wedding, which I was determined to have not long after hers, even more beautiful and romantic. My only remaining problem was securing a groom. I had already decided that none of the Ole Miss fraternity boys who swarmed around me were worthy. If I had to give up Mason Collier, then whoever I married had to be more handsome, wealthier, and smarter. As far as I was concerned, none of the boys I knew fit that description.

I agreed to go to the Christmas formal with Carter Blevins simply to have a date. This was the last event of the term before we all left for home. The semester had been so painful for me that even returning to Oak Knoll for the Christmas holidays appealed to me.

We covered the tables in the sorority house ballroom with white linen tablecloths and decorated them with white candles surrounded with holly greens and red berries. We hired a small band and set them up under a canopy of glowing electric lights. A huge Virginia pine tree stood in the corner, swathed in tinsel and shiny red balls.

I was standing behind the refreshment table; we girls had promised to guard the punch bowl until our chaperones arrived. Professor Amelia Gray, one of our single young faculty chaperones, appeared at the door with a man on her arm who instantly struck me as fitting the physical description of the husband I was searching for.

He was taller than Mason by at least six inches, towering over Professor Gray and making her look quite diminutive. He had dark wavy hair, a strong jawline like Rock Hudson, and broad shoulders. He had a sophisticated look about him, one that I found pleasantly appealing. He and Professor Gray were accompanied by another couple I didn't recognize. When the four of them approached the table, I found myself holding my breath.

"Hi, Marion," Professor Gray said, smiling broadly with her horsey teeth and pushing up her glasses. "I'd like to introduce you to my guests." I smiled warmly at all of them but was having difficulty tearing my eyes away from his. They were dark green, the color of moss. I could swear he was intrigued by me as well. I told myself even then that I was being silly. What interest would this obviously older man have in a college coed?

"This is my brother, Harold, and his fiancée, Elizabeth," she said, pointing to the other couple. "And this," she said, demurely taking the arm of her date, "is Holt Pritchett. He and Harold served in Korea together, and he's visiting for the holidays." She giggled then, not very attractive in my estimation for an adult woman who was supposed to be our role model. I discerned immediately from Holt's polite nod as he looked at her that Harold had fixed his sister up with Holt.

"I'm pleased to meet all of you," I said, giving them—and especially Holt Pritchett—my most dazzling smile. Did his eyes linger longer than would be expected for a polite introduction? I was almost certain of it. I felt something brush my elbow and saw that Carter had returned from checking his coat. I tore my eyes away from Holt to acknowledge Carter, who was fidgeting uncomfortably with his tie. Professor Gray and her party settled themselves at a central table near the dance floor and within sight of the refreshment table.

I tried to throw myself into the holiday spirit. With Carter and several other boys, I danced the pony and the monkey until my feet were sore. When the band started playing my favorite slow tune, "Our Day Will Come"—the one I had thought perfectly described Mason and me—I refused Carter and pushed him toward Jane Hubert, who was half in love with him anyway.

"Y'all go ahead," I said. "I need a break." After visiting the ladies' room to reapply my lipstick and re-tease and spray my hair, I worked my way through the crowd to the refreshment table. A ripple of excitement tingled through me as I spotted Holt Pritchett getting punch. I crossed my fingers that he would believe my bumping into him was accidental.

"Oh, excuse me," I said. "Oh, Mr. Pritchett, hello. Are you enjoying the dance?"

"Yes, very much," he said, melting me with his direct gaze. "And you?"

"Yes, of course," I replied, and then I'm not sure what possessed me. Maybe it was glancing up and seeing Laura Elise and Mason locked in a lovers' embrace, swaying to what was supposed to be my and Mason's song. "Would you like to dance?" I asked, trembling with shock at myself for being so forward. His eyes opened wide in surprise, and I was sure he would give some excuse. But instead he set his cup down, turned to me, and bowed ever so slightly.

"It would be my pleasure," he said.

I felt the other girls' eyes on us as he led me onto the dance floor for the next song. I made sure not to look at Professor Gray, but in my peripheral vision I noticed that she had stopped talking to her brother and was watching us. At that moment I felt reckless. The fact that I was dancing with a handsome older man, whose eyes were only for me, emboldened me even further. As we danced I edged him closer to Mason and Laura Elise.

"Do you like Mississippi, Mr. Pritchett?" I asked, glancing over to be sure Mason had spotted us. I was pleased to see that he had.

"Please, call me Holt," he said. "I'm not *that* much older than you." His smile was warm and even slightly flirtatious. "And, yes, I do like Mississippi. It's a nice change from D.C. Less traffic, less noise." I was aware of his hand at the small of my back and of how my own hand looked resting on his upper arm. I could feel the power in that arm through the fabric of his sport coat. I pictured a large diamond on my left third finger.

"And what do you do up there in Washington, D.C., Holt?" I asked, liking the force of his name on my lips. *Mrs. Holt Pritchett* tripped through my thoughts.

"I'm an attorney with a law firm there," he replied. This was getting better and better.

"And is your family there?" I asked.

"No, I don't have any family left," he said. "It's just me."

"I'm sorry to hear that."

Holt asked me about my family then, my interests, and my college major. He listened to each of my answers with rapt attention, never taking his eyes from me during the entire dance. The dance began with my selfish attempt to charm him. But when it ended and he held me slightly past the time the music stopped and asked if he might see me again during the holidays, I was the one who was charmed. I agreed demurely, telling him that he could reach me at the sorority house the next day if he liked. I walked back—slightly flushed and still surprised by my good fortune—to a sullen Carter Blevins waiting at the edge of the dance floor. To my immense pleasure, Laura Elise intercepted me and insisted that I tell her who that handsome older man was and how I happened to be dancing with him.

My glass is empty, and the waiter stands before me asking if I'd like another. I refuse and ask for coffee instead. I glance at my watch as he walks away; I've been here an hour already. I know that Holt will be worried. The thought of Holt brings tears to my eyes. He has been my rock, and I've never felt a rift between us except over one subject: how to deal with Avery. How would Holt handle this situation? It's one thing to be accepting of Avery's choices and of Celi as our grandchild. But this? This changes everything about our family.

This means that I am not who Holt thought I was. I couldn't bear losing Holt, but I know he'll have to know the truth. Although I don't understand it fully yet, apparently the fact that Celi has sickle-cell disease is the proof that we have a mixed-race ancestry—and I believe my mother must be the culprit in this disaster. I'm struck by a thought: Perhaps it isn't common knowledge that sickle-cell disease occurs only when both parents have black genes. I certainly wasn't aware of it.

As I sign the bill and pick up my purse to leave, I breathe just a touch easier. Perhaps there is a way to deal with this situation. A way that's worked for me so many times before—tried and true. Who says we have to reveal anything to anybody? Whose business is it but ours, anyway? That's it. We won't talk about it. Hopefully, Celi will be out of the hospital soon—I feel a stab of contrition for my selfishness, because I should be at her bedside. But if she recovers quickly, we'll get on with the wedding, and then all of the attention on our family will fade. Yes, we'll carry on. And I'm not even sure I want to know more myself. What good would it do?

Chapter 37

Avery

The seduction of a Sunday afternoon nap is pulling my eyelids closed as I scooch around in the slick fake-leather hospital chair, trying to get comfortable. Celi has polished off the part of the hospital food that she'll eat, including the green Jell-O. I've always been amazed at her particular affection for green Jell-O. Now she's snuggled under her covers, clutching Frog and dozing to the drone of the air-conditioner unit.

I feel another surge of grateful relief as I watch her eyes. This crisis has been blessedly short. The swelling is already coming down in her fingers and feet. Pain meds, a blood transfusion, fluids, and an early start on antibiotics have helped curtail the worst of it. Before he left last night, Aaron told me that the weekend relief doctor would be in to check on her this afternoon. Aaron felt certain that she'd go home today. When he asked if he could come with us to bring her back out to Will's house, I wasn't sure how to respond. It never occurred to me that he would want to be so involved. And I've never allowed myself to consider how I would feel when he was.

Aaron's interest in Celi is not a complete surprise. He's a family-oriented and loving man with a huge heart—why wouldn't he want to be part of his daughter's life? And now that he has this chance, he wants to take full advantage of it. How can I say no? I won't reveal to either of them the sting I feel each time I see them smile at each other or hear him laugh at her silly little jokes. I won't tell him how I wish I could replay the last ten years, rewrite a story in which he follows me to Colorado and we make a life together. Seeing Celi's happiness is enough to make me want that. But the truth is that my fantasy arises from more than how good Aaron is for Celi; what I felt for Aaron was much more than a girlish rebellion and infatuation, and it will be a tremendous challenge for me to find that kind of love again.

The good thing is that once I get Celi out of the hospital and we're back at Will's, Aaron can visit with her over at Sally's, and I won't need to be a part of their budding relationship. The wedding is less than a week away, and before we know it we'll be going home to Denver. Of course there will be visits. But with some time, and some distance in between, I'll manage it. I have to, for her sake . . . and his. Right now, I have to learn how.

The loud crack of the heavy hospital room door awakens me, and I turn quickly in the chair, almost falling out of it, rubbing my eyes as I'm thrown back to my childhood, seeing the man who enters the room. I haven't been face-to-face with Dr. Boggess since the day he confirmed my pregnancy. I thought he was ancient then, but now he looks almost ghostly. His thick hair has gone completely white, and the bones of his face protrude like a skeleton's. His gait is much less certain, and I can tell from his slight limp and the way he carries his left arm that he's suffered a stroke sometime during the past decade. He peers at me through the thick lenses of his black-rimmed glasses with the benign look I've come to recognize that doctors reserve for their patients—not too detached, not too familiar. He knows who I am—he has treated our family since Mother was a baby—but after the scandal I caused, I wonder if he'll acknowledge me. He's followed by a young black nurse in scrubs. She smiles at Celi, who is wide-awake now, and they chat about how she likes Mississippi.

Dr. Boggess approaches me with his hand extended. My fears of his rebuff dissipate with his warm handshake. "Avery Pritchett," he says, his eyes twinkling and his smile slightly drooping on one side. "So the prodigal daughter has returned, hmm?" he asks, and turns toward Celi. "And you've brought this sweet young lady with you." Celi smiles at him—a stiff, polite little smile—and I can see the question in her eyes.

"Celi," I say, moving toward her bed, "this is Dr. Boggess. He was my doctor when I was a little girl."

Dr. Boggess comes around to the side of her bed, and his big yellowed teeth show in his smile. "Yes, I was, and your grandmother Marion's doctor before that."

"Wow!" Celi says, her eyes wide. "You must be really old!"

"Celi!" I say, wanting to laugh but realizing I should reprimand her.

"Oh, it's okay," he says. "She's right. I am old." He pulls out a stethoscope and places the earpieces in his ears. "How about we have a listen, young lady? That is, if you think my old ears can hear anything." Celi grins. I think she's decided she likes this doctor. She sits up obediently and leans forward for him to apply the instrument to her bony little back. She immediately starts taking deep, slow breaths.

"Well, young lady," he says after he finishes listening, "do you think you're ready to go home today?"

"Yes, sir," Celi says instantly, nodding her head vigorously up and down.

"Well then," he says. "Bridget here will take that thing out of your arm and get the paperwork ready." Bridget nods, gives Celi a wink, and pulls alcohol preps and a Band-Aid out of her pocket, preparing to discontinue Celi's IV.

Dr. Boggess turns to me. "How about we walk out in the hall to chat?" he says, taking my arm. I'm confident that Celi is comfortable with this part of the discharge procedure, so I allow him to lead me from the room. "So I hear that you're a nurse," he says, fumbling slightly with the stethoscope before returning it to the pocket of his crisp white lab coat.

"Yes, I am . . . a pediatric surgical nurse."

"Glad to hear it. And your daughter here has sickle-cell anemia, I see," he says, dropping to a quieter voice as he flips through the pages of Celi's chart.

"Yes, she does," I answer, not wanting to go into detail with him, uncertain of where he's going with this conversation. Then it occurs to me. Maybe he knows more than I've considered.

"Dr. Boggess," I say, "I've been wondering how my side of Celi's family could have contributed the sickle-cell gene. Do you have any idea how that could have happened?"

He looks puzzled then and shakes his head. "We didn't test for sickle cell when you and your brother were born. It wasn't something we did, especially for white children." He scratches his wrinkly chin, pulling his face down into a frown. "No, this isn't something I would have known. They didn't start testing babies in Mississippi until the late seventies, early eighties. I suppose you're wondering how you came to have the trait?"

"Yes, that's exactly what I'm trying to figure out," I say. "Do you have any idea?"

He is shaking his head when we both look up to see Aaron approaching. He's not alone. He's carrying an adorable little boy, and walking beside him is another boy who looks to be about five and is holding the hand of the former debutante and homecoming queen of Greendale High School, Lacretia Brandon. Only now, she's Lacretia Monroe—Aaron's wife.

Meeting her brothers is not at all the awkward experience for Celi that it is for me. When Lacretia, Aaron, and their sons follow Dr. Boggess and me into Celi's hospital room, I can see Aaron's love for her written all over his face. And his boys? I've never seen a daddy prouder of his sons. Dr. Boggess quickly makes his exit after he shakes hands with Aaron and Lacretia. I can tell he is anxious to avoid any possible family drama.

Aaron plops the little one on the bed beside Celi, who is grinning from ear to ear by then, and reaches down to pull the older boy up into his lap. "Celi," he says. "These are your brothers, Louis and Brandon." He points to each boy in turn. They are impossibly cute in gym shorts and T-shirts, with New Orleans Saints ball caps exactly like their dad's.

"Hey," Celi says timidly, which surprises me. I think she is a little overwhelmed. Lacretia, who spoke politely to me when she came into the room, is now standing back watching. When Aaron reaches out for her, she steps forward to be introduced to Celi.

I have to hand it to Lacretia; she is very kind to Celi. And the boys are so sweet. Brandon, the five-year-old, sits with Celi and watches an episode of *SpongeBob* on TV, while Louis, who is just beginning to walk, toddles around the room, playing with a Nerf ball with his dad. Lacretia and I make polite conversation—each of us asking the other about work, the kids, safe topics. After the nurse comes in to give us Celi's discharge papers, Lacretia scoops up Louis, calls Brandon to her side, and prepares to leave. I get the sense that her departure has been planned, that she and Aaron agreed that he would accompany Celi home.

Now here we are, Celi in the backseat chattering excitedly, asking one question after another about her new family. Aaron, driving, is calmly answering her every query, and me . . . numb, not quite sure how I got to this point, and not sure how to take it all in. I'm anxious to get Aaron alone and hear how he convinced Lacretia to come to the hospital. I'm starting to worry about the expectations he's creating when he answers Celi's questions. Exactly when are they going to do all of the things he's promising? Basketball, fishing, even a Saints game? We don't live here. Our lives are still in Colorado. I decide to keep my mouth shut. Why burst her bubble now? She's so happy.

When we arrive at Oak Knoll, Will is waiting for us. "Come on in here, little girl," she says to Celi, giving her a big hug. When did my grandmother get so affectionate?

"Hey, Grandma Will," Celi says. "Guess what?" And Celi immediately launches into the story of meeting her brothers and her "stepmom." I know that there's an instinctive recoiling somewhere deep inside me when I hear Celi use that term for Lacretia, but I'm still so anesthetized that I can't process it right now. Aaron seems so relaxed. How can he take these developments in stride? I shake myself. I have to focus on Celi and what she needs in order to get better, so that we can get through this wedding and return home.

"Celi, time for you to rest for a while," I say. "You've had quite the morning."

"Aw, Mom," she whines. "I've been resting. I want to go outside with Grandma Will."

"Hey, come on, now," Aaron says. "Listen to your mom. You've got a big wedding to get ready for, remember?" Celi nods reluctantly. "You don't want to be getting sick during that, do you?" Celi shakes her head and allows herself to be led to our room. She insists Aaron come with us, and we both hover while she finds her book and settles into her bed. I'm vaguely conscious of the sound of a car outside. I kiss Celi and prepare to leave the room, expecting Aaron to follow me. He kisses her cheek and turns to leave, but Celi grabs his hand.

"Dad?" she says, and I can see from the glow that's returning to her face how much she loves saying that word.

"Yes?"

"I know I'm not a little kid and all, but would you read to me? Just for a few minutes?" She turns to me. "If that's okay with you, Mom?"

"Oh, well . . . sure," I say, embarrassed by my jealousy, hoping Aaron doesn't see it.

"How about I read and your mom listens?" he asks.

"That'd be great!" Celi says, her eyes shining. "Have you ever read *Hank the Cowdog* books?" she asks Aaron, who shakes his head. "Mom and I love them. They're funny. Right, Mom?" she says to me. I nod and smile, amazed at the way she seems so sensitive to my feelings. Her subtle reminder of what she and I have shared is enough for me to see no threat in having Aaron read to her.

I find myself enjoying the sound of Aaron's deep, clear voice and laughing together with Celi as we share with her dad our old friend Hank's hilarious adventures—that's how I have to think of him now. . . . *I can do this.* I will myself to relax and allow Celi her moments with him.

Aaron's voice is interrupted by another voice coming from the front of the house. It's my mother speaking in her most insistent tone. No one has heard from her since our blowup yesterday, and I'm worried about what her presence here means. Aaron finishes the chapter, and as we close Celi's door behind us, I hear, "Wil-ladean." Mother spits out my grandmother's name. "We have to talk."

"Marion, maybe we could fix a glass of tea first?" I hear Daddy say. So they're both here. I notice he's using his calming voice—the one that usually convinces my mother to back off from a tirade. As Aaron and I walk into the parlor, my mother turns to face us and I'm shocked by her disheveled appearance. Her hair is uncombed, she's not wearing any makeup, and an ordinary black warm-up suit—something she would usually reserve for the gym—hangs loosely from her petite frame. Her eyes are red, and there are dark circles underneath them. She looks as if the hounds of fear have been nipping at her heels all night.

Chapter 38

Marion

When Avery enters the front parlor followed by Aaron Monroe, I almost lose my resolve. Seeing Aaron effectively renders me speechless. I can't even be polite. Everyone is waiting for me to say something since I've demanded this confrontation. Willadean is seated in her usual chair, looking unperturbed—how typical. Holt is hovering near the doorway as if he'd like to escape. He hugs Avery and shakes hands with Aaron, clapping him on the back with all the warmth he would share with any member of the family. Only Avery looks a little worried. This doesn't surprise me, given what she revealed to me yesterday. News that has caused me a sleepless night pacing the floor, refusing to even attempt to talk to Holt for fear of his refusal to understand.

I want to launch right into what I need to say so that I won't lose my nerve. But before I do, I need Aaron Monroe to leave. This is a matter for family ears only—my family. Right now, he's busy talking to Willadean and Holt. I notice Holt catch Avery's attention and murmur something to her, and she glances over at me. She closes the conversation with Aaron, who nods good-bye to me and follows Avery out. It's not long before she returns, looking suspiciously at me. Of course, Willadean tries as usual to provoke me.

"Marion, you look like hell. What is it that you need to talk about? Are you sick?"

"No, Mother, I'm not sick," I snap. "Just sick inside about the secrets you've kept from me." I feel myself start to shake. The lack of sleep and my nervousness are getting the best of me. I try to breathe deeply, but I can't seem to get any air past the tight band around my chest.

"What are you talking about?" Willadean demands.

"Wait a minute, Mother . . ." Avery starts.

"Yes, Marion," Holt says. "Let's just calm down. . . ."

"No, I won't calm down, and I won't wait a minute. I won't wait one more second," I say, standing up so that they'll know I mean to get out what I came here to say. "What I'm talking about, Willadean, is you." She looks startled but doesn't respond. "I've struggled for years to get past your dogged insistence that mixing with blacks is acceptable to you. I've found a way to make my and Holt's life separate enough from yours that most people don't look at us as misfits. They think you're the one who's eccentric, Willadean. *Eccentric!*" She has the nerve now to smile! And Avery is smiling, too. Why is that humorous? I'm so angry, I feel my voice getting louder, but I can't stop. There's no turning back. "Yes, you can laugh. Is that what you've been doing behind my back all of these years? Laughing? Laughing because you know the truth?"

Willadean shakes her head, all seriousness now. "What truth is that, Marion?"

I can hardly get the words out of my mouth. "The truth about our family. The truth that we are mixed with blacks. And you know how it happened."

Avery is watching her grandmother and looking extremely uncomfortable. She should be; she started all this. For some crazy reason, it hits me how alike they look. In my oldest memories of my mother, she looks like Avery does now. I have a fleeting picture of her long willowy frame. I'm a little girl, probably only five or six years old, and I'm walking behind her in the garden. That was before I began to see her differently. . . . I mentally trod on the wave of sadness this memory brings. Willadean opens her mouth, but I push on, not letting her speak.

"Yes, Avery told me that our family is half the reason that child in there has this disease that blacks get." I'm standing over her now, daring her to deny it. She won't look at me. I turn and cross the room, using movement to try to get my thoughts together. "I need to know who in this town knows about this," I say. "I need to make sure that it does not get out in the community. There's already enough gossip with Avery bringing her daughter here and being in Mark's wedding, but we can deal with that. But this? If this gets out, Holt's career could be ruined." I'm getting ready to lay out the plan I've made, but I stop when Willadean holds up her hand.

"Stop, Marion!" she says. "Just stop right there." I decide to obey temporarily in order to compose myself. However, I will not let her dominate me. I have to stand up to her. Willadean turns to Avery. "Avery, would you please explain to me what your mother is talking about?"

It is somewhat gratifying to see Avery squirm. But why is Willadean acting so puzzled? Avery fidgets, pulling an elastic hair band on and off her wrist. She is obviously intimidated by Willadean. "I . . . um . . . I've been trying to figure out how Celi got the sickle-cell trait from me. And, well . . . since you were so close to Henry Johnson and you've talked about how much you cared for him, I . . . um . . . I thought that maybe you and he . . ." She looks up at Willadean and then back down. "Anyway, I hadn't had a chance to talk to you about it yet, but the other day at the hospital when Mother started blaming Celi's disease on Aaron—"

I can't help but jump in. I will not be talked about this way. "I was simply pointing out to you how mixing with blacks has caused problems for everyone in this family. You—"

"I don't want to hear it, Mother," Avery yells at me. "I don't want to hear any more about how I've brought shame on this family."

"Both of you hush up," Willadean says, and we're both silenced by her tone. "First of all, I am not going to have you creating all this commotion in my house. If you can't settle down and talk in normal tones, then you can leave—both of you. Second, Avery Louise," she says, turning to glare at Avery, "you've been going around deciding a lot of things that you have no business making assumptions about."

Avery shrinks back in her chair, and Willadean turns on me. "And you, Marion, you need to get down off your high horse and quit trying to act like you're better than everybody else. You talk about being ruined? I'll tell you what is being ruined *right now.* You're ruining any chance you'll have of being a mother to your daughter and a grandmother to that sweet little girl in there because of your damn ideas about blacks and whites!" She stops suddenly as she looks across the room at Holt. He's frowning and inclining his head toward something across the room. When I follow his gaze, I see that Celi is standing there, clutching a stuffed frog and listening to everything we've said.

Chapter 39

Avery

Daddy gets to Celi before I can. "Well, hi there, Celi," he says. "I thought you were taking a nap." He puts his arm around her, and he's guiding her over to where he was sitting. "How about you come over here and sit with me. Maybe you and I can get these ladies to talk about something more fun." He looks up at me when he says that.

Mother says, "I'm going to make coffee," and leaves the room without looking back.

Will hasn't moved. She's staring out the window and she looks far away right now.

I get up and go over to Celi, holding out my hand to her. "Come on, sweet pea," I say. "I'll walk you back to our room. Your grandparents and I have some grown-up things to talk about right now." Daddy gives her a hug, and she comes along quietly.

It's peaceful in our room. The ceiling fan makes a rhythmic, soothing noise, and the scent of dainty white phlox in a vase near the bed sweetens the air. "Mom?" Celi asks as she crawls back into bed. "Am I a black person?"

I don't know what to say. I start to answer; then I stop myself. Finally, I shrug and plop down on the side of her bed, letting out a long, exhausted sigh. "I guess the best answer I can give you for that, Celi, is yes and no."

"Yes *and* no?" she asks. "Is that because I have one white parent and one black one?"

"That's right."

"Why does it matter so much to Grandma?"

I rub my hands across my eyes. I feel so tired right now. "Celi . . . down here . . . in Mississippi . . . people tend to think of a person as one or the other. . . ."

"You mean either black or white?"

"Yes."

"But why?" she asks. "Why do I have to be one or the other? Why can't I be both? What's wrong with that?" Celi always reads my responses regardless of my words, because she says, "I'm sorry. I didn't mean to make you angry."

I place one hand on either side of her body and look down at her. "Oh, Celi," I say, "you're not making me angry. It's that I'm so frustrated. Of course you don't have to be one or the other. You *are* both. You've got your dad"—I touch her hair and her sweet full lips—"and you've got me." I pinch her nose. This makes us both smile. "And you are perfect exactly as you are." I lean down and kiss her cheek. "And it's perfect that you are both black and white."

"It doesn't seem like Grandma thinks it is. She looks at me funny. Like she's not sure what to do with me."

I roll my eyes at this. And then I stare up at the ceiling. "It's like this, Celi. For my mother, being white and the things that go with being white—"

"You mean like the big fancy house, the debutante dresses, and the maid, and her clubs and stuff?"

"Yes, all that stuff," I answer. "To her, that's all really, really important. It's like she thinks that it's actually *part of* being white, and she has always believed that whites and blacks are not supposed to mix. . . ."

"You mean like you and my dad?"

"Yes, especially like your dad and me. So your grandmother is trying to figure out how to respond to us." I drop my voice to a whisper, like it's a secret between us. "To tell you the truth, I think she's having a hard time. You know why?"

"Why?"

"Because I think that she is really impressed with her beautiful granddaughter from Colorado, and she doesn't know how to fit you into her world."

Celi thinks about this for a while.

"Now, I have to get back to our grown-up conversation and it's time for you to sleep."

"But do you think I'll ever fit in here?" she asks.

"I'm not sure." I wish I had a definite answer for her. "But here's what I *do* know." I smile at her. "Soon we'll be going home, and we won't have to worry about how people behave here. Now, you get some rest, and I'll come back and check on you in a little while."

I would rather crawl into bed beside Celi with the covers over my head than go back into that room with my mother and Will. But since I'm the one who started this trouble, I know I have to face them. By the time I return, Mother is coming back in with a cup of coffee. She sounds cold and flat as she offers to get everyone a cup, but none of us take her up on it. She plants herself on the settee across from Will, who is responding to a question Daddy has asked about her garden. He's obviously trying to lighten things up. He knows she will always talk about her vegetables.

Will looks up at me as I walk into the room. "I'm sorry Celi had to hear all that, Avery," she says. "Is she upset?"

I look at Mother, who is staring down into her cup not looking at me. "She's confused," I say. "She doesn't understand all of this talk about blacks and whites. She's never had to deal with anything like it before."

"And it shouldn't be cause for such a fuss," Will says.

This makes Mother look at her as if she's got two heads. I can tell that Mother is still fighting to maintain her composure. Daddy has opened the newspaper and is hiding behind it. As I sit down in the other chair near Will, Mother starts again.

"I don't see how you can say that," she says, and there is needle-sharp tension in her voice, even though she's keeping it low. "All my life in this town I've heard people gossip about how you carry on with blacks. Can't you see that people around here don't mix? Can't you see what happens when you do?"

Will has a resigned look on her face. I don't think she'll be fighting with Mother any more today. "Marion, what I know is that Sally Monroe is my dearest friend in the world. We've been together through thick and thin, and no amount of you telling me that white people in Greendale don't mix with blacks is going to change that. Don't you think I know what folks say about me? Don't you think I saw how ashamed you were all your life?"

I notice that Daddy glances up from his newspaper. I think he's watching for Mother's reaction.

For a split second, I think I see some remorse on her face. But then it's gone, followed by a stubborn set of her chin. "I've simply tried to make sure that my family has every opportunity to do well here, and that has meant adopting certain attitudes. Holt's practice would never have succeeded if we hadn't established ourselves with the whites in this community. You and I both know that's the truth. I want to be sure now, given this . . . new development . . . that we're able to continue to hold our heads up."

She stops as if she's waiting for a response from Will, but it's not forthcoming. I am at a loss. Will is not admitting anything one way or the other, and Mother is operating from the assumption that what I told her in anger is true.

"What we need to do now," Mother says, "is make sure that we keep this business to ourselves. There's no need for people to know that anything has changed. No one around here is going to know or understand all of this medical information that Avery does—about this sickle-cell trait and all of that. We'll carry on with the wedding, and then things will go back to normal."

"And Celi and I will go home, so you won't have to worry about us anymore," I finish. Mother looks at me guiltily but doesn't argue.

Daddy puts his paper down. "Now, Avery," he says, "I don't think your mother wants y'all to leave. Why, you just got here."

I wonder how he seems to stay above all of this wrangling and wish for some of his calm. "We don't belong here, Daddy," I say. "It makes things complicated for everyone." Mother still hasn't responded. Couldn't she say *something*? Couldn't she at least *try* to act like we matter to her?

"Avery Louise Pritchett," Will says in her sternest voice, "you *do* belong here, you and Celi both. That child has family here. She's gotten to meet her daddy, and look how well that turned out. You said yourself that Lacretia is coming around. And Sally? Sally Monroe thinks that child hung the moon. So do I, as a matter of fact." Will looks at Mother, then back at me. "That child needs her family, and so do you. Don't you let all of this foolishness run you off."

"Foolishness?" Mother asks. "You think it's foolishness? I find out that you've kept from me all my life that my own father is a black man, and you call it foolishness? What if I had sickle cell?" Mother is getting angry again. "I know that my and Holt's reputations and our success don't mean anything to you, but does our health? Does it worry you in the least that you brought a disease into this family—that you've brought your great-granddaughter all this suffering?"

"Now, Marion," Daddy starts.

"Don't you 'now Marion' me, Holt Pritchett," she says through clenched teeth as she turns on him. "It's fine for you to sit there all smug, staying above the fray, but, frankly, I could use a little support from you—especially you. I'm part of the reason you have the high social standing we enjoy in this town, and the loyalty of the wealthiest people around here. I worked like a dog to make sure every one of those high-browed women couldn't say anything disparaging about us or our children . . . until Avery's little high school drama, that is. And then I started all over again to be sure that was past us. And now this." Mother is crying now, tears are streaming down her face, and I almost feel sorry for her. She seems so broken.

Will reaches in her pocket, pulls out a tissue, and hands it to Mother. "Marion," she says gently, "what makes you think that what Avery told you is true?"

Everyone freezes, stunned into silence. Mother looks like she's been slapped, and I'm on the edge of my seat.

"Are you saying it isn't true?" I ask.

Will looks out the window again, as if she's staring off into past memories. A soft smile wrinkles up her face, and when she turns back to me her expression is unreadable. "You know, Avery, people of my generation don't talk of such things."

"I know," I whisper, wondering if this is it. Is this all she's going to say? I look over at Mother, who rolls her eyes and dabs away her tears, but she keeps watching Will.

Again Will looks away. She continues to stare out the window as she speaks. "I *did* love Henry Johnson. When he died in basic training, I was devastated. So was Sally. It was Jacob who comforted me and offered to marry me. It didn't matter one whit to Jacob Reynolds what color my best friends were."

I listen anxiously, afraid that if she gets interrupted now, she'll never speak of this again.

"I knew better than to think that I could have ever made a life with Henry," she continues sadly. She looks at Mother with such intensity that Mother is forced to return her gaze. "Yes, Marion, even *I* knew that."

"But did you—" Mother starts.

Will holds up her hand and slowly shakes her head. "I'm not going to talk about it anymore," she says, looking at me and then at Mother. "Your father was Jacob Reynolds, Marion, and he was a good father to you."

Mother sinks back into the settee, looking completely drained and confused. Daddy watches the three of us, not saying a word.

"But . . . how?" I stammer.

"I don't have an answer for that, Avery," Will says, and she gets up from her chair. "Now, if y'all will excuse me, I need a nap."

Chapter 40

Avery

I've been walking around in a fog. It's three days before Mark's wedding and as far as I'm concerned it can't come soon enough. I've gotten roped into all kinds of prewedding jobs—preparing the place cards for the rehearsal dinner, checking with the florist for last-minute changes, making sure Will has the right Marion-mandated dress. Celi's been loving it, of course. She's been feeling much better and I've taken her with me on errands whenever I can. Aaron's called a couple of times to check on her—I usually hand the phone to her right away and let them chat. They need to form their own relationship without me in the middle. And I have to learn to let go. He's asked to bring her over to Sally's for dinner with Lacretia and the boys, and of course I said that would be fine. But it's still painful to know Celi will have a whole other family that doesn't include me.

I'll be dropping Celi off at Sally's before I head into town, which still feels strange. But not as strange as the phone call I got this morning. It was Daddy, calling at seven o'clock, speaking quickly, as if he wanted to be sure that Mother didn't catch him making the call.

"I need you and Mark to meet me down at the office today at eleven. Can you do that?"

"Sure, Daddy," I answered, still sleepy. "What's up?"

"I'll explain when you get here, darling," he said. "I've already called your brother."

"Um . . . okay . . ."

"And one more thing—please don't mention this to your mother."

As he was saying good-bye, I heard a noise in the background as if she was coming into the room. I still have no clue what he's up to, but I'm following instructions.

Celi is so thrilled to be spending time at Sally's house that she was out of bed this morning and eating a bowl of cereal without me having to coax her. She skips happily off to our room to get dressed while Will and I finish our coffee.

"That child is contented here," Will observes.

As if I can't see that? As if Celi hasn't begun to ask me every day, "Mom, are you sure we have to go back home? Can't we stay here?"

I've told myself that if I continue to give her the same answer, eventually we'll both believe it: "Our life is in Colorado—my work, your school, our friends." What I don't say is that I couldn't bear the prospect of living here. What would it be like for her? How would she be treated? But I decide not to get into that with Will right now.

"She is content," I agree. "I'm glad things have worked out for her."

"And you?" Will asks. I can feel her looking at me, but I don't return her gaze. I get up to clear the table, focusing on the dishes and trying to come up with some general, noncommittal comment.

"I know it's good that Aaron and Celi met," I finally say. "He's a great dad. And it's also good that Lacretia is so accepting of Celi. And, of course, Sally is terrific, and she loves her to death. . . ."

"But what about you, Avery?" she presses. "How are you weathering all these changes?"

"I'm doing okay," I answer, and reach to turn on the kitchen radio, hoping she'll get the hint. She does, and we work in silence for a while, me doing dishes, her working the crossword puzzle in the newspaper. I feel a bit of remorse for cutting Will off. Of anyone in the family, she has been the one to fight for me. I stop with the dishrag in my hand and turn to wipe off the kitchen table.

"I'm sorry, Will," I say, not able to look at her. "To tell you the truth, I feel more confused than ever. I thought this trip was about finding answers. And I have gotten some. But I still don't know how we're going to both be parents to her, long distance. I can't stand the thought of spending long periods of time away from my own daughter while she visits Aaron here. And I'm no closer to knowing how I passed on the sickle-cell trait to Celi." I stop wiping the counters and look at her. "Funny, I thought that was my main reason for coming down here."

After our big confrontation with Mother on Sunday, Will and I haven't discussed any of this. I left that conversation still feeling that she was keeping something from us. But she's not going to talk about her relationship with Henry Johnson. It's not going to happen. She is watching me calmly, letting me talk. "Now I don't even know if it matters," I say.

But it does matter, because until I know for sure, the uncertainty will be a constant source of upheaval in my family.

As I pull my car into the tree-shaded lot behind the old building that houses Daddy's law offices, I'm filled with curiosity about why he's called me and Mark here. What can possibly be so important? The first thought that occurred to me this morning was that he's going to tell us he's sick. *Please, dear God, don't let it be that.* As I'm getting out of the car, Mark drives up, gets out, and walks over to hug me.

"What do you suppose this is all about?" he asks. "I was supposed to be at a meeting with a client over in Mound Bayou today, but Daddy had me cancel it. He never cancels meetings."

"I have no idea," I answer, keeping my fears to myself. "I guess we'll find out soon."

Daddy is talking to Merle when Mark and I enter the reception area. He tells us to go on in; he'll be right there. In his office, redolent with the familiar, comforting smells of old law books and leather, we sit in the two chairs across the desk from his. My hands are shaking. This is strange. As a nurse, I've always prided myself on my steady hands. Why am I so nervous? Is something wrong with Daddy? I can't tolerate the idea of him not being there for Mark and me. I'm conscious of how I count on certain things staying the same—while being the first to complain when other things don't change.

"So do you have any theories?" Mark asks. "I mean, when was the last time Daddy wanted to, you know, *talk* to us?" He actually looks a little scared, too, and it triggers a memory that makes me laugh.

"I had forgotten this, but there was one other time. I remember him having a talk with us when you and I were . . . hmm . . . I think we were ten and twelve. Remember? We were in the backseat of the car, driving home from church, I think, and we passed that old black man who used to walk around downtown?"

"Oh, yeah," Mark says, the memory coming to him. "He was the crazy guy who talked to himself all the time. . . . We were laughing at him, or making fun of him or something, weren't we?"

"Yes, we were mocking him, and when we got home, Daddy told us to go into the den and sit on the couch and not move until he got there."

"I remember how scared we were when he came in," Mark says. "Then he told us how that old guy had been one of the first black foot soldiers in World War Two, and that we had no idea what he had gone through in . . . wherever he was—that part I don't remember." Mark shakes his head. "I'd never seen him so mad."

"Me, either," I say. "But he told us he'd better never see us disrespect a person like that when we had no idea what his life was like."

"Yes, and if he ever caught us doing it again, we wouldn't see the outside of our house, except for school, for a very long time. He said that he was sure Mother could find plenty for us to do. He knew that would get to us."

Our conversation stops when Daddy comes in, shrugging out of his suit jacket, his starched white shirt crinkly from sweat. I notice that he moves slowly, as if his joints are stiff, and as I study his hands placing his jacket on the back of a chair I mentally calculate his age—ten years older than Mother would make him sixty-eight. I can't believe my own father is almost seventy years old. He sits down heavily in his leather chair and pulls it toward the desk. Mark and I wait expectantly. I think we both sense his tension, and we remain silent.

He leans forward, props his elbows on the desk, folds his hands together, and rests them on his chest for several seconds as he stares at a folder lying in front of him. As he drops his hands and picks up the folder, he says, "I've got something I need to tell the two of you, and . . ." He stops, holds the still closed folder, and looks up at us. He looks exhausted, the way he used to look when he came home after trying a particularly hard case. I stare at the folder, wondering if there's a diagnosis written in it, one that will shorten my father's life. He continues, "I need you to listen. I know you'll have questions, but hear me out first. Can you do that for me?"

Chapter 41

Avery

As Daddy starts to talk, I'm reminded of why he's been so successful as a lawyer. Mother thinks it's her determination and social connections, but Daddy's ability to tell a story, to pull a person into the rhythm of his voice, is mesmerizing, and I find myself transported to a hot, dusty Georgia day in 1951 when my eighteen-year-old father decided to register for military service.

"I remember how hot it was that day, standing in the recruitment line," he says. "The Georgia sun was beating down on our heads, and we couldn't wait to get to the part of the line that was in the shade of this big oak tree. By the time you got to the shade, you were within spitting distance of the recruiters. There were two of them with tables set up under the tree, but the one that caught my eye was a sharp-looking young buck with slicked-back blond hair and a crisp uniform. I remember thinking how important he looked, like a man of distinction, as if men would straighten up and pay attention when he had something to say. I wanted to be that man. I wanted to be able to order other men around. I knew I could be good at it."

I'm having a hard time imagining my father not in control, and I've never thought of him as young. My heart fills with sadness for my father, a young man whose parents had already died, wanting so much to make his mark in the world. But why is he telling us this now?

"What you two don't know is that in all my eighteen years before that time I hadn't done anything but follow orders. I've led y'all to believe that my parents came over from Poland and died young and that I didn't have any family here." Daddy pauses, rubs his chin and eyebrows, and takes a deep breath. "Fact is that my mother and father were not Polish. They were both born and raised in Georgia. My father owned a grocery store in a tiny logging community in the hills near Clayton."

I gasp, startled at this sudden shift in what I've always believed. Wait a minute. Why would he hide that his parents were from a small town in Georgia? What difference does that make? This conversation is not at all what I was expecting.

Daddy continues. "By the time I was twelve years old, all I had ever done was work in that store, stocking and cleaning and wrapping up bologna and cheese to sell to loggers when they dragged themselves in from those deep woods for their dinner breaks. I wanted a taste of adventure and I knew that the only way I could get out of there was to leave against my daddy's will. He was a hard man, my father. He had the constitution of a preacher—went about everything like it was the work of God himself—and the hard-driving determination of a drill sergeant." When Daddy pauses for a moment, I'm still trying to wrap my mind around the fact that I had other grandparents—grandparents who lived only eight hours from where I'm sitting right now.

"The loggers always told me I looked like my father. Tall and well muscled, kind of like you, Mark," Daddy says with a weary smile. I look over at my brother, and he appears as stunned as I feel. "I inherited Daddy's hair and eyes, too, black wavy hair and green eyes," he adds.

"Matter of fact, it was only in the last year that I lived at home that I was able to lift more flour sacks than him," Daddy says as he leans back in his chair and spins it slowly toward the window, where he stops to look out over the street. "I didn't go into town as a child. If we needed anything, Daddy went without us. My mother refused to make the trip down the mountain into Clayton. She said she had no use for townsfolk. But when I got to be twelve years old my father announced one day that I was to go with him on his trip into Clayton. I was about as excited as a young boy could be."

I'm following along with this story, imagining my father's pride in strutting around a small town with his own handsome father. I start to interrupt to ask about his mother, but Daddy turns back toward me and holds up his hand. "Now, Avery, I need you to let me finish. This is hard enough as it is." I stay quiet, determining to ask my questions later, wondering why this is so hard for him.

"We made the trip into town together in our old wagon, loaded up the supplies we needed, and then my father and I stopped into the drugstore for a chocolate milk shake. Now, back then that was quite a treat. My father must've been feeling generous that day for some reason, and I was beside myself because I'd never had a milk shake from a soda fountain.

"The counter was crowded with people, and I noticed when we came in that an older well-dressed woman gave us a funny look and immediately got up from the counter. I couldn't understand why she looked at us that way and I wondered if she could tell that I'd never been to town before. My father and I sat down on stools to wait our turn, and I watched her out of the corner of my eye whispering something to the soda jerk behind the counter. He looked over at us and nodded his head, and then she glared at us with this smug expression as she walked out. My father didn't seem to notice any of it. In fact, he seemed to be ignoring everyone around him. But then the soda jerk came over to where we were sitting and said to my father, 'Sir, I'm going to have to ask your boy to leave. We don't serve colored at this counter.' The whole crowd at the counter went quiet then, and every set of eyes turned to stare at me. I'm here to tell you, I was stunned."

I feel my lips going numb, my hands tingling, and I've been breathing so fast and shallow that I'm close to hyperventilating. Daddy seems very far away, and his voice sounds hollow, like he's speaking from the inside of a barrel.

"Avery!" I hear Daddy say from a distance, and I feel Mark's hand close over mine, which is gripping the arm of the chair so tightly that my knuckles are white. "I need for you to breathe, darling. Just breathe and listen." I take a deep, ragged breath and try to focus. My mind is screaming now; questions are buzzing in my ears like gnats on rotten fruit.

"And do y'all know what the worst part was of all that happened that day?" Mark and I both slowly shake our heads. "My big, strong father didn't say a word. He looked at me with a sad expression in his eyes, and knowing that I looked as white as he did, he did something I'll never forget. He simply got up and we left. Right then and there, he admitted to that whole town that I was colored. At that time, one drop of black blood was all that was needed to change your race in people's eyes. It didn't matter what color your skin was.

"We proceeded straight to our wagon, loaded up, and started out of town. My father didn't utter one word, and neither did I. When we finally reached the outskirts of town, he pulled the wagon off the road into the shade. That was when he told me the whole story.

"What I learned was that my white grandfather was a prominent lawyer in Clayton. My black grandmother had been his maid. When his wife found out about the pregnancy, my grandmother was fired, of course. She found work in another nearby town, married a black man, and raised my mother there, along with her darker-skinned brothers and sisters who came along later.

"The whispering older woman at the drugstore was my maternal grandfather's white wife, and what my father didn't know was that she had been jealously keeping abreast of the details of my black grandmother's life through her own sister, who had been the one to hire my grandmother when she was pregnant with my mother. I think the old woman must have espoused the philosophy 'Keep your friends close, but keep your enemies closer.' That day when we came into the drugstore, she recognized my father as the man who married her husband's bastard daughter. Even though I didn't look black and my mother didn't look black, one whispered comment from a vindictive betrayed woman was all it took. In the instant that soda jerk publicly kicked me out of the drugstore I became black in the eyes of the citizens of Clayton, Georgia."

Daddy looks exhausted. He pulls off his glasses to rub his eyes and squeeze the bridge of his nose. When he opens his eyes, I notice how red they are.

"My whole notion of who I was changed that day. Up until then I'd lived my life believing I was white. Mother and Daddy had never told me any different. Daddy knew about my mother's parentage when he married her, but he said that it didn't matter to him. My mother chose to pass as white in our small community, and no one ever had any reason to question it." Daddy stops and takes a drink from a cold cup of coffee sitting on his desk.

"Interestingly enough, my best friend ended up being a black boy named Jed Taylor. Jed was as anxious to get out of Clayton and see the world as I was. When Jed and I turned eighteen we got ourselves on the bus out of town and went to Macon to sign up for military service. We had heard that a black man could do all right for himself in the army. Not as well as a white man, but it beat selling bologna and cheese to loggers.

"So we were waiting for our turn to sign up. Jed was sweating so bad his shirt was stuck to him and he was starting to stink, and I wasn't doing much better. We were standing beside each other in the line, but we weren't saying much, when one of the white boys started to talk to me.

"'Ain't it a shame they'll take anybody in the army these days,' he said, and tilted his head ever so slightly toward Jed. I glanced over at Jed, who hadn't heard him because he had struck up a conversation with another black man in the line. Right then and there something inside me snapped. This man talking to me obviously took me for a white man. And now, three other white boys were gathering around and talking, and they thought I was one of them. My head was swimming so badly, I couldn't even hear what they were saying. I inched my way a little farther from Jed and slowly turned away from him, facing those white boys. I felt myself nodding to their comments about how the president had ordered integration, but thank God, the army wasn't rushing to do it.

"Just then, the line split, and I found myself drifting into the line with those white boys. Jed was so busy talking, he veered off into the other line without realizing I wasn't behind him anymore. I kept my back turned and continued to nod and smile and make the occasional comment. And when one of them asked me my name and where I was from, I instantly invented a story that I was from a little community near Savannah. That's when I think Jed heard my voice. I saw him out of the corner of my eye turn his head toward me. I think he was straining to hear what I was saying, but I kept my back turned to him. By then, we were at the front of the lines and he went to one table and I went to the other.

"'Race?' I heard the recruiter ask Jed.

"'Negro,' Jed answered, waiting patiently for the next question.

"My turn was next, and as I stepped up to the recruiter and gave him my name and date of birth, I made a decision that has changed the course of my life since that moment. When that army recruiter asked me my race, I answered, 'Caucasian.' In my peripheral vision I saw Jed's head jerk in my direction, but he didn't say a word and I wouldn't look at him. After that, all I remember is the hurt in Jed's eyes the last time we saw each other. We were loading on buses to go to basic training. He was getting on the bus for the colored recruits, and I was getting on the bus for the whites.

"After that, I kept getting more and more distant from my Georgia family. I went over to Korea for two years, then came back and lived in D.C.—went to law school on the GI Bill. I'd write to my mother about once a year, but I never went back to Clayton. I think they knew what I was doing—knew from the tone of my letters that I was passing. And then one of my army buddies invited me down to visit him in Mississippi. That's where I met your mother. Y'all know that part of the story."

I'm intensely focused on my hands. Daddy is waiting for me to look at him. I can feel it. I look up and blink, trying to convince myself that this is real and not some movie I'm watching.

"Anyhow—and Avery, I need you to hear me when I say this. I had absolutely no idea about this sickle-cell problem. After that argument on Sunday between your mother and Willadean, it hit me that maybe it was me that had passed along that trait. So I made an appointment with a doctor up in Memphis and drove up there and had myself tested."

He picks up the folder that he had dropped while he was talking and opens it slowly. He runs his finger along a line of print on the paper and says, "According to the doctor, my blood tested SA. He says that means I have the sickle-cell trait." He looks up at me, "So you must have inherited the trait from me, Avery."

Chapter 42

Marion

When I make my way from the rose garden to the front door, I'm a little irritated to find Avery standing sheepishly outside her own home, ringing the doorbell as if she's a stranger. Mark never rings; he simply strides in calling, "Mama, where are you?" as if he still lives here. I can't say that I'm glad to see Avery, but I am relieved that she made the first move. We haven't spoken since that disastrous confrontation on Sunday. It was as if everyone in this family has retreated to his or her own personal corner to lick our respective wounds. Even Holt has been distant from me during the past couple of days.

I'm exhausted from the emotional extremes of the past weeks. I thought I was doing so well, bringing Avery back into my life and learning to love Celi, even plucking up my courage to stand up to Mabel Waverly. Granted, I was still struggling, especially after yet another scene at the engagement party, but Celi's hospitalization and that awful confrontation about our family genes completely set me back. I'm ashamed to admit to myself that it was one thing to accept that we would have a black child as a member of the family, but a completely different and devastating notion to find out that we could *be* part black. I feel beaten down and uncertain, wondering what Avery will confront me with today.

"Hi, Mother," she says, continuing to stand there looking at me with a strange expression, one I don't quite recognize. This I *can* tell: The fight has gone out of her. I can hear in her voice that she did not come here for more quarreling.

"Avery," I say, "come in. Where's Celi?" I glance behind her.

"She didn't come. She's actually playing with Brandon and Louis over at Sally's." Written all over her face is how difficult she finds sharing Celi with her newfound family. Part of me wants to throw my arms around her and comfort her, but I assume that's the last thing she would want right now.

"Oh," I say, forcing myself to keep still. I'm confused because she doesn't seem to have her usual agenda; rather than her usual forthright questions, as if she intends to handle business and leave, she seems hesitant and not sure why she's come.

"What were you doing?" she finally asks, taking in my long-sleeved shirt and jeans.

"I was working with my roses," I say. "Lots of deadheading this time of year."

"That sounds nice," she replies, as if she means it, which surprises me.

The awkwardness of our conversation is making me anxious so that I decide to move us toward the kitchen. I've got to do something besides stand here and stare at her. "Would you like something to eat or drink? I have some chicken salad left from lunch, and there's lemon icebox pie—"

"No. No, thanks," she says. "I'm not hungry . . . and I don't want to pull you away from your gardening."

"Oh, I don't mind. I could—"

"How about I help you?" she asks. With that question, I'm beginning to think this must not be my daughter. But here she is, offering to share an activity that I hoped for years she would show an interest in. Only now, I'm suspicious. I try to set aside my skepticism and be gracious.

"That would be lovely, dear," I say. "Come on outside. I'll show you how it's done."

After I find an extra pair of gardening gloves for her and show her the basics of deadheading roses, we work in silence for several minutes. I wonder if she's able to allow the sights and scents of my garden to soothe her like they do me—the delicate sweet scent of roses, the tinkling of the water in the fountain, the cool piney scent of the mulch under our feet, and the ever-present chorus of birds constantly moving from trees to fountain to the feeders I have hung in the lower garden. I watch her surreptitiously and she seems to be relaxing. Her shoulders have dropped some and the deep lines between her eyes have softened.

She's on her knees, clipping dead blossoms from the bottom of a particularly loaded New Dawn, when she stops, clippers poised in midair, and turns to where I'm standing about four feet away working on a hybrid tea rose. "I'm sorry that I've never tried to understand your point of view," she says.

I stop what I'm doing to look at her. "What point of view is that?" I ask, sincerely not understanding.

"On what was best for me—that you were trying to protect me from getting hurt. I could have at least tried to understand . . . not pushed you completely out of my life."

Years of turmoil over how to deal with the young woman kneeling near me, looking so vulnerable, seem to fade away with Avery's words. Recrimination and "I told you so" are about as useless to me now as one of the withered blossoms at my feet.

"I've made a lot of mistakes," I say softly, having difficulty finding my voice.

"Me, too," says Avery, fixing on a cluster of roses and carefully pulling away the spent ones from the new buds. I sense openness in her today, a willingness to talk in a way that we haven't before. Is it possible that we could start over? I can't let this opportunity pass, no matter how difficult it is.

Instead of risking losing our momentum by leaving the garden and returning to the terrace where the comfortable chairs are, I drop my clippers and sit right where I am in the shadow of the wooden arbor leading to the lower garden.

"Avery, I want you to know that I was afraid for you. I know it seems silly now, but I was so worried about your future in

Greendale," I say, pulling off my gloves and removing my hat to try to catch the slight breeze. She comes to sit across from me, leaning on the arbor's other wooden support. She studies me intently. "But I never meant for Aaron to get hurt like he did," I continue. "I was horrified by that whole incident."

She sits quietly for a moment, then says, "For a long time I've wondered how you found out about Aaron and me."

The day so long ago, when a local gossip sent my world into a tailspin of fear, comes back to me in a flash, and I tell Avery exactly what happened.

May 1991

A group of us women were having lunch at the country club when Mabel pulled me aside on our way to the ladies' room and said in a low voice, "I thought you should know. . . ." She hesitated then; I thought she was trying to be dramatic. "Your daughter has been seen . . . we're not sure by whom, mind you . . ." She was so nervous about whatever it was, she was making me ill.

"What is it, Mabel? What are you talking about?" I was losing my patience with her.

"Avery has been seen out at Alligator Lake with a black boy." In her doughy face, her mouth was puckered and pink with disapproval. Her eyes gleamed with the thrill of passing on such weighty news. When I glanced up to see if anyone was watching us, my eyes met Laura Elise's, and I wondered right then if she already knew, if she'd encouraged Mabel to tell me.

"What do you mean 'seen with a black boy'?" I asked.

"All I know is that they were seen together in a truck, driving around to the back side of the lake. I thought you should know."

Thank goodness I kept my wits about me. "I'm sure there's a perfectly good explanation," I said. "Willadean has been having some work done on Oak Knoll. The boy was probably one of the workmen." Mabel didn't look convinced, but she dropped it and I was able to get through the rest of the luncheon—barely.

I couldn't see for one minute how this gossip could be true. Avery might be a willful teenager, but to think she would be involved with a black boy was simply ridiculous. She was due for her coming out in the spring and I'd been planning it for a year. She'd gone along with all the activities for preparation: dance lessons, parties, meeting all the right people. I was even hosting a tea the next day.

I wondered if Laura Elise had started the rumor. There was something about the way she had looked over at us when Mabel was telling me. Laura Elise was my best friend, but that didn't mean I trusted her. When Mason threw me over for her all those years ago, she thought she'd won our rivalry once and for all. But then I married Holt, and that assured my standing in the community. She'd always been jealous of me. Since the day I started going out with Holt, I'd known that she was plotting my social demise. But this was so vicious! If it was true, it could ruin us.

When I arrived home, I walked down the hall to Avery's bedroom and knocked. Of course, she didn't answer. Avery didn't come home much these days. She was always saying she was going out to Oak Knoll to visit Willadean. Could this boy be why she'd gotten so interested in spending time with her grandmother? I knew what they said around town about my mother: that she was always involved in civil rights causes, that she was somehow involved when my aunt Jerrilyn died, that Daddy married her out of pity, that she had lots of money but lived—and dressed—like a pauper. I didn't know how many of the rumors about the past were true because I'd never wanted to go checking into her history. Some stones were better left unturned. It occurred to me that maybe Willadean was the cause of this foolishness about Avery.

I turned Avery's doorknob gently and noticed that the door was unlocked. I peeked in to make sure she wasn't in there sleeping. The room was empty. If I took a look around, I might find some clue as to what was going on. Her desk under the window was cluttered with spiral notebooks, a couple of textbooks, and what looked to be a paper she was writing for school. She was such a smart girl. It was a good thing she was smart since she paid no attention to her looks.

I glanced out the window to check for Avery's car in the driveway. Not there. I was against it, but Holt had had to go and buy her that vehicle. Now she could jump in it any time of the day or night, and we didn't have any idea where she went.

Her bed was unmade and there were T-shirts and shorts, a nightgown, and a pair of jeans all scattered across the comforter. I noticed the jeans had mud stains on the hems and knees and I wondered what she'd been doing in them—probably working out in that silly vegetable garden of her grandmother's. That woman had plenty of money and plenty of food. Why she wanted to continue to labor out in the heat like a field hand was beyond me.

Avery's nightstand held a John Grisham novel and a half-empty glass of flat Coke. I resisted the urge to remove the glass. Leona would be coming in tomorrow to clean, and besides, if I moved the glass, Avery would know I'd been in here. I was about to leave, thinking this had been a waste of time, when out of the corner of my eye, I spotted something.

What appeared to be a newspaper article was sticking out of the top of the novel. I almost missed it, thinking it was a bookmark. I opened the novel and turned it upside down on the bed to keep her place and unfolded the article. When I saw what it said, my heart sank. *It was true. How could it be?* Panic rose in my throat and my knees started shaking. *How could she do this?*

The headline read LOCAL ATHLETE WINS SCHOLASTIC ACHIEVEMENT AWARD. The short article from the *Delta Democrat Times* described how Aaron Monroe, a senior at Greenville High, was recently awarded top honors in a scholastic competition. Aaron reported his plans to attend the University of Mississippi after graduating from high school. His grandmother, Sally Johnson Monroe, stated, "We are so proud of Aaron. He'll be the first in our family to go to college."

I stopped reading; waves of nausea were washing up from my stomach. I sat down on the edge of the bed to collect myself and try to think what I was going to do next. The sound of a car outside made me jump. I quickly refolded the newspaper article and placed it back in Avery's book. I tried to remember how the book was positioned on the nightstand, but I was running out of time, so I replaced it the best I could and slipped out of the room, closing the door quietly behind me. When I reached the first step of the staircase, I heard the front door slam.

"Mother, I'm home," Avery called. "Are you here?"

I forced myself to take the next step down toward her, but I had to clutch the rail to keep from tipping forward. I considered hurling myself down the staircase. If I was in the hospital with a broken leg or hip, I wouldn't have to follow through with the tea tomorrow. Then I wouldn't have to face them. How many of the other mothers knew and hadn't told me?

Avery appeared at the bottom of the stairs, and I looked at her with new eyes. All this time I thought she didn't date any of the boys from the old families because she was such a tomboy. Even today, she had her hair yanked up into a scraggly ponytail and she was wearing cutoff blue jeans and a T-shirt with something written on it I couldn't read without my glasses. The T-shirt didn't look very clean and I noticed she was wearing those awful plastic thongs from the dollar store. She looked up at me and frowned.

"Are you okay? You look like you're sick," she said, starting to come up the stairs toward me.

I felt flushed and my head was spinning, so I gripped the stair railing harder. I could not avoid this situation, but I could certainly discuss it with Holt before I got into an argument with Avery. I somehow never seemed to be able to win any argument with her. She'd probably end up being a lawyer like her father. That was probably for the best, because unless Holt and I could do some damage control, she certainly wouldn't be marrying anyone from around here. I took a deep breath and told myself to remain calm.

"I'm fine, honey. I've got a bit of a headache, that's all. Let's go out to the kitchen and you can have a Coke and I'll have a cup of coffee. We need to talk about the tea tomorrow and what you're going to wear."

Avery groaned and threw her keys on the foyer table. "Okay, but can I go up and pee first?"

I winced at her casual use of language but nodded my head as she squeezed past me. I tried to catch the scent of her as she quickly dropped a kiss somewhere in the vicinity of my ear. I wasn't sure what I was looking for. She certainly didn't smell like perfume; she never wore it. But other than a slight smell of outdoors, I didn't notice anything else.

"I'll be in the kitchen. Don't take too long, now," I called to her back. She was already at the top of the stairs because she took them two at a time.

What brought this on? She never mixed with black children in school. We'd always sent her to the best private schools in town. Everyone knew your children didn't get a good education around here if you sent them to the integrated schools. So how did this happen? Then I remembered the name from the newspaper article. *Sally Monroe.*

Sally Monroe was that old black woman Willadean always visited. So Sally had a grandson. Now I knew. This really *was* because of my dear mother. She had somehow managed to corrupt my daughter by having her mix with blacks like she did as a young girl. Well, I'd have none of it. As soon as Holt got home he'd get an earful.

I walked into the kitchen and checked to see if Leona had left any of those brownies she made, looking for food to calm my nerves. I had to focus on the next day's event. I had eleven women and their daughters coming over here. The caterers would arrive at ten o'clock in the morning and the company that set up the tables would be even earlier, at eight. No time for worrying over this now. I heard Avery's heavy tread on the stairs and pulled my face into a smile. *Drown them with sugar,* I'd always heard. My mouth filled with honey as the stranger who was my eighteen-year-old daughter walked into the kitchen.

"I remember that conversation," Avery says now. "I knew you were trying to find out what was going on, but there was no way I was going to admit to you that I was seeing Aaron."

"I know that now," I say. "How could you have talked to me when you knew what kind of response I would have had? And I was busy holding my mother responsible for your interest in Aaron."

"I always thought you somehow found out about our plan. You know, for all these years I've blamed Seth Collier for what happened to Aaron, and I blamed you for telling Seth, or more likely his parents, what you thought we might be planning." Avery tells me then how Seth was waiting for her outside the mansion on the night of the ball and how he threatened her.

I'm sickened by the picture of abuse she paints, and I know I have to tell her the rest. "It's true," I say. "I did go to Mason for help, once I heard the rumor about you. But you've got to believe that I had no idea that Aaron would be beaten."

"I believe you," she says. "Aaron told me the names of the guys who beat him up. Seth wasn't involved."

I'm relieved that he wasn't directly responsible for Aaron's injuries. But I know his father encouraged Seth to intercept Avery, and it's still possible that something Seth said triggered a darker violence in the other boys. I'm not surprised when she tells me that Farley Cole and Landon Hornsby were at fault. I know their fathers—*and* their mothers.

Avery gets a hard, angry look of recognition on her face. "I don't know why I didn't think of this before," she says incredulously, "but it had to have been Merilee Waverly who betrayed us. She was the only other one who knew," she says, as if talking to herself. "I wonder if Seth threatened her."

She shakes her head slowly. "I've got to let it go. It doesn't matter now. Aaron has moved past it; I need to as well." We sit silently, each of us struggling to find a place for the revulsion we feel at the ugliness of that night.

Avery breaks our silence. "I do have a question for you," she says.

I try to set aside my defenses. This new openness is difficult for me to tolerate in large doses. I watch her, waiting for what she'll ask.

"You mentioned earlier that Mason threw you over for Laura Elise. Will gave me the impression in one of our conversations that you and Mason had a thing for a while in high school and college. Is that true?"

I tell her that, yes, Mason Collier and I dated for a while. That he lost interest when we went off to college, and that ironically, he did date Laura Elise, and I, of course, dated many other boys. I tell her that Laura Elise and Mason announced their engagement about the same time I met her father, and how I was smitten with Holt from the moment I saw him.

What I don't tell her is the real reason Mason broke my heart, that his father was a member of the white Citizens' Council—not to mention the Ku Klux Klan. That he would not stand for his son dating the daughter of an activist like Willadean Reynolds. I don't tell her about the way I ignored my mother's warnings and threw myself at Mason because I was convinced he was my ticket to acceptability. I don't tell her about the fall we returned to school for senior year at Ole Miss when Laura Elise came to me with her eyes full of manufactured tears to say that she and Mason had fallen in love over the summer. After which, she immediately produced a ring and could hardly contain her gloating over their engagement.

Avery doesn't need to know all of that history. I sometimes think her preoccupation with finding the truth is tedious. She would never understand how I have remained friends with Laura Elise and Mason all these years. I'm not sure I understand it myself. I'm relieved that what I do tell her seems to satisfy her. After all, Nicki Collier is about to be a member of this family.

"It seems as if all of us have been struggling with the past lately," she muses. "About the other day . . ." she starts.

I pull myself up from the ground as she begins this new tack and start to dust off my jeans. "Honey, I understand that at some point I will probably need to understand about Celi's disease and all that business about genetics and traits and the like, but right now I've got about all on my plate that I can manage," I say, hoping she'll tolerate my ambivalence. I'm relieved when she nods.

"Okay," she says. "I can understand that."

"You know, after fifty-eight years of seeing the world one way, it's going to take me a little while to change my perspective."

She smiles as she gets up and joins me in a walk through the arbor into the lower garden. "There seems to be an epidemic of that lately," she says.

"What's that?" I ask.

"Changing perspectives," she answers. I nod in agreement as we both turn at the sound of her father's voice calling from the terrace.

"Hello, y'all out here?"

We both smile and Avery reaches to embrace me. "Thanks for talking with me," she says, and my heart warms with a renewed glimmer of hope for our family as Holt's sweet, familiar face appears through the arbor in search of us.

Chapter 43

Willadean

Sally and I are sitting on her back porch watching Celi play with her stepbrothers. When Avery called Sally today asking to bring Celi to visit, Sally immediately called Aaron and asked him to bring the boys over. It makes my old heart glad to see those children together. I look over at Sally, and she looks happy, too. "You reckon Avery might think about moving back here?" she asks.

I consider her question for a while. "I'm not sure. I think she's having a hard time with her feelings for Aaron. She knows he loves Lacretia; don't get me wrong. But she has to find a place for him now in her life."

"That doesn't surprise me. As hard as I tried to keep them apart after he got hurt, sometimes these days I half wish they'd been able to stay together. I was so afraid that what happened with you and Henry could happen to them—especially to my Aaron. I'd already lost Henry. I couldn't bear to lose Aaron." She looks at me, counting on my understanding. Henry's was the hardest loss we've shared all these years.

I nod. "I know that, Sally. I reckon I knew it then. I just couldn't accept it."

"Maybe Avery will understand now why I was so scared for Aaron. I was so afraid that Aaron would have to leave town like Henry did when he signed up for the marines," Sally says. "I was afraid Aaron would run away with Avery and I'd never see him again."

"I know, I know," I say. "Seems like everywhere I turn someone's digging up old memories. I don't know that any of us ever quite understands even when we try to look at things through each other's eyes. I guess the best we can do is try."

"Willie, I reckon there's been a lot of water under the bridge, and you and I know things that don't ever need to be told," Sally says. "Was Marion relieved when you told her that Jacob was her daddy?" she asks.

"Seemed to be," I say, focusing on the children, trying to hide my hurt out of habit.

"Do you suppose having Celi around might soften her up a little bit? Maybe help her see that skin color doesn't matter that much?" Sally asks.

"I'm hopeful. I see little changes in Marion, but it's going to take some time." The children are squealing and splashing each other now with the water hose. "It *could* have been me, Sally," I say, and I'm irritated when I can't keep tears out of my eyes.

Sally hands me a clean handkerchief out of her pocket. "What do you mean?" she asks.

"If I hadn't miscarried early, after we found out Henry had died, it could have been me raising a mixed-race child."

"Yes, it could have," Sally answers, knowing that being with Avery and Celi has got my old pain all stirred up.

"What would I have done, Sally? What if I had had Henry's baby and not married Jacob? You and I both know I didn't love Jacob when I married him. I was heartbroken over losing Henry, and Jacob was devastated over losing his twin sister. We came together out of pain. Was that the right thing to do?" I stop to blow my nose.

"But you learned to love him, didn't you?" Sally asks. Sally loved her brother, Henry, but she's always been right defensive of Jacob Reynolds. He was one of the best-hearted men either one of us ever met. His only hard spot was the hate he carried for George Collier.

"I did." I nod. "I did grow to love him. But I have to say, I understand how Avery is struggling to let go of Aaron. I even understand why Marion reacted the way she did after she lost Mason. I reckon none of us gets what we want."

Sally and I sit quietly contemplating. When the children come running up to the porch, all wet and thirsty, we stir ourselves to hand out cups of Kool-Aid. After they're back at their water games and we're settled in our chairs, Sally says, "I'm not so sure it's that we don't get what we want, Willie. Sometimes I think we don't *know* what we want until it slaps us in the face."

I nod. "Maybe so."

Chapter 44

Avery

The antique white satin of Nicki's wedding gown glows in the soft afternoon light slanting through the floor-to-ceiling windows of Laura Elise Collier's elegant master bedroom. Laura Elise fusses around Nicki like an anxious mother bird, causing Nicki to roll her eyes and Celi to giggle. The photographer waits patiently while Laura Elise moves a single strand of Nicki's hair into place.

The wedding coordinator opens the bedroom door and pokes her harried head inside. "Ten minutes," she warns.

"We're coming," Laura Elise answers, still lingering.

"Now, Mama, shoo," Nicki says, waving her mother aside. "I want this one last picture with Celi." Laura Elise looks prickly but reluctantly steps away from her daughter.

"Mother of the bride, time to go," the wedding coordinator barks.

Laura Elise makes her exit, and the other bridesmaids and I stand back as the photographer perfects the final scene before the ceremony. At his instruction Celi and Nicki stand facing each other, their profiles beautifully backlit by the window. Each holds out the skirt of her dress, as if they are comparing. The photographer identifies the perfect angle to highlight the tiny white rosebuds woven into Celi's braids and directs Celi to look up at Nicki, which is a simple instruction for her to follow since she is mesmerized by every detail of Nicki's wedding attire.

I'm so proud of my beautiful daughter that I feel as if my heart will explode out of my tightly fitted bridesmaid dress. I must have eaten more of Will's excellent cooking than I thought over the past month, because I could swear this dress was more comfortable when I tried it on two weeks ago. At least Nicki's taste is simple. Our strapless dresses are elegantly cut in deep blue satin, with the obligatory matching pumps, which I'm making a point to leave off until the last possible minute. There are six bridesmaids—four of Nicki's friends from college, Alicia, and me. As five of us watch the photographer complete this last prewedding shot before we start the processional, Alicia waits outside in the hall, trying to contain her fidgeting twins and make sure they don't lose the ring pillows.

I look through the window at the scene that spreads out below us. Beyond the white reception tent erected on the Colliers' expansive lawn, a twenty-foot-long arbor covered in wisteria vines opens to a path into the Colliers' hydrangea garden, where the wedding will take place. Deeply shaded by a grove of twisting oaks and clean-scented pines, hundreds of white lace-cap and deep blue mophead hydrangeas grace a pine-needle-covered path winding through the trees. At the end of the path, an ivy-covered gazebo will serve as the site for the ceremony.

From my upstairs vantage point, I can see the valets busily parking cars in the field to the north of the house as the wedding guests make their way toward the garden. My casual perusal stops abruptly when I spot Aaron and Lacretia each carrying one of their sons. Even from a distance, it is clear what a stunning family they make. Aaron wears a perfectly cut gray suit and coordinates beautifully with Lacretia in an elegant lemon-colored dress. The boys are each dapper in suits and ties.

"Mom, it's time," Celi says, grasping my hand and pulling me away from the window.

"Your dad and Lacretia are here," I say, pushing my feet into my waiting satin pumps.

"Cool," Celi says, dropping my hand and pushing past me to look out the window. "Wow! They look great," she exclaims. I smile, remembering Mark's description of Laura Elise's terse reaction when he and Nicki announced that they needed to make some additions to the guest list—including Miss Sally.

We walk carefully down the stairs and across the brick terrace toward the entrance to the shade garden. The wedding coordinator orchestrates our every move, using her two-way radio to communicate with the worker stationed near the gazebo. Her minions flit about the garden, holding up Nicki's train, straightening Alicia's too-tight skirt, replacing a flower in a bridesmaid's hair, checking Celi's basket of petals, and making sure that all of the guests are seated in the rows of chairs placed in front of the gazebo.

The string quartet initiates the processional music, and I am the first bridesmaid to emerge from the arbor. I'm a little intimidated as one hundred sets of eyes turn toward me. I gather my courage and don a wedding smile, trying to focus on the joy of this occasion rather than on my nervousness. Up ahead, in the first row, I spot Mother and Daddy, and I tell myself to breathe. Will's kind eyes come into focus from her seat next to Mother and my heart begins to lighten. Aunt Lizzie, who flew in yesterday from Colorado, is all smiles as she squeezes Will's arm and gives me a big wink.

Mark, standing between the minister and his groomsmen, looks a little dazed, and I wonder if he's recovered from the tequila shots he and his friends were consuming last night after the rehearsal dinner. I glance briefly at Seth, who stands at the outer edge of the groomsmen, and it strikes me that his sons look exactly like him—portly penguins stuffed into their black tuxedoes. When I assume my position, awaiting the remainder of the bridesmaids, I begin to relax and take the opportunity to study the crowd, whose backs are turned toward me in anticipation of Nicki's entrance.

Mother already has Daddy's handkerchief in her hand, forestalling tears, but she looks poised and radiant in her midnight blue silk suit. Daddy beams proudly as he looks down at her and I'm reassured that Daddy, Mark, and I made the right decision not to tell her yet about Daddy's history. My mother is an intelligent woman, but her preference for avoiding what makes her uncomfortable is legend. We all agreed that there was no reason to push this issue—especially with the wedding so close.

Last night's rehearsal dinner was a huge success. Mother's tireless work with the ancient event planner Marjory Dean paid off, and everyone raved over the food catered by Mark and Nicki's favorite restaurant, Doe's Eat Place. Afterward, Daddy and I took a walk through the quiet neighborhood streets together while Mother, Will, and Celi curled up in the den with bowls of ice cream to watch *Father of the Bride*.

Daddy and I hadn't talked since the day he told Mark and me his story. We agreed then that we all needed time to think about what this meant for each of us and for our family. Given the nature of the South in 1951, I thought I understood why Daddy made his spontaneous decision to answer "Caucasian" to the army recruiter's question. I was more curious to know what it was like for him to live all those years denying his family, cutting off all ties with them.

He talked last night about how the years melted into each other and how it became easier and easier to distance himself from his origins. "As I told you before, I think they probably knew I was passing. But there's an unspoken creed in the black community not to reveal another's heritage—even when it means losing them." This left me saddened for my young father and what he must have gone through, and even more for his mother. I couldn't imagine losing Celi that way.

For Daddy, meeting my mother at the Delta Gamma Christmas formal was the event that sealed his fate. "Here stood this beautiful young woman in a red velvet dress, smiling up at me. I'm telling you, Avery, she was so bold. She even asked *me* to dance." He laughed. "But there was something vulnerable about her, too—something that made me want to protect her." He said he knew that even if he reached a point where his racial background didn't matter anymore to him, it would always matter to Mother.

"And, Avery, I couldn't live without your mother," he said.

Daddy's statement touched me deeply. My father initially made the choice to pass for selfish reasons—for a chance at career success and financial security—but he continued to make the choice because of his love for Mother. It struck me how we all make choices out of love or fear, or both, which send our lives in whole new directions.

Daddy said that he came close to revealing everything when I got pregnant with Celi, but then I moved away and detached myself from all of them so completely that he figured I was probably doing the same thing he had done when he left Georgia—putting enough distance and time between the community and the family to make an entirely new life, one that didn't include the prying eyes of those who knew my secret.

"Having you come back . . . meeting Celi . . . it's made me ashamed of hiding who I really am," he said. "Would I be a better grandfather to her if she knew that I'm mixed-race too?"

How could I answer that question? Would the consequences he'd no doubt suffer be worth the added sense of family identity the knowledge might give Celi, especially considering that Celi seems to be the least troubled of all of us?

What I realized after I recovered from my initial shock and contemplated everything I've learned over the past month—about Will and Henry, about what happened to Aaron the night of my debutante ball, and about Daddy's grandmother—was that maybe we're all just trying our best to protect our children. I've been trying to protect Celi; Sally was trying to protect Aaron; Mother was trying to protect me. Or maybe we're all just protecting ourselves, trying to shield ourselves from hurt when that's pretty much impossible.

The last of the bridesmaids takes her place and Trey and Troy strut to the altar, puffed up with the importance of their tasks and trying to look as macho as a boy can look carrying a lacy pillow that holds a wedding ring. I look over at Alicia, who frowns, purses her lips, and slightly shakes her head as Trey nudges Troy, causing him to sway off balance into an elderly woman craning her neck to try to catch a glimpse of the bride. The music changes and Laura Elise rises from her seat, signaling the crowd to follow suit. Celi appears at the arbor opening and I watch the varied reactions of Mark and Nicki's wedding guests. Most of them smile warmly and whisper to one another. Some of the older women of Laura Elise and Mother's set raise their eyebrows.

My beautiful daughter is oblivious to them. She carefully reaches into her blue-hydrangea-and-white-peony-studded basket, pulls out handfuls of white rose petals, and sprinkles them confidently along the path before her. I observe her searching the crowd, and when she spots Aaron she raises her hand in a tiny wave and beams at him.

Aaron and Lacretia are sitting with Miss Sally, who sports an amazing pink hat, complete with feathers and a satin ribbon. Heads in the audience turn to see who the pretty little flower girl is waving to. Aaron's older son points in recognition and loudly says, "Look, Mom, it's Celi!" causing the guests to chuckle. Any concern I once had about the response of this crowd of people to my daughter seems trivial now—eclipsed by the joy I see in her face, the pride in Aaron's eyes, and the warm smiles on my parents' and grandmother's faces as Celi turns her attention to them.

Nicki's entrance evokes a ripple of admiration, and I watch my brother swell with pride as she nears him and takes his hand and Mason Collier affirms for the minister that he is giving his daughter in marriage. As Mason turns to take his seat beside Laura Elise, I see his head turn toward Mother. The look in her eyes as she watches him makes me wonder what she's feeling. She immediately shifts her gaze back to Nicki and Mark.

As the minister recites the words of the ceremony and Mark and Nicki state their vows to each other, I reflect on the four of us: Will, Mother, myself, and Celi, four generations of Reynolds-Pritchett women. Will lost her Henry but learned to love my grandfather Jacob. I suspect there was more to my mother's relationship with Mason Collier than she has revealed, but she chose my father instead. Much of Mother's history remains a mystery to me, and I mull over how in the coming years I might learn more about the girl she was in the 1960s. I loved a boy and lost him under what seemed impossible circumstances at the time. And Celi? Her world is wide open with possibility.

Everyone is flushed with pleasure—and champagne—in the candlelit glow of the reception tent. Small children run around among the tables, entertaining themselves as their mothers stealthily slide out of their high heels under the cover of floor-length tablecloths. Men who have shed their suit coats stand in shirt-sleeved groups outside the tent, smoking and telling stories. Mark and Nicki, along with their circle of close friends, glide expertly across the floor in a country-music line dance. I look over and see Alicia pulling Trey's chubby hand away from the wedding cake, since he's probably had about three slices already. Of course, while she's focused on him, Troy is behind her stealing yet another slice.

I'm sitting at a table with Will, Aunt Lizzie, and Miss Sally, who are enjoying a second glass of champagne and laughing uproariously at one of Sally's fishing stories. I'm feeling a little out of sorts, relegated to the old ladies' table while Nicki and her friends claim the dance floor, which seems to be filled with particularly good-looking young Southern men, one of whom looks my way and winks. A little disconcerted by the attention, I decide to go in search of Celi. She's rebounded beautifully since her sickle-cell crisis, but being watchful of her is a habit I can't break.

I look across the tent to see Celi holding a cup of punch and tugging a complaining Brandon back toward the table where Lacretia sits, looking slightly exhausted and holding his brother, Louis, whose entire face is covered with chocolate groom's cake. Celi plops Brandon into a chair, hands him his punch, and sits down beside Lacretia. Before I reach the table, two older ladies I recognize as members of Mother's garden club stroll past Lacretia and smile benevolently down at her.

"It looks like you have your hands full, dear," one of them says.

"Yes, they're busy, busy boys," Lacretia replies, trying to wipe some of the chocolate frosting from Louis's face.

"It's a good thing you have your daughter to help you with them," the other lady comments, smiling at Celi.

I freeze in place behind the ladies and stop myself from blurting out the correction that leaps to my lips. That's *my* daughter. Lacretia has her back to me, and Celi looks up and sees me standing there transfixed. It takes everything within me to arrange my face into a familiar, conspiratorial smile for Celi's benefit. I watch as Celi and Lacretia exchange the briefest of glances. Celi's anxious expression turns into her usual charming grin as Lacretia calmly says, "Yes, that *is* a good thing, isn't it?"

I loudly push aside a chair to alert Lacretia to my presence as the Garden Club ladies move on. "There you are," I say to Celi. "I was wondering where you'd gotten off to." I try to hide the nervousness I still feel around Lacretia.

"I've been helping with Brandon and Louis," Celi says.

"I hope that's okay, Avery," Lacretia says. "Aaron's on call and he was paged a few minutes ago. He's gone off to find a quieter place to return the call."

"No problem," I say, trying to decide whether to stay and attempt to make conversation with Lacretia or to feign seeing someone I urgently need to speak with. My problem is solved when Aaron returns.

"Handled it over the phone," he says, smiling at all of us. "Look at your face," he says to a fretting Louis as he reaches to take him from Lacretia. Louis pushes Aaron's hands away and refuses to leave his mother's arms.

"He's tired," says Lacretia.

"We'd better get these boys home," says Aaron.

"Oh, Dad, don't go," Celi says, moving over to him and allowing him to pull her close to his side. I'm still standing awkwardly beside Aaron and Celi when the roaming photographer snaps a shot of us. This will become Celi's favorite photograph from the wedding—the one she insists be framed for her nightstand. She will guard it faithfully over the years to come, it will leave for college with her, and years later I will see it surface once again on the mantel in Celi's own living room. In the photo I have a somewhat startled expression on my face as I look up at the photographer—so indicative of the surreal feeling I am experiencing. Celi looks up at me, joy evident in her small features, and Aaron looks at Celi, his eyes full of love.

Celi says good-bye to her brothers, Aaron, and Lacretia. I can sense her conflict as they start to leave, wanting to go with them, worried that she should show more interest in being with me. I do my best to ease her loss, promising that she'll see them lots next week before we leave. Aaron and his family make their way toward Miss Sally so that she can tear herself away from Aunt Lizzie and Will long enough to kiss her grandbabies good-bye.

Celi and I follow, and I'm surprised to see Seth Collier stop Aaron and pull him aside. Aaron motions for Lacretia to take the boys and go ahead to Sally. He stops and faces Seth. From his body language, I feel Aaron's apprehension as if it were my own. As Celi and I come into earshot of the two of them, she forges ahead toward her great-grandmothers, and I try to move subtly and slowly enough not to be noticed as Seth offers his hand to Aaron. After only the slightest hesitation, Aaron grasps Seth's hand and shakes it. I hear only snippets of what Seth is saying over the din of Aaron's boys and Celi: ". . . and I heard about what happened. . . . I just want you to know that I'm really sorry. What those boys did was wrong. I hope you and I can . . ."

I'm amazed at how graciously Aaron nods at Seth and simply says, "Thanks, Seth." But I'm even more incredulous that Seth, blushing bright red above the too-tight collar of his tuxedo shirt, is trying to make amends with Aaron. Could this scene get any stranger? That's when I spot Laura Elise nearby with Mason standing coolly at her side sipping bourbon. She and Mason, along with Mother and Daddy, are chatting with two other couples their age.

Daddy looks up, sees us gathered around the table, and bends down to speak in my mother's ear. She turns our way and immediately excuses herself. Laura Elise and Mason remain deliberately distant from our strangely cohesive family scene, each with aloof expressions on their faces as they make small talk with wedding guests. Mother walks purposefully toward Aaron, and I hold my breath.

"I . . . we . . . just wanted you to know that if there's anything Holt and I can do to help get our families together . . . for Celi . . . we'd be happy to do that," Mother says, placing her hand tentatively on Aaron's arm. He looks surprised but recovers quickly and nods appreciatively at my mother, taking her hand in his. Lacretia looks surprised and a little suspicious but remains quiet. Will and Sally, who are sitting behind where Mother stands with Aaron, look at each other with shocked expressions. By now, I'm pretty much numb.

After Aaron and his family leave, Daddy asks a thrilled Celi to dance, and we all sit smiling and watching from the table. He towers over her as he guides her to the floor, and she giggles as he encourages her to stand on his feet for a waltz. Aunt Lizzie sits back and crosses her arms over her large breasts.

"Avery," she says, "I suppose you'll have a hard time convincing Celi to come back to Denver."

"Right now she's certainly dropping tons of hints about staying," I answer. "But things will probably look different after we've been back home for a while and she's had a chance to settle into her routine with school and friends and all."

"You know, I've heard Mabel say that nurses can get jobs just about anywhere," Mother says. "It sure would be good to have you back home to stay."

"I agree with that," Will says, and Sally nods.

"Well, what am *I* supposed to do without them?" Aunt Lizzie says, making everyone laugh.

"You'll just have to come visit more often," Sally says.

"I've got plenty of room," adds Will.

"So do I," says Mother, more relaxed than I've seen her in a long time.

Celi and Daddy return to the table, and Celi, finding herself without a chair, perches on my lap. At that moment the photographer finds us again, and this photo will be the one that I choose to frame for the mantel in my home in Denver and, later, the mantel at Oak Knoll, when I eventually inherit the grand old place from Will. The four generations of us—Will, Mother, Celi, and I—all smile up at the photographer, while Daddy, Aunt Lizzie, and Sally look on. The photograph marks the beginning of the close-knit family we will learn to be.

I really don't know what's best. When things seem impossible, do you make a clean break from an old life? I tried that at age eighteen. Or is it better to live with our history and learn to embrace it? We all embody our past in one way or another—literally in our cells as Celi does; or in the recesses of our souls in the form of fears hidden away, sometimes unacknowledged; or in old loves and broken hearts, sealed off from our feeling selves, tucked away from view.

They're all there, waiting to surface at any moment—teeming with life just beneath a smooth facade like the water of Alligator Lake on a hot summer day. Why reinvent a self somewhere else when getting to know the one rooted in the history of where you started out is so full of surprises? We can't change the past, but we can add to the story. Maybe it's time for Celi and me to start a new chapter in our lives.

ACKNOWLEDGMENTS

I would like to thank the following:

First of all, my family, who patiently allowed me to disappear into my studio, or into my imagination, for hours on end so that *Alligator Lake* could become a reality.

My dear friend and department chair, Lea Gaydos, who gave me not only her friendship and support, but also that much-needed summer off.

My sisters Karen and Margaret for patiently carting me all over creation to book signings and bookstore visits. We had a grand time, didn't we?

Ellen Edwards, my amazing editor. How can I ever express my gratitude for your belief in my writing, even when what I believed to be a completed manuscript was actually a rough first draft? Thanks for seeing me through *Alligator Lake*.

My terrific agent, Kevan Lyon, for her support and never-failing encouragement.

All of the bookstore owners, book clubs, book reviewers, and book bloggers who have been so supportive of my work and, through their enthusiasm, have inspired me to keep writing.

And most of all my readers, whose gracious responses push me forward and make even the most difficult writing days a joy.

I would also like to acknowledge all of the following resources for providing invaluable information during my research for *Alligator Lake*:

1. Anderson, Henry C. with essays by Shawn Wilson, Clifton L. Taulbert, and Mary Panzer. *Separate, but Equal: The Mississippi Photographs of Henry Clay Anderson.* New York: Public Affairs, 2002.

2. Brown, David H. Conjure Doctors: "An Exploration of Black Discourse in America, Antebellum to 1940." *Folklore Forum* 23 (1990): 3–46.

3. "Changing the Face of Medicine: Dr. Dorothy Celeste Boulding Ferebee." National Library of Medicine. Retrieved from http://www.nlm.nih.gov/changingthefaceofmedicine/physicians/biography_109.html.

4. *Eyes on the Prize: America's Civil Rights Years 1954–1964.* Produced by Henry Hampton, Blackside, Inc. Arlington, VA: PBS, 1987.

5. Kroeger, Brooke: *Passing: When People Can't Be Who They Are.* New York: Public Affairs, 2003.

6. Larsen, Nella. *Passing.* New York: Alfred A. Knopf, 1929.

7. Montgomery, Jack G., Jr. "Chapter One: Beneath the Spanish Moss: The World of the Root Doctor." *Western Kentucky University Top Scholar, DLTS Faculty Publications,* Paper 3 (2008). Retrieved from http://digitalcommons.wku.edu/dlts_fac_pub/3.

8. *Prom Night in Mississippi.* Directed and produced by Bob Saltzman. Franklin, TN: RTM Productions, 2009.

9. Sickle Cell Disease Association of America. Official Web site. Retrieved from http://www.sicklecelldisease.org/index.cfm?page=home.

10. *Sickle Cell Research for Treatment and Cure*. Bethesda, MD: National Institutes of Health, 2002. Retrieved from http://www.nhlbi.nih.gov/resources/docs/scd30/scd30.pdf.

11. Smith, Lauren A., Suzette O. Oyeku, Charles Homer, and Barry Zuckerman. "Sickle Cell Disease: A Question of Equity and Quality." *Pediatrics* 117, no. 5 (May 1, 2006): 1763–1770. Retrieved from http://pediatrics.aappublications.org/content/117/5/1763.full.

12. Sokol, Jason. *There Goes My Everything: White Southerners in the Age of Civil Rights, 1945–1975*. New York: Vintage Books, 2006.

13. Stitt, Van J. "Root Doctors as Providers of Primary Care." *Journal of the National Medical Association* 75, no. 7 (1983): 719–721.

14. Thompson, Wright. "Ghosts of Mississippi." *ESPN Online Magazine* (2010). Retrieved from http://sports.espn.go.com/espn/eticket/story?page=mississippi62.

15. Wailoo, Keith. *Dying in the City of the Blues: Sickle Cell Anemia and the Politics of Race and Health*. Chapel Hill: University of North Carolina Press, 2001.

16. Washington, Harriet A., Robert B. Baker, Ololade Olakanmi, Todd L. Savitt, Elizabeth A. Jacobs, Eddie Hoover, and Matthew K. Wynia, for the Writing Group on the History of African Americans and the Medical Profession. "Segregation, Civil Rights, and Health Disparities: The Legacy of African American Physicians and Organized Medicine, 1910–1968." *Journal of the National Medical Association* 101 (2009): 513–527.

Marion Zachary, Blue Sky Designs Web Development

Lynne Bryant grew up in Columbus, Mississippi, and has lived for many years in Colorado Springs, Colorado, where she teaches nursing at the University of Colorado.

CONNECT ONLINE

lynne-bryant.com
facebook.com/lynnebryantauthor

CONVERSATION GUIDE

Alligator Lake

LYNNE BRYANT

This Conversation Guide is intended to enrich the individual reading experience, as well as encourage us to explore these topics together—because books, and life, are meant for sharing.

A CONVERSATION WITH LYNNE BRYANT

Q. Like your first novel, *Catfish Alley, Alligator Lake* is set in your home state of Mississippi. What inspired this particular story?

A. For me, a story typically begins with a question. I found myself wondering what it would be like to be of mixed race in a culture that sees in only black and white. Historically, the infamous Southern "one-drop rule" meant that a person was automatically categorized as black if he or she had any known black ancestry, no matter which cultural group he or she felt more affinity toward, and no matter what physical traits that person exhibited.

The idea of mixing blood was so abhorrent to white supremacists that they went to great lengths, even murder, to discourage interracial relationships from tainting the white race. Ironically, white men could rape black slave women at will, because of proprietorship. But the mixed-race children who were born of those unions, and who were variously labeled over the centuries as high yellow, quadroon, octoroon, and mulatto, were considered black. They could attempt to claim the privileges of being white only at great risk.

The exclusion and discrimination that have accompanied being black often led people of mixed race to attempt to pass as white—an act that was highly controversial in both black and white communities. Two books on the subject offered fascinating insights to me: Nella Larsen's *Passing*, published by Alfred A. Knopf in 1929, and the 2003 nonfiction work by Brooke Kroeger, a journalism professor at New York University, also titled *Passing*, published by Public Affairs. Kroeger defined passing as "when people effectively present themselves as other than who they understand themselves to be." To pass as white often meant living in fear of being discovered, and of having to completely disconnect from one's family and any association with blacks.

Inevitably, somewhere along the way, someone in a Southern family chooses to love someone of another race. I wanted to explore the emotion that accompanies that decision. How would a family deal with it? How would successive generations, each raised in the changing eras of the South—Jim Crow, the civil rights movement, and the years afterward—experience interracial relationships?

Q. Although *Catfish Alley* is set in fictional Clarksville and *Alligator Lake* in fictional Greendale, are both towns based on your hometown, Columbus?

A. *Alligator Lake* is set in a different part of the state, in the Mississippi Delta, located in the northwest. The delta is a flat plain of fertile, fine-grained soil created by thousands of years of flooding. The delta was one of the best areas for growing cotton, and before the Civil War, it was home to some of Mississippi's wealthiest plantations. Although the delta is now one of the poorest areas of the state, it is rich in history. Jazz and blues greats like B. B. King, Charley Patton, and Muddy Waters hail from the delta, as well as writers such as Hodding Carter, Jr., Walker Percy, Shelby Foote, and Ellen Douglas. Civil rights leaders Charles and Medgar Evers were born in Decatur, and actor Morgan Freeman is from Charleston, both delta towns. This is to name just a few. The Mississippi Delta has been called by author James C. Cobb "the most Southern place on earth." The towns in western Mississippi tend to have a larger percentage of blacks—for example, Greenville is seventy percent black. Given the history of segregation in the state, this racial imbalance brings unique challenges to both races. Because of its location on the Mississippi River, the delta is subject to periodic flooding; it was the site of the great flood of 1927, and more recently, the flood of 2011.

Q. Three different women, from three generations, narrate *Alligator Lake.* Why did you choose to tell the story that way?

A. First of all, I love narrating in first person because I get to put myself into the mind and body of a character and experience the world through his or her eyes. And having three women—all in the same family—gave me a chance to look at Mississippi's culture during three different historical periods. Because it is often said that change comes slowly, or not at all, in Mississippi, I wanted to examine how these women saw their world and how their perceptions might have changed over time. I find that telling a story through individual characters brings abstract issues such as separate but equal, segregation and integration, and interracial relationships into the personal realm. We get to see firsthand what has not changed and what has. I hold the belief that none of us are in a position to judge how we would respond to a situation until we've experienced something similar.

The generational points of view also fascinate me because how one sees race is determined partly by one's personality, partly by the historical context, and partly by whether one accepts the status quo or questions it. I have characters who do both, with all sorts of consequences.

Q. Can you share some personal experiences of growing up in a segregated society and during the civil rights movement in Mississippi?

A. Like so many Southern white children, I was oblivious of the issues of race raging around me in the sixties. Until my public school was integrated when I was in the sixth grade, in 1970–1971, I had no occasion to mix with blacks. I can only imagine how difficult it was for the black kids, who lost the school they had attended for years and were thrown in with a bunch of white kids who had no knowledge of their lives and no appreciation of their struggle. Forces outside of us pushed Mississippi toward integration. I'm not sure it ever would have happened otherwise. Even after civil rights legislation was passed, and laws supporting segregation were abolished, in most ways our lives remained separate. We played separately, ate separately, shopped separately. And when my own daughter graduated from the same high school that I did, twenty-five years later, in 2002, there was still a black homecoming queen and a white homecoming queen.

Q. So, when you return to Mississippi for visits, what strikes you about it now? How have race relations changed and not changed? What factors can you see that might influence change in the future?

A. Mississippi is a paradox of change and stasis. Since Mississippians tend to remain in place, so do their attitudes and culture. Yet there is evidence of change here and there. More blacks are elected to public office now, and there is increased integration in churches and social settings. However, many public schools remain predominantly black, with whites attending private schools, and overall academic performance remains low, as do economic indicators. Mississippi has a rising black middle and upper class, but this is coupled with an increasing use of drugs and rising poverty.

Last year, the Ole Miss student body chose a new mascot, the Rebel Black Bear, to replace Colonel Reb, who was associated with the Confederacy. It remains to be seen whether the Black Bear will be accepted by the Ole Miss alumni and fans. Ole Miss had already banned the controversial rebel flag from sports events.

Q. Is there more tolerance for black-white friendships and romances in Mississippi today than when Alligator Lake takes place in 2002?

A. The *New York Times* reported in March 2011 that Mississippi led the nation in growth of mixed marriages during the last decade; however, persons of mixed race are still a very small percentage of Mississippi's population. Another poll early that year, conducted by Public Policy Polling, reported that forty-six percent of Mississippi Republicans support a ban on interracial marriage.

Sometimes, each race looks upon a person who chooses to date outside of their race as rejecting their own people. Exclusivity among whites seems to stem from historical notions of privilege, of believing that one's whiteness is accompanied by certain rights. White supremacist groups, in particular, use biblical references to justify their contempt for interracial relationships, citing that they are frowned upon by God. Mississippi did not repeal its ban on interracial marriage until 1987, even though the Supreme Court declared miscegenation laws unconstitutional in 1967.

As I mentioned, there are still separate debutante balls and proms. In 2008, Morgan Freeman traveled to his hometown of Charleston and offered to pay for the senior prom on the condition that it be integrated. The Charleston kids agreed and the event was successful, but several white families still chose to hold a separate prom. Bob Saltzman produced a documentary about these events called *Prom Night in Mississippi.* When the filmmakers revisited one year later, both the integrated and all-white proms were being held for the second time. Both are now annual events.

Q. Physical ailments have a huge impact on people's lives in the novel, and they rarely receive effective treatment. Elixirs, root doctors, illnesses that remain undiagnosed and largely untreated, and the failure to receive timely help from those of a different race all contribute to the characters' suffering. Is that just how it was back then?

A. Unfortunately, yes. After *Plessy v. Ferguson* established the separate but equal doctrine, segregation of health care was codified into law. However, separate did not mean equal. Blacks were barred from medical schools, hospitals, and doctors' offices. Root doctors and conjure doctors were often the only source of health care available to rural Southern blacks. Health care remained primarily segregated well into the 1960s. For example, the Jim Crow laws typically barred white nurses from caring for black patients, specifically black men. If blacks were allowed into white hospitals, they used a separate entrance and were treated in a basement, or in a separate wing, with substandard care.

Q. The novel traces the tragic appearance of sickle-cell disease through several generations. Can you share some background on the medical breakthrough that led to identification of the disease and modern treatments for it?

QUESTIONS FOR DISCUSSION

1. What was your response to *Alligator Lake*? What did you like best about it?

2. Willadean, Marion, Avery, and Celi are four generations of mothers and daughters who often don't understand one another. Discuss how they succeed and fail to meet one another's needs. Is it inevitable that a mother will fail her daughter at some point?

3. Henry Johnson and his grandnephew Aaron Monroe live very different lives. Discuss those differences and the factors that make Henry's so tragic and Aaron's so hopeful.

4. When even one drop of so-called black blood meant that society considered you black, there were those of mixed race who "passed" as white. Discuss what would tempt someone to choose that path, and the dangers and sacrifices involved. Can you think of other stories (novels, poems, plays, movies) that explore that experience? Or maybe you know of someone who passed. . . .

5. Sickle-cell disease has haunted the Johnson-Monroe family. Has your family, or a family you know, been marked by a recurring ailment? How has that affected the entire family? Has modern medicine changed the situation?

6. When Avery and Aaron fall in love in 1990, mixed-race relationships are still taboo in Mississippi. What about where you lived then? What about now?

7. Willadean has defied social convention all her life. Do you know anyone like her? Do such people end up changing the rules?

8. Marion doesn't intend to hurt blacks; she just wants to fit in. Do you sympathize with her? Have you ever behaved in ways that left you feeling uneasy, but you did it because you were told to, the rules said you should, or you wanted to fit in?

9. Avery thinks she does the right thing when she leaves Mississippi, becomes financially independent, and raises her mixed-race daughter in a more welcoming environment. But what mistakes does she make? What would you do in her shoes?

10. Compare Lynne Bryant's depiction of the Deep South with other depictions in literature. You might consider Kathryn Stockett's *The Help*, William Faulkner's novels, and Eudora Welty's short stories. How about *To Kill a Mockingbird* by Harper Lee or *Their Eyes Were Watching God* by Zora Neale Hurston? Can you think of others?

11. What do you want to happen to the characters after the book ends? Should Avery and Celi move to Greendale?

has been extremely supportive. I am most gratified to hear from Southern African-Americans, who have assured me that the voices in *Catfish Alley* are on target and believable. People from my hometown have told me that they learned about their own local history by reading *Catfish Alley*, as I did by researching it. Equally exciting are the responses I've received from readers expressing their affection for the characters of *Catfish Alley*.

Q. Has your life changed since you became a published author?

A. Despite the discipline and hard work that writing requires, I walk around every day feeling so fortunate to be able to see my work in print. I continue to learn so much about writing and about myself as a writer—and I've developed a thicker skin for criticism, which is so important to becoming a better writer. The most satisfying response I hear is when readers say that they lost themselves in my book, or that they couldn't put it down. These words are music to a writer's ears.